VESTIGES OF VALOR

A MEDIEVAL ROMANCE

By

Kathryn Le Veque

Print Edition

Text by Kathryn Le Veque
Cover by Kim Killion

Kathryn Le Veque Novels

Medieval Romance:

The de Russe Legacy:
The White Lord of Wellesbourne
The Dark One: Dark Knight
Beast
Lord of War: Black Angel
The Falls of Erith
The Iron Knight

The de Lohr Dynasty:
While Angels Slept (Lords of East Anglia)
Rise of the Defender
Steelheart
Spectre of the Sword
Archangel
Unending Love
Shadowmoor
Silversword

Great Lords of le Bec:
Great Protector
To the Lady Born (House of de Royans)
Lord of Winter (Lords of de Royans)

Lords of Eire:
The Darkland (Master Knights of Connaught)
Black Sword
Echoes of Ancient Dreams (time travel)

De Wolfe Pack Series:
The Wolfe
Serpent
Scorpion (Saxon Lords of Hage – Also related to The Questing)
The Lion of the North
Walls of Babylon
Dark Destroyer
Nighthawk

Ancient Kings of Anglecynn:
The Whispering Night
Netherworld

Battle Lords of de Velt:
The Dark Lord
Devil's Dominion

Reign of the House of de Winter:
Lespada
Swords and Shields (also related to The Questing, While Angels Slept)

De Reyne Domination:
Guardian of Darkness
The Fallen One (part of Dragonblade Series)

Unrelated characters or family groups:
The Gorgon (Also related to Lords of Thunder)
The Warrior Poet (St. John and de Gare)
Tender is the Knight (House of d'Vant)
Lord of Light
The Questing (related to The Dark Lord, Scorpion)
The Legend (House of Summerlin)

The Dragonblade Series: (Great Marcher Lords of de Lara)
Dragonblade
Island of Glass (House of St. Hever)
The Savage Curtain (Lords of Pembury)
The Fallen One (De Reyne Domination)
Fragments of Grace (House of St. Hever)

Lord of the Shadows
Queen of Lost Stars (House of St. Hever)

Lords of Thunder: The de Shera Brotherhood Trilogy
The Thunder Lord
The Thunder Warrior
The Thunder Knight

Highland Warriors of Munro
The Red Lion

Time Travel Romance: (Saxon Lords of Hage)
The Crusader
Kingdom Come

Contemporary Romance:

Kathlyn Trent/Marcus Burton Series:
Valley of the Shadow
The Eden Factor
Canyon of the Sphinx

The American Heroes Series:
The Lucius Robe
Fires of Autumn
Evenshade
Sea of Dreams
Purgatory

Other Contemporary Romance:
Lady of Heaven
Darkling, I Listen
In the Dreaming Hour

Multi-author Collections/Anthologies:
With Dreams Only of You (USA Today bestseller)
Sirens of the Northern Seas (Viking romance)
Ever My Love (sequel to With Dreams Only Of You) July 2016

Note: All Kathryn's novels are designed to be read as stand-alones, although many have cross-over characters or cross-over family groups. Novels that are grouped together have related characters or family groups.

Series are clearly marked. All series contain the same characters or family groups except the American Heroes Series, which is an anthology with unrelated characters.

There is NO particular chronological order for any of the novels because they can all be read as stand-alones, even the series.

For more information, find it in **A Reader's Guide to the Medieval World of Le Veque**.

AUTHOR'S NOTE

Welcome to Val and Vesper's tale.

This is a true knight's tale – a powerful knight with the world at his feet who suddenly finds himself in a terrible situation. One decision and his life seems to follow a string of terrible luck. As much as it is about the downfall of a man, it's also about his redemption and the value of friends and family.

Since this novel is set on the very early end of my family timelines, you won't see many crossover characters in it (most of them haven't been born yet), but Tevin du Reims from "While Angels Slept" appears as a man in his sixties by this point. Our hero, Val de Nerra, is related to Braxton de Nerra of "The Falls of Erith" as a direct ancestor about one hundred and thirty years before Braxton is born.

A few things to note, as always –

There is a mention of a *clavichordium* – or clavichord – about one hundred years or more before it was really documented. Of course, there could have been a piano-type instrument this early on, but any records of it have faded. Medieval people really had a great many instruments at their disposal and a keyed instrument – like a piano – is not out of the realm of possibility this early on.

Also, the murder of the Archbishop of Canterbury, Thomas Becket, is somewhat central to this novel. That event made for some very interesting research on my part because I discovered through my reading that the four knights who assassinated Becket weren't actually ordered to by Henry II. They heard Henry mumble something about "will no one rid me of this priest?" or something to that effect, and they took it literally. Most historians agree that Henry never actually gave the order.

It was a very messy affair and the knights mentioned in this novel were actually the knights who carried out the deed, including a knight named Hugh de Morville (or de Moreville, depending on the source). In my book, Hugh is the “ringleader” of the knights, although some historians have pointed to another knight in the group. The locations and timeline of this are historically accurate for the most part. And – fun fact – Le Veque means “The Bishop” in French, and it was the Archbishop of York, Roger de Pont L’Évêque, whose coronation of Henry the Young King kind of threw everything into action, resulting in Becket’s death. Another fun fact – Le Veque really is my name – I didn’t steal it from Roger!

As always, I sincerely hope you enjoy this story. It’s not a huge epic like some, but it’s a lovely story about love and loss and, most of all, hope. Val de Nerra is quite the hero.

Hugs,
Kathryn

TABLE OF CONTENTS

PROLOGUE

November, Year of Our Lord 1170 A.D.
Bures Castle
Normandy, France

A KNIGHT WITH dark red hair barely ducked in time to be missed by a flying cup.

But not just any cup. It was heavy and well-made, pewter, because it was the cup of the king. A man descended from kings, queens, and conquerors, a cup belonging to Henry Curtmantle, also known as Henry II of England. A short, stocky man of legendary stubbornness and legendary temper, as he was currently displaying.

Zing!

Another cup went flying and Henry's advisors were simply trying to stay out of the way. His personal guard, the knights who both protected and served him, were also trying to stay clear of the king's rage but in the solar of the king in the keep of Bures Castle, there wasn't much room to move around. It was a cluttered room, with rushes and furs on the floor, tapestries on the walls, and rather cramped for so many men. Therefore, it was much like a shooting gallery when Henry began to hurl things.

It had happened before.

"My lord, what can we do?" the Earl of East Anglia, Tevin du Reims, was the only man not trying to protect himself. He was an older man, massively built, with his long hair tied off at the nape of his neck. He controlled most of Norfolk and Suffolk. "Surely you knew that Canterbury would respond when he discovered York had crowned Young Henry. In fact, you and I discussed this very scenario. You should not be surprised."

Henry looked at du Reims, a man he trusted almost more than anyone else. "Nay, I am not surprised," he hissed, pounding his right fist into the palm of his hand. "But he has excommunicated L'Évêque!"

"I know."

"This move nullifies my son's coronation!"

Du Reims sighed faintly. "It does not matter in the grand scheme of your world," he said calmly, hoping Henry would stop throwing those heavy cups. He'd already clipped one of his clerks and the man had a bloodied eye because of it. "Henry's time will come and he shall be coronated before God and the church to rule in your stead. Canterbury will not have the last word on this; you know that. The best thing you can do now is simply ignore him."

"I will *not* ignore him!"

"If you do not, then you will give him what he wants – a reaction. Canterbury expects you to react to this and then he will condemn you for it."

Henry knew that, but he was so angry that it was difficult for him to focus. His once good and dear friend, Thomas Becket, had thwarted him in yet another situation in a long line of situations that had been happening since Becket had been appointed to the position as the Archbishop of Canterbury. When the former archbishop died, Henry had moved swiftly to fill the position with a man who had formerly held the position of his chancellor. He had been certain that his old friend, Thomas, would side with him on all matters, giving him control over the church. That had been the hope, anyway.

Instead, Becket had opposed Henry on nearly everything.

Henry saw his mistake now; putting Becket in charge of the church had turned the man power-hungry. He now competed against Henry for control of the entire country and Henry, a stubborn and abrasive man, raged at Becket regularly. This latest incident – the coronation of Henry's heir by the Archbishop of York, Roger de Pont L'Évêque – had not only been condemned by Canterbury, as such a thing was historically his right, but Canterbury then went ahead and excommunicated York because of it.

The vindictiveness of a man who felt he was within his rights.

Truthfully, rage didn't quite encompass what Henry was feeling. It was the last straw as far as he was concerned and everyone in the room could sense that. Not only were the advisors and the knights on edge, waiting for the next object to go flying, but the dogs were huddled under the table, sensing the tension in the room. But it was more than tension and more than fury.

It was the desperation of a man pushed beyond his limits.

"Damn him," Henry finally hissed, turning away from du Reims because the man made sense and, at the moment, he didn't want any sense. He wanted satisfaction. "He has gone too far. I will not let this go unanswered."

Du Reims realized his advice for calm would go unheeded. "Then what would you have us do?"

Henry wasn't so sure what, exactly, he wanted done. All he knew was that he needed an end to his problem. "Why do you ask such questions, Tevin?" he said. Then, he threw his hands up as if clawing at the sky. "It is *not* a question to be asked. It is an action to take on behalf of your king. For the love of God, *who* will rid me of this troublesome priest?"

It was a forceful shout that reverberated from the very stone walls of the solar. A few of the dogs even bolted out from beneath the table, running from the room. As du Reims endeavored to calm the irate king, the last eight words spoken by Henry seemed to reverberate most of all. Unlike most words, disappearing with the breath they were spoken upon, these words had substance.

They had merit.

To one of Henry's knight, the words were a call to action. They hung in his mind, lingering, and as he mulled them over and over, they began to paint a picture he could clearly see. He'd served with Henry for several years and he'd seen the contention between Canterbury and Henry. He knew their history. Finally, Henry was making a plea. He needed help and he needed peace.

To Sir Hugh de Morville, those words sounded very much like a command. Glancing at the comrades standing nearest him – FitzUrse, de Tracy, le Breton… he could see their expressions. They were looking at Hugh as if they, too, had understood Henry's plea. These men who guarded the king, who had sworn an oath to obey and to serve.

They, too, heard the command. As knights of the king, they could not ignore it.

Something had to be done.

CHAPTER ONE

"Even in a hero's heart, discretion is the better part of valor…"

December, nearing the Christmas celebration
Selborne Castle
Hampshire, England

THE MORNING WAS bright, with ribbons of sunlight streaming in through the lancet windows of the small hall of Selborne Castle. Although the castle had a large great hall, a separate structure that was only used for soldiers and for major feasts, the smaller hall built into the keep was used for family meals. Even now, as he came down the narrow stone steps, built into the wall of the keep, he could see the sunlight through the hall doorway and smell the fresh bread. His mother demanded hot bread in the morning and the smell told him she was already at the table eating.

He braced himself.

Not that he didn't love his mother. They had an excellent relationship. But she could be a bit overbearing at times. That was the kind way of putting it. Last night, she'd had too much to drink and had harped on one of the many subjects she liked to harp on, which had chased him from the room. He was wondering if she would remember how he'd fled in frustration or if the drink had erased that part of the evening for her.

He was hoping it was the latter.

Entering the chamber, he forced a smile as he kissed his mother on the head. "Good morn to you," he said pleasantly. "How did you sleep?"

A woman with a severe wimple sat at the table, focused on her food and not her unnaturally cheery son. "Unwell."

"Unwell? Why?"

She tore apart a small bread roll, sending steam into the air. "Because I dreamt that I had grandchildren and awoke to a dark room and a cold bed," she said. "I have been dreaming of grandchildren a good deal as of late, Val. One would think you would take the hint."

Sir Valor de Nerra sat across the table from his mother, resisting the urge to roll his eyes. It was too early in the morning to start on that subject. Sometimes, he gave himself a headache with all of the eye rolling he did when his mother began to preach to him. One of these days, he was going to roll an eyeball right out of its socket.

"Are you going to start this so early in the morning?" he asked, his smile leaving him. "I have only just walked into the room. You could at least bid me a good morning and tell me that you love me. But instead, all I hear is that you have no grandchildren and a cold bed. The cold bed is *your* fault for not remarrying."

His mother flicked her eyes up to him, eyes the same color as his. "But the lack of grandchildren is *your* fault."

Val took his own hot bread roll and pulled it open. "I will make a bargain with you. If you get married, then I will, too."

His mother cast him an expression that suggested she didn't like that bargain at all. "I am too set in my ways, Val. My heart is not strong, nor is my health. It would be foolish to remarry."

"My heart is strong and my health is fine, but I am too young to marry. It would be foolish for me to do it, too."

"You have seen thirty-four years," his mother pointed out. "If you do not marry soon, you will be an old spinster and no woman will want an old husband like you. For shame!"

Val fought off a grin. "Men cannot be spinsters."

"They can if I say they can!"

He started to laugh. "Can we please defer this until after I eat? You are going to give me a sour stomach if you keep hen-pecking me."

Lady Margaretha Byington de Nerra eyed her son most unhappily. Such a beautiful, beautiful boy who had turned into a man that was the most eligible bachelor in all of England. At least, in her opinion he was. Val was tall, muscular, and broad, with a head of dark, wavy hair and brilliant green eyes. He was excruciatingly handsome, the subject of many a maiden's affection, and he soaked it up but never seemed to grow serious about any of it.

And he was successful… Sweet Mary, so successful! Having served the king for many years in France, her son had come home two years ago with a royal appointment. Itinerant Justice of Hampshire he was called, and Margaretha could not have been more proud of him. Prestige and wealth had been given to him by the royal hand.

But Margaretha soon began to realize that the royal appointment was not an easy thing, at least the way Val carried out his duties. Never one to delegate tasks, he was in the middle of whatever was happening that fell under his jurisdiction – chasing down outlaws, holding judgment over them, and even executing them. Val took his duties very seriously and, with that diligence, his reputation in the area grew.

Valor de Nerra was a man to be reckoned with.

Now, he was the most powerful man from Basingstoke to the sea, a vast area where he had several men in patrols that kept order in a lawless time. Margaretha was still hugely proud of her son but she was afraid that his attention to duty was causing him to lack foresight into his future. *Marital* future. As his mother, it was her duty to make sure he understood the importance of it. But after two years of her trying to beat it into his head, she was afraid she wasn't making much of an impression on him.

"I am not hen-pecking you," she said as she put butter on her bread.

"It seems to me that you fail to understand the importance of your future. You are the last of your father's line, Valor, not to mention the last of my line. In fact, my line is far more important. You understand that it must be continued."

Val was quickly growing exhausted of the conversation. When the servant poured him watered wine, he down the entire cup and demanded more.

"I understand," he said with exaggerated patience. "I understand that your family line can be traced back to Pontius Pilate when the man was brought by Roman galley to Porchester, whereupon he fathered a child with a local Saxon woman, a child who happened to be your forbearer on your mother's side. I also understand that there is Wessex royalty in your blood, Mother, and I give thanks to God daily that you did not name me after the wyvern in your family crest. Instead of Wyvern, you named me Valor because that is what you wished for me. How could a man with the name Valor be anything other than valorous? Therefore, I understand clearly what you have been telling me for thirty-four years."

Now, his irritation was showing and Margaretha was feeling scolded. Still, she had her pride and that meant her son would never see her in the throes of submission or defeat. Even if what he said was true. She eyed him before returning to her meal.

"I do not think I like your attitude this morning," she said. "I sense disrespect."

"And I sense the same."

She looked at him, surprised and confused. "What do you mean?"

He sighed. "Evidently, you do not respect my judgement or intelligence enough to know that I realize I must take a wife at some point. We have had this conversation so many times that my head is swimming with your expectations. I know them all too well, Mother. Therefore, may we drop the subject, at least for this meal?"

Margaretha returned her focus to her food, trying not to sound hurt. "If that is your wish."

"It is."

Margaretha took a bite of her bread with butter as a servant spooned out an egg dish onto her trencher. Val, too, delved into his bread, eyeing his mother and feeling some remorse for the turn of the conversation.

She meant well; he knew she did. She wasn't really the harpy that she seemed to be at times. In truth, she could be very wise and generous. But the situation with his lack of a wife was starting to create tension between them and, for that, he was, indeed, sorry. But, as he'd told her many times, she was going to have to let him make his own decisions where that was concerned.

The meal continued in silence for a few minutes until another man entered the hall and Val found himself looking up at his second in command. Sir Calum de Morville had been on patrol the evening before, for whenever Val wasn't out attending to his duties, Calum was there in his place. Still in his mail breeches and still armed, Calum smiled wearily at Val.

"Good morn," he said. Then, he looked to Margaretha. "Good morn to you, Lady de Nerra. It 'tis a fine morning. In fact, I passed a woman on the road who gave me some bulbs for your flower garden when the spring comes. I have left them at the door for you to inspect."

Margaretha seemed pleased. "How fine," she said. "My thanks, Calum. Will you eat with us? My son and I were just discussing my lack of grandchildren. Since you have a wife, mayhap you can stress to him how pleasant it is to have a woman in your bed every night."

So much for keeping her mouth shut. Val, who had a knife in his hand that he'd been eating with, suddenly flipped it to the dull side and sawed it back and forth across the inside of his wrist, evidently trying to kill himself. Calum caught the gesture and struggled not to laugh.

"We have discussed the issue many times, Lady de Nerra," he said, biting off a smile. "I am confident that Val will select a fine wife someday. You must be patient."

Margaretha cocked an eyebrow at the knight. "Bah," she said. "He had better do it before I die or I will not be able to rest in peace. With my bad heart, there is the very real possibility that I shall not live to see the morrow. Do you hear, Valor? If you do not marry before I die, then I shall be forced to haunt you."

Unable to slit his wrists with the dull side of the knife, Val gave up and stabbed a piece of boiled apple, plopping it into his mouth. "It cannot be any worse than the way you haunt me right now," he said, chewing. He looked at Calum. "Sit down and eat. Give her another target to aim for so she will leave me alone."

Calum couldn't help the laughter then. "I cannot," he said, chuckling. "I have come with news, Val. Do you recall the missive we received from Lord Horsham about the knight who had killed one of his sons?"

Val nodded. "Latham de Wyck was the name, I believe," he said. "He'd come to court one of Horsham's daughters. When the girl's brother tried to intervene, de Wyck killed him."

Calum nodded. "Indeed," he said. "We have reason to believe that de Wyck is in Whitehill. One of our patrols sent word about the horse that Horsham described as belonging to the knight being in the livery in Whitehill. I thought you would want to see for yourself."

Val nodded. "I do," he said, quickly downing the rest of his watered wine and rising to his feet. "We will take a full contingent of men with us. Forty men, fully armed. If this is the knight, then he will more than likely fight to the death rather than be captured alive. I want the men prepared and protected. Gather them now and I shall meet you in the bailey."

Calum nodded and, begging leave from Margaretha, fled the small hall. Val wasn't so quick to leave; he rounded the table and kissed his mother on her smooth cheek.

"I will return when I can," he said.

He was halfway to the door when Margaretha called after him. "Valor," she said. She was the only one who ever called him by his full name. "You will take care."

He winked at her. "I always do, love."

He was hurrying to leave but Margaretha stopped him again. "Wait," she said. When he stopped to look at her, impatience in his features, she softened. "I do love you, my dear boy. Surely you know that."

"I know."

"I simply want you to be happy. But I want to be happy, too."

Val softened his impatient stance, but only for a moment. "I promise you that, someday, we shall both be exquisitely happy. I would stake my life on it."

"Then you shall marry someday?"

"Of course I will."

"Soon?"

"If I meet her tomorrow, then mayhap soon. But if I do not… be patient, dearest Mother. I will not disappoint you."

Margaretha knew that. He'd not disappointed her yet; he'd always been a son to be very proud of. Well, most of the time. He flashed her that devilish smile, the one he always flashed her when he got his way, and dashed from the chamber.

When he was gone, Margaretha sat in silence, pondering their conversation and listening to the distant shouts of the men in the bailey of Selborne Castle. Men sworn to the king and, through the king, to her son. He was a favored of Henry and a man who could have anything he wished simply for the asking. It was a charmed life that Val led, in royal favor, something he worked his entire life to attain. Aye, she was proud of him. Overwhelmingly so.

But pride wouldn't bring her any grandchildren.

With a heavy sigh, Margaretha returned to her morning meal, one she found she no longer had an appetite for. Something in Val's expression as he'd left, in that brilliant smile of straight, white teeth, had given her a sense of doom. She didn't know why. Perhaps, it was only her imagination and nothing more. But something in his face had had a shadow of dread upon it.

Today is a day for dread.

It was just a feeling she had.

CHAPTER TWO

The village of Whitehill
4 miles east of Selborne

UPON SEEING THE blue roan Belgian warmblood, a very rare color of horse, Val and Calum were convinced that they had happened upon the knight Lord Horsham was seeking. Horsham had described the horse and the knight in detail, a man he wanted brought to justice for the murder of his beloved son.

It was Val's intention to see that Lord Horsham got his wish.

In the old stone livery in a part of the village that had two popular inns, they were inclined to believe that their man was in one of the taverns but the livery keep couldn't tell them which one. He did, however, describe a tall knight with a long red beard and curly red hair, which made finding de Wyck a little more certain. A man of that description would stand out.

It was still early enough in the morning that men were just awakening and preparing for the coming day. From their vantage point at the livery, the knights could see both inns; one was to the north about one hundred feet away across a vacant lot and the other one was directly across the road. From the rain the previous night, the road was muddy and the air cold, the breath of living creatures creating puffs of fog upon the air. As the livery keep scurried off, fearful of all of the armed soldiers, Val and Calum gathered men at the rear of the livery to produce a plan of action.

"You were briefed on our purpose for coming to Whitehill," Val said to the forty-three men he'd brought with him, including three knights. "Based on a discussion with the livery keep, we believe that the man we are seeking is in one of the two taverns on this road. The tavern to the north, one-storied, is The Peacock and the Flame. I believe most of you men are acquainted with it. Probably more intimately than I would care to know."

The men snorted, looking at each other knowingly. Val was generous in the time and freedom he allowed his men for service well-rendered and The Peacock and the Flame had a host of lovely women from which to choose. It was popular with travelers and locals alike. Val grinned because his men were.

"But no such distractions today because we have work to do," he said, looking pointedly at his smirking soldiers. He threw a thumb over his shoulder. "Across the road is The Golden Pheasant. That one is bigger and less expensive to lodge in. Since we cannot know where the man is staying, our best option is to flush him out. Calum will take Kenan with him along with twenty men down to The Peacock and the Flame while I will take Mayne with me and the remainder of the men to The Golden Pheasant. Now, separate yourselves into two groups of twenty and await further orders."

The soldiers did as they were told as Val turned to his knights, the three best knights a man had ever had the privilege to serve with. He'd brought them all back with him from France when he'd returned with his royal appointment, so these were men proven in battle. Along with Calum, a big blonde stud of a man, there was Kenan de Poyer, built like a bear with big hands and shaggy brown hair, and Mayne de Garr, a knight who was handsome to a fault and took great care in his personal appearance.

Mayne could fight with the best of them. But if a hair was out of place on his combed head in the process, he would become furious. It was often quite entertaining to watch Kenan ruffle Mayne's hair, only for Mayne to light Kenan's tunic on fire. That had happened three times that Val knew of, and probably more that he didn't. Mayne didn't take kindly to Kenan's taunts and there was a subversive war going on between them when Val wasn't looking. But in battle, they would both kill and die for one another, making it an odd relationship, indeed.

But on this morning, both men were primed for what was to come. The ride from Selborne had been hard and fast. Even now, they awaited their orders. Val didn't keep them in suspense.

"It is my suggestion that you have men surround the tavern and cover all windows and doors," he said to the three knights. "Have a group of men go in from the rear and flush everyone out through the front. These taverns will be crowded this early in the morning, so be on your guard. We are looking for a man with long red hair and a beard to match, and he will be in no mood to be taken prisoner. He's killed once and it is my suspicion he will not hesitate to do it again if threatened. But we want him alive for Lord Horsham's good justice."

The knights absorbed the orders. "The Golden Pheasant has two floors," Calum said. "As I recall, there were at least eight sleeping rooms above the common room."

Val nodded. "Eight plus a communal loft," he said with confidence. "I will send Mayne and a contingent of men to roust that floor but ultimately, everyone will be driven out of the front door. I would suggest you follow a similar tactic."

The situation was clear to them all. As Calum and Kenan went to collect their group of men, Val turned to Mayne.

"Pick your men to take to the second floor," he told the man. "But remember that sleeping men, when caught off-guard, can often act before thinking. Watch your head."

Mayne nodded. "I have every intention of doing that," he said. "Some men consider scars a mark of honor. I, for one, do not."

Val fought off a grin at the vain knight. "Then let this operation not mar your tender skin," he said, a dig at Mayne's pride. "Get on with it. I will position men around the inn and wait at the entry for you to drive the mob towards me."

"Aye, my lord."

As Mayne went to pick his men, Val took the remaining fourteen with him towards the tavern. Off to his left, he could see Calum and Kenan heading towards the other tavern, moving through the mud and debris that had collected overnight along the road. They made a concerning sight, armed for battle as they were. Villeins going about their business were intimidated by the sight of so many armed men.

Val knew that word of their appearance would quickly get around, so he emitted a soft whistle between his teeth, motioning to Mayne and his men to quickly enter The Golden Pheasant. As Mayne and his soldiers ran past him, entering the front of the tavern in a well-organized group, Val hurriedly positioned his men around the perimeter and instructed six of them to enter from the rear along with Mayne. That way, both floors would be covered. That left eight on the perimeter, watching doors and windows. Val was just about to give them the signal to move, another one of those piercing whistles, when the entry door of the inn lurched open.

A man and a woman spilled forth into the early morning, bearing satchels and heavily robbed against the cold. But it wasn't just any man and woman; Val immediately recognized an old ally with an unfamiliar young woman at his side. In fact, the sight was rather surprising and all Val could think of was getting the pair out of the way before a mob of terrified people trampled them as his men chased the patrons from the tavern.

"D'Avignon?" Val said as he moved quickly towards the man. "McCloud d'Avignon?"

Sir McCloud d'Avignon, hearing his name, turned in Val's direction. He had been moderately concerned when he came out of the tavern and saw all of the armed soldiers. But when Val called to him, his concern turned to both surprise and relief.

"De Nerra?" he boomed, grabbing the young woman by the arm as he headed in Val's direction. "Is it really you?"

"It 'tis."

"I've not seen you in years!"

"It has been a long time."

"What are you doing here? And who are all of these men?"

Val reached out to take the man by the arm. "Come away from the door," he said, not really answering his question. "I do not want you to become caught up in what is surely to come."

He pulled McCloud and the young woman away from the tavern just as screams began to erupt inside. Hearing that his orders were already being carried out, Val signaled to one of his men to commence and the man emitted a shrill whistle in response. With that, there were the sounds of a massive crash and more screams coming from the rear of the tavern.

It all sounded quite harrowing. Val increased his pace, pulling McCloud and the woman across the road and towards the livery as the entire tavern began to erupt.

"God's Bones, Val," McCloud said, realizing there was some danger going on behind them. "What is happening?"

Val's attention was on the tavern, distracted as he spoke to McCloud. "A fugitive," he said. "A knight who killed Lord Horsham's son. I have been asked to bring the man to justice."

McCloud was eyeing the tavern with great concern. From the sound of it, whatever was happening inside wasn't good. "The poor man," he muttered. "My daughter and I were just inside the tavern and it was very crowded. What does the man you seek look like?"

Val took his attention off the tavern for a brief moment. "A tall knight with red hair and a red beard," he said. "Did you see anyone that fits that description?"

McCloud shook his head. "Alas, I did not," he said. "But that means nothing. The sleeping rooms were all full. He could have been in one of those."

Val simply nodded, his focus returning to the tavern. "I will find him," he said. "Meanwhile, it was good to see you. Pleasant journey to you."

McCloud sensed his distraction. "And I wish you well in your endeavor to bring about law and order," he said. "A pity we do not have time to speak and become acquainted again. I have missed you, my old friend."

Val was torn now, because he did want to speak with McCloud. But he was focused on the task at hand. Therefore, he did the only thing he could.

"Then come and sup with me this evening," he said. "Please allow me to extend the hospitality of Selborne Castle."

McCloud looked at the young woman with him, who was nearly completely obscured by the hooded cloak she wore. There was some indecision on his face as the young woman shook her head. "We… well, we were traveling home but I would very much like to feast with you this evening," he said. "Where is Selborne?"

Val's attention was back on the tavern because the front door had burst open and screaming men and women were being purged from the innards of the tavern.

"Four miles to the west," he said. "You cannot miss it. It sits like a great lioness crouched on a hillside overlooking the land."

McCloud was still looking at the young woman, who was still shaking her head as if she very much didn't want to feast with an old friend of her father's. But before McCloud could reply, sounds of a great swordfight came from within the tavern and Val unsheathed his broadsword, running towards the tavern only to be met by a fight spilling out into the street. Men with swords were battling the men he'd sent in to roust the tavern and there was no sign of Mayne.

Very quickly, the situation turned very dangerous.

Val didn't stop to ask questions. He and the men who had remained outside now jumped into the fight that had turned into a nasty brawl. The sounds of swords engaged, metal hitting metal, filled the morning air as men strained against their opponents.

Val plowed into the group, using his big right fist when he wasn't using the sword in his left hand. If one wasn't flying, the other one was. He wasn't exactly sure why there was such a big fight going on when they were only searching for one man, so he made his way through the crowd until he came to one of his sergeants.

"What is happening?" he demanded, ducking when one man took a swing at his head. He retaliated by kicking the man in the gut only to punch him in the face when he doubled over. "Who are all of these men?"

The sergeant had a nick on his shoulder, bleeding through his mail and tunic. "There was a contingent of soldiers inside, breaking their fast," he said. "They did not take kindly to the fact that we burst in from the rear and threatened them."

So it was a group of men unrelated to their fugitive. "Damnation," Val hissed. This was a complication they hadn't needed and he had to get the situation under control. "Try to calm everyone down. Spread the word amongst the men to try and calm these men down rather than fight them. Is that clear?"

The sergeant nodded, avoiding a sword that was aiming for him and trying to talk to the man rather than respond. As Val pushed his way back through the fight, he caught sight of Mayne just inside the door of the tavern, tossing a limp body outside. Val didn't know what happened and he didn't ask, but he was heading in Mayne's direction when he caught a glimpse of someone on the road, running for the livery. A second glance showed a man heavily armed, in well-worn mail and a tattered tunic. It was just another soldier until Val caught a glimpse of the man's red hair peeking out from his helm.

Red hair!

Val veered away from Mayne and the roiling mass of fighting men, pushing his way through and bursting free, heading in the direction of the livery. With his men tied up fighting a group of unhappy soldiers, Val realized he would be the only one to confront the knight who had just dashed into the livery. He was running so fast that he didn't even notice McCloud and the young woman, still standing where he had left them at the mouth of the livery. Val burst into the stable and nearly crashed into the knight who had just claimed his blue roan warmblood.

"Hold," Val said steadily, his broadsword poised but not raised, at least not yet. "I have a question before I permit you to leave, if you will indulge me."

The knight turned to him, his pale face flushed. Noting Val's broadsword, he immediately unsheathed his weapon.

"Get out of my way," the knight growled.

Val remained cool. "Give me your name and I will consider it."

"Get out of my way!"

Val didn't budge. He could see the man was vastly nervous, for his upper lip had beads of sweat on it and his breathing was coming in heavy pants. He could see the man's facial hair, reddish-blonde in color, and the red curls were spilling over his shoulders from beneath his helm.

But it was the eyes… something in the eyes bespoke of rage and fear. Val knew he had to treat this situation very carefully if he wanted to accomplish his goal. The punishment of this man, this murderer, was Lord Horsham's right, but if the knight moved against him, Val would be forced to defend himself. He didn't want to kill him. Therefore, he had to be smart about the situation.

He took a deep breath, his mind working quickly.

Be clever!

"Alas, I cannot," he said, more calmly. "My name is de Nerra. I am the Itinerant Justice in this area and I am hunting for a man who is due a fortune. I am told he had red hair and a blue roan horse. I only wish to give this man the money, so could this man I seek possibly be you?"

It was a manipulative way to not only lower the knight's guard, but to, perhaps, even cause him to give his name. Val was brilliant in that sense. As he watched, the fear in the man's eyes flickered with confusion.

"A fortune?" he repeated. Then, he shook his head firmly, struggling with his horse's saddle in order to cinch it up. "Nay, I am due no money."

"But you fit the description," Val insisted, lowering his sword so he could prove he wasn't a threat. "Your red hair and your horse's color fit the description perfectly. I received an edict from a lord to the north, in Alton I believe, who swore that his nephew was due money. His name was de Wyck."

The knight came to a halt, looking at Val with wide eyes. He was torn between suspicion and glee; Val could see it in his eyes. The knight knew very well that he wasn't due any money but the mention of his name had him questioning that knowledge. Did he, in fact, have an uncle he knew nothing about? A *rich* uncle? Seeing the indecision, Val sought to press his point.

"Will you please come with me to see if we can settle this matter?" he asked. "I am told it is a great deal of money. If it were me, I would certainly want to find out if I had a fortune coming. But mayhap you are wealthy enough that you do not need any more money?"

That was a ridiculous question considering the state of the knight's clothing. The horse, as fine as it was, was even wearing well-repaired tack, tatters of once-fine regalia. It was, therefore, clear that the knight had no money. Val was counting on that fact, with the lure of money being enough to force the knight to trust him.

"De Wyck," the knight finally mumbled. "*Who* is this lord?"

Val shook his head. "I do not recall," he said. "The name is on the edict but I do not recall. All I know is that the lord is north, towards Alton. Do you have relatives up there?"

"I do not."

"Is your name de Wyck?"

The knight paused. "It is possible," he said, "but I have no uncle to the north."

"But you fit the description I was given. Clearly, someone knows of you."

The knight eyed him. "Is that why you are here in Whitehill? Searching for me?"

"Indeed. I'd heard rumor of this blue roan and sought to locate you."

It wasn't exactly a lie. In fact, it was very close to the truth. The knight opened his mouth to reply but he was interrupted when Mayne came charging into the livery in the company of several soldiers. One look at Val standing next to a knight with red hair and a red beard was all he needed to continue his charge with heavily-armed men at this side, all of them rushing towards Val and the knight.

It was an ambush. Instantly, the red-haired knight went into defensive mode, grappling for the broadsword at his side. Val knew that he had to prevent the man from producing the weapon because he, personally, would be the first target. Therefore, Val's sword came up as fast as he could possibly move it, the tip of it coming to bear on the face of the red-haired knight.

In that instant, everything seemed to come to a blinding halt.

"Move and I shall drive this blade through your eye," Val hissed. "Drop your weapon. I will not tell you again."

The red-haired knight looked at Val with a mixture of terror and fury but, to his credit, he did as he was told. He let go of the hilt of his sword and the weapon slid back into its sheath.

"Who are you?" the knight hissed. "What do you want of me?"

Val never took his eyes off of the knight's face but he could see in his periphery as the blue roan was moved away and Mayne appeared, coming up behind the fugitive from justice. As Mayne and a pair of soldiers grabbed the knight and began to strip him of his weapons, Val stood back and watched.

"Lord Horsham has something to say to you," he said, watching a look of disbelief ripple across the knight's features. "You murdered his son. He wants his vengeance."

The knight's pale face turned red with anger. "Then all of that about a fortune...."

"Was a lie."

"It was to keep me here until your men arrived!"

"Possibly."

Mayne threw the knight onto his face, down into the muddy floor of the livery as he tied the knight's hands behind his back with hemp rope. With the suspect subdued, Val turned away from the scene and headed out of the livery to see what had become of the battle in front of the tavern. He was feeling smug in his accomplishment, pride in a job well done. He had his man. As soon as he emerged from the stable, he could see that the tavern battle had essentially come to a halt although there were still several men out front, including his own, who were talking and pushing each other about. But at least they were no longer fighting.

Relieved to see that the skirmish had died down, he looked off to the north to see if Calum and Kenan had been faced with similar obstacles when raiding the tavern they were charged with. He could see men milling around in the distance, out in the road, but he couldn't really tell what was going on. Given that Val had accomplished his goal, he sent one of his soldiers to The Peacock and the Flame to call off Calum and Kenan. As he stood there and watched the man run off, he heard a quiet voice behind him.

"Wherever you go, trouble follows," McCloud said quietly. "It has been a long time since I have seen the tempest that you bring about, Val. It reminded me of days of old."

Val turned around to see McCloud and the young woman standing a few feet away. He'd completely forgotten about them. There was a smile on McCloud's face, which caused Val to smile in return.

"This was nothing," he said with feigned arrogance. "You should have been with me last week when we captured a gang of outlaws who had been robbing travelers on the road between Holybourne and Ropley. That was quite a fight, I must say. They were not very cooperative."

McCloud laughed softly. "I remember now," he said. "You are the law in this area. I had forgotten about that appointment until now."

Val nodded. "Indeed, I am," he said. Now, the arrogance was real. "I have been the Itinerant Justice of Hampshire ever since I returned from France. There is not much that goes on in my jurisdiction that I do not know about. I am proud to say that I have made it a safer place for all, now with the capture of this murderer."

McCloud could see the pride in the man. That was the Val he knew, prideful and confident. "Is the invitation still open to sup?" he asked.

Val nodded. "I would be hurt if you did not accept," he said. Then, his gaze moved to the cloaked woman at McCloud's side. "Your companion is welcome also."

McCloud looked at the woman standing next to him, reaching out a meaty hand to grasp her arm and pull her closer, as she seemed to be standing off on her own. "This is my daughter," he said. "I have been rude not to introduce her to you but it did not seem quite proper in the middle of your fight."

Val grinned. "Now is the perfect time," he said, his gaze lingering on the woman well hidden by the hood of her cloak. All he could see was her chin and part of her mouth. "My lady, I am Sir Val de Nerra. I am honored."

McCloud beamed at his child. "This is Lady Vesper d'Avignon," he said. "I am returning her home from fostering, in fact. That is why we are on this road."

"Oh?" Val said, increasingly interested in the woman who didn't seem apt to show her face. "Where did you foster, my lady?"

Since he was addressing her directly, it would have been poor manners not to reveal herself and answer. A white hand with long fingers reached up to pull the hood away and Val found himself staring into the face of an exquisitely beautiful woman. Her dark hair was long and wavy, the front of it pulled away from her face, and big hazel eyes sat above high chiseled cheekbones and a bow-shaped mouth.

"Eynsford Castle, my lord," she said.

Her voice was deep for a woman, but smooth and silky. Val rather liked it. "I know it well," he said. "I know your lord, William de Eynsford. How long were you there?"

"Since before my father went to France," she said, looking at her father. "Eight years."

"I do not seem to recall your father mentioning he had a daughter in all the time we served together."

"It is easy to forget girl children."

McCloud snorted, a forced laugh. "I could never forget my daughter. You will have Val thinking that I am neglectful."

The woman didn't reply. She simply looked at her father as if she saw no humor in his statement. Val couldn't seem to take his eyes off of her; the more she spoke in that deep, husky tone, the more he wanted to listen. He didn't even notice that Vesper seemed to be looking at her father rather hostilely as McCloud gazed at his daughter with a mixture of anxiety and humor. It was an odd combination.

Had Val had eyes for the situation at that moment and not Vesper in particular, he would have seen the mixed signals between father and daughter. But he didn't. His inspection of the lady was cut short when his men emerged from the livery with the prisoner, heading into the corral where their horses were.

"I am afraid that I must attend to some business at the moment, but please continue on this road until you come to a fork," he said. "Take the fork to the right and that will take you directly to Selborne Castle. My mother is in residence. Tell her I have invited you both to feast with us tonight and she will make you comfortable."

"We shall look forward to it," McCloud said. "Thank you for your hospitality."

Val smiled although it was clear he was distracted with his prisoner. He bowed briefly to them both.

"I am eager to return home and hear of your adventures since I last saw you," he said. His gaze inevitably moved to Vesper. "My lady."

With that, he excused himself, heading towards the corral where his men were gathered. McCloud and Vesper watched him walk away, a very big man with a brilliant smile. Confident, seasoned, he radiated power.

He was a man with the world at his fingertips.

HE WAS ALSO a man that Vesper wanted nothing to do with.

When the big knight was finally out of earshot, heading back to his men and their struggling prisoner, the lady turned to her father.

"Why did you accept his invitation?" she hissed. "We must go home, Papa. We cannot delay."

McCloud's gaze was on Val in the distance. "Nay, Daughter," he muttered. "Not yet. Did you not hear the conversation? God has put us here, today, so that I could see my old friend, Val. This moment could not have been more fortuitous."

Vesper sighed heavily, hanging her head. "It is *not* fortuitous," she insisted. "Why would you want to walk into the lion's den? He is the law in this area. Or did you not hear him?"

"I heard him."

"Then why must we sup with him?"

McCloud took his daughter by the arm and, together, they began to walk out onto the road. They had no horses to transport them; horses were expensive and they had not the money to spare on them. The only horse they had belonged to McCloud's son and Vesper's brother, Mat, and he needed the animal for his activities.

Unspeakably dark activities concealing a ghastly family secret.

"You are not looking at this as a great moment," McCloud said. "I firmly believe that God put us here, today, so that we could meet with Val. I have not seen him in two years and, suddenly, here he is right in front of us. This is the answer to our prayers, Vesper. You cannot know how I have prayed for… help with your brother."

Vesper shook her head. "It is *not* the answer to your prayers," she said, coming to a halt and facing him. "And it is not help you ask for Mat, but absolution for his heinous deeds. Do you know why I am coming home, Papa? Do you even understand? It is because you and

Mat have gotten yourself into a terrible situation that must be stopped."

McCloud tried not to look too remorseful, guilty at his daughter's scolding. "Mat is doing what he needs to do in order that we should survive," he said quietly. "I have told you that."

Vesper was growing angry. "You are *not* surviving," she hissed. "What you are doing… Papa, it is horrific. We have had this conversation many times over the past week, ever since you came to Eynsford and revealed this horrible life you and my brother lead. Now, we must have this conversation again – are you so blind that you do not even realize that what Mat is doing is wrong?"

McCloud was having difficulty looking her in the eye now. "If you were starving, you would see things differently."

Vesper threw up her hands in frustration. "Are you truly so complacent?" she asked. "Do you truly not know right from wrong? Mat is killing in order to survive and he is going to be caught. You will be hanged with him because you do not stop him!"

So she had spoken of the situation aloud, the truth behind the horrible family secret. It was painful to the ears, like a stab to the eardrums, but now it was out in the open; *Mat is killing.*

Was it true that the House of d'Avignon had sunk so low?

Truth be told, McCloud had been wrestling with the very same conflicts. He had for some time now, ever since he and his son began to starve and Mat, in order that they should eat, had taken to murdering men, women, and entire families in order to take whatever they had to bring home to his father.

Simply put, Mat killed so that he and his father could survive.

McCloud was complacent. Indeed, he was. But he was a sick, old man who was no longer worth anything with a small farm his family had kept for over one hundred years all dried up. The orchards no longer produced and the livestock had gradually been killed for food. Everything the d'Avignon family had stood for was gone now, as if it had never existed, leaving a starving man and son, as desperate as desperate could be.

And Mat… poor, simple Mat… had never been smart enough or diligent enough to train as a knight. God knows, McCloud had tried. He'd sent his son away to foster only to have the boy sent home because he was dense. He had no skills, no way of learning anything that would elevate his status or create a future for himself, so he'd gone out one night in search of food and had ended up killing a shepherd who had been tending a flock of sheep. Mat had stolen one of the sheep, which had kept him and his father fed for almost a month.

McCloud had been horrified by the event but his hunger had been stronger than his horror. He ate the ill-gotten sheep because it was all they had. But when there was nothing left but the hide, Mat had gone out again to seek food and had come across a farmer and his wife taking their produce to market. Mat had strangled the wife and bashed the husband's head in with a rock, taking the cart of produce back to his father's home. The produce went into the root cellar and the cart was used for kindling. The vegetables had lasted even longer than the sheep had, but once they were gone, Mat was forced to go out and procure food again.

And kill again.

It was a horrific cycle that McCloud, as a seasoned knight, should have stopped. He knew he should have stopped Mat and that he should have brought his simple son to justice. He began to hear whispers from those in the towns surrounding his farm that an angel of death was on the loose. People were living in fear. But the will to do what was right had left McCloud when he realized he could no longer feed his family. So his son continued his killing spree unimpeded.

Still, McCloud had one hope in a child who had been sent away to foster eight years earlier. A daughter who was more of a stranger to him than a child he was close to or fond of, but a daughter who could marry well and carry them all out of poverty. Aye, she was his only hope. But instead of being sympathetic to their plight, all he'd found when he'd visited Eynsford after all those years was a daughter who was repulsed by what her father and brother had become. She hadn't been sympathetic in the least.

Now, she was once again speaking loud of their plight and McCloud didn't like it. He didn't like feeling judged. He needed her help in all of this and he was going to get it. She was going to do her duty as a daughter should. With the reacquaintance with Val de Nerra, perhaps that opened up an entirely new world of opportunity.

It was all he could think of.

"Let us not speak of such things now," McCloud said after a moment, pondering what was to come. "We have the opportunity to eat a fine meal and sleep in a warm bed this night. Let that be the only thing we think of this day."

Vesper looked at her father; he seemed far too calm about the situation, as if nothing in the world was amiss. He spoke of a fortuitous meeting with the Itinerant Justice of Hampshire. She was starting to wonder what he meant. Even though she didn't know him very well, something in his manner bespoke of a man with more on his mind than the fine meal and warm bed he spoke of.

"So de Nerra is your friend," she said, studying his face for any hint of what he might be thinking. "I fail to see why you think this is such a fortunate meeting. Why do you not think that supping with the law in this land would not be opening yourself up for trouble?"

McCloud simply shook his head. "Because he is my old friend," he said. "We shall not speak of your brother this night. I will ensure that nothing suspicious is discussed. We will speak of our adventures in France. Look, now, a sparrow has flown across the morning sun. That is a good omen. It will be a fine day."

Vesper lifted her eyes to the sky, seeing a variety of birds flying overhead. It seemed to her that her father was trying to distract her now, unwilling to speak any more on Val de Nerra. Truth be told, she had about all of the arguing she could handle with her father. This journey had been an exhaustive one and the more she thought on a warm bed and a fine meal, the better she began to feel. It would be lovely to experience those things because she knew that once they left the Justice's home, they would be faced with cold nights and hardship until they reached Durley. God only knows what they'd find when they got there.

Vesper couldn't even think about it.

Spending the night in a safe and warm haven was looking better and better.

CHAPTER THREE

Selborne Castle

IT WAS NEARING the evening meal, late in the afternoon, when Val and his men returned to the castle.

As they approached from the east, they could see the pale-stoned walls of the fortress gleaming in the sunset, protecting the enormous keep and hall within her bosom. It was a sight that Val never got tired of, a castle that had belonged to his ancestors, built by Saxon lords but fortified by the Normans. His blood ran within those stone walls with the lineage that his mother repeatedly preached to him. Truthfully, he was as sentimental about the place as she was.

Only he'd never tell her that.

The gates of the fortress were open, great iron panels lodged within a stout gatehouse. Beyond was the vast bailey with its large stables near the gatehouse. While further back by the keep, there was a stone troop house for the soldiers, two small cottages for the married knights, trade stalls, and the kitchens – butchery, buttery, store house, garden, and more. The keep itself was enormous, built of stone by an ancestor who adapted the Norman way of building and had constructed an impenetrable tower in the middle of the castle grounds.

The keep was unique in that it was fairly self-sufficient, built to withstand a siege even if the enemy gained control of the bailey and walls. An enormous iron gate protected an equally massive oak door, forged with iron rivets, which protected the small hall, a well and kitchen on the sub-level, several chambers that were small but well-ventilated, and even a chapel.

In all, the keep was a stunning example of functional Norman construction, as was the great hall next to it, built with heavy stone and a sod roof. To Val, the sight of his ancestral castle was something he drew strength from. Even as he reined his horse to a halt, he found himself surveying his castle as a Caesar would survey his empire. This was *his* empire. It was true that he had inherited this property, but he had worked hard for everything else. He didn't consider Selborne a gift or simply his inheritance; he considered it something only he was worthy of.

Handing his steed off to a stable groom who had rushed out with other grooms to greet the incoming horses, Val began to make his way towards the keep, already inhaling the smells of the coming meal. He could most definitely smell pork. Smoke from the kitchens hung heavy in the air. Crossing the bailey, he was hungry already, thinking of the night ahead and conversation with McCloud. He was looking forward to an evening with someone he'd not seen in a long time and conversation with someone other than his mother and his knights.

Just as Val neared the steps leading up to the entry level of the keep, his mother appeared in the entry door. Val removed his helm, running his fingers through his damp hair as he mounted the steps.

"Valor," his mother said sternly as he came within earshot. "Where have you been?"

Val paused at the top of the stairs. "Horsham," he said. "We were fortunate to capture our fugitive in Whitehill so we took the man to Lord Horsham. It is a long ride there and back."

Margaretha eyed her son, disapproval in her expression. "I see," she said. "While you have been rushing about all over Hampshire saving the world from cutthroats, a man and his daughter showed up on our doorstep demanding food and lodgings. He says he is a friend of yours."

Val began to loosen his gloves. "Did he give his name?"

"McCloud d'Avignon."

Val eyed her. "He is, indeed, an old friend of mine," he said. "I saw him in Whitehill and invited him to sup. You were not rude to him, were you?"

Margaretha scowled. "Of course not," she snapped. "I did not question him, although I wanted to. The man wears rags and appears destitute. Are you certain he is a friend of yours?"

Val sighed. "Not all friends come with coffers of gold," he said. "D'Avignon comes from a very old family that lives somewhere to the south. Down by Southampton, I think."

Margaretha didn't appear convinced. "Why have I not heard of this friend until now?"

Val simply pushed past her. "Because I cannot tell you of every single friend I have ever had," he said. "I knew many men in France, men I have not told you of. But rest assured, McCloud d'Avignon is my friend. I intend to sup with him tonight to become reacquainted with the man and I would like for you to be polite to him."

Margaretha followed him into the keep. "I have been. I am the model of decorum."

Val wasn't entirely sure of that. His mother came across like a shrew most of the time, so he was hoping McCloud and his daughter hadn't been offended by her manner. But to say something about it would only bring about an argument, so he kept his mouth shut. He pulled off one of his gloves, heading for the spiral stairs that were built into the thickness of the wall.

"Where did you put McCloud and his daughter?" he asked.

Margaretha pointed up. "On the top level," she said. "The Priest's Chamber and the Constable's Chamber."

Those were designations that, one hundred years ago, were rooms that had once actually housed the castle priest and the castle constable. Selborne no longer had a resident priest or a need for a constable, so these days they were chambers meant for guests but were still referred to by their formal designations. Val began to mount the steps.

"Are we supping in the great hall tonight?"

"We are."

"Then I shall return to my chamber, strip myself of my weapons, and escort McCloud's daughter to the great hall," he said. "You will escort McCloud. It will give you time to amend your opinion of him."

That was proper etiquette with guests but Margaretha wasn't thrilled about it. She didn't want to amend her opinion about anyone. She began to follow her son up the stairs.

"They can only stay the night, Valor," she said sternly. "I do not like your friend's manners. You should see the way he looked over Selborne when he arrived."

"What do you mean?"

"I mean that he looked it over most greedily. And he commented on it."

"What did he say?"

"He said you must have done very well for yourself."

"Well, I *have*."

Margaretha wasn't finished. "It was the *way* he said it," she stressed. "Almost… envious. He even asked if you had married."

"There is no crime in that."

"Nay, there is no crime in that question, but it seemed to me that it was a rather bold question to ask. Furthermore, do you know they arrived on foot? They did not even have a horse between them."

They had reached the floor above and Val came to a pause. "On foot?" he said, surprised. "When I saw them in Whitehill, it was near the livery. I assumed they had horses in the livery."

"Nary a one."

Val thought that was strange but not overly so. He didn't give it much thought, truthfully. He was simply looking forward to the coming meal and conversation, and that was all that occupied his thoughts at the moment.

"Well," he said as he turned for his chamber. "If the man wants to borrow a pair of horses to make it home, I will happily loan them to him. McCloud d'Avignon saved my life more than once in France so he can have whatever he wants. You should be grateful to him, too."

"Valor, I…."

He cut her off. "*Please*, Mother. For my sake. Just… be kind."

Margaretha didn't reply as she watched him walk into his chamber, leaving the door open as he began to strip down of his weapons and mail. He was unbuckling and unstrapping things, tossing them onto his bed or even onto the floor. When he began pulling off his tunic, she turned away and headed back down the stairs, heading to the kitchens to ensure the evening meal would be on time.

As she made her way out of the keep, crossing the bailey beneath the clear, dusky sky, her thoughts were lingering on the man her son had called his friend. A slovenly man who smelled of compost. Old, grizzled, she didn't like the look of him one bit. How her beautiful boy could befriend such a decayed example of a man was beyond her comprehension.

But Val was magnanimous that way; he tended to make friends easily, a likable man that was greatly esteemed by all. In truth, she envied that quality about him. He was a good judge of character and she was proud of that. But in this case, she simply thought he had lost his mind. She'd have to keep an eye on Val's friend to ensure the man didn't make off with anything of value when he left Selborne. Even if Val was unconcerned with the man's obvious poverty, Margaretha was not so blind.

She fully intended the man and his daughter would be gone at sunrise.

VESPER WAS FAIRLY certain she had died and gone to heaven.

The tiny chamber that the gruff older woman had put her in had a small bed, but very soft, a basin for washing, and a hearth that a servant had stoked when she'd arrived. Vesper had asked the same servant for hot water to wash with but the woman evidently thought she'd meant a bath, so one had been brought up to her, complete with soaps and towels.

It was a type of bath where it was basically a copper pot with tall sides and a stool in the middle of it, meant to sit on and bathe sitting up. Before Vesper could protest the trouble of an actual bath, servants filled the copper pot with hot water, several inches of it, and Vesper was able to have a hot bath, something she'd not had in weeks. The lure of that luxury was stronger than her protests.

Aye, this was heaven.

So, she sat on the stool and poured the hot water over her body, lathering up the soap that smelled of lavender and scrubbing every inch of skin. She even washed her hair with it. Living at Eynsford Castle for the past eight years, she'd grown up with access to a fair amount of luxuries – baths, soaps, fine wines and sweets, things that most people considered extravagances. Lady Eynsford had expensive taste and her husband indulged her. And being that Vesper had been one of the woman's wards, she, too, was the recipient of some fine things on occasion.

In fact, she'd loved her life at Eynsford Castle. She didn't want to leave it. When her father had shown up two weeks ago, purely by surprise, she hadn't been all that glad to see him. After her mother had died, Vesper had been sent to Eynsford while her father had gone to France, burying his grief fighting Henry's wars. Vesper had been glad of it, though. She was so glad that for six straight months after coming to Eynsford, she wept with joy every night while saying her evening prayers.

Giving thanks she no longer had to face unspeakable shame and pain at her home of Durley.

It was shame that she had forced from her mind, unwilling to remember it or speak of it, well forgotten until her father had shown up again, acting as if he wanted to renew his relationship with her. Vesper wanted nothing to do with him but Lady Eynsford had pleaded with her to try. He was her father, after all, and people do change. They grow older and realize their regrets in life. Perhaps McCloud had realized his, as well.

Aye, she'd listened to Lady Eynsford because she'd had little choice. But her heart wasn't in it because every time she saw her father, she saw a man who had refused to protect her from a simpleton brother who liked to crawl into her bed at night.

God, she couldn't even think about that.

But here she was, heading back to Durley with her father, back to the place where those horrific memories were lodged. But this time, it was different – her simpleton brother had graduated from trying to fondle his sister to murdering innocent people.

When her father had gotten drunk one night and confessed Mat's wicked activities, Vesper knew she had to do something. She wasn't exactly sure what she could do, but something had to be done. She had to stop her foolish brother from destroying himself and taking the entire family with him, for no man would want to marry a woman whose brother was a known murderer.

Therefore, it wasn't Mat's life she was saving but her own.

She could admit that to herself. She was selfish and she knew it, but she had her whole life to live and dreams to fulfill, and she wouldn't let Mat ruin her prospects. There wasn't an altruistic bone in her body when it came to her father and brother.

Sweet Jesù, what has my family become?

So, she took comfort in something as simple as a warm bath, trying not to think of what lay ahead for her. After washing every scrap of skin and hair, she dried off before the warm fire and dressed in a dark green surcoat that she'd made herself with fabric supplied by Lady Eynsford. Her damp hair went into a braid, trailing down her back. Sitting by the hearth, she was warm, clean, and content for the first time in days. Somehow, it made facing her coming tribulations more bearable.

A knock on the door roused her from her thoughts. The chamber was so small that the door was literally right next to her. Rising from her stool, she cautiously opened the panel to find a handsome man standing there. Their eyes met and he smiled timidly.

"My lady," he greeted. "I have come to escort you to sup. Are you ready?"

Although Vesper really didn't recognize the man, she recognized the voice as that of her father's friend, the very man who had invited them to feast. She opened the door wider, rather surprised by the vision in front of her. The man she'd seen back at Whitehill had been a big man with piercing green eyes and a bright smile of straight white teeth, but she'd been unable to see much more than that because he'd had a helm on that had obscured much of his face. Truthfully, she hadn't paid any attention. But the man standing in front of her...

Now, she wished she'd paid more attention.

As she'd noticed at the first meeting, Val de Nerra was a very big man, broad-shouldered, but now that he wasn't wearing his mail protection, she could see that he had a head of curly, dark hair and a square jaw. His skin was darker, too, as if he spent a lot of his time out in the sun, which made his bright eyes even brighter.

And that smile... Vesper wasn't one to find attraction with men. In fact, they rather frightened her. But Val was the most attractive man she'd ever seen and that smile was a large part of it. Something about those big teeth made her heart flutter strangely.

"I am ready, my lord," she said quickly, realizing that her mind had been wandering at the sight of him. "I am extremely grateful for your hospitality."

Val's gaze lingered on her, perhaps as appraisingly as hers had lingered on him. "It is my pleasure for my old friend and his daughter," he said. "I only returned home a short while ago so I've not seen your father yet. Was your trip from Whitehill uneventful?"

Vesper nodded. "Uneventful, my lord," she replied. "The weather was excellent and we suffered no difficulty."

Val stepped away from the door, extending his hand to the stairs as if to invite her to follow him. "I am glad to hear that," he said. "My mother said you were traveling on foot. What happened to your horses?"

Vesper faltered a bit, trying to appear as if she wasn't. But she couldn't think up a reasonable answer swiftly enough because she never thought this question would be asked. It was too close to the reason for their journey altogether.

My brother kept the horse....

"My… my father does not have any," she lied. "I am sure he will tell you more about his situation this evening. Since it has been such a long time since you have seen him, I am sure there will be much to speak of."

Val could see that he'd unbalanced her with a simple question. But her answer made him curious. "What situation?" he asked, but then it began to occur to him – his mother had mentioned how slovenly McCloud had appeared. *Poverty*, she'd said. Was it possible his old friend had fallen on hard times? "Forgive me, my lady – I do not mean to pry, but I am genuinely concerned for your father. He was a great friend to me in France. Is… is he in need of money? Of work?"

Vesper was growing increasingly uncomfortable. "Truthfully, I do not know," she said. "Until last week, I'd seen my father only once in the eight years I was at Eynsford. I do not know what he needs. He will have to tell you."

Val could see that he'd upset her with his questions, for she seemed nervous now, unable or unwilling to look him in the eye. Perhaps he had been too inquisitive, asking her things he should not have. He paused just as they reached the stairs.

"I am truly sorry," he said. "I did not mean to offend you. I did not realize… well, I did not realize you'd not seen your father in so long. I thought you knew his needs."

"Alas, my lord, I do not."

"Then I will, once again, apologize for asking. But I am sure it has been a blessing for you coming to know him again."

Vesper had to bite her tongue. *If you only knew!* "It was surprising to see him again," she said, forcing a smile. "I hardly recognized him.

He has a great bushy beard now that he'd not had before."

Val laughed softly, taking the stairs first and reaching out to take her elbow to help steady her as she followed him. "That is nothing new," he said. "He had that terrible beard in France. It grew wild, like a forest, and he used to say that after each meal, he could run hot water through it and make soup from the crumbs."

That brought a genuine smile to Vesper. "How disgusting," she giggled. "Now I will have this terrible image in my mind all night about my father making soup from his beard."

She continued to giggle and Val found himself completely upswept in her silly little laugh. It was enchanting. More than that, when the woman smiled, she was quite beautiful. The prospect of staring at her across the feasting table all evening did not distress him.

"So I have said the wrong thing again, have I?" he said, taking the steps slowly because she was. "I must apologize yet again. It seems that I have been completely clumsy in my attempts at conversation. Do not tell my mother or she will take a strap to me."

Vesper was still grinning, looking into his glimmering green eyes now. "You are quite a bit larger than she is," she reminded him. "Surely you can best her."

Val's dark eyebrows flew up. "My mother? God help you, my lady, for you do not know what you are saying. My mother is so fearsome, the devil himself would run from her."

Vesper remembered the brusque woman who had showed her to her chamber and she could understand why Val would make such a statement. But she would not agree with him. To do so would be impolite.

"Your mother was very kind when we arrived," she assured him. "I found her very pleasant."

They had reached the landing with a second flight of steps leading down to the entry level. Val cocked an eyebrow at her.

"Are we speaking of the same woman?"

Vesper fought off a grin. "I believe so. A white wimple and round cheeks?"

"And she carried a pitchfork?"

Vesper burst out into laughter. "She did *not*."

He grunted. "Then she must have hidden it away." His hand was on her elbow as he began to take the second flight of steps down. "Believe me, she has a pitchfork. It is her weapon of choice."

Vesper shook her head at him reproachfully. "Do you slander your mother, my lord?"

He shook his head quickly. "It is not slander if it is the truth."

"Should I ask her, then?"

"If you do, you may see both the pitchfork and the strap come out at me. You would not want that, would you?"

There was a twinkle in his eye as he spoke. He was deliberately flirting with her and Vesper couldn't ever remember having such an engaging conversation with a man. There were rare occasions when she would receive flattery from any one of Eynsford's men and, in particular, one man who seemed to be quite solicitous of her, but it wasn't something Vesper reciprocated. Therefore, she was badly out of practice when it came to the art of flirting. All she could do was speak of the first thing that came to mind.

"Nay, I would not," she said, watching him flash a smile at her. "I suppose I would not ask if it would mean your downfall."

Val bowed exaggeratedly. "You are most gracious, my lady," he said. "I will be forever in your debt."

Vesper smiled coyly. "I am sure that is not necessary," she said. "In fact, my father and I should be the ones in your debt to show us such hospitality. It was most kind of you."

Val hit the bottom of the stairs, helping her down the last few slippery stone steps. "We rarely have guests, so this is a special event. Your company is most welcome."

Vesper came off the stairs, her skirt lifted slightly so she wouldn't step on it. Something about his last few words sounded very inviting and almost personal. It was enough to bring a blush to her cheeks.

"I am glad," she said, noticing that he hadn't let go of her arm. Not that she minded. "I… I am sure it will be a memorable evening for us all."

"Of that, I am sure."

Val led her towards the keep entry, with the mild evening sky above and the hall across the bailey, light emitting from the lancet windows. Val moved through the entryway but Vesper paused, drinking it all in. It was a beautiful night.

"This place reminds me of Eynsford," she said wistfully, looking across the torch-lit bailey. "Such a lovely castle. Have you ever been there, my lord?"

Val nodded. "I have been there on business," he said. "But I have never seen you there."

Vesper looked at him, smiling weakly. "That is because Lady Eynsford was very careful with her ladies, my lord," she said. "Whenever Lord William had visitors, we were kept away. I would have never known you were there."

Val lifted his eyebrows. "I do not blame Lady Eynsford for keeping you away from male visitors. One look at you and men would lay siege to the castle simply to gaze upon your beauty."

Even in the moonlight, Vesper flushed violently. "I cannot imagine such a thing, my lord," she said. Then, she began to walk, heading to the steps that led down into the bailey. "I hope they are not waiting for us to arrive. I do not mean to be late."

She was trying to change the subject, embarrassed that Val's gentle flirting had caused her to blush. She loved it and was unnerved by it at the same time.

But Val figured that out fairly quickly. Vesper had moved out of his range, her head lowered as she descended the steps, and his hand had dropped from her elbow. The reason for her behavior began to occur to him. He followed.

"You have no idea how lovely you are, do you?" he asked softly.

Vesper wouldn't look at him, having no idea how to gracefully answer him. "I… I would not know, my lord."

"Stop addressing me formally. We are old friends now. You may call me Val."

She came to a stop, looking at him with great surprise. "I… I am not sure that is proper, my lord."

He cocked a disapproving eyebrow at her, reaching out to take her hand. He tucked it into the crook of his elbow, possessively. "It is proper if I say it is proper," he said. "It is impolite to refuse to call me by my name when I have asked you to. Did you ever think of that?"

She hadn't. She continued to wallow in embarrassment as he resumed their walk towards the great hall. "I did not mean to offend you," she said. "I will call you Val if that is your wish."

"It is. And I would like to call you Vesper but mayhap I will wait until your father gives me permission. I should not like to become too familiar with you and anger McCloud. I have seen what that man can do with a sword and I have no desire to be on the receiving end."

Vesper's lips twitched with a smile as she dared to look up at him. "Val," she repeated as if mulling over the name. "Is that your Christian name? The name you were given at birth?"

He shook his head. "My given name is Valor," he said. "I am the only son of Sir Gavin de Nerra and Lady Margaretha Byington de Nerra. I was named Valor because that is what my parents wished for me – a life of strength and valor. And you? I did not realize that McCloud was so pious that he would name his child after evening prayers."

Vesper's smile grew. "It was my mother's idea," she said as the entry to the great hall loomed before them. "She was very devout. I also have a brother named Matins."

Val could see the door to the hall looming, too, and he slowed his pace. He was enjoying their conversation so much that he didn't want it to end, knowing that the moment he set foot in the hall, he would lose her company all to himself. He would have to share her.

He didn't want to.

"I never met your mother," he said, "nor have I met your brother although I recall McCloud speaking of him on occasion. Where does he serve?"

Vesper quickly realized they were treading into the exact territory she wanted to avoid. Any subject of her brother made her vastly nervous and she struggled not to show it. She silently cursed herself for even bringing him up but the deed was done. She couldn't take it back. She labored to give him an answer that sounded relatively benign where Mat was concerned.

God help me not to give anything away!

"Mat was born simple," she said quietly. "He was never capable of serving as a knight should."

It was a truthful response. Val seemed sympathetic. "I wondered why he did not serve with your father in France," he said. "He is older than you, is he not?"

She nodded. "He is five years older than I am."

Val pondered that. "Then I am sure he is proficient at whatever profession he chose," he said. He came to a halt, looking at the entry door. "It seems we have arrived."

Vesper was vastly relieved to be off the subject of her brother. She took to the change readily. "Shall we go in?"

Val gave her a half-smile but he didn't move. "They are expecting us."

"Are you not hungry?"

He shrugged. "A little. But I was very much enjoying speaking with you."

The flush in her cheeks returned. "And I, you, my lord."

"Val."

"I mean Val."

His smile grew. "I will not let you starve. Let us go in but do not be surprised if I sit next to you. It is not often I have the opportunity to speak with so lovely and accomplished a lady."

Vesper simply smiled, that charming gesture she wielded like a shield when she wasn't sure what to say to him. But that smile seemed to say everything to him, at least everything in his own mind. Who knew what was really in her thoughts? He could dream, couldn't he? Chuckling at her modesty and liking very much her coy manner, Val escorted her into the great hall.

He hoped it would be an evening to remember for them both.

CHAPTER FOUR

THE MOMENT VAL and Vesper entered the great hall of Selborne, they were hit in the face by the heat from not one but two blazing hearths.

Given that the night was so mild, the heat was nearly oppressive. Dogs roamed the hall, looking for a handout, as servants bustled about to deliver food to hungry diners. The hall was big enough for a few hundred people and, given that it was where the soldiers usually ate, it was full of men noisily eating and drinking.

The difference, however, was that on this night Lady Margaretha wasn't dining in the small hall, as was usual, but was sitting at the table reserved only for the family and honored guests. The table was in better repair than the four others in the hall and could seat nearly thirty people at any given time. It was also positioned in its own alcove off the main hall, with its own small hearth, for a measure of peace and privacy.

It was to this table that Val escorted Vesper. Already, Margaretha and McCloud were there, as were Kenan, Mayne, and Calum and his wife, Lady Celesse de Geld de Morville. Calum and Celesse had been married six months and Celesse was already with child, a pregnancy that had caused her great illness. Val was surprised to see her, in fact, as he brought Vesper to the table. Celesse usually didn't deal well with food. He specifically sat Vesper down next to Celesse so Vesper would have a female at her side to make her more comfortable. He could have sat her next to his mother but he feared that would only terrify the young woman.

"Good men, if you have not yet met this lady, permit me to introduce you to Lady Vesper d'Avignon," he said as Vesper took her seat on the bench. "Lady Vesper has been a ward of William Eynsford and is now returning home with her father, my dear friend, McCloud. My lady, this is Sir Calum de Morville and his wife, Lady Celesse, and across the table is Sir Kenan and Sir Mayne."

Vesper smiled politely to those around the table, relieved when Val took up a seat at the end of the table, right next to her. Since he was the only one she knew at the table other than her father, she hadn't wanted him to go far and was pleased when he didn't.

"Good evening," she greeted those at the table.

Immediately, servants appeared with trenchers of boiled pork and cups of tart red wine. The food was quite generous – in addition to the pork, there were boiled apples, carrots, and big hunks of bread. In fact, it was more food than Vesper had seen in a week and her mouth was already watering. When a servant presented a bowl of warmed water with rose petals floating in it so she could wash her hands before eating, she could barely take her eyes off the food to accomplish the task. Wiping her hands on the towel that the servant offered her, she was preparing to rip apart the pork when she heard a soft voice from her left.

"Welcome to Selborne, my lady," Celesse said. "Your father was just telling us of your trip from Eynsford. He said you passed through a town that had a troop of entertainers with trained apes."

Vesper looked over at the woman. She was pale and willowy, with skinny arms and long fingers. Her enormous blue eyes were looking at Vesper with kind interest.

"That is true," Vesper said pleasantly. "They were performing in the street for the coinage people would toss them. I saw at least two monkeys and a bear that danced on its hind legs. It was in Guildford, I believe, so it is possible the troop is moving this way. Mayhap you will have the opportunity to see them."

Celesse's pale features lit up. "I would like that," she said. "I have always loved to watch animals perform. Once, a man with trained dogs came to Selborne to stay for the night. He entertained us with his dogs."

"And she tried to steal them," Calum put in from the other side of his wife. "The man brought five dogs. The next morning, I woke up and four of those dogs were in my bed sleeping peacefully."

Everyone at the table grinned to varying degrees except Celesse; she frowned at her husband. "I told you that I do not know how they got there."

"Lies."

Across the table, Kenan and Mayne chortled, their mouths full of food. "Are you sure it is not one of those dogs that is the father of your wife's child?" Kenan asked.

Mayne burst into guffaws as Calum threw a bread crust at Kenan, hitting the man in the forehead. "At least I *have* a wife, de Poyer," he said.

The insults began to fly but Margaretha suddenly slammed her pewter cup on the table two or three times, breaking up the building argument with her banging.

"I will not listen to your filthy conversation this night," she said pointedly, looking at Kenan. "Not only are we close to the day of the Christmas celebration, but we have guests. If you cannot behave yourself, then you can eat out in the stable with the rest of the animals. Is this in any way unclear?"

Kenan was instantly rebuked. Lady Margaretha wielded more power than her son in times like this. "It is clear, my lady," he said, lowering his head back to his food.

Satisfied that the knights would behave, Margaretha's gaze moved over her son and the lovely young woman sitting next to him. She'd not seen the woman clearly when she arrived for the sheer fact that she had been wearing a cloak. But now she could see the woman plainly – a beautiful creature with high cheekbones and silken hair.

Now, Margaretha was coming to see the real reason behind Val's invitation to these guests – *a beautiful woman.* Her son had always had an eye for lovely women, much as his father had. Now, she understood everything perfectly. It wasn't so much an old friend he'd invited to sup but his old friend's beautiful daughter.

Now, it all makes sense....

The truth was that Margaretha resented the intrusion of her son's friends and she hardly said a word to McCloud since she went to escort the man to sup. But now with Val present, she thought to, perhaps, amend that attitude. She thought to prove a point to her son about this man he had called his friend, a man who dressed in rags and who had commented about the richness of Selborne. Not all men, regardless of the beauty of their daughters, were worthy to be at Val de Nerra's table.

Perhaps it was time for Val to realize he needed to be more careful when it came to befriending men. She'd been stewing about it ever since their arrival; aye, perhaps it was time to teach her son a lesson.

"Val," she said, her focus on her food. "I was hoping that your friend would tell us about himself. Since you have not seen him in so long, mayhap there is a good deal to tell of his peace and prosperity."

Val looked at McCloud, who was seated down the bench from his mother. It was as if Margaretha was deliberately isolating herself from the others, sitting off as she was. It was his mother's way of disapproving of his guests.

"McCloud," Val said politely. "My mother wants to know why you have come to Selborne. She believes you are plotting to marry me and inherit my property. Will you please tell her you are not plotting anything?"

McCloud's head snapped up from his food, looking at Val in shock as Margaretha's manner turned sour.

"I said nothing of the kind," she hissed. "Val, you will apologize for slandering me in front of your guests!"

Val was fighting off a grin. He could see that Calum and the other knights had their faces turned away from him, no doubt fighting smiles of their own. It was always great fun to rib Margaretha until she began throwing things, in which case it was all fun and games until someone lost an eye. But nothing was thrown as of yet, so Val was still confident in jesting with his mother. Lazily, he sighed.

"My apologies, Mother," he said, sounding as if he didn't mean it at all. "McCloud, my mother said nothing of the kind. But I would still like to hear of your life since last I saw you. Surely you have seen great adventure and prosperity."

McCloud swallowed the food in his mouth. He'd been steadily stuffing his belly since they'd arrived in the hall, starving as he was. It had been years since he'd has so much to eat at one time. He was loathed to take the time to converse, but he did so out of courtesy.

"There is not much to tell, truthfully," he said, realizing they were on what could be a very sensitive subject. "Durley is my home and, although I do not believe you have ever been there, it is a farm. It has been in my family since before the Normans came to our shores. We have apple and pear trees and flocks of sheep. At least, we did. I will admit that times have been difficult the past few years."

Val was listening with interest. "I am sorry to hear that," he said, putting bread in his mouth. "What happened?"

McCloud shook his head. "Truthfully, I do not know. The orchards had a blight move through them. It has been difficult for them to bear fruit. But I do not complain. We have food in our bellies and a roof over our head. God sees to our needs."

Considering the state of his friend's clothing and the fact that he had no horses for transportation, Val wondered if that was really the truth but he didn't question the man further. He would leave the man with some semblance of pride and not force him to bear his soul in front of strangers, even if Val was asking the questions out of concern. He forced a smile.

"Then I am happy to hear that God has shown you such fortune," he said. "In speaking with Lady Vesper, she mentioned your son. Why did he not travel with you to Eynsford?"

McCloud held a steady expression even though he was shocked to hear that Vesper had mentioned Mat. "Because… because someone must remain at the farm to tend it," he said. "My son does not like to leave home. He prefers to remain there."

It was a reasonable explanation, one that Val believed. He had no reason not to. "I hope to meet him someday," he said.

McCloud forced a smile, vastly uncomfortable on the subject of his son. "He is not very sociable, unfortunately," he said. "But… but we would, of course, be honored with your visit."

Val was chewing on his pork now, using a broad knife to shovel it into his mouth. "Durley," he said thoughtfully. "Did you tell me once that it was near Southampton?"

"I did."

Val continued to chew. "I've not been to Southampton in quite a while," he said. "I have heard the weather is quite fair there. Mayhap my mother and I are due for a visit."

Margaretha was sipping at her hot, mulled wine, her favored drink. "There is nothing in Southampton that I could want for," she said, making it clear she had no intention of visiting the d'Avignon homestead. "Much like your friend's son, I prefer to remain at home."

McCloud turned to her. "I do not blame you in the least, my lady," he said. "Selborne is a beautiful place. I would never want to leave it, either."

Margaretha looked at the man, hearing that appraising tone again, the same one she'd heard when he'd first arrived at Selborne. She didn't like it in the least and her eyes narrowed as she responded.

"The castle has been in my family for well over two hundred years," she said. "My family heritage is Saxon, a long and distinguished line. We managed to keep our lands when the Normans came and when I die, the estate shall be passed to Valor."

McCloud wasn't oblivious to the woman's suspicious nature; he could read it in her expression. Not that he blamed her, for in this case, she was absolutely right – he was quite envious of Selborne. He had been since he'd walked through the gates and, in seeing the great castle, the plans that had been working in his mind since Whitehill began to take definitive form.

He'd had the entire afternoon to think on his scheme and plan what was to come. It was a pity for greatness like Selborne to belong only to one man, one family. But confident in his plan as he was, he also knew that he had to be very careful about his words or actions if Lady Margaretha was already suspicious of him. Yet his plan, for all of its unsophisticated beauty, was so very simple….

If he could marry Vesper to Val, his troubles would be over.

Even if McCloud's body didn't move swiftly these days, his mind did. It was clear that Val wasn't married and McCloud was seeking a husband for his daughter. That has been his whole purpose of going to Eynsford – a marriage for his daughter that would lift their family out of their poverty-stricken state. What could be better than a marriage between Vesper and his dear friend, the Itinerant Justice of Hampshire? Not only would it ensure the survival of the House of d'Avignon, but if Mat's ghastly deeds were ever discovered, surely Vesper's husband could not punish his wife's brother.

It was the perfect situation.

But he had to be more clever than Lady de Nerra for his plans to come to fruition. He didn't want her blocking his attempts. In truth, there was something to be said for him marrying again as well. And with Lady de Nerra being a widow, that might be another avenue to pursue.

Ah, yes… be clever!

"Then your son and his future wife are very fortunate to not only have such a distinguished matriarch, but such a fine estate," he said after a moment, throwing in a little flattery for the old bird. "In fact, Val never told me he had such a lovely mother. I shall become very angry at him for not telling me."

Ripples of surprise rolled across Margaretha's face, stumped for a reply for the first time in a very long while. But that surprise quickly turned to annoyance. "Flattery will not work on me," she told McCloud. "I am too old to fall victim to such things."

McCloud grinned. "That cannot be true," he said. "For certainly, when I first saw you, I believed you to be Val's sister."

Margaretha nearly choked on her wine, but her round cheeks flushed a bit. "Then your eyesight is terrible."

"That is possible, but I still know a lovely woman when I see one, Lady de Nerra. You can deny it all you want, but I know the truth."

Margaretha hadn't been complimented in so many years that the soft praise poked holes in her brusque matter. Perhaps McCloud was only feigning his flattery, perhaps he wasn't. Perhaps he really meant it. Margaretha was so unused to such things that she simply didn't know what to think and her feminine vanity, long buried, began to awaken, just a little.

As his mother flushed and pretended not to care that a man had paid her a compliment, Val watched the entire scene with a grin on his face. He loved seeing his mother ruffled.

"Keep talking, McCloud," he encouraged the man. "Mayhap you will cause her to smile. I think she likes it."

Margaretha waved a hand at her son as if to brush him off. "You are a beast," she told him. "Flattery is the product of a weak male mind."

Val's eyebrows lifted, looking at the other men around the table, including Calum. "Did you hear that?" he said to the knight. "Your mind must be horribly weak because I know for a fact that you flattered Celesse most sickeningly when you were courting her."

Calum laughed. "And I thought I was being rather clever about it."

Celesse patted his cheek. "You were, my love," she said. "You were so clever that I believed every word."

"And now look at you."

Celesse sighed and patted her pregnant belly. "Aye, now look at me," she said. Then, she looked at Vesper. "Are you married, my lady?"

Vesper, who had been paying less attention to the conversation and more attention to her food, looked at Celesse as if startled by the question. Mouth full, she struggled to swallow her bite.

"N-Nay, my lady, I am not," she said.

Celesse didn't sense that she might be embarrassing the guest. "I cannot believe such a thing," she said, meaning it as a compliment. "You are quite lovely, which I am sure has not gone unnoticed by any of the unmarried knights here. Are you betrothed?"

Vesper was starting to flush again, her cheeks turning hot. "I am not, my lady," she replied, praying this woman would move to another subject. Not wanting to take the chance that she wouldn't, she sought to change the focus herself. "May I ask when your child is due to be born?"

Any mention of her baby and Celesse was more than willing to speak on it. She forgot about the unmarried lady at the table and beamed as she rubbed her belly.

"Early next year," she said. "Calum wishes to return to Scotland to present the babe to his father, who is the Constable of Scotland. Have you heard of him? His father is the Lord of Westmoreland."

She said it proudly and Vesper shook her head. "Alas, I have not heard of him, but that is a very prestigious association," she said. "Was your husband born in Scotland, then?"

From Vesper's other side, Val spoke. He found he simply couldn't keep out of a conversation with Vesper involved, not even when the subject didn't directly concern him.

"Calum was born in Scotland but he has spent most of his life in England," he said. "He does not sound like a Scots, nor does his brother, Hugh. Calum, what has become of Hugh as of late? He used to visit us quite often because we are on the road between Winchester Castle and London, but now we never see him."

The women were pushed out of the conversation completely as Calum replied. "He has been with Henry in Winchester as far as I know," he said. "But my father has also been ill so it is possible he has returned to Scotland. I am not for certain."

Val's gaze lingered on his friend. "I told you that you could return to Scotland, too, to see to your father."

Calum shook his head, looking at his wife. "I do not want to take the chance that I will not return before my son is born."

Val understood his point of view, but his thoughts inevitably turned to Scotland. "I would like to return to Scotland someday," he said. "I always thought I would like to live in the north. It is such a wild place but it is also a place of such beauty. Have you ever been north, Lady Vesper?"

Vesper shook her head as the conversation swung back to her. "Never," she replied. "But I have heard it is quite lovely."

"Then mayhap you should ask your husband to take you there for your wedding trip." Mayne suddenly entered the conversation from across the table. He'd been staring at Vesper through the entire conversation with something more than polite interest. "I must agree with Celesse. I cannot believe that you are not married or at least betrothed. What fool has allowed you to get away from him?"

Vesper had never been around so much flattery in her life. She was certain her cheeks would be a permanent shade of pink after this. But before she could answer, Val stepped in.

"That is a rather impertinent question, don't you think?" he asked Mayne, frowning. "You will apologize for being rude."

There was a flicker of jealousy in Val's eyes, which surprised Mayne. Still, in hindsight, he shouldn't have been surprised. Lady Vesper was quite lovely, something that wouldn't have gone overlooked by Val. He had an eye for pretty women. Opening his mouth to plead the lady's forgiveness, Mayne was interrupted when Vesper lifted a hand to him.

"Apologies are not necessary, truly," she said to both Val and Mayne. "Lady Celesse also suggested disbelief that I am not betrothed. I suppose it is true that, at my age, I should be, but it does not distress me that I am not. I have had a very good life at Eynsford Castle as a confidant of Lady Eynsford. My life is very full with my duties and I have not felt wanting in any fashion, truly."

Val and Mayne were both looking at her, both of them thinking nearly the same thoughts – a beautiful, accomplished woman who was not already spoken for was a prize, indeed. Val knew simply by looking at Mayne what the man's thoughts were because had the expression of a hunter about him.

But Val wasn't about to let Vesper fall prey to the man. *He is interested in her*, Val thought. He was grossly offended by it.

"I would be very interested to hear of your duties at Eynsford," Val said, leading into a much more pleasant line of conversation instead of her lack of a betrothal. "Do you hope to return someday?"

Vesper nodded. "I would like to," she said. "Lady Eynsford would like for me to continue attending her. I have been her ward for so long but she would like for me to be one of her ladies, which would be a tremendous honor. It is through her that I have learned so many things, but I am particularly fond of sewing and music. Whenever Lady Eynsford requires something new to wear, she always has me produce it for her."

She seemed very proud and Val was impressed. "That is an exacting skill," he said. "You must be excellent."

"I do like to sew and create garments."

"And the music?"

"I have learned to sing and accompany myself on a *clavichordium*," she said. "Lady Eynsford had one brought all the way from Italy and, although she did not know how to play it, I was quite fascinated by it. She gave me permission to play it and, soon enough, I learned how to. Lady Eynsford was very pleased."

Val's gaze lingered on her for a moment before leaping to his feet and taking her by the wrist.

"Come with me," he said quietly.

Vesper had no choice but to follow as he practically yanked her from the table. Val ignored his mother calling after him as they disappeared into the rear of the great hall where there was a wooden staircase that led to the minstrel's gallery above. In truth, Vesper hadn't even noticed the minstrel's gallery, a loft on the north side of the vast hall, until Val had pulled her up the staircase. Even then, the gallery seemed to be more for storage than anything else.

There were old trunks, an old wardrobe, and other things, neatly arranged but quite obviously forgotten up in the darkened gallery. Val led her to the balcony where the gallery overlooked the hall, coming to a halt in front of something that was covered up with a great length of canvas made from hemp. It was dusty from not having been disturbed in quite some time and Val had Vesper stand back as he yanked the canvas away.

Dust flew up in the air but beneath the fabric sat a small *clavichordium*. It was quite small, built as a boxy wooden cabinet on four spindly legs that, at one time, had been highly polished. Now, it was lonely and forgotten. On the plate above the ivory keys were the words *Aurelius Cato Anno MCXXXIX* etched into the plate, perhaps once painted with gold paint. It was difficult to tell because time had faded away some of the gold, but in all, it was a magnificent piece. Vesper was enchanted.

"It is beautiful," she said softly as she bent over to inspect the old keys. "Is it yours?"

Val watched her as she studied the old instrument. "Nay," he said. "It was my father's. He, too, was musical and had a talent for instruments, but this has sat here unused since his death. Mayhap, you would be kind enough to play it for us. I am sure my mother would like to hear the sounds again."

Vesper looked at him, smiling timidly. "If you do not believe she would mind."

Val shook his head. "She would love to hear you play it," he said, suddenly looking around as if he was missing something. "There is a stool that goes with it but I do not… ah, here it is."

He yanked a small three-legged stool out from beneath a stored table, setting the stool in front of the instrument and indicating for her to sit.

"My lady?" he said, an encouraging smile on his face. "If you please?"

Vesper couldn't resist. She really did love playing music so she carefully sat, timidly pressing one of the keys to see if the old instrument even worked. A soft, slightly out of tune note echoed in the loft and also down into the hall, where it was heard above all of the noise and eating. Sensing that entertainment was about to come, the room quieted down and Val smiled at her when she seemed too hesitant to play another note.

"Go ahead," he said softly. "Play something as beautiful as you are."

Vesper looked at him, seeing purely by the man's expression that he was sincere. It made her heart leap strangely, that same feeling he'd caused within her once before. It also fed her courage as she very much wanted to please him now, as her host. Or perhaps it was even more than the fact that he was simply a generous host; perhaps it was because he'd been so kind to her. *I like the way he looks at me.* Placing her hands on the keys, she played four or five chords before finally lifting her voice in song.

I dreamt that you loved me still
And loved me forever and a day.
From beyond the mellow sea
I felt your spirit calling to me
And I dreamt that you loved me still.

She had a pure, true voice, like the sound of angels singing. It was very sweet and high. Val couldn't help the grin that spread across his face as she continued to play the instrument but her singing had stopped for the moment. Now, she was simply continuing the song without words but her sweet voice lingered in his ears. He wanted to hear it again.

"Surely that is not all you are going to sing for us," he said, moving up beside her as she played. "I have never heard anything so lovely in my life. Please sing something else."

Vesper paused in her playing. "If you wish," she said, clearly flattered at his praise. "I am sorry, but the instrument is slightly out of tune. I am afraid my singing might sound poorly because of it."

He shook his head before the words were even out of her mouth. "You open your mouth and angels pour forth," he said. "Nothing you could sing could sound poorly, my lady. Please sing another."

Vesper was back to blushing again. Val was a charming man and not afraid to heap praise upon her, something she was very quickly coming to like. His words made her feel very special and honored in a way she could never remember feeling. Wondering if he truly meant what he said never crossed her mind; surely he meant it.

She wanted to believe him.

O lovely one… my lovely one…

The years will come… the years will go…

But still you'll be… my own true love…

Until the day… we'll meet again….

Seeing Val's enthralled expression, she continued with the next verse.

O lovely one… my lovely one…

My love for you… will never die…

My heart is yours… 'til the end of time…

When you will be…my own true love…

The song was glorious and endearing, a love song that was typical of the songs in these times, written and sung by troubadours or young maidens like Vesper. Songs that spoke of lasting affection, undying love, or sad partings. All Val knew was that those words, words he'd heard before, had never really had any meaning to him until Vesper had sung them. As he watched her sing, he couldn't help but wonder what it would be like to have the affection of a woman like Vesper.

My heart is yours… 'til the end of time….

Those thoughts had never occurred to him until that very moment. What a lovely thing that would be… with the right person.

Rather startled at his turn of thought, Val looked over the side of the balcony to see that the room below had come to a halt. Faces were turned upward, towards the minstrel's gallery, all of them waiting eagerly for the next bit of music to come. Val looked over to see what his mother's reaction was to Vesper playing Gavin's old *clavichordium* and he could see his mother looking up at the gallery as well, a rather wistful expression on her face.

He hadn't seen that expression from her in a very long time and Val had to admit that he was touched. His mother, for all of her gruffness and petulance, had a soft heart beneath that she liked to keep hidden. He was pleased that Vesper had given the woman a moment to find that soft part of her again. He was more impressed that she could bring a room full of people to a halt with her sweet singing voice. Returning his attention to Vesper, who was just playing a few chords now and not singing, he knelt down beside her.

"You have a captive audience below," he said. "Play and sing to your heart's content. Everyone is enjoying it very much."

Vesper kept her eyes on the keys as she played. "To tell you the truth, I have never played for anyone other than Lady Eynsford. It is good that I cannot see the hall from where I sit for if I could, I would surely faint of fright."

He laughed softly. "You seem brave enough to me," he said. "Moreover, you sing and play so beautifully that it is a genuine tragedy for you not to be heard. McCloud must be very proud of your accomplishments."

Vesper thought of her father and her good mood faded. Nay, her father wasn't proud of her accomplishments or if he was, he'd not said so. He was as wrapped up in life at Durley as she was wrapped up in life at Eynsford and the two did not meet. They didn't even come close.

Not wanting to get on to the subject of her relationship with her father, she sought to change the focus, realizing she had done a good deal of subject changing when in conversation with Val throughout the course of their association. She hoped he hadn't noticed.

"As I am sure your mother is very proud of your accomplishments as well," she said. "My father did not tell me much of how you and he met. Mayhap we should return to the table so I may hear some of those adventures in France that you spoke of."

But Val did, indeed, notice that she always seemed to change the subject away from her and especially away from her father. He realized she didn't know McCloud very well but he was coming to suspect it was more than unfamiliarity that made her shy away from discussing her father. There was some kind of sullenness there, as if she not only didn't know her father but didn't *want* to know him.

There was resistance.

However, the lady spoke so fondly of Eynsford Castle that Val was coming to think she hadn't wanted to leave it, that perhaps McCloud might have forced her to. But for what purpose? His curiosity about the lady, and about McCloud, was growing. There was something odd afoot that he couldn't quite put his finger on as if to say "*Aye! That's it*!" Nay; it wasn't anything definitive.

But it was there.

"There is all evening to speak of France," he said after a moment. "I do believe everyone would rather listen to you play. It has been so long since we've had good music in this hall. Won't you please indulge us?"

Not strangely, Vesper didn't feel much like singing anymore. Her thoughts were leaning heavily on her father and on leaving this wonderful place and wishing she didn't have to.

"I… I am a bit tired after traveling today," she said. "I hope you will forgive me that I am too tired to continue. But I would be happy to play something for you to sing."

Val lifted his eyebrows at the irony of that request. "I do not know any fine songs. Moreover, I am a terrible singer. How can you punish everyone in this hall with such a request?"

Vesper burst into soft laughter. "I do not believe you," she said. "All knights are trained in courtly accomplishments. Did you not learn to sing when you were younger?"

He made a face that suggested she was asking him something most distasteful. "Aye, I did, but I do not want to speak of it. I was teased mercilessly. My master told me that a goose sounded better than I did when I sang."

Vesper bit her lip, trying to keep from laughing at him but it was to no avail. "I am sure that is not true," she said. "Please sing something. I insist. What can I play for you?"

Val didn't want to deny her but he truly didn't want to sing. Therefore, he sought to teach her a lesson. Perhaps if he sang a terrible and shocking song, she would never ask again. He eyed her thoughtfully.

"Do you know *Tilly Nodden*?" he asked.

Vesper's brow furrowed in thought. "I do not. How does it go?"

With a mischievous gleam to his eye, Val went to the balcony and called down to the men eating there. "The lady has never heard *Tilly Nodden*," he boomed. "Who here is brave enough to sing it?"

Suddenly, most of the men eating below had the same mischievous gleam in their eye that Val did. An older soldier stood up, grinning, and lifted his cup to the chamber as he belted out a tune that was better suited for the walls of a tavern.

"A young man came to Tilly Nodden,
His heart so full and pure.
Upon the step of Tilly Nodden,
His wants would find no cure.
Aye! Tilly, Tilly, my goddess near,
Can ye spare me a glance from those eyes?
My Tilly, sweet Tilly, be my lover so dear,
I'm a-wantin' a slap of those thighs!"

Almost every man in the hall had joined in by the second line, so by the time the song was finished, it was being sung by everyone. When it was over, the hall burst out in bawdy laughter as some of the men began the next chorus. Up on the balcony, Val turned to Vesper, who was looking at him with very wide eyes.

"That is an example of the songs I know," Val told her. "I pray you do not think me too crass."

Vesper stared at him a moment longer before slapping a hand over her mouth to stifle the giggles. "I have heard the soldiers at Eynsford sing that tune," she admitted. "I simply did not know the name of the song. *Tilly Nodden*, is it? That is a naughty song."

Val snorted. "More than you know," he said. "There are more verses that are even worse. Now, will you sing something lovely or do I have my men sing that terrible song all night long?"

Vesper grinned at him, knowing he had her cornered. She couldn't refuse. "Can I at least finish my meal before you make me sing?" she asked. "I am rather famished and I've not yet eaten my fill."

Val was appalled at his behavior. "Of course," he said, reaching out to snatch her hand again and pulling her away from the instrument. "Forgive me, my lady. I was only thinking of myself. And my ears."

Vesper easily forgave him. "It is no trouble," she said. "And… and you may call me Vesper when we are not in front of my father. I would be honored if you would."

Val's featured softened into something quite warm. "'Tis I who am honored, my lady," he said with soft sincerity. "Permit me to escort you back to the feast where you can eat as much as you wish. I will make no more demands upon you."

Vesper shook her head as they began to take the steps down to the main level. "I do not mind singing for you, truly, but I would like to eat first. When I am satisfied, I shall sing as long as you wish."

"That could be a very long time."

"It cannot be too long because I must return home on the morrow."

Val knew that but to hear it from her lips… well, he didn't like that one bit. He found that he wanted to spend more time with this enchanting woman. "Then mayhap you and your father will come back again, very soon, to visit. I enjoy his company very much."

"But you have hardly spoken to him."

He cast her a rather coy glance. "If I said I enjoy your company very much, it might be too forward. I do not wish to chance that. So let me say that I enjoy your father's company tremendously and I wish for him to return as soon as possible."

Vesper knew he was speaking of her even as he used her father as the example. She gave him a coy glance of her own.

"I am sure he would like that very much."

"Would he truly?"

"Indeed."

They had come to the bottom of the stairs. With a broad smile, meant only for Vesper, Val escorted her back over to the table where she could finish the remains of her meal.

It was one of the more memorable evenings he'd ever had.

CHAPTER FIVE

IT WAS VERY late and McCloud was so full of pork and beans and bread that he was close to bursting. It was well after midnight when he returned to his borrowed chamber, where the fire was low and the tiny room was warm and cozy. He'd taken his shoes off and fallen into bed, lacking the strength to remove anything else. He'd had such a perfectly wonderful evening of food and conversation that all he wanted to do was sleep. He was nearly there when a soft knock on the chamber door roused him.

"What?" he growled, exhausted.

"Papa! Open the door!"

Hearing Vesper's voice, McCloud struggled up from his bed in the darkness and staggered across the chamber, throwing the bolt. He yanked the door open just as Vesper burst in, hitting him with the panel and nearly sending him into the hearth. He caught himself on the wall and, scowling at his child, stumbled back to bed and threw himself on the mattress.

"What do you want?" he demanded, grumpy. "Be quick. I must sleep."

Vesper was tired, too, but she also had something of vital importance to speak to her father about. Much like her father, she'd just returned from the feasting hall but instead of going to bed, her father's behavior was weighing heavily on her mind. She could not sleep until she spoke to him about it.

"I will be swift," she hissed, keeping her voice down lest they be overheard by nosy servants. "I want to know why you were so solicitous to Lady de Nerra this evening."

McCloud peeped an eye open. "What do you mean?"

Vesper cast her father a long look. "I mean that I watched you flatter that woman all night, sickeningly so," she said. "Why did you do that? Everyone at the table was thinking you were foolish for it."

He closed his eye, sighing heavily because he very much wished to sleep. "I was not being foolish."

Vesper eyed him as he lay there and tried to ignore her. "What are you up to, Papa? Why did you pay so much attention to Lady de Nerra?"

"Because she is our hostess."

Vesper was fairly certain that wasn't the truth. If she'd come to know one thing about her father over the past week, it was that he had a scheming mind and didn't seem to have any conscience about it.

"So you peppered her with sickly sweet flattery all night?" she asked. "I do not believe that you had no motive."

He grunted and rolled onto his side. "I do not care if you believe me or not," he said. "She is a handsome widow. I am also a widow. There is no harm in flattering the woman."

It struck Vesper what he was driving at, the reason behind the spray of compliments he'd aimed at Lady de Nerra all evening. "I *knew* it!" she hissed. "You mean to endear yourself to her to… Sweet Jesù, Papa, are you trying to woo the woman because she is rich?"

Both of his eyes flew open at her. "No more than you were trying to woo Val," he shot back. "Do not deny it. I saw the smiles and laughter that passed between you two this night."

Vesper was taken aback at the accusation. "I was not attempting to woo him," she said. "He is a kind man. I was simply enjoying the conversation."

McCloud sat up, his eyes blazing at her. "You foolish wench," he growled. "Can you not see a perfect opportunity before your eyes? Val is interested in you; that is clear. Do you even understand what I am telling you? He is trying to woo you also, Vesper. You need a husband he needs a wife – what could be more perfect?"

Vesper stared at him. "Husband?" she repeated, astonished. She would have condemned the entire shocking idea had it not been for one thing – she liked Val. She was very attracted to him. Was it true that he was actually interested in her? She struggled not to fall victim to the excitement racing through her mind. "Papa, surely you cannot be serious. Why would he be attracted to me?"

McCloud was in no mood for her guileless question. "He considers you beautiful and accomplished," he said. "God's Bones, Vesper – the man spent the entire evening hanging on every word out of your mouth. Do you honestly mean to tell me that you did not realize that?"

Vesper's suspicion towards her father was fading fast as a new subject was brought to light – *Val is trying to woo you*. Now, the focus was on her and the giddiness she was trying so hard to suppress was fighting to let loose.

"I simply thought we were having a conversation," she said. "It did not seem to me that he was being more polite to me than anyone else."

McCloud shook his head. "Listen to me, girl," he said, his voice low. "There is a grand opportunity here for you to marry a rich and prestigious man. I had hoped that Val would find attraction to you and, without you even trying, you have endeared yourself to him. I can tell that he is very interested in you. If we plan this correctly, not only will you be married to the Itinerant Justice of Hampshire, but I will be married to his mother. We shall never have to worry about anything ever again!"

Vesper listened to him with mounting horror. "So… you see this as an opportunity to gain wealth? To put food on the table and coins in your purse?"

"What else is of matter in this world, Vesper? Do not be so naïve."

Vesper wasn't surprised at what she was hearing, to be truthful, but somehow her father's words were hurtful. She was a woman of deep feeling with, perhaps, a rather foolish view of marriage – she wanted to at least like the man she was married to. With Val, there was a very strong like there already, even after knowing the man so short a time. But her father held no such view – he simply viewed it as a business transaction.

"I see," she said, her manner hardening now that she realized what her father was after. "You have a son who murders and steals, but that is not your problem. You want to hide that fact by marrying a rich widow so Mat's deeds will be buried by a wealthy marriage. Is that it?"

McCloud looked at her as if he had little more than contempt for her. She may be his daughter, but he was coming not to like her very much because of her rather righteous and inexperienced view of the world.

"When you have children and one of them is less than perfect, see if you would not do anything to solve the issue," he said quietly. "If we have money to buy food, then Mat will no longer have to do what is necessary to feed us."

Vesper was starting to feel a good deal of disgust for her father. She'd hoped to return home to solve the issue with Mat, but it was becoming increasingly apparent that her father had his own help in mind where she was concerned. *Marry a rich woman.* Feeling sickened, and foolish, she simply turned for the door and, without a word, quit the chamber.

When his daughter was gone, McCloud lay back down on his bed but found that he wasn't as tired as he had been. His mind was racing with their conversation, with what was discussed. Now, Vesper knew what he expected of her. A rich bachelor was within her grasp and she would be stupid to reject him.

As for McCloud… he wouldn't be stupid enough to let Margaretha de Nerra slip through his fingers.

The hunter had sighted his target.

"HE FLATTERED ME into the evening. You were there. You saw it, Valor."

It was sunrise in the small hall of Selborne after a night of song and feasting. Val was awake because he normally slept very lightly and was up well before dawn. But in this case, it was because his guests were leaving and he didn't want to miss bidding them farewell. In fact, this wasn't the end as far as he was concerned. He wasn't ready to let Vesper slip away.

"He was being very kind to you, Mother," he said, sipping at warmed, watered wine as the servants brought forth his mother's fresh bread. "I would think you would simply enjoy it. How often does an attentive man sit at our table and lavish praise upon you?"

Margaretha grunted but Val couldn't tell if it was in agreement or disapproval. "He still seemed quite envious of Selborne."

Val sighed heavily. "And why shouldn't he? It is a magnificent fortress."

"I do not like the way he salivated over it."

"What does it matter if he did?"

"It was the *way* he did it, Val. You did not see him."

It was too early in the morning for his mother's usual rot and Val quickly reached his limit. His thoughts were on the coming day, and the departure of McCloud and Vesper. He had little patience for his mother's nonsense.

"Mother, I do not know where your suspicions come from but I want you to cease," he said pointedly. "I find it deeply offensive that you do not trust my judgement in people enough to know that I would not associate with an unsavory character. Every time you voice your suspicions about McCloud, you are effectively slandering me and I am tired of it. God only knows what has made you so bitter at this point in your life that you must find fault with everything around you; if it is not me you are condemning because I have not yet married, then you are condemning a man who was a great friend to me in France. You have absolutely no cause to do that. Are you truly such an unpleasant person to be around?"

Margaretha looked at her son with some astonishment. "If being truthful is being unpleasant, then I suppose I am."

Val shook his head and stood up from the table. "You are *not* being truthful," he said. "You are being a shrew. Stop finding fault with everything around you because if you continue on this path, then I may choose not to spend so much time around you. I grow weary of your negativity and am nearly at my limits of tolerating it, so if you want me to stay around, I would suggest you change your attitude."

With that, he turned away from the table, making his way out of the small hall just as Calum and Celesse were entering. Val waved Calum off when the man tried to follow him, leaving both Calum and his wife confused at his departure. When they saw the expression on Margaretha's face, however, some things were explained. Lady de Nerra looked as if she was verging on tears, keeping her head down as she barely acknowledged the pair at the table. An argument or two between Val and his mother was not an unusual occurrence, but usually not so early in the morning.

Outside the keep, the air was fresh and brisk, the sky above a crystal shade of blue as Val descended the steps into the bailey. They were heading into the winter season and the days would begin to get cooler now. Forcing his irritation at his mother aside, Val headed for the stables to pick out a pair of mounts for McCloud and Vesper to borrow. He had a particular horse in mind for McCloud, an old and scarred war horse who spent his time in the pastures these days, chasing fillies around. It would give McCloud a dignified mount. He also had several palfreys for Vesper's use but he wanted to pick just the right one for her. Something pretty and soft, like she was.

The stable master knew just which horses Val wanted and, soon enough, the enormous and fat war horse was brought forth, his hide dusty from where he'd been rolling around in the dirt. As the grooms set about cleaning up the beast and saddling him, a lovely white palfrey was brought forth for Vesper. She wasn't in season but the old war horse was very interested in her, which Val thought was rather funny. The old war horse would sniff and the filly would kick. It would make the ride home very interesting.

On impulse, he asked the grooms to bring out his horse as well. Durley wasn't more than a day's ride so Val thought to ride escort with McCloud and Vesper part of the way. At least he might be able to speak with Vesper more. Since he didn't have any pressing duties at the moment, it would be time well spent.

He'd made up his mind last night after the feast had concluded and his guests had gone to bed that this would not be his last contact with Vesper d'Avignon. He'd toyed with the idea during the meal but as he lay alone in his darkened chamber, he'd come to the conclusion that, most definitely, this would not be the end of their association. There was something about the woman he didn't want to let go of. As his own horse was brought out and tended, Val headed back to the keep to check on his guests.

But there was no need; as he headed across the bailey, he immediately spied McCloud and Vesper over near the great hall, presumably in search of a morning meal. Picking up his pace, he jogged across the dusty bailey, closing the gap. McCloud was the first to see him, raising his hand in greeting.

"Good morn, Val," he said. "We were just looking for you and the servants said you were going about your duties. We were hoping to find you in the hall."

Val's attention was drawn to Vesper. Glowing in the early morning sun, she was wearing a mustard-yellow garment and her dark hair was pulled back away from her face, braided to keep it neat on her journey. Val swore he'd never seen such a beautiful woman in his life and his limbs seemed to go weak with joy. Everything felt like jelly but in a most wonderful way.

Smitten? Indeed, he was. He liked what he saw.

"My lady," he greeted Vesper before he even said anything to

McCloud, but considering the man had spoken to him, he figured he should at least try to speak to them both. "Did the servants give you food for your journey? I told them to make sure they gave it to you before you departed."

McCloud nodded, lifting up a basket that was overflowing with cloth-wrapped items. "They did, indeed," he said. "Thank you, Val. It was very kind of you to provide for our journey."

Val's gaze drifted back to Vesper no matter how hard he tried to keep it on McCloud. "It is my pleasure," he said. "In fact, I have just been at the stables. They are saddling up horses for you to ride home. I thought I would ride part of the way with you. I did not have much time to speak with you last night, McCloud. There are a few things I wish to discuss with you."

"Horses?" McCloud looked astonished. "Val, that is most generous, but we…we cannot take your horses from you."

Val held up a hand. "A loan, I assure you," he said. "Besides, if I am to accompany you, I do not intend to walk, so you may as well ride with me."

McCloud seemed rather stumped by the suggestion of the loan of horses, but more so by the suggestion that Val would accompany them home. He didn't want Val and his son to come into contact with each other. In fact, he didn't want Val around his home at all. He was fearful of what might come to light. Although any evidence of Mat's activities had long been burned, McCloud was still nervous. Val was a very smart man and he didn't want any suspicions raised. Yet, he knew discouraging Val from riding with them would be suspicious in and of itself.

Therefore, McCloud knew he had to accept the man's offer. The only positive aspect was that it would give Vesper more time to charm the man, so he supposed it was a good thing in the long term.

"Then we are very happy to have your company," he said after a brief hesitation. He turned slightly, moving aside as the first of three horses was brought forth. But along with the horses, he caught sight of something near the keep. "Ah! Your mother, Val. I would like to bid the woman a farewell."

Val turned to see his mother descending the steps from the keep. After their harsh words earlier, he was on his guard. He hoped she hadn't followed him out to continue picking at him so he sent McCloud to intercept the woman. It was a calculated move, on many levels. His mother would be prevented from continuing their conversation and it would give McCloud one last chance to charm the woman.

"I am sure she would like to bid you farewell, also," Val said, sounding sincere. "You made an impression on her last evening, McCloud. She was quite taken with your kind words."

McCloud grinned. "She is a handsome woman," he said. "Val… I do not suppose you would let me return to Selborne to keep company with your mother, would you?"

Val almost laughed; he was actually quite thrilled over the request. To have McCloud court his mother might make his life more bearable, not to mention making Margaretha happy. Nay, he couldn't imagine anything more wonderful. But he couldn't resist teasing the man.

"For what purpose?" he asked innocently.

McCloud cleared his throat as if embarrassed. "Well…," he said, struggling, "I rather like your mother's spirit. There are not many women my age who are as fine as your mother, and widowed, so I was hoping… I know it is a foolish thought, but…"

"Go," Val interrupted him, waving him on. "By the time you finish telling me that you want to court my mother with the consideration of marriage, I will be an old man. Go and tell her how much you fancy her."

"Then I have your permission?"

"God, yes. Best of luck, McCloud. You will need it."

McCloud snorted, relieved that he had Val's permission to pursue his interest with the man's mother. He wondered if is glee showed overly, trying not to feel guilty that his intentions were not altruistic. He had no intention of harming the woman, of course, and he would be kind to her. But the fact that her money was the most attractive thing about her him feel as if he was betraying Val somehow.

The truth was that he was.

But he pushed aside the guilt as he headed towards Margaretha, who by now had come down off the stairs and was heading in their direction. When he was halfway to his intended target, Val turned to Vesper.

"I thought he would never leave," he said, a glimmer in his eye. "Now I may speak with you privately."

Vesper had been watching her father as he headed towards Margaretha, thinking terrible thoughts about him. Pretending his intentions were honorable when they weren't. She couldn't believe he'd been so bold to say what he had but, in hindsight, nothing about him surprised her any longer.

Looking at Val, she resisted the urge to tell him everything she knew. But in the same breath, she knew that telling the man that her father was preying upon his mother, and the reasons behind it, would kill whatever warmth Val had for her. It would destroy her family and it would destroy her future; she knew that as surely as she knew the sun would rise on the morrow.

God, it was all so disheartening. As a person of undying honesty, it was mortifying to Vesper to realize that she was related to a den of immoral characters and, in that sense, she felt trapped. Trapped because she was unable to tell Val what was truly going on and guilty as hell because she was being selfish in not telling him.

To tell him would be to lose that gleam in his eye forever. Instead of telling him the truth, she simply replied to his statement.

"You and your mother have been such wonderful hosts," she said. "I do hope we shall see you both again soon."

Val cocked an eyebrow. "Sooner than you think."

"What do you mean?"

A smile played on his lips. "My lady, I am not entirely sure if you are aware that you have captured my attention since the moment I returned to Selborne yesterday."

Vesper knew what he meant. It only confirmed her father's observations. She was thrilled to hear it from Val himself.

"I… I am not entirely sure how to answer you," she said, the familiar mottle creeping into her cheeks. "I feel that if I admit I have, you might think me arrogant in my assumption."

He chuckled. "Your modesty is admirable, but unnecessary. I have done everything but throw myself at your feet, so surely I have made it obvious."

She looked at him. "Then I might have noticed."

That wasn't exactly what Val was looking for. She seemed rather noncommittal about it and his male pride was about to take a hit. "Is it something that has pleased you?" he asked. "If not, all you need do is say the word and I shall not pursue you further. I do not want to be persistent if it is not welcome."

Vesper's heart was thumping against her ribs, excitement and happiness she'd never before experienced. She never imagined that on this terrible trip home, she would find something redeeming and lovely about it. Something utterly unexpected but utterly wonderful. Truthful as she was, she couldn't toy with him.

"It is welcome, Val."

His breath caught in his throat. "I have never heard my name sound quite so beautiful," he murmured. "Your voice has such a beautiful quality about it."

Her smile broadened. "I have never in my life been so flattered as when I met you."

"You will hear it quite often from me. You had better become used to it."

"I believe it is something I could grow quite accustomed to."

He smiled at her, a giddy smile that caused her to giggle. He laughed because she was, both of them giddy with the attraction they were feeling between them, something new and delightful to explore. But Val caught a glimpse of McCloud heading back in their direction and he quickly sobered.

"I wanted to escort you and your father home today because it is my intention to ask your father if he will permit me to visit you at Durley," he said. "Will you be receptive to that?"

"Of course I will."

Val very much wanted to take her hand and kiss it but he was afraid it might alert McCloud, or worse, offend the man. So, he clasped his hands behind his back to lessen the temptation.

"Thank you," he said softly. "I am very much looking forward to it. And to you."

Vesper averted her gaze, both delighted and embarrassed by the man's attention. She was in new territory and struggling to adapt.

"I hope to return to Eynsford soon," she said. "I… I hope that is not too far for you to visit."

He shook his head. "You could go to the moon and I would find a way to get there. Do not worry about me; where you go, I will follow."

It was a very sweet thing to say. Vesper didn't think her heart could get any lighter. This was better than anything she could have ever dreamed. Before she could reply, however, McCloud joined them and disrupted their conversation.

"Your mother is most gracious, Val," McCloud said. "She has invited us back next month to visit again and stay for a few days. She says the forests in the area still have game in the winter and that you and I will hunt."

Val liked that idea very much and he was, frankly, surprised his mother had suggested it. Perhaps McCloud's flattery had softened her up, after all.

"That sounds like an excellent suggestion," he said. "I welcome it."

McCloud seemed very happy about it, as well. "I am pleased to spend more time with you, my old friend," he said. "But, for now, must return home. Shall we depart?"

Val nodded, turning to indicate the stables over by the western wall. "If you are ready, then we shall," he said. "It seems that we have a great deal to discuss on the ride home."

They started walking towards the stables. "Oh?" McCloud said. "What about?"

Val and McCloud were walking together with Vesper following. Val turned to glance at Vesper before answering, just to make sure she was there. She smiled sweetly at him when their eyes met.

"A position with me," he said, tearing his gaze away from her to look at McCloud. "I need a man to cover the extreme southern portion of my territory and I was hoping to hire you for that task. I pay two pounds a month in silver. It would make a nice income, McCloud. Would you be interested?"

McCloud stumbled, faltering as he came to a halt. His wide-eyed gaze was on Val. "An… an appointment? With you?"

Val nodded. "I have needed a man in the south for some time now but I have found no one I can trust. Forgive me for not thinking of you all along. Are you interested?"

McCloud was speechless for a moment. "Two pounds a month?"

"Is that enough?"

A look of joy rippled across McCloud's features. "It is more than enough," he said, his voice hoarse with emotion. "You… you would not want a younger man for this task?"

Val shook his head. "Younger men often do not have the experience. I need someone older, with such experience as you have. Will you do this, McCloud? You would be doing me a great favor if you did."

The old, tired man that McCloud had become suddenly felt a resurgence of life through his veins. He saw the potential of redeeming himself in a way he could have never expected. And the money… God's Bones, the money! It would keep them from starving. But it did not deter him from his plans for Margaretha; nay, that was a much bigger prize. But for now, Val's offer would do.

It was a start.

"Of course I will do it," he finally said, reaching out to shake Val's hand eagerly. "I cannot tell you how grateful I am."

Val patted the man on the shoulder as they resumed their walk towards the stables. "Good," he said. "I am comforted. We shall discuss your post on the ride to Durley. And there is something more I wish to discuss with you."

"God's Bones, what more could there be?"

Val didn't hesitate. "Much as you wish to keep company with my mother, I wish to keep company with your daughter. Will you permit me? I assure you that my intentions are entirely honorable."

They had reached the stables and McCloud paused again, facing Val. "I could ask for no finer man for my daughter," he said sincerely. "If Vesper is agreeable, then I give you my blessing."

Val smiled in a gesture of a man who had what he wanted. "I have already asked her and she is agreeable."

"Then there is nothing more for me to say. I will ride ahead of you two on the way home so that you may speak privately."

As McCloud went to mount the fat old war horse that the stable master indicated, Val turned to Vesper and victoriously winked at her.

She winked back.

CHAPTER SIX

Saltwood Castle
Kent, England
Quartier de Chevaliers (Knight's Quarters)

ON THE CROWDED grounds of Saltwood Castle, what was kindly termed the *porcher* was actually the building that housed the knights for the king and traveling soldiers of an upper rank. *Porcher* loosely meant pig's sty and the building was just slightly above a mud pit for the livestock to wallow in. The dirt floors could be muddy at times because the drainage was poor and this attracted flies when the weather was warmer and misery when it was colder. Mold grew on the floors and up the walls, a black mold that the servants tried to remove because it had been known to make men sick. In all, it was a nasty and cold place.

But it was the one place where Henry's knights could come for privacy away from their duties for the king, and Henry carried a large retinue of seasoned knights. While Henry was inside Saltwood's great stone keep for the night as his court traveled from France to Winchester Castle, his seat in England, the knights who were not on guard retreated to the *porcher* to drink and sleep until their time to tend the king came once again.

But this night was different.

Six knights had originally been sitting in the common room of the *porcher* on this dark and clear night, men who had served Henry for many years. These were six of Henry's most trusted. While the king slept, other knights were on guard and the six retreated for a well-deserved rest.

But sleep was difficult to come by for men who were constantly on duty, constantly on guard, so they sat in the common room before a hearth that belched black smoke into the room and tried to tire themselves with pitchers of sweet red wine. Eventually, towards midnight, two of the knights retired, leaving four still sitting up and talking.

In the weak light of the chamber, lit only by a bank of tapers that dripped tallow all over the dirt floor, those four men had something serious on their minds.

They had for several days.

Now that they were finally alone, it was time to speak of it.

"Thank God François and Etienne have retired," Hugh de Morville spoke softly. "Good men, we must speak of this and speak quickly. This may be our one and only opportunity."

The other three knew what he meant. They'd been speaking of the subject on and off for over a week, muttering to each other when others weren't around but, now, they had some privacy as a group. It was unexpected and welcome. It was time to bring the subject out in the open and do it swiftly.

"Then I shall begin," a knight with shaggy dark hair and a bushy beard spoke. "We all heard our lord speak at Bures. We all heard him declare his wish for Canterbury's removal. Will we continue to ignore it?"

The first man looked at his comrade. "Reg, we will not ignore it, which is why we must speak of this now, before too much time elapses," he said. "We have stood by for years while the contention between Canterbury and Henry goes on. Canterbury used to be an ally of the king but he continues to prove that he is a foe. Now, has excommunicated those who crowned Henry the Young King and he continues to wreak havoc for the king. As Henry's protectors, it is our duty to protect the king and rid him of his enemies. Do you agree with me on this?"

Those around the table nodded. "Hugh, there is no doubt that Canterbury has become a foe," the third knight, a man with a receding hairline, spoke softly. "But what are you suggesting, exactly? That we actually rid Henry of Canterbury?"

Hugh nodded his head. "That is exactly what I am suggesting, William," he said quietly. "You heard Henry's plea; we all heard it. He said 'who will rid me of this troublesome priest?' It was a command, I tell you. Certainly, he could not come out and order us to rid England of Canterbury and the cancer he has become. To do so would incur God's wrath, for certain, and Henry needs God to govern this fractured country."

"So you are suggesting we carry out this – this *command*?" The fourth knight spoke, a heavyset man who was older than the rest. "We are to rid Henry of Canterbury? Can we not simply arrest the man and bring him to Henry for punishment?"

Hugh gazed at the man. "Richard, we are sworn to the king," he emphasized. "Would you agree with that statement?"

Richard le Breton nodded reluctantly. "I would," he said, sighing heavily. "But by assuming Henry has ordered us to rid him of Canterbury, we are, by nature of that act, assuming responsibility for it. God will punish *us,* not Henry. Does Henry's sin become our own?"

Reginald FitzUrse, with the shaggy brown hair, held up a hand. "We have sworn to uphold Henry's will upon this earth," he said, siding with Hugh. "We are sworn to the king above all else. We must carry out his wishes."

William de Tracy sighed heavily, running his fingers through his receding hair. "That is essentially true, but we are also sworn to uphold the church," he said. "Our oath is to God and the king."

"It is the king we must face today and God at a later time," Hugh pointed out. "I, for one, am committed to my king. Henry has been good to me; he has been good to all of us. It is a prestigious post we hold. Is it now a post for cowards who are afraid to do the king's will?"

Those words echoed in the small room as the hearth crackled and smoked. For several long seconds, the snapping of the flame was the only sound heard as the men pondered the subject at hand.

"To assassinate the archbishop would have far reaching consequences," Reginald said softly because no one else seemed willing to speak. "Henry would be avenged and, perhaps, he would even be pleased, but the church would be out for blood. Do you think Henry would protect us then?"

Hugh pondered the dregs in the bottom of his cup. "I have no wife to consider hardship for, no family," he said. "My vocation is my life. There is little else. But there is my brother to consider, I suppose."

The others looked at him. "Calum is not far from here," William said. "Selborne Castle is a two days' ride from here. Hugh, do not hate me for saying this, but mayhap we should seek assistance from your brother."

Hugh's head came up, his brow furrowed. "Why? This is not his task."

William's eyebrows lifted. "Think on it," he said quietly. "We all want to carry out Henry's wishes but we do not wish to become hunted men in the process. I have my family to consider, lands and titles that will become mine upon my father's death. I do not wish to lose that. The same can be said for Richard and Reg. And you – you will inherit the Lordship of Westmoreland when your father dies. Do you truly wish to lose that, Hugh?"

Now, Hugh was beginning to feel some doubt. "Of course not," he said. "But why must we seek assistance from my brother?"

William sat back in his chair, his gaze upon Hugh intense. "Because Calum has nothing to lose," he muttered. "And because he serves Val de Nerra, who is Henry's Itinerant Justice in Hampshire where Winchester Castle is located. De Nerra is the law and, instead of killing Canterbury, we will simply have Val arrest him."

It was an intriguing thought, one with great possibilities. "And do what with him?" Hugh asked.

William's dark eyes glittered. "Whatever Henry wants him to do. Val has the authority to administer justice on behalf of the king. You are very aware that Henry feels that he must have jurisdiction over the clergy. It will be Henry's right to punish Canterbury however he wishes and he will see how loyal we are to him because we had Canterbury arrested and brought to him. That way, we avoid being ruined by killing the man. If we only arrest him...."

It made sense; Hugh could see the logic. "Henry would still be avenged," he murmured.

"Exactly."

Hugh's thoughts moved to Val de Nerra, a knight they all greatly respected. He was also a favored of Henry, which meant if Henry became angry for the arrest, he'd be less apt to punish a man like de Nerra.

"And how are we to convince Val that this is what Henry wants?" he asked.

William shrugged. "It is simple. We tell him that Henry has ordered it."

Hugh digested that suggestion. He had said, in his opinion, that Henry's rhetorical cry had been a direct command. He couldn't go back on that, not when he truly felt as if it had been Henry's order to knights who would hopefully interpret it as such and carry it out. But it was possible that an arrest was what Henry really meant and that consideration brought about some doubt in his actions.

Arrest? Or assassination?

In any case, de Nerra was the law. It would be his responsibility to arrest Canterbury on behalf of the king, but de Nerra was no fool. He would fully understand the implications of such an action. He would want proof.

"Val is trusting but he will want evidence of such a command," Hugh finally said. "We have no such evidence but a few coins to one of

Henry's clerks and we would have an arrest warrant. I will swear upon my oath that I truly believe that Henry's plea was a command to us, as his loyal men, to rid him of Canterbury. We all heard him say it. Therefore, we will issue a warrant for Canterbury's arrest and ride to Selborne for de Nerra and my brother before continuing on to Canterbury. Do you all agree?"

He was looking particularly at William and Richard, who had seemed more reluctant than Reginald. Reginald, in fact, was nodding and so was William. Eventually, Richard nodded, but it was with great hesitation.

"Very well," Richard said, sounding frustrated. "We ride for Selborne and then to Canterbury, and we arrest Canterbury. We stand by our belief that this is what Henry wishes."

Hugh was relieved that everyone was finally in agreement but he couldn't help feeling guilty, as if they were deflecting the responsibility in this action onto de Nerra. But that could not be helped now, not if they truly wanted to carry out what they believed to be the king's orders.

It must be this way.

"Henry departs for Winchester tomorrow and hunting after Christmas," he said. "We shall take that diversion to do what needs to be done."

The door to the *porcher* suddenly opened, spilling forth a pair of knights who were heading in to sleep and the conversation at the table abruptly quieted. But before it died completely, Hugh spoke softly.

"It is as the king wishes," he muttered, lifting his cup.

Three more cups were lifted as a dark bargain was struck. They would fulfill Henry's command to the best of their abilities, unwilling to acknowledge again that they were bringing two innocent knights into their mix to deflect their rogue deeds. But the die was cast.

It was time to end Henry's torment with Canterbury once and for all.

CHAPTER SEVEN

Bishop's Waltham, two miles from Durley

VAL HAD RIDDEN further with Vesper and McCloud than he'd intended to, but the journey had passed so quickly that he'd lost track of the miles. The first half-hour after they departed from Selborne had been filled with conversation with McCloud, but after that, Vesper had monopolized his time and, before he realized it, they were entering Bishop's Waltham, a large village that wasn't far from the d'Avignon home of Durley.

The village was, in fact, the seat of the Bishop of Winchester, Henry de Blois, and he'd built a large castle there about thirty years before. Val had been to the bishop's palace a few times in his capacity as Itinerant Justice and it was a very large place, rich with wealth from the bishopric of Winchester. He knew de Blois only through his legal dealings, and the man's grandfather had been the Duke of Normandy, so he was an important man in southern England.

But Val didn't intend to stop to socialize with the bishop on this day. He was more concerned with Vesper and the fact that, very soon, he would have to leave her company, which he was genuinely not looking forward to. She was so easy to talk to and the warmth between them, starting the evening before, had only grown and now led them into a rather comfortable repartee.

It was joy beyond measure.

The more the hours passed, the more determined Val became to see her as often as he could, as much as his schedule would allow. McCloud had given him permission to court her and the sheer delight he felt was something he'd never known before. All he knew was that he wanted to see Vesper every hour of every day. He wasn't entirely sure he could even leave her on this day, returning home to his shrew of a mother and an empty fortress. Now, something would be missing without Vesper there.

It was something he intended to rectify sooner rather than later.

At this part of December, the weather was remarkably mild as they rode into the outskirts of Bishop's Waltham. The roads were passable and there were people out conducting business or simply visiting family or neighbors. Children played in the road, laughing and screaming, as dogs chased them about. When one child ran too close to Vesper's palfrey and startled the horse, she pulled the little animal to a halt.

"It has been a very long time since I have visited this village," Vesper said, watching a little girl with a kitten standing alongside the road before giving her horse a kick to get it going again. "It seems to have grown quite a bit since I last remember it."

Val was inspecting their surroundings. "With the Bishop of Winchester seated here, it has, indeed, grown quickly over the past several years," he said. "I seem to remember hearing that the Danes burned the town about two hundred years ago, but I do not see any evidence of that. McCloud? Did you hear that as well?"

McCloud, who was riding ahead because he wanted to leave Val and Vesper some privacy to their conversation, turned around when he heard his name.

"Indeed, it was," he said. "I can recall my grandfather speaking of such things. His father was here when the Normans came, you know. He'd come from France to establish his orchards before the Duke of Normandy came and then he found himself fighting off his countrymen. But he managed to save his lands, poor old fellow."

Val smiled faintly. "Fortunately for you," he said. Then, he glanced off to the southwest where the towers of the bishop's palace could be seen over the trees. "Have you ever had any contact with the Bishop of Winchester? It seems to me that you may have, being that your home is so close to this town."

McCloud considered that question; had he had any contact? He hadn't. He didn't want any. Given what he was trying to hide, he didn't want contact with anyone of authority, including Val, which made this journey an increasingly anxious thing. He didn't want Val coming to their home and had spent the past hour trying to determine how to discourage him from doing just that. Given that the man was on the scent of Vesper, he suspected he would not be easily discouraged.

But he had to try.

"Nay, I do not know the man," McCloud said. "Do you?"

Val nodded. "I have had some contact with him in the capacity of Itinerant Justice," he said. "He is not a pleasant fellow."

"I have heard that about him."

Val wouldn't say anything more, simply because they were in the bishop's town and he didn't want to be overheard gossiping about the man. He changed the subject slightly. "I mostly have contact with the sheriff of the village, a man named Benton. I hold court in Winchester, Fairfield, and Waterlooville about once a month and Benton brings his prisoners to Fairfield, mostly."

"Is that what you do?" Vesper asked curiously. "Travel around and render judgement in towns?"

Val nodded. "That is exactly what an Itinerant Justice is, so I travel to the larger towns in Hampshire and hold court. I also hold court at Selborne once a month."

"Any kind of justice?"

"From someone stealing a pig to a wife beating a husband and more. Anything."

Vesper thought that all sounded quite interesting. When her eyes met Val's, he winked, causing her to flash that smile he was coming to love so well. But as he smiled in return, they came to an intersection of two streets and Val seemed to catch sight of something over the top of Vesper's head.

It was a busy merchant area, a prosperous village bustling with commerce. With thoughts of Vesper and her sweet smile on his mind, it occurred to Val that he now had an excuse to remain with her a little longer. He'd been given permission to court her, had he not? And it would not be unseemly for him to give her a gift from any number of these merchants, a small token of his esteem and intentions. Moreover, McCloud was present so he could do it in full view of the woman's father so it wouldn't seem as if he was doing anything subversive.

But, truth be told, he was most excited to purchase something for Vesper that would remind her of him during the times they could not be together. Still, he didn't want to come right out and say that. It seemed a little too sentimental considering how long they'd known one another.

Therefore, he would have to be clever about it.

"My lady," he said, pointing to the merchant street beyond, "I was wondering if you might help me with selecting a gift for my mother. With the day of Christmas upon us and being in a village with a selection of merchants, this is a prime opportunity to find something for her."

Vesper nodded eagerly. "I would be most happy to," she said. "What do you think your mother would like to have?"

Val began directing his horse in the direction of the street, as did Vesper. "Fabric," he said without hesitation. "My mother loves to sew, whether it is garments or scenes to display on walls or looms. Mayhap there is a merchant that will supply material and threads of different colors."

Vesper was already looking around, leaning forward on the small white palfrey. "I am sure there is someone like that around here. Papa, do you know of a merchant where Sir Valor can purchase fabric for his mother?"

Trailing along behind the pair, McCloud was embarrassed by the question. He had no money to spend on anything and, therefore, wouldn't have any idea about the merchants in town. But he would not admit that.

"I have not purchased fabric in many a year, Vesper," he said, trying to brush off the question as a subject he didn't care about rather than one didn't know about. "Not since your mother was alive. You will have to find such a merchant yourself."

Val wasn't distressed that he and Vesper had a bit of an adventure ahead of them. Reining his horse over to the side of the avenue, he dismounted his steed and went to help Vesper dismount, his big hands around her slender waist as he lifted her from her horse. She was warm and firm beneath his hands and it was a struggle to let her go once her feet hit the ground. He very much wanted to keep his hands on her. But he forced himself to release her, removing his hands and taking the reins of both horses and handing them over to McCloud.

"Do you mind waiting here for a few moments?" he asked. "I promise I shall not keep your daughter overly long."

McCloud shook his head. "I shall wait here for you."

Pleased that the father hadn't insisted on coming along to chaperone, Val dug into the coin purse at his belt and pressed a silver coin into McCloud's hand.

"There is a food stall there," he said, pointing to the next stall over where pies of some kind were sitting out, cooling after having been removed from the fire. "Consider that coin part of your stipend for managing my southern territory. Find something to eat and we shall return."

McCloud didn't have the strength to protest. He was hungry and the coin in his hand bespoke of a fully belly, so he simply nodded his head as he watched Val and Vesper head down the avenue. The more time they spent together, the better for the chances of a marriage sooner rather than later, so McCloud was in full support of the pair spending time together. All of this was going better than he had anticipated.

With a lingering glance at Val and Vesper, he turned for the food stall.

With McCloud involving himself in meat pies, Val took Vesper's hand and tucked it into the crook of his elbow as they headed down the avenue. It was a bright day, a cloudless sky, and people were beginning to wind down their business for the day as the afternoon waned. The weather was still cool, however, in spite of the sunny skies and a cool wind blew off the sea, stirring the drifting leaves.

But to Val, it was the most beautiful day he'd ever known. With Vesper on his arm, he was as proud as a peacock. He glanced at her once, twice, three times, finally meeting her eye. She smiled and so did he.

"I have not had the chance to tell you how beautiful you look today," he said. "Your gown is most becoming."

Vesper looked down at the dark yellow garment. "You flatter me, my lord," she said. "I am pleased that you like it. I made it myself."

"You are extremely talented."

Vesper simply grinned, draping her free hand onto his elbow as well, now gripping him with both hands as they made their way down the avenue. They weren't even really paying attention to the merchant stores; the only had eyes for each other. Val was thinking on paying her yet another compliment because he liked how her dark hair glimmered in the sunlight when the glint of something else caught his eye. He turned to look, seeing that they had ended up in a cluster of jeweler stalls.

These stalls were more fortified than usual merchant stalls because of the value of the contents. Even though they were actual structures, small one-room shops or even two-room shops, the windows and doors were fortified with iron grates. The stall in particular that Val was looking at had two armed men at the door and he could see that there were necklaces being displayed behind the barred windows. Pulling Vesper along, he went straight to the armed men.

"My lady and I wish to inspect the wares," he said. "Will you admit us?"

The armed men looked him over; Val was wearing full complement of mail protection including his heavy de Nerra tunic, colors of crimson and white with a gold lion stitched on the front that had exaggerated claws. He was also wearing his broadsword, an enormous and very expensive piece of equipment. The men pointed to the broadsword.

"No weapons inside," one man said. "Leave it with me."

Val shook his head. "I will not," he said flatly. "I am the Itinerant Justice for Hampshire and this sword is worth more than what you will make in your entire life, so you will either admit us entrance or I will find another jeweler who will happily take my money. Make your choice."

The men eyed him, indecisive, but the fact that his sword was, indeed, expensive and fine told them that he was more than likely who he said he was. Begrudgingly, they unbolted the iron gate and admitted him and the lady into the small business. Then they locked the door tightly behind them.

Once they were inside the structure that smelled strongly of dirt, a small man with a strange cap on his head swiftly approached them. "My lord?" he asked. "May I serve you?"

Val nodded. "Something pretty for my lady's neck," he said. "I see that you have necklaces you are displaying in your window."

The old man with the stringy hair nodded eagerly. "Indeed, m'lord," he said. "Are you looking for anything in particular?"

"Nay. Just bring what you have."

The old man turned for the rear of the shop. "Then you will sit. I shall bring you a selection."

He dashed off, leaving Val and Vesper standing in a rather barren room with a table and a few crude seats around it. As Val led Vesper over to the table, she balked a bit.

"What do you mean to ask for something pretty for *my* neck?" she asked quietly, concerned. "I thought we were looking for something for your mother?"

He looked at her squarely. "I lied," he said. "I wanted to purchase something for you because… well, you will not laugh at me, will you?"

"Of course I will not laugh."

He took a deep breath. "I wanted to get you something that will remind you of me. Something that brings a smile to your lips every time you look at it because you know it is something I gave to you as a token of my esteem for you."

Vesper fought off a grin. "I already know of your esteem for me," she said softly, although she was deeply touched. "Just as you know of my esteem for you. I do not need a gift from you to remind me of that."

He nodded. "Aye, you do," he insisted. "Although it is my intention to see you a great deal, there may be times when my duties make that impossible. I do not want you to forget me."

A smile spread across Vesper's lips as she looked up at him; she'd spent the past six hours with the man, leisurely traveling, speaking on everything from the weather to the new additions to Eynsford Castle. She'd come to know a man of sharp wit and great intellect, but a man who seemed somewhat challenged by the thought of pursuing a woman.

At times, he seemed uncertain about what to say, and how much to say, and Vesper thought that was infinitely charming. He had pride and a grand knightly arrogance when it came to his position as Itinerant Justice. But when it came to his feelings or anything personal, that was where he was most untried.

Truth be told, Vesper was untried, too, so it was a little like the blind leading the blind. All they could do was what came naturally and what propriety allowed. But the more they became acquainted, the more comfortable with each other they became.

The moments, like this, were turning into magic.

"How could I forget you?" she wanted to know. "You took my father and me into your home, fed us, entertained us, and now you are escorting us home because my father has given you permission to keep company with me. Surely, I will never forget you. There is no need to give me a gift to ensure that."

The corner of Val's lips twitched. "I cannot be certain that a handsome man on a dashing white horse will not ride up and steal you away."

Vesper laughed. "If he does, I will tell him to go away because the Itinerant Justice of Hampshire will run him through if he does not."

"Would you really tell him that?"

"I swear that I would."

Val beamed. He took her elbow again, continuing their journey to the table where he pulled out a stool for her to sit upon. "Then I am grateful and honored, my lady," he said. "Will you still allow me to purchase a small token for you? Not much, but a little something."

She had to chuckle at him because he looked so sincere. "If you absolutely must."

"I absolutely must."

"But what about your mother? Do you truly intend to buy her nothing at all?"

He grunted. "Let McCloud buy her something. He wants to court her, after all. That is his business now."

Vesper's smile faded, knowing that her father purchasing something for Margaretha was impossible because of his lack of coinage. She seriously wondered if Val understood that, although he had offered her father a fine job that paid very well. Perhaps, that was his way of ensuring her father had money to spend on his mother or, more than likely, it was because he was a truly generous individual. She sensed that about him.

A fine and generous man who was about to find himself in a family full of vipers.

Vesper had been increasingly wrestling with that thought on the ride to from Selborne. It was true that she had vowed not to tell him anything about her father's conniving and her brother's murdering, but only because she didn't want to lose what they were building between them. But the more she came to know him, the more her thoughts began to shift in his direction – was it fair that so fine and true a man unknowingly enter into a deal with such unsavory characters?

As much as a marriage to the man thrilled her, she could only imagine that look of horror on his face when he discovered what her father and brother truly were. Val was too noble, too accomplished to associate with what her father and brother had become. Worse still, would he believe she had lied to him by omitting the truth about her family?

Because that was exactly what she was doing – lying by omission. More and more, she was coming to realize it wasn't fair to Val.

... but what about *her*?

Was she not entitled to marry a fine knight with a prestigious post? She'd done nothing wrong. It had only been by misfortune that she'd been born into this family but she certainly had never participated in their deeds.

It was a dilemma that was starting to overwhelm her.

Mulling over thoughts of right versus wrong, Vesper was distracted when the old man with the strange hat emerged from the rear of the stall, bringing forth a wooden box which he laid carefully upon the table. As Vesper and Val watched, the old man unfastened the hinge on the box and carefully opened it.

Vesper couldn't help but gasp. The case contained several fine necklaces of gold and pearls and colored stones, all of them exquisitely made. She looked up at Val, almost in a panic.

"These are far too expensive," she whispered. "Please... you do not have to...."

Val ignored her protests. "These are perfect," he said to the old man. "Do you have more? The lady might not like any one of these."

The old man nodded eagerly. "Aye, I do," he said. "Shall I get them?"

Vesper would not be ignored any further. "Nay," she said loudly, somewhat embarrassed when both Val and the old man looked at her as if surprised she had asserted herself. Val grinned as she appeared contrite for yelling. "I will look at these. I do not need a vast selection."

Val simply shrugged, pleased he'd forced her to his will, and Vesper bent over the case, not touching anything. But her eye was drawn to a necklace of pearl and a blue stone that flashed red in the light. It was an unusual stone and the old man saw where her attention was.

"A dragon's fire stone, m'lady,' he told her in his thin, scratchy voice. "That is called a dragon's fire."

Vesper sighed. "It is beautiful," she said. "Where does the stone come from?"

The old man flashed a toothless smile. "Far to the east, m'lady."

It was quite exotic sounding. Moving in on to the necklace next to it, Vesper found herself looking at a chain of gold interspersed with beads of a pale green stone. At the end of the chain was an exquisite gold charm shaped like a key and inlaid with pale green and pale purple stones. The stones were so pretty and glittery that it immediately caught her eye and she bent over even further, inspecting it, seeing the craftsmanship. When she reached out to touch it, timidly, Val spoke softly.

"Do you like that one?" he asked. When she looked up at him, he smiled at her expression of awe. "I like it, too. In fact, I believe it is perfect for you."

Vesper could feel the warmth from his gaze, reaching out to grab her, turning her limbs to mush. The man had a smile that could devastate and eyes that could render one completely helpless. But Vesper didn't mind; surrendering to her feelings for him was one of the easier things she'd ever done.

"Why?" she murmured.

Val didn't answer her; he simply smiled, as if he knew something she didn't. But he tore his eyes from her long enough to look at the old man. "We shall take the key," he said. "Polish it for her and I shall pay you handsomely."

Excited at the prospect of a hefty sale, the old man scurried off, leaving Val and Vesper at the table. When they were alone, he answered her question.

"Because it is the key to my heart," he whispered, reaching down to take her hand. Lifting it to his lips, he kissed it tenderly. "It is symbolic, I know, but so very perfect. Wear it around your neck, always, and think of me."

Vesper was having difficulty breathing as he kissed her hand again, bolts of excitement shooting through her body, a delicious pleasure-pain sensation. Unconsciously, she licked her lips, wondering what it would be like when he finally kissed her mouth. Would his lips feel as warm and gentle as they did upon her hand? She'd never been kissed by a man, at least not like this, and all she could think of was the sensation of his heated lips. Her trembling body must have given off an invitation to Val because, suddenly, he was pulling Vesper from her stool, his mouth slanting over hers hungrily.

Somehow, she became boneless. Val's arms went around her and it was as if she had no bones, caving against the man as he squeezed the life from her. His mouth suckled hers, first her lower lip, then her upper lip, and then her tongue when she gasped because he was squeezing her so hard. He was overwhelming her with his power and masculinity, but as quickly as he grabbed her, he was forced to retreat because the old man was returning to the table with the necklace in his hand.

Vesper nearly fell down when Val let her go. She tried to stand up straight but she couldn't seem to keep her balance. She could feel Val's hands on her, steadying her, as the old man extended the necklace to her.

"There, m'lady," he said with satisfaction. "This shall be a necklace you will be proud to wear."

With trembling hands, Vesper took the necklace, a magnificent piece that she put over her head, watching it settle against her bosom. The key came to rest right between her breasts, a heavy golden piece with the green and purple stones. She lifted it up, looking at glisten in the light.

"It is so beautiful," she said sincerely. Then, she turned to Val. "I have never in my life had anything so beautiful. Your generosity humbles me, my lord."

Val touched her cheek affectionately. "You are worth all this and more," he said, looking to the old man. "What is your price?"

The old man eyed the necklace, seeing how happy the lady was with it. "It is an expensive piece, m'lord, made in France by the finest craftsmen."

"Aye, it is exquisite. How much?"

"Five pounds, m'lord."

That was quite a bit of money but Val didn't hesitate. In fact, he dug into his coin purse and pulled out two gold coins, which was almost twice what the man had asked for the necklace. He wanted the man to remember him so when he returned again to purchase more jewelry, and perhaps a wedding ring, that the man would show him the very best he had. Putting the coins into the man's palm and watching the old man's eye's bulge, he took Vesper by the hand and led her to the locked door.

The two armed soldiers were there and quickly opened the door for him, having come to realize that the Itinerant Justice of Hampshire was an important and wealthy man. Val took Vesper through the door but she almost tripped because she was looking at her necklace. She couldn't take her eyes from it. Val kept her from falling to her knees and she smiled gratefully.

"I am sorry," she said. "It is simply that I cannot take my eyes off of this. I have never seen anything so lovely."

Val was looking straight at her. "Nor have I."

At first, she thought he meant the necklace, too, but she soon realized he meant her. Instead of flushing and looking away, which was what she usually did, she met his gaze steadily. She was coming to trust him now and to trust that his compliments weren't empty ones. That gave her the courage to face him.

"I told you last night that I have never known such flattery," she said. "At first… at first, I did not believe you were sincere, but now I am coming to think that you might be."

He laughed softly. "Did it take me buying you an expensive piece of jewelry for you to realize that my words to you are genuine?"

She laughed because he was. "Nay," she said. "I did not mean that to sound as trite as it did. I simply meant… is this real, Val? Do you truly wish to keep company with me?"

He nodded, slowly, his smile fading. "And with time, more than that, even."

She knew what he meant. God, she knew and it was like music to her ears. *Marriage!* Already, she could see a strong son with his father's handsome features and a daughter with her sensibilities. She could see all of this, already, and the solitary life she'd known all of these years began to seem like hell. Before she realized it, tears filled her eyes.

Val noticed because she quickly lowered her head. He put his hands on her upper arms, comfortingly.

"What is the matter?" he asked gently. "What did I say? Did I say the wrong thing again?"

She sniffled, shaking her head. "You said the right thing," she assured him. "'Tis only that I did not realize how terribly lonely I was until now. I did not know what I had missed in my heart until I met you."

His grip on her lessened and he began to caress her. "My sweet lass," he murmured. "You will no longer be lonely, I swear it. You have me now; you shall always have me, evermore."

Vesper smiled at him, still watery-eyed, and he leaned forward to kiss her forehead. It was a brazen move in public but far less brazen than kissing her lips again, which is what he wanted to do. In fact, he was already plotting how to get her alone before he had to return to Selborne when they both began to hear the distant roar of a crowd.

It was a faint buzz of many voices in the distance. The sound caught Val's attention and he looked off to the northwest, towards the center of the town. He knew there was a well there. There was also a vast grassy area where farmers and others conducted daily business. But now, there seemed to be something else afoot. He could just tell by the buzz that it wasn't something good.

People began running past him, towards the town center, while more people were running away from the center, screaming at others to come and see. Val strained to hear what they were saying.

"What is going on?" McCloud walked up behind the pair, leading the three horses. "Val, what is amiss?"

Val shook his head; he was trying to make out what people were shouting about. "I am not entirely sure," he said. "But there seems to be a great deal of excitement."

"Shall we go and see?" McCloud asked.

Val pondered that a moment. If it was something grim or serious, he didn't want to drag Vesper into it. A delicate lady didn't need to be exposed to the whims of a mob. He finally shook his head.

"Nay," he said. "Durley is not far from here. Mayhap we should simply take Vesper home."

McCloud didn't like that response. He'd spent the past several minutes trying to think up an excuse as to why Val couldn't come to Durley and he thought he had concocted a fairly believable one. There was only one way to find out.

"Nay, Val," he said quietly. "I will take Vesper alone. My son, you see… he does not deal well with strangers and I am afraid the sight of you would greatly upset him. I never told you this, but Mat is… he is a simple man. He has the mind of a child and a great many things upset him, so until I can get him used to the idea of your presence, I would prefer you not come to Durley."

Some of what McCloud said was true but not all of it. Mat was actually very friendly but therein lie the problem – Mat could very easily tell Val of his murderous activities without even realizing what he'd done, so that was another reason to keep Val away from Durley and away from Mat. McCloud held his breath, watching Val's expression and praying the man would honor his request. Given that Val was a gracious man, he really wasn't surprised by his answer.

"If you feel that is best, then I will do as you ask," Val said. "But I will admit it will be difficult. May I send a messenger to Vesper at least?"

McCloud looked at his daughter, now bearing a spectacular gold necklace on her shoulders. Nay, he didn't want Val or his messengers near Durley. It would be too risky. Therefore, he shook his head.

"Not now," he said. "But I would like to see your mother very soon. You will recall that she invited us to return to Selborne and visit. May we return to Selborne in a week or two?"

Val's gaze had inevitably moved to Vesper, lingering on her sweet face. "Make it next week," he said. "In case you have not yet noticed, I am smitten with your daughter. Any time away from her will seem like an eternity."

McCloud could see the expressions of warmth and joy passing between Vesper and Val. *I could not have planned this better*, he thought gleefully. "Then it shall be next week," he said. "Tell your lovely mother that we shall come to visit and stay for a time. We shall look forward to it."

Val sighed, realizing this would be his last glimpse of Vesper for at least a week. He didn't like it in the least. "Very well," he said. "Since you do not want anyone to approach your farm, my men and I shall come back to Bishop's Waltham in eight days. We shall meet you in the square and escort you to Selborne. Will that be acceptable?"

McCloud was precluded from answering when the buzz of the crowd grew to epic proportions and people began screaming about the capture of someone, or something. It was difficult to know because there was such a frenzy going on. Val was coming to think he should probably go and see what the fuss was about as shouted words filled the air around them.

"The Angel has been caught!"

"Come and see! We have him!"

Val let go of Vesper and stepped into the street, grabbing the next frantic person who tried to run past him. It was a man, poorly dressed, flushed about the face. Val had him by his skinny arm.

"Hold, there," he commanded. "What has happened?"

The man was panting, out of breath. "The Angel of Death has been caught! He was caught in the act and brought into town! They will hang him now!"

Val frowned. "Angel of Death?" he repeated. "Who is that?"

The man pointed to the center of town where everything was in an uproar. "The man who has been killing," he insisted. "He killed two children near the river this morning and he was caught!"

Val still wasn't clear. "Where is Benton, the town's sheriff?"

The man was still pointing frantically towards the mob. "He has him!"

With that, Val let the man go. The man ran off down the street. Scratching his head, Val made his way back over to McCloud and Vesper.

"It seems as if they have caught a criminal," he said. "I must go and see what has happened. You will return to Durley and remain there. I will see you in eight days, here in town. Is that understood?"

McCloud nodded, as did Vesper. "Indeed, Val," McCloud said. "But I have been thinking – since you asked me to be your man here in the south, would you not like for me to attend you also? I should know what is happening as well where it pertains to the law."

He had a point but Val was reluctant to involve Vesper in this, simply because she couldn't be left alone while they went off to see what had happened. He was very conscious of the lady's delicate senses when it pertained to distasteful matters.

"Mayhap we should leave Vesper with the jeweler while we tend to this," Val suggested. "She would not be interested in our business. My lady, would you like to pick out more pieces of jewelry until we return?"

Vesper shook her head. "I am not a weakling woman," she said firmly. "I am not easily bothered so if you do not mind, I shall go along with you. I find what you do very interesting and I should like to see you as you carry out your duties."

"There is nothing exciting about it, I assure you."

"May I not admire you as you complete your sworn duties?"

When she put it that way, he could hardly refuse. More than that, Val could see such strength in her. But he could also see a taste of his life to come with her, which truthfully didn't bother him. He rather liked a strong woman.

"Very well," he said, "but stay close. Do not wander off."

She nodded. "I will not, I promise."

His eyes twinkled at her, secretly glad he would not have to be separated from her yet. He took her over to the palfrey and lifted her up onto the horse's back. Then, he mounted his steed as McCloud climbed onto the fat war horse.

Everyone was still running towards the center of town – men, women, children, and the mood was something between a delighted frenzy and a terrified rant. It was odd to say the least, but once Val and Vesper and McCloud reached the end of the avenue where it opened up into the town square, they could see just how many people had really gathered.

The winter-dead grass of the square was being trampled by the excited group as Val spurred his horse onward, skirting the edge of the square and trying to catch sight of the town's law, Benton St. Lo. This was actually called St. George's Square, christened by the original Bishop of Winchester since this was his town, given to him by a long-dead king, and it was the usual gathering place for the town's business, including executions.

Val paused a moment, watching the flow of the crowd because that would more than likely lead him to the people he sought. He could see that the crowd was moving to the northeast where there was a great gathering on the other end of the square. Spurring his war horse in that direction, he loped along the edge of the square with McCloud and Vesper following him.

Benton St. Lo wasn't difficult to find; the man was exceedingly tall with a crown of frizzy red hair, so right away, Val caught sight of him. Forcing his horse forward to push through the crowd, he came upon St.

Lo and his men, who had a man down on the ground, face down, bound tightly. Val could see that St. Lo's men were beating on the man.

"St. Lo!" he boomed in a controlled, commanding tone. "What goes on here?"

Benton St. Lo turned to see the Itinerant Justice of Hampshire in his midst. His eyes widened at the sight and he stopped whipping the prisoner with a silver-tipped cat-o-nine-tails to hurry in Val's direction.

"My lord!" he said, clearly surprised. "I did not know you were in town!"

Val peered around St. Lo as his men abused the prisoner. "Who is that man?"

St. Lo turned to look this prisoner also. "A devil," he said. "This man has been murdering for the past year, at least. He has been murdering villages and stealing their property. This morning, he drowned two children over in the Bishop's marsh and he was caught."

There were so many people around that Val couldn't really see the prisoner. Villagers were hitting him. All the while, St. Lo's men continued to beat him.

"Have you questioned the man?" Val asked.

St. Lo nodded. "When he was brought to me, I asked him if he was the man the people were calling the Angel of Death," he said. "He said that he wanted to go home."

Val's brow furrowed. "And you took this as a confession?"

St. Lo nodded. "People witnessed him killing the children," he said. "He drowned them and stole their possessions. That is what the Angel of Death has been doing for a year around these parts."

"Why was I never informed about this outlaw?"

St. Lo shrugged. "It was something my men and I were aware of. We knew we could capture him."

"But an entire year? You did not tell me?"

St. Lo could see that he was in a rather precarious position; as the law of Hampshire, Val de Nerra should have been notified. Val was a powerful man with powerful connections and Benton didn't want to fall from the man's good graces.

"I apologize if this offends you, my lord," he said, "but I viewed this as a village matter. I did not want to bother you with it because I was sure we could find the man. And we have."

Val cast the man a look that suggested he was frustrated with his answer. Then he turned around to see McCloud several feet behind him and Vesper directly behind her father.

"Did you hear that?" he called back to McCloud.

McCloud put a hand to his ear, cupping it as if to hear better. "Hear what?"

Val didn't want to shout above the frenzied crowd. He simply motioned to McCloud to come forward. As McCloud tried to push through the hordes of people, Val dismounted his steed.

"Get your men off of the prisoner," he snapped quietly to St. Lo. "Bring the man to me."

St. Lo barked at his men, who were slow to stop kicking and punching the man on the ground. They were paid henchmen, really, a brute squad that Benton used to enforce peace in the town. Val pushed through the crowd, shoving people aside, as Benton walked beside him and did the same.

Meanwhile, St. Lo's men had hauled the prisoner to his feet and turned the muddy, beaten man in Val's direction. Val could feel McCloud beside him, turning to see that Vesper was directly behind him. He found himself concerned about Vesper because of the crowd, reaching out to grasp her elbow and pull her up beside him. He didn't want the woman touched by this rabid mob. Even though he was in the process of his duty, he still wanted to protect her.

But the moment the prisoner was thrust forward towards him was the moment Val's world changed forever.

CHAPTER EIGHT

"PAPA!" THE PRISONER screamed, tears and spittle flying from his face. "Papa, help me!"

Val had no idea who the man was talking to. He reached out and grabbed the man by the chin, forcing him to look at him.

"Who are you?" he demanded. "Tell me why these people believe you have murdered two children this morning."

The man was filthy, covered in mud and blood and bruises. He wasn't particularly tall, but he was stocky. It was clear that he was strong. But he wasn't looking at Val; his gaze kept moving to McCloud.

"Papa!" the man cried again. "Take me home! I want to go home!"

It occurred to Val that McCloud had this man's attention for some reason. When he turned to look at McCloud, the man's face was sickly pale. He looked as if he was going to become physically ill.

"McCloud?" he asked, confused. "Do you know this man?"

McCloud tore his eyes from the prisoner, turning to look at Val. God help him, his worst nightmare had come true. This was a moment he'd been dreading, hoping to avoid, doing everything he could to make sure none of this came to pass. He'd almost made it home without Val coming to his farm, or seeing Mat, and he'd been counting on the fact that he'd kept the law of Hampshire away from his home where terrible things had happened.

But… oh, God… it was not meant to be.

He must have gone out to kill again, McCloud thought as he recognized his son's muddy, bloodied face. *He must have gone out to kill again and now he has been caught!*

McCloud had no idea what to say. To affirm Val's question would only throw him into the mix of this rabid crowd, a criminal who had been an accomplice to a murderer. But to deny it would mean he would have to make that lie convincing. He would be lying to his long-time friend, a man whose money and support he wanted. He had to have it. Val was about to make it possible for him to lift his family out of poverty, but now, his murdering son had ruined everything.

Mat had ruined everything!

"Aye," came the soft answer behind McCloud. "He knows the man. So do I."

Both Val and McCloud turned to Vesper, who was looking at the prisoner with a great deal of sorrow and contempt. When McCloud looked at her, looking as if he wanted to strangle her, she refused to meet his eye. Her gaze remained on the prisoner.

"Will you tell him the truth, Papa, or shall I?" she asked softly.

McCloud began to tremble. He had no choice now, forced by his honest daughter. "Vesper," he hissed. "You will keep silent."

But Vesper wasn't listening. Although she hadn't seen her brother in eight years, she would never forget the man who had made her life miserable for so many years. He didn't look all that different. But what was the most sickening was that he was about to make her life miserable for eternity as his shocking crimes were about to be revealed to a man she had come to adore. It didn't matter that she'd only known Val for just a few short days; in that time, she'd come to clearly and unabashedly adore him.

But now, it was at an end.

All of it had been dashed in a mere few seconds as Mat d'Avignon's face came into view. Her terrible, murdering brother had ruined her life again, this time for good. All of those hopes and dreams of marriage, of living happily as Val's wife, had vanished like dust upon the wind.

She had nothing left to lose with a confession.

"They were starving," she said as she turned to Val, her features pale and her lips trembling with emotion. "The d'Avignon farm is in ruins and my father and brother were starving. I told you my brother is a simpleton; he is. His mind is like a child and, along with that mind, he has no sense of right or wrong. All he knew was that he was hungry, so he began to kill people to steal their food. That is how he and my father have kept fed this past year – by killing and stealing. The prisoner before you is my older brother, Matins d'Avignon, and, according to my father, he is, indeed, guilty of what he has been accused of."

Val felt as if he'd been hit by a giant fist, straight into his gut so that he could hardly breathe. It was a struggle not to stagger from the force of the blow. He looked at McCloud, who was hanging his head, eyes closed, as the reality of his once-proud life was laid bare. Val's gaze lingered on McCloud's head in shock before returning his gaze to Vesper.

"Is this true?" he asked, his voice hoarse with emotion.

She nodded, feeling defeated. So very defeated. "It is."

"And you have known this all along?"

She shook her head. "Nay," she replied. "Only since my father came to Eynsford two weeks ago. He told me what had happened and explained to me that it was my duty to marry well so that I could provide for him and my brother, so my brother could stop this murder spree. He made it sound as if it was my responsibility to fix the situation. That was why I was coming home, Val. It was my intention to return to Durley to see if something about the farm was salvageable, something that would feed my father and brother so that my brother would stop committing these crimes. Meeting you was purely accidental, I assure you, but you fell into my father's plans quite well. He saw in you salvation for him and marriage for me. He also saw marriage to your mother as an added bonus."

If Val didn't think he could be any more shocked, he was wrong. All he could think of was his mother warning him about McCloud and how the man seemed envious of Selborne and all that Val had. *My God… was my mother right?* Val began to reel with the wider implications of Vesper's confession, on how he'd been too trusting of an old friend he'd not seen in years. Situations change; people change. Wasn't that what his mother had been trying to tell him?

"Then you knew," he said raspily, "and you did not tell me. That means that all of this… everything we have spoken between us – has been a lie."

Vesper shook her head. "Nay," she insisted softly. "Everything we spoke of was true. My feelings for you are true, Val. Never doubt that. But I am selfish – I wanted you and your adoration. I knew that if I told you about my father and brother, you would see how low my family has become. Even though I have not had any part of their dirty dealings, I knew you would see me as part of that situation. I knew it would change your feelings for me and I could not bear it. I was simply hoping all of this would fade away and it would be something we would never have to discuss, but I see that I was wrong. My brother has been ruining my life ever since I was a small lass. He continues to ruin it, now ruining my future with you. I apologize that I did not tell you any of this, of my father's schemes and my brother's crimes. I was hoping to fix such things so you would never have to know."

Val just stared at her. She was calm in her confession but he could see how emotional she was about it; pale and quivering. But he was so confused and upset that he didn't know what to believe.

Was she even telling the truth now?

Or was she trying to manipulate him?

"Whatever you think of me, Val, do not think poorly of Vesper." McCloud finally found his tongue. "What she says is true, all of it. She has no part in my dealings. She did not even know about them until I went to Eynsford."

Val looked at him. "Then your son really did murder people?"

"He did." It was a painful confession for McCloud. "But Vesper… she is a righteous and accomplished young woman, much too good to be related to someone like me. She deserves you and you deserve her, so do not judge her for knowing about this situation. You will blame me; I should have told you but I could not. I was ashamed and frightened to. A man will do most anything to protect his name and his family. I fear that I have lost my sense of moral character."

Val's gaze moved to McCloud, hearing the man's words and feeling both rage and pity; rage at McCloud for lying to him, pity for Vesper, but anger at her as well for not telling him what she knew. He was so torn that he could hardly think straight. As he stood there, his body so tense that he was grinding his jaw, Vesper removed her necklace.

"Here," she said, extending the jewelry to him. "I cannot keep this. I *will* not keep this. I am sure your mother would love to have it. You need not tell her how you came into possession of it."

Val looked at the very expensive necklace she was extending to him. "Vesper…."

"Take it. If you do not, my father will take it from me and sell it back to the jeweler for the money. It will feed him and my brother for the next year."

Val still wouldn't take it back, indecisive, but Vesper wouldn't wait. She opened her fingers and let it fall to the ground before turning away and fleeing through the crowd. Val bellowed after her.

"Vesper!" he roared. "Vesper, come back!"

Vesper ignored him, pushing through people, running past the palfrey she'd ridden from Selborne. She was running wildly, trying to escape the horror she'd been forced to confess. Val grabbed McCloud.

"Go and find her," he commanded. "Bring her back."

McCloud was torn; a fleeing daughter and a captured son. He didn't know what to do. "My boy…."

Val cut him off. "Leave him to me. Find Vesper. If even half of what she says is true, then you owe her at least that. What has happened to the man I once knew, McCloud? Since when did you become so dishonorable?"

McCloud knew he deserved the harsh words. Val would have done less damage had he physically struck him. Beaten, devastated, McCloud simply did as he was told, following Vesper's path as Val watched him go.

Thoughts of Vesper were echoing through his mind, rattling his brain with the shock of the entire situation. But something at his feet caught his attention and he reached down to pick up the necklace where it had fallen. Looking at the necklace and pondering what he'd been told, all he could manage to feel was confusion and devastation. Devastation for Vesper, for him, and even for McCloud. He'd always had a great deal of respect and admiration for McCloud.

A man will do most anything to protect his name and his family.

Val couldn't even relate to that. To lie? To hide the truth? Nay, he couldn't relate to that at all. He couldn't imagine falling so low that he'd do anything to save himself. And Vesper… poor Vesper, not seeing her father for so many years only to be thrust into the man's desperate scheme.

I was hoping to fix such things so you would never know.

Something told him that she was telling the truth.

But he couldn't focus on that now, as much as he wanted to. He had a situation on his hands and men were waiting for his judgment. Still clutching the necklace, he returned his attention to St. Lo and the weeping prisoner.

Val took a good look at Mat d'Avignon; shaggy, dirty, stocky, he barely looked human. He looked like an animal, in fact, and fully capable of doing what his sister and father said he did. He took a step in the man's direction.

"Are you Mat d'Avignon?" he asked in an authoritative tone.

The prisoner was weeping profoundly. "I want to go home!"

"Tell me who you are."

The prisoner either didn't understand the question or didn't want to answer. "Where is my papa going?"

It was obvious to Val that everything he'd been told was true – this was McCloud's son. Hearing the man speak, it was also clear that he was, indeed, a simple-minded man. His speech was slurred, inelegant.

"Matins d'Avignon," Val said, louder. "Did you murder children this morning?"

Mat continued to weep, trying to see where McCloud had gone. Val moved so that he was blocking Mat's view of the crowd and of his father, so he was the only thing filling up Mat's vision. He grabbed the man by the chin and forced Mat to look at him.

"Did you kill those children this morning?" he asked again. "Answer me."

Mat looked at him as if he didn't understand the question. "Where is my papa?"

"Your papa is not returning unless you tell me what happened. What did you do this morning?"

Mat understood the threat of his father not returning. In fact, the young man had been living in terror for the past few weeks, ever since his father left him. He didn't understand why McCloud had to leave and he was terrified of being left alone, so he was obsessed by his recent glimpse of his father. *His world.* But he took Val's threat very seriously.

"They… they had food," he finally stammered. "I could smell their food!"

"What did you do?"

"I was hungry!"

"*What* did you do?"

Mat frowned, confused by the question, trying to remember what he'd done. He was so frightened that he could hardly think. "I took it," he said. "They hurt me. I hurt them back!"

"You killed them."

"They hurt me!"

"What about the others you killed? Do you remember them?"

Mat's brow furrowed as he seriously considered the question. "They would not give me their food," he said. "I wanted it. They would not give it to me."

"So you took it."

"I took it."

"This is not the first time you have stolen. Do you remember how many people you have stolen from?"

Mat couldn't grasp that question. He began to whine again, panicking. "Where is my papa? I want my papa!"

It was all Mat was capable of saying. To Val, he had his confession but he was greatly distressed over the situation now for an entirely new reason – he had a simpleton who was a murderer. He was coming to think that the man had no grasp of what he'd done, only that he was justified in whatever had happened. He was hungry, he took their food, they obviously fought back, and he killed them. In Mat's mind, that was evidently all that happened and he was perfectly right to do what he did.

But Val knew, upon hearing those words, that Mat had consigned himself to death.

The crimes had to be punished. Val couldn't stop that, simpleton or not, because the man had killed and that meant his punishment would be the same. The families of the victims and the townspeople who had lived in fear of becoming his next victim would demand justice.

Therefore, Val knew he had no choice in the matter. If he balked at delivering the sentence, then it was quite possible he'd lose credibility with St. Lo. Word like that would get around and he'd be viewed as weak, or worse. It would make keeping law in Hampshire even more difficult if men thought he was weak.

Even now, they were all looking at him, wondering why he'd even questioned the man. He could see their confusion in their eyes. That confusion would soon turn to disdain.

The prisoner had to be dealt with.

Val turned to St. Lo. "Before I render judgment, you said there were witnesses to the murder this morning?" he said. "Where are they?"

St. Lo gestured to a huddled group of children several feet away. They were wet and looked terrified. "There," he said. "Two of their friends were murdered."

Val made his way over to the gaggle of skinny children; half of them were wet, but they were all trembling, looking at him with utter fear in their eyes. Val looked them all over very carefully, a rag-tag group of peasant children.

"Tell me what happened this morning," he said. "Tell me what you saw that man do."

The children were huddled, quivering. A boy about eleven or twelve years of age spoke.

"We fished at dawn, m'lord," he said. "We often go to the marsh to fish and we caught many fish. We were cooking them and that man came out of the trees and took the fish we were cooking on sticks. He just started eating them. When we tried to stop him, he pushed my two young brothers into the marsh. They couldn't swim, my lord, and he went into the water and held them down. Then he tried to do the same to us but some people from the village heard our cries and came to save us."

Val was listening seriously. "Then you saw him drown your brothers?"

The boy nodded, wiping furiously at his eyes, as he didn't want to be seen weeping. "Aye, m'lord."

That was all Val needed to hear. He had what he considered a confession and now he had witnesses. There was no doubt as far as he was concerned. He turned to St. Lo, standing beside him.

"Then we must render punishment," he said quietly. "Move the crowd back and away."

St. Lo seemed surprised. "Now?" he asked. "You will not announce a time?"

"Nay."

"But what of the bishop? He will want to know."

"We have caught a murderer. That has been confirmed. Why would you delay carrying out his sentence?"

St. Lo was still surprised at the swiftness of the command but he didn't question further. He began barking orders to his men, who shoved the crowd back from the prisoner. The two men standing on either side of Mat kicked out his knees and forced him to kneel.

"I will get the ax," St. Lo said. "It is at my house. I will send a man for it right away!"

Val shook his head. "Nay," he said, putting a hand on the broadsword strapped to his side. "I will use my sword. This man is a simpleton, obviously, so I am not entirely sure he understood that what he was doing was wrong. I will therefore grant him a measure of clemency and use my sword rather than an ax. It will be swifter and cleaner that way."

St. Lo peered at him curiously. "You will execute him personally, my lord?"

Val sighed faintly, hating the sound of what he had to do. "Aye," he said. "It is my sword. Only I will use it."

"Shall we at least send for a priest to pray with him?"

"Nay. There is not enough praying that can save that man's soul after what he has done."

St. Lo shut his mouth after that. De Nerra was delivering swift and brutal justice. He left Val's side, going to help his men push the crowd back as two of his men remained with the prisoner, keeping him down on his knees because he kept trying to rise. Mat's wailing filled the air, adding to the harrowing atmosphere.

The truth was that Val wanted to carry out the sentencing swiftly for one largely predominant reason – McCloud and Vesper were not in view of it. That was his primary reason for doing it so fast, for not sending for a priest. It would take time, precious time, and give McCloud a chance to return with Vesper only for them both to see what he had to do to their son and brother. It was a small mercy he would give to them, handling the execution himself so there would be no torturously long execution with a sloppy axman and to do it when they couldn't see it.

But there were other reasons. Even though Val suspected Vesper's relationship with her brother was not a good one, he doubted their budding relationship could survive her witnessing him execute her brother. It would be a stain always between them and even if he couldn't overcome her lack of forthrightness in the long term, he didn't want her to end up hating him.

That wasn't something he could stomach.

Therefore, he looked around one last time to see if they were near and, not seeing them in the crowd, he unsheathed his magnificent broadsword. Sharp as a razor, it was more than up to the task that would soon be asked of it. The crowd was jostling around, trying to gain a better look at what was to come as St. Lo's men held back the throng. Val knew he had to act. There was no more time to delay. Taking the hilt in both hands, he came up behind the kneeling prisoner.

God forgive me for what I am about to do, he prayed silently. He felt so much angst and sorrow and confusion that it was difficult to push it all aside. Was he doing the right thing? Was he rushing through this? He tried to imagine if this was someone else, someone who wasn't related to a woman he was coming to adore. Would have acted so hastily? Probably. With such evidence, there was no reason not to. It was that realization that give him the confidence to do what he needed to do.

The men guarding the prisoner backed away as Val approached from behind. Mat's head was still lifted, still searching the crowd desperately for his father, having no idea that death was stalking him.

But that last glimpse of his father was not to be. Mat never even knew what hit him; one moment, he was looking for his father, and in the next minute…

Nothing….

CHAPTER NINE

VESPER WAS HALFWAY down the Street of the Merchants, where the jeweler stalls were located, when McCloud caught up to her.

"Where are you going?" he demanded, reaching out to grab her arm. "You are not leaving until you and I discuss what has happened."

In tears, Vesper yanked her arm from her father's grasp. Standing in the middle of the street as they were, she didn't care who saw them. So much of what they'd tried to keep private had come out, so there was no privacy left to be had.

No pride left to salvage.

"There is nothing to discuss," she hissed. "Your evil has finally caught up with you. I am glad Val knows; *glad*, do you hear? I am going to return to Eynsford and pretend I do not have a father and a brother who murder and steal. I am going to forget about everything over the past few weeks and if you do not leave me alone, I will tell Lord Eynsford about you. I will tell him what a despicable creature you are."

McCloud had his entire world rocked that morning and was in no mood for his daughter's dramatics. Reaching out, he grabbed her by both arms now so she couldn't get away.

"Listen to me, you foolish wench," he muttered. "Regardless of what you told Val, he has sent me after you. Do you know what the means? It means that he still cares for you. It is very possible that he will forgive you. I will not let you ruin your life because you hate me. If Val will marry you, then so be it. I will not see you again. But do not run from a man who still wants you."

Vesper was wrought with such anger and grief that she could hardly hear her father's words.

"Damn you," she snarled, trying to pull her arms free. "Damn you for coming back into my life with your schemes and horrors. Why would you do this to me? I was happy at Eynsford; I had respect and a good position. And you came and ruined it all! I shall never forgive you!"

McCloud was having a time keeping his grip on her. Vesper was strong for a woman, that strength now fed by her anger at him.

"I do not care if you do not forgive me," he said. "But if you want to salvage your life and not live with regrets for always, then think about what I have just told you – Val still cares for you. I believe he will forgive you. You had no role in what has happened and he will understand that with time. Are you going to throw that all away in a fit?"

His words were starting to sink in. Vesper's struggles lessened but she wouldn't look at her father. The sight of him sickened her. She was convinced that everything was ruined and her only thought was to leave this place, to run back to the safety of Eynsford. Perhaps there, she would forget about the dark-haired, green-eyed god that was Val de Nerra. Perhaps in time, she could convince herself that he had been a dream and nothing more. But she was in such agony at the moment that it was difficult to think clearly.

"I do not understand how he could forgive such a thing," she said. "He discovered that which you were attempting to keep from him. And my brother… when you came to Eynsford, you left him alone. Did you not think he would wander and strike again? Did that not occur to you?"

McCloud sighed heavily, with great emotion. "What was I to do?" he asked. "Bring him with me? Mat does not function well outside of his world at Durley. He would have been a miserable fit of a man. I had no choice to leave him behind when I set out for Eynsford."

"You should have caged him!" Vesper shouted. "Did you hear what they were calling him, Papa? The Angel of Death. Did you know that? Did you know what terrible things he was called?"

McCloud was struggling to keep above the guilt and regret that was grasping at him. "I heard," he muttered. "I knew. But I will be truthful – I did not expect to find him in town this day. Even when the mob gathered, it did not occur to me that it was for him."

Vesper was beside herself with frustration. All of it was too much to take for a young woman who'd had so little excitement in her life. "If you did not restrain him before you left, then you should have known he would leave," she said. "Now he has killed again? All of that blood he has spilled is on *your* conscience, Papa. It is your soul these deeds have stained."

McCloud knew that. He was a condemned man and he had resigned himself to that long ago. "It is as you say," he said. "There is no use speaking on what has already been done. I cannot change anything. What matters now is what the future will bring. You must return to Val… reconcile with him. He is a good man, Vesper. He is everything I am not. Go back to him now and I shall leave you alone. You will not see me again."

Vesper considered that. She genuinely did not want to see her father again, not after the havoc he'd brought to her life in just the short time they'd been reunited. Maybe he was right; maybe there was the possibility that Val would forgive her for not having told him what she knew. Was he worth the attempt? With every breath she drew, she believed he was.

Perhaps her father was right for once.

"Very well," she said, taking a deep breath and endeavoring to calm herself. "I will return to Val to see if anything can be salvaged. But you will keep your word – return to Durley and stay there. Do not speak to me or contact me. I do not ever wish to see you again."

McCloud was grieved to hear those words but he knew it was for the best. "You will not, I swear it," he said, depressed. "But allow me to return with you to see to your brother, at least. I must see what has become of him."

"You *know* what has become of him."

"Val promised me he would see to him. He will spare your brother, I know it."

Vesper didn't say a word. With a lingering glance at her father, one full of disgust, she turned and headed back the way she had come, back to the square where hundreds of people were still milling about.

The crowd hadn't disbursed but it had grown eerily quiet. Vesper skirted the group, straining to catch a glimpse of Val where she last saw him, over on the north side of the square. It seemed very densely packed over on that side as people crowded in to see the murderer who had been captured.

The *Angel of Death* she'd heard the people call her brother. She was grateful that no one knew who she was as she moved through the crowd lest she be attacked for being related to the murderer they were all so fearful of. It would be great irony for her to be caught up in her foolish brother's punishment.

The closer she drew to the last place she saw Val, the more her stomach twisted into knots. She began to second guess herself, wondering if this was a wise thing to do. Did her father tell her the truth when he said that Val was still concerned for her even after what had happened? Or was it a lie designed to manipulate her? She didn't want to face Val only to be condemned. She'd run away from him for a reason – so she wouldn't have to face him. Was it cowardly of her? It was. But she didn't care. Better a coward than to see hate in Val's eyes when he looked at her.

Vesper must have slowed her pace when her indecision began to overwhelm her because McCloud grasped her by the arm, pulling her through the crowd, forcing her into Val's presence. When they finally entered a dense portion of the mob, McCloud began pushing people out of the way, dragging his daughter behind him. Soon enough, they were through the thick of it but they ran headlong into St. Lo's hired men. They were kept back just as the crowd was, away from the prisoner and the scene beyond. McCloud could see Val standing several feet away.

"De Nerra!" he shouted over the crowd.

Val's head snapped in his direction and he caught sight of McCloud and Vesper at the edge of the crowd. Leaving St. Lo, he quickly made his way over to them, telling St. Lo's men to let them through. McCloud had a tight grip on Vesper as he pulled her with him.

"I found her," he declared the obvious. "She did not want to come but I told her that she must."

Val's gaze was on Vesper. Her head was down and she was clearly reluctant, even as her father dragged her along. "Thank you," he said to McCloud. Seeing that Vesper was pulling against her father, or digging her heels in at the very least, he spoke softly and calmly to her. "Vesper, I will tell your father to release you if you promise not to run. Will you do that? Will you promise to remain?"

Vesper couldn't even look at him; guilt was consuming her, but she managed to nod. "Aye."

Her tone was barely above a whisper. Val spoke to McCloud. "Release her, if you will."

McCloud did so against his better judgement. He still wasn't entirely sure Vesper would keep her promise. He waited a few seconds for her to start running again but she didn't. She remained rooted to the spot, her head lowered in a gesture reminiscent of a beaten dog. But that was as much concern as McCloud could spare. He began looking around for his son, his primary concern at the moment.

"Where is Mat?" he asked eagerly. "Did they take him away?"

Val knew his question would come and he thought he could muster some pity for McCloud, but he couldn't. He had absolutely no pity for a man who would knowingly get himself into such a predicament and allow a son to murder unimpeded. He wasn't even tactful in his reply.

"Do you know what *Infangenethef* is?" he asked.

McCloud hesitated before shaking his head. "Nay."

"It means that I have the authority to render judgement over any and all crime committed within my jurisdiction."

McCloud knew this had to do with his son. "I know, Val. I know that you must punish my son for what he has done. Where is he?"

Val pointed to a heap of something covered up by a dirty horse blanket they'd taken from the livery across the square. "He is there," he said. "Based on your son's confession and the testimony of witnesses, a judgement was rendered and the sentence carried out. Before you think me unfair, be grateful that you are not beneath that cover, also, as an accomplice to your son's deeds."

McCloud's eyes widened, his jaw going slack. His dark eyes fell on the dirty horse blanket and he could see a hand poking out beneath it. With a wail that set Val's hair on end, McCloud rushed to the covered corpse and threw the blanket back, weeping loudly at the sight of his son's headless body.

His cries were enough to mute the crowd into an uncertain buzz. It was an unearthly howl, grief in the purest sense. The hushed villagers watched as McCloud collected the corpse of his son, still warm, and held it to his chest as he wept. Mat's head was on the other side of the body, getting rolled around as McCloud sobbed.

Val watched the scene without emotion but Vesper couldn't look. She kept her head turned away, hearing her father's cries, knowing that it was a pain of his own making. Still, it didn't make it any easier to listen to. She very much wanted to leave.

"You had my father bring me back," she said to Val, her voice hoarse with emotion. "Please say what you need to say so I can leave this place."

Val looked at her, seeing her distress. He moved slightly, blocking her view of her father and brother. "You did not give me a chance to say anything before you went running off," he said quietly. "Will you not at least look at me when I speak to you?"

"I cannot."

"Why?"

She let out an ironic choke. "Because I cannot see your hatred for me. Please say what you must and let me go."

Val sighed heavily. "I do not hate you," he said. "But I want to know why you did not tell me any of this. Did you truly believe you could resolve it?"

Vesper nodded, her lower lip trembling. "I was going to try."

"But… your brother has committed serious crimes," he said softly, pleading with her. "I admire the fact that you thought you could resolve the situation, but did you not understand how serious it is?"

She wiped quickly at her eyes, flicking away the tears angrily. "Of course I understood how serious it is," she hissed. "But I thought I could stop it because I was afraid… afraid of the damage it would do to my reputation if and when the activities became public. I was trying to save myself, Val. Do *you* understand that?"

In truth, he did. "Aye, I do," he replied. "But… you could have told me. I could have helped you."

She sighed sharply, frustrated by his statement. "Is that really true?" she nearly demanded. "I have known you a matter of two days. How would it seem if I suddenly came out and told you that my father and brother had been starving so my idiotic brother had taken to murdering people to steal their food? You do not know me and know that I am as reasonable and honorable as a woman can be. You would have thought I was mad for telling you such things. Worse still, you might have thought I was even in league with them. Of course I could not tell you; I did not know you well enough. And I did not want to ruin what we had building between us."

It made perfect, utter sense to Val. "I suppose I do see your point," he said reluctantly. "I suppose I cannot blame you for not telling me. But you do see how shocking this was to me – to discover all of this. And McCloud… God's Bones, what has happened to that man I knew?"

It was a rhetorical question, perhaps not really seeking an answer, but Vesper chose to answer it. "I do not know," she said. "You can imagine my horror when he told me."

"I believe I can."

Silence fell between them, a painful silence that left them both wondering if there was anything else to say on the matter. Vesper finally sighed faintly, a sound of misery.

"Will you please permit me to leave now?" she asked.

Val looked at her; her lowered head, her slumped shoulders. It was killing him that she refused to look him in the eye.

"I told you that I do not hate you," he murmured. "Will you *please* look at me?"

She shook her head. "Nay," she responded, the tears coming once more. "Please do not make me."

Val's heart was breaking. "Then what can I do?" he asked. "Is it because of your brother? I had no choice, Vesper. The man was guilty. It is my duty to render judgement and carry out sentencing, which is what I did. I will not apologize for doing my duty."

Vesper shook her head, peeping an eye open to see her father several feet away as the man cradled a headless corpse. She quickly shut her eyes again. "You do not have to," she said. "I understand that you did what you had to do. As for my brother, I have no love for him. He was a wicked man and my father never disciplined him, not even when he… suffice it to say that my brother has caused me years of misery. If it is wicked to be relieved for another's death, then I am wicked. I am relieved."

Val had to admit he was glad to hear that. At least she bore no grudge against him. "Then what can I do to make things right again? I understand you had no part in this. I understand this was your father's doing. Will you please look at me now?"

Vesper opened her eyes but she stopped short of looking at him. "Please," she whispered, "you must understand that I discovered something about myself over the past two days. I never believed that I could feel for someone the way I feel for you. You make me… happy. So very happy. But I feel as if I have betrayed all of that by being part of a family who murders and lies. You asked to court me, Val; I cannot allow it. You do not deserve to be related to a family of murderers. As the Itinerant Justice, that would be most shameful if people discovered your association. Do you not understand that? It is for your own good that I must do this."

He was shocked to hear this. "You will let me decide what is in my best interest," he said. "I am unconcerned with being related to the House of d'Avignon. The name still stands for something, something good, at least to most people who remember your father and grandfather, and their honor as knights."

Tears were running down Vesper's face as she quickly wiped them away. He just didn't seem to understand that she was only thinking of him. "But someday, it will not. Word of this will spread and it would be most shameful for you."

Val couldn't help it. He reached out and grabbed her by the arms, giving her a shake so her head rolled back and he finally found himself looking into those beautiful hazel eyes.

"Listen to me," he said. "I have never felt for anyone as I feel for you. I do not give my affections frequently or easily, and I have done both with you. I know that I was shocked earlier when I discovered what you knew of your father and brother, but that has been forgotten. I still intend to court you and, God willing, marry you someday. This incident with your brother and father… it is over now. Justice has been rendered and I will deal with McCloud appropriately. But that is wholly separate from my feelings or intentions towards you. Is that clear enough?"

Vesper shook her head, turning her gaze sideways so she wouldn't have to look at him. "I cannot let you."

"Is it because you do not feel for me as I feel for you? I thought you did. You were clear that you did. How has that changed, Vesper? I have not done anything wrong and neither have you."

She tried to lift her hand to wipe at her watery eyes but the way he was holding her arms made that impossible. She finally gave up. "I care for you *too* much; that is why I must spare you."

"You will let me decide my own risks. And you are well worth anything I have to endure. Please believe me, Vesper."

His last few words were pleading with her, a man who had lowered his guard and was now vulnerable. Vesper could hear it in his voice and it was enough to give her a small measure of hope. Was it true? Did he really feel as if she wasn't a liability to his work and reputation? Her heart, so shattered by the recent turn of events, began to feel stronger. But she still wasn't convinced. She swallowed away the last of her tears.

"Will you do something for me, then?" she asked.

He didn't hesitate. "Anything."

"Let me return to Eynsford. Let me put some distance and time between us, and let us both think very hard on whether or not we still wish to pursue this relationship. Something has happened to it, Val; something dark and terrible. It has been damaged. Please…let us both decide if it can be mended."

"I know it can be mended."

She lifted her hands, putting them on his chest in a pleading manner. "Much has happened today and you are full of emotion," she said earnestly. "You are, mayhap, not thinking as clearly as you should. Let me return to Eynsford and you return to Selborne. Ponder what a relationship with me will really entail, the sister of a murder. If, after a time, you still feel the same way, then send for me."

Val could see that she was probably correct. Today had been an important event in his life. He was still riding high on the emotion of it. Perhaps he would go home and, after thinking carefully about everything, decide that he wanted to put it, and Vesper, behind him. But he felt so strongly for her that he couldn't imagine that would be the case. He was fairly certain that he loved her, even after knowing her such a short time, but he would not say so.

Perhaps she was right – perhaps they both needed time to think.

He thought of the necklace he'd given her, tucked into the belt at his waist. Reaching down, he pulled it out, holding it up between them.

"I will return to Selborne as you ask, and I will think," he said quietly. "But I already know what my decision will be. That has not changed. In a week's time, I will send a messenger to Eynsford with this necklace. If your decision is to permit me to continue courting you, then you will keep it. If you have decided against it, then simply send it back and I will trouble you no more. Agreed?"

It was a fair enough arrangement. Vesper's gaze drifted over the magnificent necklace before looking him in the eye.

"Agreed."

Val's focus fixed on her for a moment before taking the necklace and tucking it into his coin purse for safe keeping. Once he'd done that, he looked at her again. There was so much he wanted to say, so much he was fearful to tell her. His mind was muddled by everything that had happened that day.

"I will have some of St. Lo's men return you to Eynsford," he said. "It should take about four days so I will pay them well to ensure you sleep in a good bed nightly and are well protected. Are… are you sure I cannot accompany you?"

Vesper almost agreed but she reconsidered. It would defeat the purpose that they had already established; of deciding whether or not this courtship was damaged beyond repair. Everything had happened so fast that they both needed time to think.

Only time would tell.

"I believe it would be best if you did not," she said. "But thank you for being generous enough to hire men to return me to Eynsford. I am grateful."

Val simply looked at her. Then, he lifted his hands, cupping her face between his two enormous palms. Before Vesper could pull away, he kissed her sweetly, tenderly, in front of the entire town of Bishop's Waltham. But Val didn't care; he was afraid this might be the last time he ever kissed her and his heart was filled with both the joy of her touch and the sorrow of their parting. His heart hurt as he never imagined it could.

"Nothing I am feeling for you has changed," he whispered before reluctantly dropping his hands. "I want you to understand that."

Vesper was left breathless by his kiss, her heart racing in her chest. "Nor have my feelings changed for you," she said softly. "But I believe this is for the best."

"I do not agree with you, but I will respect your wishes."

Vesper knew that. It was in everything about him; he wanted things the way he wanted them but he didn't want to push her. She was grateful. But the cries from her father caught her attention for they were still going on. The crowd around them had shifted somewhat and they had moved over to where McCloud was embracing the executed man. She peered around Val to see her father in the same position, now being surrounded by people who were spitting on Mat's corpse. Although St. Lo's men were trying to hold them back, there was a great deal of rage in people who had lived in fear for a year.

Val could see what was going on, too. He reached out, grasping Vesper's arm to give her a reassuring squeeze.

"I will make sure your brother is taken care of," he said. "And I will deal with your father appropriately. For now, go over to where the horses are and wait there. I will speak with St. Lo about your escort."

Before he could turn away, Vesper stopped him. "Val," she said, fighting the lump in her throat. "Whatever happens, I want you to know how very grateful I am to you. You have shown me… you have helped me to understand what it means not to be lonely any longer. If for no other reason than that, I thank you for giving me that gift. It was the best blessing you could have ever given me."

Val's throat was rather tight, too. He smiled wanly. "Even better than the necklace?"

Vesper nodded, a single tear popping from her eye. "Even better."

"Then I am glad."

Vesper swallowed hard, struggling not to weep again, as Val headed over to McCloud and that horrific scene. She could see him talking to the red-haired sheriff of the town, pointing to McCloud before finally turning around to point at her.

Feeling far more settled about the situation than she had minutes earlier, Vesper turned for the horses, who were over in a corner of the square, tearing out the fat green grass and munching happily. Her satchel was tied to the white palfrey and she wandered over to the horse, standing by it as she'd been directed. But her gaze inevitably returned to Val as he ordered men about.

It made her heart swell simply to look at him. He was so strong and tall and proud, but every second she looked at him, she was reminded that he didn't need to be associated with a family of murderers. Was she being a martyr in all of this, sacrificing her happiness so that Val's reputation would remain clean? In truth, her intentions were altruistic. She firmly believed he would be better off without her association.

But the fact remained that she didn't want to be without him. She'd risked much to keep his opinion of her intact and she'd almost lost that when he'd discovered the truth. But the man had an unnatural capacity for forgiveness, as she'd discovered.

Such a man deserved something far better than she could provide.

Soon enough, a wagon was brought around and Mat's body was put into the bed for transport to the church. McCloud climbed in with his son and Vesper wondered if that would be the last she ever saw of her father as the wagon lumbered down the road, heading for St. Peter's Church. Although Mat would not be buried in the church yard, the priests would ensure he had a proper burial outside of the walls.

Once McCloud and Mat had disappeared, Val continued to give what appeared to be instructions to St. Lo and his men. Men would dash away, obviously off to complete a task assigned to them by Val, while still others completely disbursed the crowd which, by now, had thinned out considerably.

Still, Vesper stood by the horses, ignoring the hunger she felt now that the evening meal was approaching, looking up to the sky to see that it was, in fact, a glorious sunset. *How ironic,* she thought. A beautiful sunset as if to signify a new future now that Mat, the Angel of Death, had finally been punished. Even God was celebrating her brother's death. For the people of Bishop's Waltham and the surrounding area, it was a new future, indeed.

Val eventually returned to Vesper with six men who had been assigned as her escort. They were older men, heavily armed, used to being paid for their protection and men that St. Lo trusted. So, Val instructed the six in the strongest possible language that they were to ensure that Lady Vesper reached Eynsford without incident. Vesper watched Val pay them all extremely well with the promise of more coinage when the job was complete. Wanting to please the Itinerant Justice of Hampshire, the men firmly agreed.

But night had fallen and they would not begin their travel at night, so Val took Vesper over to The Crown Inn, the oldest and best inn the village had to offer. He asked twice to remain with her, at least for sup, but she politely declined both times.

Heartsick, but understanding that she was trying to stick to their bargain when he was fully prepared to ignore it, Val paid the innkeeper for his finest room and a meal. He stood in the corridor while Vesper went inside her rented room and bolted the door. Only then did he feel comfortable enough to leave her there, although it was killing him.

He very much wanted to stay with her.

Dulled from the events of the day and thoroughly exhausted, Val quit the inn and went across the street to a livery where he had a birds-eye view of the inn and of Vesper's chamber window. Although he could only see the faint glow of the taper, he was comforted by knowing she was behind the shutters. Even if she didn't want him in the inn, near her, that didn't mean he couldn't watch out for her through the night.

And that was exactly what he did.

In a stall next to his war horse, Val spent the entire night watching Vesper's window and the inn in general. No one went in or out without his knowledge. When dawn hinted over the eastern horizon, he saw Vesper and her six guards emerge from the inn and head to the livery to collect their horses. Val stayed out of sight while the escort gathered their beasts, helped Vesper mount her palfrey, and departed the city just as the sun began to rise in the east.

After that, Val left the livery astride his horse, leading the old war horse he'd loaned McCloud, and followed the escort at a good distance as far as the tiny settlement of West Meon where there was a fork in the road. As Vesper and her party continued east, Val headed north towards Selborne.

Once Vesper was out of his sight, Val realized, with a heavy heart, that he'd never felt so empty in his entire life.

He began to count the minutes until he would see her again.

Please, God… let me see her again!

CHAPTER TEN

Selborne Castle

"GOD'S BONES, HUGH. I've not seen you in ages. Where have you been?"

Hugh grinned at Margaretha de Nerra, a woman he genuinely liked. She was feisty and strong, everything a well-bred mother should be. But he had to admit that he felt sorry for Val sometimes the way his mother came down on him. But he was very patient with his mother and mostly taunted her in return, which had resulted in some truly hilarious conversations that Hugh had witnessed. Here at Selborne, he felt truly at home and truly in the presence of friends. He enjoyed it here.

But now, he was about to violate that trust.

"I have been with the king in France, Lady de Nerra," he said, greeting the woman with a kiss to the hand. "We have only just returned. Henry is heading to Winchester, in fact, and plans to hunt through the new year. And you? How is it you become younger every time I see you?"

Margaretha cocked a dark eyebrow. "You have the silken tongue of a viper," she said. "Do not flatter me. I shall beat the foolishness right out of you."

Calum was standing beside his brother, as he had escorted the man from the gatehouse to the keep so Hugh could pay his respects to Lady de Nerra. Both he and Hugh laughed softly at Margaretha's threat.

"It would be a pleasure to be beaten by such lovely hands, Lady de Nerra," Hugh teased.

But Margaretha simply rolled her eyes. "I see you get your manners from my son, you beastly boy," she said, mostly because that was how Val reacted to her threats. "Where have you been keeping yourself? Why have we not seen you?"

Hugh shrugged. "The king has kept me very busy," he said. Then, he gestured to the group of knights by the gatehouse. "Being that it is the Christmas season, he has kept us busier than usual. We are on an errand for him, in fact. It is something I must speak with your son about. Is Val here?"

Margaretha shook her head. "He is not," she replied. "But I expect him back shortly. Is it something I can help you with?"

"Nay, Lady de Nerra."

"Then you shall enjoy the hospitality of Selborne until he returns."

"Thank you, Lady de Nerra."

Margaretha gestured towards the keep. "Will you come inside and refresh yourself?"

Hugh shook his head. "You are most gracious, but I must speak with my brother first. Will you excuse us?"

Well aware when it was time to conduct business and that she was not wanted, Margaretha gathered her heavy silk skirts and headed for the steps to the keep. "Calum, bring your brother inside when you are finished," she commanded. "And where is your wife?"

Calum turned to her. "She is lying down in our cottage," he replied. "She has not felt well this morning."

Margaretha shifted course. "Then I shall see to her," she said, heading off across the bailey. "I shall see you both later."

The men let her go, watching her as she headed to the western wall where the cottages of the married knights were situated. Calum waited until she was out of earshot before returning to his brother.

"What is amiss?" he asked, glancing at the gatehouse where the other knights were gathered. "FitzUrse? De Tracy? Le Breton? It must be something serious if those three are with you. What has happened?"

Hugh's gaze lingered on his younger brother. "Is there someplace quiet that we may speak?"

That request did nothing to ease Calum's curiosity. If anything, it was now joined by a measure of apprehension. "Aye," he said. "Inside."

He began to take the steps up to the keep and Hugh turned to his men, off by the gatehouse, and emitted a shrill whistle. When the three turned to look at him, he indicated for them to follow him with a big wave of his arm. When he could see the three men in motion, he followed Calum into the keep of Selborne.

The interior was dark and cool, smelling the same way most keeps did – of dust, of dirt. Sometimes, there was a snippet of smoke from the hearths, or even food. Sometimes, there was even incense if the owner liked to burn that kind of thing. But this keep smelled like any other.

Hugh had been inside Selborne many times before and he knew the layout. Entering into the lobby took one immediately into the small hall which, at this time of the morning, was full of servants sweeping floors and scrubbing the tables in the room. There was a doorway on one side of the hall that led to a corridor, built into the thickness of the wall, that led to a chamber that was used by Val as his private solar. It wasn't a big room but it was comfortable. The room was packed with shelves that contained decrees and laws, all rolled up in yellowed vellum, plus a pile of maps, two cow hide rugs on the floor, and a big table that was pocked and marred from years of use.

There were also two big chairs with backs on them and a smattering of stools near the hearth. Hugh planted himself in one of the chairs before the others arrived and confiscated them. No one wanted to sit on stools. He watched his brother as the man bent over the hearth to light a fire.

"The weather seems to have grown cold suddenly," Calum said casually as he struck the flint against stone. Sparks flew, igniting the kindling. "Did you see any frost on your ride here?"

Hugh shook his head. "Nay," he replied. "We left Winchester before dawn but we saw no frost."

Calum blew on the fire to feed it. "So you've been at Winchester?" he asked. "We were just speaking of you only a day or so ago, wondering where you'd been. I thought you might have gone north to see to Father."

Hugh watched his younger brother, knowing he was simply making conversation until the others arrived and the serious discussion began. Calum had always been so eager to please, something that made him a very good knight. He was noble and true, and obeyed without question, which made him perfect for the message that Hugh was about to deliver.

"Nay," Hugh replied, leaning back against the chair. "I have not gone north but I have been planning to. However, Henry keeps me so busy that there hasn't been the opportunity. I was fortunate that I was able to come to Selborne today."

Boots were heard in the doorway as Reginald, William, and Richard entered, pulling off gloves and removing cloaks. Calum stood up from the hearth, brushing his hands off and summon a servant for food and wine. When the servant fled, Calum took the cloaks and hung them up by the hearth to both dry them off and warm them.

"Well," he said with a grin, looking at the men in the chamber, "this is not a sight I expected today. I know you have come to see Val but I will do what I can for you. He should not be long."

"Where is he?" Reginald asked, moving to warm his hands by the fire. "I thought he was chained to this place."

Calum shook his head. "He is chained to Hampshire, but not Selborne," he replied. "He leaves quite frequently to render justice throughout the shire. That is why they call him an itinerant justice. In case you do not know what that means, it requires him to travel."

Reginald grinned, lopsided. "Now I remember why I do not like you," he said. "You have your brother's smart mouth."

Calum laughed softly. "He learned everything he knows from me."

"Now I *really* do not like you."

Chuckles filled the chamber as William and Richard went to warm their hands, feeling the delicious warmth from the fire lick their flesh. Calum came away from the hearth when he saw the servant return with refreshments, taking the pitcher and cups from the man and setting them onto Val's big table. Wine was poured, men were satisfied. When the servant left, Calum turned to the group.

"Now," he said, his voice low. "Will you tell me why you have come? You did not leave Henry's side and ride all the way to Selborne simply to drink my wine and warm yourself by my fire. What has happened?"

Reginald, William, and Richard looked at Hugh, who remained seated on the big chair. But Hugh's gaze was on a pair of saddlebags that had been brought in. He stood up and went to the bags, unlacing one of them and pulling forth a faded yellow roll of vellum. It was tied with a red silk ribbon and he brought it over to his brother, handing it to the man. Calum accepted it, looking at his brother in puzzlement.

"What is this?" he asked.

Hugh was grim. "I already know what it says. You had better open it."

Calum did. Unrolling the vellum, he was met with the perfectly scribed letters from the king's clerk. At the bottom was the big red waxed seal of Henry II. Moving into better light, he began to read.

Most Wanted Notice

Upon this First Day in December, Anno Domino Eleven Hundred Seventy, Sir Valor de Nerra, Itinerant Justice of Hampshire with jurisdiction granted by the king for all of England, is hereby ordered to arrest Thomas à Becket, Archbishop of Canterbury, for crimes against the king and his descendants. Failure to do so constitutes a refusal of the king's wishes and a criminal action by the Itinerant Justice.

Becket is to be brought to Winchester Castle with all due haste to face the king's good judgement.

Calum read it three times. He wasn't the fastest reader, but he took particular time with this. The missive was signed at the bottom with Henry's distinctive seal. To Calum, it looked official. When he was finished, he looked at his brother in shock.

"Is Henry serious?" he breathed. "He wants Val to arrest Canterbury?"

Hugh nodded calmly, but in truth, he was vastly relieved. The missive, forged by the same clerk Henry had clipped with a pewter cup when he'd first learned of L'Évêque's excommunication, was done with great skill, exactly as the king would have done it, down to the signature of the monarch. Calum may not have been a fast reader but he had a good eye and he had seen Henry's missives before, many times. If it was able to pass his scrutiny, then surely it would pass Val's. At least, that was the hope.

"He does," Hugh replied. "I do not know if you've yet heard, but Canterbury excommunicated York, London, and Salisbury for crowning Young Henry at the king's request. As you know, Canterbury was out of the country when Henry had his son crowned. When Canterbury returned, he excommunicated the clergy who did it. This power struggle between the two of them has to stop, Calum. Henry has ordered Canterbury arrested."

Calum was astonished. "My God," he hissed. "So he will send Val to do it?"

"Val has been ordered to."

Calum looked at the other knights; FitzUrse, le Breton, de Tracy… these were men deep in Henry's inner circle, men who had served the king flawlessly for many years. The weight of the order began to push on Calum, so much so that he sought the nearest chair, sinking into it as he digested the contests of the missive.

"God's Bones," he finally hissed. "So it has come to this. All of these years of the king and the man who used to be his closest ally and it has come to this – the arrest of Becket. But why Val? Henry surrounds himself with hundreds of men of greater rank."

"But Val is the law in Hampshire, which includes Winchester," Hugh pointed out. "It is his duty to carry out the king's arrest warrants when they are issued from Winchester Castle. As unsavory as this is, Val has no choice."

Calum knew that. He looked back at the warrant, still in his hand, and sighed heavily. "The church's anger will not be directed at Henry for this," he muttered. "It will be directed at Val. It was very clever of the king to order another man to do his dirty work."

Hugh was aware. He'd said the same thing, essentially, and therefore struggled against the guilt of it. It was he who was putting Val's neck on the line in the name of justice, not Henry. But he still stuck to the belief that Henry had ordered this; all of the four of the knights still did – him, FitzUrse, le Breton, and de Tracy. They all were still under the firm belief that Henry had ordered Canterbury arrested. Therefore, he pushed aside the guilt.

It had to be done.

"It is the wish of the king, little brother," Hugh said with resignation. "We are not to question him. We simply carry out his commands. Agreed?"

Calum didn't look convinced but he nodded nonetheless. "Agreed," he said begrudgingly. Then, he stood up and went to Val's table, putting the warrant on it. "Val should be home soon. Will you not stay and greet him?"

Hugh shook his head. "The four of us intend to go on ahead of Val to Canterbury and attempt to talk Becket into peacefully surrendering," he said. "There is no time to waste on the king's order, so we must go today. As soon as Val arrives, he is to follow us. We shall procure rooms at the West Gate Inn. Hopefully, by the time he arrives in Canterbury, we will already have Becket in our custody. It is our hope that the man will not put up a fight."

From what Calum knew of Thomas Becket, that would not be an easy thing. "He will not surrender," he said. "The man has been in contention with Henry for years. What makes you think he will peacefully surrender to you?"

Hugh stood up from the chair, stretching his body as he did so. "Because we will tell him that Val de Nerra is coming for him," he said simply. "If he does not wish to be confronted by a man who can use a sword better than almost anyone in England, then it would be in his best interest to surrender peacefully."

Calum cocked his head curiously. "So you are using Val as a threat?"

"It is a good threat."

Hugh winked at his brother when he said it, which caused a resurgence of Calum's shock. So they were going to threaten Canterbury with violence from the Itinerant Justice of Hampshire if the man did not surrender? That was putting Val in an extremely precarious position that he wasn't even aware of yet. Val's world was about to change dramatically and the man had no idea. Calum felt a great deal of pity for him.

"Then I am sorry you cannot be here to tell Val the course his life is about to take," he said. "If I did not know better, I would think you were cowardly in leaving so soon. It is as if you do not want to face Val with this."

Those words would have had swords drawn had they come from anyone else, but Hugh didn't draw his sword, mostly because what Calum said was true. But he would not acknowledge that. He simply reached out and patted his brother on the cheek.

"Tell Val that he must come to Canterbury immediately," he said evenly. "We will see him there."

Calum watched his brother leave the solar, a rather baleful expression on his face. He didn't even acknowledge FitzUrse, le Breton, or de Tracy. He thought they were all cowardly for dropping the warrant and then departing for Canterbury. It felt very much as if they were fleeing, as Calum had said; men who didn't want to face Val because of the seriousness of the situation. Much like Henry, they were pushing off the responsibility to Val.

Now, it would be Val who would intervene in perhaps the most volatile situation in England at the moment. He would literally be putting himself between the king and the church, a place that no man wanted to be. Two powerful factions vying for control of the country, two very stubborn institutions that refused to give ground, now with Val caught between them.

It was more than likely going to tear Val apart.

Calum fervently hoped not.

IT WAS CLOSE to sunset by the time Val reached Selborne.

Usually, the sight of his fortress brought him great comfort, but not tonight. Looking at the structure, all he could feel was emptiness. No Vesper, no joy. The last time he was here, she was here and he'd become quite smitten with the lovely young woman. Odd how even her short stay here had somehow impressed itself on him until all he could think of was the evening they'd shared in the great hall, with feasting and music. Precious hours he'd spent with her, not realizing they might be his last.

As he approached the gatehouse, the sentries on duty began to take up the call and the iron gates were opened. Men with torches were moving about, greeting him in the dark passageway beneath the gatehouse, taking the horses from him as he headed across the bailey.

It was relatively quiet in the bailey at this time of night. Men were being fed in the great hall and patrols were on the walls, the flickering torches warding off the darkness. There was very little activity in the bailey itself. Val made his way up the steps of the keep, slowly, his mind heavy with the sorrow of the past two days. This wasn't something he was used to and he was, therefore, having difficulty dealing with it. Just as he reached the top of the steps, a figure appeared in the doorway.

"So you have finally returned," Margaretha said. "Where have you been?"

Val looked at his mother, feeling a stab of shame and sorrow. There was so much he had to tell her. In spite of the fact that she could be harsh and antagonistic, she also had the ability to be wise and calm. She had helped him through many a crisis with her sage advice. He trusted her.

"I took McCloud and Lady Vesper to Bishop's Waltham," he said, his tone dull. "I had not expected to go so far with them, but it was a good thing that I did. Come inside, Mother. I must speak with you."

Curious at her son's tone, Margaretha permitted him to take her by the arm and turn her around, entering the keep and heading for the small hall beyond. Already, she could feel his sorrowful mood.

"Valor, what is the matter?" she asked. "Why do you sound as if you have been beaten?"

Val could only shake his head. The dimly lit small hall greeted them and Val released his mother, heading straight for the pitcher of wine on the table. He didn't bother to collect a cup; he drank straight from the pitcher, great gulps of the sweet red wine. Margaretha stood by the table, watching him with increasing concern.

"Valor?" she asked, her voice considerably softer. "What has happened? Please tell me."

Val took another gulp of wine. He didn't seem apt to look her in the eye. "You were right," he said quietly. "About McCloud, I mean. You were right in your assessment of his character and I was wrong. I knew the man from years ago when he had honor. You saw that the man before you had none. You were correct about that, Mother."

Margaretha, surprisingly, wasn't one to gloat, not when the mood was as heady as it was. She was wise enough to know that there was no point. "Sit down," she said softly. "Tell me what happened."

Val did as he was told but he kept a firm grip on the wine pitcher. After a moment, he snorted ironically. "I hardly know where to start," he said. "It seems that McCloud has changed much over the years. His farm has fallen into poverty and he and his son were starving. His son, being a simple-minded man with no sense of right or wrong, proceeded to go out into the countryside to kill people and take their food. This has been going on for a solid year, evidently, and the locals down in Bishop's Waltham had taken to calling this murderer the Angel of Death. McCloud hid that from me, all of it. But that is not the worst part."

Margaretha was listening with growing horror and struggling not to show it. "How did you discover this?"

Val looked at her, then. "When we entered Bishop's Waltham yesterday, as it is only a short distance from McCloud's farm, the locals had captured their Angel of Death. It seems that while McCloud was gone, his son killed again, this time two children, and he was discovered. By the time we got there, he'd been restrained and the town was going mad over the capture. That prompted McCloud's confession. Or, shall I say, Vesper's confession."

Margaretha swallowed hard. "Sweet Mary," she breathed. "She was complicit as well?"

Val shook his head. "Nay," he said. "Not complicit. She had only just found out about her brother's activities when McCloud recently visited her at Eynsford. That is why they were coming home; Vesper thought she could stop whatever was happening. I feel a good deal of pity for the lass, in truth; she enjoyed a good reputation at Eynsford as a trusted woman of character, and then she finds herself part of a family of murderers. She thought she could fix the problem, as she put it, but it was bigger than she imagined. It was she who confessed the situation when it became obvious that both she and McCloud knew the man known as the Angel of Death."

Margaretha was truly astonished by the tale. "What did you do?" she asked. "Did you punish them all?"

Val shook his head. Then, he downed what was left in the wine pitcher, wiping his mouth with the back of his hand.

"Not all of them," he said. "I had a confession from the murderer and eye witness accounts from people who saw him kill the children in his most recent killing spree. Based on that, I executed him on the spot.

I will deal with McCloud at a later time; I simply didn't have the will to do it. Discovering a longtime friend was an accessory to murder has not settled well with me. Worse still, he was evidently plotting to marry you for your money and marry Vesper to me so he and his son would never have to worry about food or money again. Even though you are a handsome woman, Mother, McCloud was trying to manipulate you. And I let him. I should have protected you against it and I did not."

Margaretha was disappointed to hear that. Not disappointment in her son, but disappointed that she no longer had a male suitor. She had been rather pleased about that, in truth. It had been a very long time since a man paid her flattery but now to discover it had been with an ulterior motive in mind was disheartening.

"As you said, you saw the noble man you used to know," she said, trying to sound as if McCloud's flattery had not affected her. "You did not know what he had become, Val, although I tried... well, I will not say that I tried to warn you. Even I could not imagine how horrific your friend's life had become. But I am sorry for you. I know he was your friend."

Val just sat and stared into space, the wine in his veins starting to have some effect. It was giving him a bit of a foggy head, which he'd hoped for. Perhaps it would dull his angst.

"People change," he said. "Did you not tell me that? You were right."

Margaretha wasn't going to confirm something he already knew. "What of Lady Vesper?" she asked. "What became of her?"

Val sighed heavily; that question seemed to affect him even more than the situation with McCloud. "She has returned to Eynsford," he said with sadness. "She is under the opinion that it would not do for me to be keeping company with a woman from a family of murderers. She feels that by my courting her, it will destroy my reputation. She is afraid of what people will think."

Margaretha was rather surprised to hear that. It spoke to her of a young woman who was more ethical than her father and more level-headed than her son. She knew Val was smitten with the girl; that had been obvious. He was thinking emotionally. But she tried to be sympathetic.

"And you?" she asked quietly. "What do you think?"

His jaw ticked faintly. "It is not her fault that her brother killed and her father let him," he said. "She had no part in it. I still intend to court her, Mother. You may not want to hear that, but it is my intention. She has gone back to Eynsford, at her request, and I am to stay away from her for a time so we can each decide if we want to continue this courtship. I have already made my decision."

"It was her decision that you should stay away from her?"

"Aye. She does not believe that I am thinking clearly on how a relationship with her will affect my future and my reputation."

Margaretha was starting to like Vesper. She'd truly not had much contact with the young woman but hearing that she'd been most reasonable in this situation, Margaretha approved. Whether or not she actually approved of the woman herself was another matter, but at least she approved of her decision making. She had a feeling, however, that Val didn't want to hear that.

After a moment, she stood up.

"Then mayhap it is for the best, if only for a short time," she said. "I agree with your lady, Valor – mayhap some time apart will help you see things more clearly."

Val's thoughts were on Vesper, of the last time he saw her in the early morning light. "Did you hear me?" he asked. "I still intend to court her."

"I heard you."

"But you do not agree?"

"It does not matter if I do or not. You will do as you wish."

That was true. Val was grateful that at least she wasn't arguing with him. She had remained uncharacteristically silent throughout his sordid tale but he took that as a blessing. He wasn't sure he could have handled anything else other than an ear to listen.

"She is a good woman, Mother," he said quietly. "I do not want the actions of her father and brother to mar your opinion of her. She had not seen them for years prior to this incident and knew nothing."

"I understand."

He didn't like the way she said it. There was judgement in her tone in spite of her words. He turned to look at her as she went to summon a servant, no doubt for food. "Shall I have Lady Eynsford come and tell you of the Vesper she knows? Lady Eynsford is quite fond of her."

Margaretha sent the servant to the kitchens and turned to her son. "Mayhap in time," she said. "But there is no need at this moment. Let us eat and then you shall sleep. You need rest."

He did. In fact, he was too tired to argue with her about anything. He'd told her what he needed to say and now there was an odd sense of emptiness because of it, emptiness because his usually controlled world had veered out of control. The excitement he'd built up over the past few days about Vesper had taken an unhappy turn. Perhaps when he'd eaten and slept, his mother could help him sift through the situation for a resolution. Wearily, he stood up from the table.

"Then I shall change my clothes and wash," he said. "As I recall, I am not allowed to eat at your table looking like a filthy animal."

"I will make you eat in the stables if that is the case."

That brought a grin to his weary lips. "I do adore you, you cruel woman," he said. "I will return shortly."

He was barely to the chamber door when he saw Calum enter the keep, heading in his direction. Calum was moving very swiftly.

"Val," he said, both relief and a sense of urgency in his tone. "I was just told that you had returned."

Val came to a pause, weaving about in his exhaustion. "Aye," he said. "I am going to eat sup and go to bed. I did not sleep last night."

Calum shook his head. "I must speak with you before you do," he said. "Did your mother tell you that Hugh came this morning?"

Val frowned. "Hugh?" he repeated, surprised. "Your brother?"

"Aye."

"Where in the hell has he been?"

Calum could see that Margaretha had not told her son anything and he was frustrated. Although he had not told Margaretha the contents of the missive, still, she knew that Henry had sent her son a message. Calum thought the lady might have placed some importance on that.

"He came with a missive of great importance to you from the king," he said. "It is in your solar."

That seemed to snap Val out of some of his weariness. "Henry has sent me a missive?" he said, suddenly agitated. "Well, *Christ* – why didn't anyone tell me?"

He spun on his heel, heading back into the solar where his mother still lingered. He looked at her accusingly.

"Why did you not tell me I received a missive from Henry?" he asked.

Margaretha looked straight at Calum. "Because it has not yet come up," she said, her anger at Calum obvious. "Clearly, you have returned home with much on your mind and Hugh's visit this morning was not a priority. I was going to tell you once you'd had a chance to wash and eat something. Whatever Henry has sent you can wait, Valor. You cannot do anything about it tonight."

Calum, surprisingly, didn't back away. "It is imperative, Lady de Nerra," he said as if to remind her. Then, he looked at Val. "In your solar, Val. I have much to tell you."

Leaving Margaretha irritated that Calum would agitate her exhausted son, the knights quickly moved past the woman and into the short corridor that led to Val's solar. The chamber was dimly lit, only by embers from the dying fire, and Calum went to light a bank of tallow tapers as Val headed straight to the table.

"That one," Calum pointed out the one that was unrolled, right in front of him. "See Henry's seal on the bottom?"

Val did. He snatched it, bringing it over to the tapers that had just been lit, giving forth their soft warm glow into the chamber. Calum watched his face as he read it; he read it once, twice, and then just stared at it. After a moment, he lowered the missive and looked at Calum with an odd expression on his face – something between disbelief and horror.

"God's Bones," he hissed. "I take it that you read this?"

Calum nodded solemnly. "Hugh told me to," he said. "Henry has ordered you to arrest the Archbishop of Canterbury because you are the law in Hampshire, where the missive was written and where the trial shall be carried out. Hugh brought FitzUrse, le Breton, and de Tracy with him and they have already gone ahead to Canterbury to talk the man into surrendering peacefully before you get there. But we know he will not. My God, Val… what has Henry put you in the middle of? If Canterbury refuses, Henry will blame you and if he complies, the Church will blame you because you arrested him. What are you going to do?"

Val simply stared at him as if he had no real answer. His exhausted face gave forth a rainbow of emotions as the implications of the missive sank deep. While Calum had been given time to think about every angle, Val hadn't. Now, Calum had slapped him across the face with the reality of the situation and he turned away, missive in hand, struggling to collect his thoughts.

"I am going to obey his missive," he said after a moment. "That is the only thing I can do. But for something like this, Henry should have summoned me to Winchester at the very least. He should have told me to my face that this was to be my duty. To send a missive is cowardly at best. In fact, mayhap I should ride to Winchester to discuss it."

Calum shook his head. "But he has already sent my brother and the other knights on ahead," he said. "Hugh told me that you should meet them at the West Gate Inn. Do you know it?"

"I do."

"Then if you seek Henry to discuss the contents of the missive, it will delay you in going to Canterbury and I would wager to say that you will anger Henry. He wants this done quickly; otherwise, why would he have had my brother bring you this missive? To go back to Winchester would cost time and my brother is already heading for Canterbury."

Val understood that. Evidently, this was something Henry wanted done very fast so it could be over and done with before church supporters were rallied to protect Canterbury. But Val knew of the troubles Henry had with Thomas Becket; hardly a fighting man in England hadn't heard of it, troubles that went back for years. He knew about the excommunication of York and Salisbury, something that a knight traveling to Winchester from London last month had told him when he'd stayed a night at Selborne. That same knight was traveling to Winchester to inform the king.

It never occurred to him that the message the knight bore would someday involve him.

But it did. The excommunication of those who had crowned Young Henry had evidently been the last nail in the coffin as far as Henry was concerned. Was he surprised by the directive? Nay, he was not. But he was deeply concerned about it. Calum had been correct; Henry was putting him in a very bad position.

"Henry knows he has placed me in the jaws of the lion," he muttered. "Did you see the portion of the message that threatened me? If I do not do my duty, then Henry will consider it a refusal of his command. He had to do that because he knew I would not swallow this command easily."

Calum watched the man carefully, looking for any signs of rebellion. But Val was very good at covering his emotions. More than that, it would be unheard of for him to refuse an order from the man who had done so much for him. He was loyal to Henry until the end.

Even his.

"I am sorry, Val," he said quietly. "This is not something you should be mixed up in."

Val was oddly calm about the situation, mostly because it hadn't fully sunk in yet. His exhaustion had prevented that, as had the events with Vesper. Even now, when he should be thinking about the king's directive, it was competing in his mind with thoughts of the lady who was now halfway to Eynsford.

But he had to shake himself of thoughts of her. He needed all of his focus because he had a very serious duty to undertake. He looked at the missive again, still in his hand, reading those words yet again.

"I am the law in Hampshire," he said. "Henry made me so. I cannot pick and choose those laws and royal directives I decide to enforce. I suppose I am the logical choice when it comes to arresting Canterbury although I do not relish it. This will be trouble for me, if I refuse or if I comply. Either way, I am doomed."

Calum knew that. He was feeling a great deal of pity for Val. "Kenan and Mayne do not know of this directive," he said. "It is up to you if you wish to tell them. Do you have any thought as to who will go with you to accomplish this task?"

Val looked at him as if surprised by the question. "No one will," he said. "I will go alone. This directive is for me and me alone. I will not allow the rest of you to be sucked up into it."

Calum was concerned. "But you must take some men with you," he said. "What if Canterbury resists? How will you overcome him?"

Val sighed heavily. "Before I was a justice, I was a knight and a very good one," he said. "I spent years on the battlefields of France, as you well know. Now, do you truly believe a cleric like Canterbury can fight me off?"

Calum quickly shook his head. "I did not mean that," he said. "I know you can handle Canterbury, but he has men that surround him. What will you do about them?"

Val turned for the table, reaching out to set the missive atop it. "You said your brother and the others have gone on ahead of me," he said. "I think between the five of us, we can subdue any guards that Canterbury might have."

Calum didn't like that at all. "Please, Val," he begged softly. "Take one of your knights and a hand-picked contingent with you. For your own safety, please. I know you do not want to get any of us mixed up in this, but we serve *you*. We are already mixed up in it. Please do not go it alone, I implore you."

Val was too weary to fight off his words. He made sense and he knew Calum would pester him until he agreed. Worse still, he might even tell Margaretha and then she would enter the fray. Nay, that's not what he wanted. Therefore, he gave in to Calum's soft pleas simply to shut the man up.

"You are an old woman, Calum," he said sternly. Then, his face cracked into a smile. "But I understand your concern and I will respect it. If you were hoping to go with me, I will not permit it. You have a wife and a child to think of, so you remain here. But I will allow you to select the knight and contingent who will attend me. Tell them not why; I will do that. We will leave before dawn, so have them meet me here in the solar before dawn breaks. I will explain the situation to them. Even if Henry did not tell me to my face what his wishes were, I will show my men more respect than that. They will know what they will soon be facing."

Calum was disappointed that he would not be going with Val but he understood. He did have a wife and child to think of and this mission would have far-reaching implications to those who participated. He didn't want to jeopardize his family, or worse, leave them completely. He very much wanted to see his son born.

"Very well," he said reluctantly. "What about your mother? Will you tell her?"

Val nodded. "I must," he said. "She will have to know why she will no longer be welcome in church."

It was the truth. The House of de Nerra had always stood for piety and devotion to the church but, after this, they would become an enemy of the godly. There wasn't much more to say after that and Calum patted Val on the shoulder comfortingly before heading to the solar door. He suspected the man needed time to his thoughts. But he paused before leaving entirely, turning to Val one last time.

"I did not ask you how your journey was with Lady Vesper and her father yesterday," he said. "Are you officially courting the woman now?

Celesse likes her a great deal, by the way. She is looking forward to another young woman here at Selborne."

Val looked at him, sharply. He had only just succeeded from chasing thoughts of the woman from his mind. Now, they were back again, full-bore. They mingled with thoughts of Henry, beating him down. Leaning against the table, he hung his head in a defeated gesture.

"That is another matter altogether," he said. "You are not going to believe what happened."

Calum was intrigued. He came back into the chamber. "Is that so?" he said. "Do tell."

Val had been right; so great his surprise, Calum hardly believed him and wondered, secretly, how much more the man could take. Val de Nerra was strong but he wasn't invincible.

That strength was about to be put to the test.

CHAPTER ELEVEN

IT WAS A winter's dawn, complete with ice on the ground and a pewter-colored sky. The weather this winter had been so mild that only now, in the midst of the Christmas season, was it starting to truly feel like winter.

Val was in his solar in the hours before dawn, waiting for the men Calum had selected to join him. He knew they would be here soon, eager to know their directive and Val had been wracking his brain for the past two hours on how to ease them into the seriousness of the orders. He'd hoped to soften the blow. But he'd come to the conclusion that he couldn't; any way they were to look at Henry's missive, the situation was plain – Val had been asked to intercede in something that, so far, only the Pope had made an attempt to intercede in. It was a feud that had been going on for years. And now, Henry was hiding behind the law in this case or, more specifically, behind Val.

A man who could take the fall for him.

It was a realization that had cost Val sleep that night. He'd been horribly exhausted from no sleep the night before in Bishop's Waltham and had managed just a few hours before thoughts of Henry and Canterbury woke him. He hadn't been able to sleep with those two on his mind, so he'd arisen, shaved, and dressed, preparing to meet his men before heading out to Canterbury.

In the weak light of the tallow tapers, Val was seated at the table, once again going over the missive sent from Henry. He'd already read it fifty times; he didn't know why he needed to read it again. When he'd read it the first few times yesterday, he'd been in a bit of a fog, and this morning he was only starting to think clearly about it. If Val was one thing, it was decisive – and he always had a plan. He'd come up with a plan for the arrest, one which relied heavily on logic. He could only hope he could stick to that plan before Canterbury's guards rushed him.

As he was mulling over what was to come, a figure appeared in the solar door and he looked up to see the silhouette of someone carrying a tray. He assumed it was a servant until it came into the light and he saw his mother enter, carrying a tray with food and drink upon it. Puzzled, as his mother hadn't served him food and drink since he was a child, he stood up and took the tray from her as she approached his table.

"I am flattered," he said, setting the tray down and looking at the contents – bread, porridge, warmed wine. "Since you have not brought me food in some time, I feel a little as if you are bringing me a last meal."

He meant it in jest but Margaretha saw no humor in it. Wrapped tightly in soft blue wool, her features were pale and strained in this early morning hour. She'd been told of Henry's missive the night before and had been unable to sleep because of it. Her beautiful, strong son was to be used as a scapegoat by a stubborn and vile king… those horrible thoughts had been rolling around in her mind for hours. It hurt her heart to know that her proud boy would soon be facing an unwinnable situation. Therefore, she had to see him before he left.

God only knew if he would return.

"It may be poisoned for all you know," she said seriously, as she was coming to appreciate his attempt to lighten the dark mood. "I would be careful eating it if I were you."

Val gave her a half-grin. "That is what I like about you, Mother," he said. "You show no mercy. You would poison me rather than let me carry out Henry's order."

Any levity Margaretha might have been feeling was dashed. "It might be a blessing," she murmured, pulling her shawl more tightly around her shoulders. "Although we did not discuss this much when you told me, I find that now I must. I have been thinking about this all night, Val. You know that you are going to be punished for this. You are being ordered to involve yourself in a family squabble. When it is all over, Henry and Thomas shall forgive each other and you shall be imprisoned."

"I am doing what I have been ordered to do."

"But you cannot win!"

Val didn't want to argue with her, not now. But he'd had the very same thoughts so it was difficult for him to hold out against her. "Then what do you suggest?" he hissed. "That I refuse? I will find myself imprisoned faster if I do that. You saw the missive for yourself; he threatened me if I refused the order. Or shall I side with Canterbury on this? We would lose everything if I did."

Margaretha watched him as he moved about the table, his movements full of the frustration he was feeling. "Your father still has family in Le Ruau," she said quietly. "Go, Val. Go to France and remain there until this situation goes away."

Val looked at her as if she'd gone mad. "Leave?" he repeated. He could see the concern on her face and he labored to ease her. "Mother, I know you are frightened but running away is not the answer. I would be a coward if I did and I am not a coward. You named me Valor for a reason, did you not? I would not be living up to my name if I ran from this."

Margaretha was starting to feel some desperation, unusual for the usually cool woman. "Sometimes caution is the better part of valor," she muttered.

"What does that mean?"

"It means that I have one son," she said. "I do not wish to see him caught up in Henry's personal battles. There are some battles that you cannot win and this is one of them."

He snorted. "You are fine when I am in the king's favor but the moment he asks something of me that requires bravery, you want me to fold like a weakling. I am sorry, Mother, but you did not raise a fool. I will fulfill my duties and I will face whatever the consequences are. I thought you knew me better than that."

"And Lady Vesper?" Margaretha went for the jugular. "What about her? You said you wanted to court her, Val. How are you to do that if you are in prison?"

Val was off-balance with her attack now. He hadn't expected her to bring Vesper into the mix. In fact, he'd been doing admirably well – he hadn't thought of Vesper in over two hours. Now, Margaretha was throwing the woman in his face, trying to weaken him. They were good tactics from a woman who was used to winning.

But not this time.

"I do not know," he said honestly. "I suppose I shall seek a resolution to that situation when the time comes. Mother, nothing you can say will change my mind. So, before you and I start arguing and say hurtful things, I suggest you stop trying to talk me out of this. I am sorry you do not understand my sense of duty."

Margaretha fell silent for a moment, but only for a moment. Her son's words had wounded her. "I know your sense of duty all too well," she said quietly. "Your father had the same sense of duty. Do you recall how I met your father?"

"I do. He served your father."

Margaretha nodded. "Indeed, he did. Gavin de Nerra was an astonishing sight, Val. Tall and dark, he was beauty and power personified. He served Matilda's husband, Geoffrey, as the Count of Anjou because he was a cousin to Geoffrey. The House of de Nerra is kin to the Counts of Anjou. Your father was gifted to my father in a treaty with the Saxon house of Byington to secure an alliance and that is how he came to serve here at Selborne. You know that you are related to the king, Val. He is your father's cousin and yours as well."

Val knew that. "How do you think I have been in favor all of these years?" he asked. "Of course, my sword has played a larger role in that but I received opportunities many did not because of my relationship to the king. I am well aware of it, Mother. You are telling me nothing I do not already know."

Margaretha took a step towards him, her eyes riveted to him. "So Henry believes that because you are his family, that he can send you out to attack his enemy in Canterbury?" She was becoming emotional, which was very rare for her. "I lost your father to Henry. Gavin went to France to help Henry protect some of his properties against the French king and he was killed for it. You were there, Val; you held your father as he died upon the field of battle."

Val was becoming less and less patient with his mother. He didn't want to relive that horrible day when his father, in the midst of trying to reclaim a very minor castle in France, was hit in the neck with an arrow. Val watched his father die and it was something he didn't like to be reminded about.

"Aye, I was there," he said.

"I will not lose my son to Henry as well!"

Val had to stop her before she became completely irrational about the situation. "Your husband was a knight and so is your son. You cannot dictate our duties, Mother. I am fulfilling an order from the king just as my father was. And you know that Papa would agree with me."

Margaretha stared at him a moment before backing down, perhaps realizing that she'd reached a dead end. Or perhaps she realized that what her son said was true. Whatever the case, she was shaken and frightened by Henry's orders. She didn't want to lose her son but she was positive that would happen. It was tearing her up inside.

"So I am to lose my other love," she murmured, turning away. "You and your father have the same sense of honor, the same sense of suicide. You do not think of yourselves first."

Val could hear the tears in her voice and was coming to feel badly for her. He knew that he was all she had left.

"Mother," he said quietly. "What is our family motto?"

Margaretha closed her eyes, tears stinging. "*Ante mortem animo.*"

Val nodded. "Courage before Death," he whispered. "I can promise you that I will show much courage before death can catch up to me. It may be tomorrow or it may be in thirty years. Who is to say? But I want you to know something… I have a great deal to live for. There is a woman at Eynsford that I very much wish to marry and I am going to do everything in my power to ensure that I live long enough to do that. I do not like these orders, either, but they are from the king and I have no choice. But mark my words… I shall return. I will do my duty and I shall return."

Margaretha believed that he believed he would. Whether or not he did… only God knew. Before she could reply, men began entering the solar and she knew her time with her son was ended. She had said what she wished to say and now it was in God's hands. Val's sense of duty was stronger than most, no matter how terrible the orders.

Without another word, she left the chamber as Val began to speak to his men. She could hear her son's soft baritone as he began to explain a mission that most sane men would run from. *I am to arrest the Archbishop of Canterbury.*

Sane or not, no man in England had the courage her son had. Valor's character was his namesake.

And he would have that innate sense of courage until the very end.

CHAPTER TWELVE

Four days later
Canterbury

THE WEST GATE Inn was empty at this time of day, at least empty of the men Val was looking for. De Morville, FitzUrse, le Breton, and de Tracy were nowhere to be found and a particularly solicitous barmaid could only say she'd seen them earlier, returning to their rooms and then emerging again swathed in cloaks.

Although the weather was cold, there was no snow on the ground and Val wondered why they had returned to the inn for their cloaks. Men bearing mail and heavy tunics were often quite warm in these temperatures, so it seemed odd to him. It was nearing late afternoon and, soon, Vespers would be upon them at the cathedral, which meant Becket would be there to perform the mass. Val couldn't really think of anywhere else the four knights would have gone so he and his men quit the inn, mounted their horses, and tore off in the direction of the cathedral.

Being that they were in the days approaching the Epiphany, a day that was celebrated as the Three King's feast, there were more people gathering near the cathedral than normal. Clusters of pilgrims swathed in wool against the cool temperatures were drawn to the warmth and light emitting from the cathedral like a moth to the flame.

The city of Canterbury was walled but so was the cathedral, with a fairly large barrier that was built around it and then inside, a vast open bailey with a cloister and the massive cathedral in the middle of it. It was an extraordinarily impressive monument to England's veneration of God and even though Val had been here before, he was still impressed with the size and architecture of the cathedral and even the surrounding city. Canterbury was a very cosmopolitan city.

The faithful were gravitating towards the entrance to the cathedral but Val paused at what was called Christ's Gate, a massive gatehouse which had a statue of a dove representing the Holy Spirit. This was the main entry, and he plus eighteen heavily-armed men made quite a conspicuous sight. Not wanting to create a massive uproar by charging into the grounds and terrifying everyone, he turned to Kenan, the only knight that had accompanied him.

"You and I will go in," he said. "We will take ten men with us. It should be enough to do what needs to be done. Have the rest wait out here with the horses and prepare to fend off any papal soldiers who try to intervene."

Kenan nodded firmly, relaying the message to the soldiers behind them. A fearless man, Kenan hadn't taken issue with Henry's directive in the least. He wasn't a great supporter of the church, feeling that it was more a hotbed of greed for men pretending to be pious, so he was more than willing to help Val subdue Canterbury. Once the orders were delivered and he selected the men to accompany them inside, he turned to Val.

"Awaiting your move, my lord," he said quietly.

Val silently dismounted his horse, handing the reins over to one of the soldiers remaining behind as he, Kenan, and ten men proceeded onto the grounds of Canterbury Cathedral. They were armed and it wasn't usual to enter a house of worship armed, but since Val was here on official business, he maintained his weapons and so did his men. He also brought with him the warrant for Canterbury's arrest, preparing to read it to the man before he took him into custody.

"Canterbury should be heading into the cathedral from the cloister by now," Kenan said, looking around the grounds and spying papal guards spread out over the area. "Shall we intercept him before he gives mass?"

Val, too, was very attuned to their surroundings but he was mostly looking for the four knights who had come ahead of him. "Nay," he replied. "We wait until he is finished and arrest him when he emerges from the cathedral. He will return to the cloister and that is where we shall wait for him. The less attention we draw to this, the better. I want to get the man out of Canterbury before we are mobbed by those trying to protect him."

Kenan understood. He could tell Val was on edge, which had him on edge as well. There was prudence in a sense of fear in this situation. Fear equated to caution and, for something like this, they needed an abundance of it. This had the potential to be more volatile than they could imagine. Kenan quietly relayed the orders to the soldiers behind him, men bearing the colors of de Nerra of Hampshire.

Since it was dark, most of the worshippers had already gone into the cathedral as Vespers was about to begin. Only a few people saw the gang of soldiers led by two knights heading towards the cloister. But Val knew that, sooner or later, word would get around regarding their presence and it could, quite possibly, alert Canterbury or, worse, his guards.

Val had the law on his side but Canterbury had the church, and they were on church grounds, so the sooner they get in and out, the better. He fought down the apprehension he felt. Instead, he focused on what needed to be done. The moment was upon him and he would not fail. He and his men were just approached the cloister entrance to the cathedral when they began to hear grunts and cries.

It sounded like a fight. Men were crying out and moaning. And the unmistakable sounds of weapons could be heard. Val and Kenan looked at each other in shock before breaking into a run, dashing to the cathedral entrance and entering into the dark, cold corridor that connected the cloister to the cathedral.

It smelled like earth and death in the corridor, linked to the vaults as well as the church beyond. Smells of the dead were permeating the very walls. Even though the corridor was weakly lit by intermittent torch light, they could immediately see a body prone on the ground, surrounded by men with weapons.

As Val watched in horror, someone – it wasn't clear because of the darkness of the corridor – brought their weapon to bear on the prone form's head. Bone and tissue went spraying onto the floor. The blow was so hard that a piece of skull ended up right by Val's foot. Shocked, he unsheathed his weapon and charged forward only to see men he recognized standing over the body.

De Morville… FitzUrse… le Breton… de Tracy.

As their features became clearer in the weak light, Val could hardly believe the scene he was witnessing. Horror turned to confusion until he looked at the body on the ground and saw the unmistakable regalia of an archbishop – deep blue robe, red lining, and white under garment. Bile rose in his throat.

"Stop!" he gasped, reaching out to grab the man's hand before he could come down again on the clearly dead body. "Clearly, this man will arise no more. What in the hell have you done?"

It was Hugh's hand that he had grabbed. At the sound of Val's voice, Hugh and the three knights looked at Val with great surprise.

"Val!" Hugh gasped. "You – you have come!"

Val's astonishment and fury was written all over his face. "You knew I would," he boomed. "You gave Calum Henry's missive and told him that I should follow you to Canterbury with all due haste and here I am. But – dear God, what havoc have you brought about here?"

Moans and gasps caught his attention. It was becoming evident through the weak torchlight that there were other men who had been wounded in the fight. Val could see at least four priests, possibly more but it was difficult to tell in the weak light. Priests who had undoubtedly been attending Canterbury as he'd headed into the cathedral for Vespers and men who had fought back when the knights attacked. Of the four men Val could see, two were not moving, one was cringing against the wall in shock, and the last man – cut across the shoulder brutally – was trying to push himself into a sitting position.

"They have killed him," the man wept, blood staining his clerical tunic. "Our most holy lord has been murdered!"

Those words hit Val as surely as if they had taken the form of a fist, driving into his chest and expelling the breath from him. He was stunned. He looked down at his feet, at the man in the archbishop's robes whose head had been bashed in. The features were barely recognizable but in that mess of tissue, he saw features that were familiar.

It was Thomas Becket.

"My God," he breathed. "Hugh, tell me what happened."

Hugh was breathing heavily, still worked up from the fight. He struggled to answer the question. "It happened so quickly."

"Tell me!"

Hugh swallowed hard. "This morning, we tried to convince Canterbury to surrender to you," he said hoarsely. "We – all of us – had hoped to deliver him to you peacefully but he refused, so we returned this evening with weapons in the hope of forcing him to surrender. He… he fought back, Val. We had no choice."

Val's jaw ticked as he gazed down at the bloodied head. There was so much emotion pent up in him at the moment that he hardly knew where to begin with it.

"Was he armed?" he asked, teeth clenched.

Hugh glanced at the knights around him, the three he'd been in collusion with. "That staff," he muttered. "That holy staff. He tried… I am not exactly sure, but I believe he tried to ram Reg with it. After that… after that, I do not recall what happened. It happened so quickly."

Val looked around and saw no staff. At least, not obviously. He pointed to the dead man. "You killed him," he hissed. "You lost control and you killed him. By all that is holy, Hugh, do you realize what you have done?"

Hugh just stared at him, either unable or unwilling to answer. He seemed to be in a degree of shock, just like the others. It was as if they'd all been in a bloodlust frenzy, something they were only now coming to realize. They were all looking at Val as if the man held all the answers but Val had no answers to give, at least not at the moment. But he knew he had to come up with something.

As he stood there, several monks who had heard the commotion came down from the quire of the cathedral and down the stairs to see what had happened. One look at Canterbury on the ground with his brains spread out over the stone and they retreated back into the cathedral in a panic. Val could already hear their cries. He knew they had to get out of there.

"Go," he commanded, turning Hugh for the door that led out to the courtyard. "Get on your horses and get out of here. Ride back to Henry and tell him what you have done. I will follow you and if you do not tell Henry, I will tell him in your stead. If you think to kill me to silence me, I have eleven men with me who have seen this also. Get out!"

He shoved Hugh, hard, and grabbed Reginald behind him, yanking the man to the door. William and Richard quickly followed and, soon, the four of them were fleeing into the darkness of the evening, murderers who had committed the most atrocious of crimes. But Val remained even as Kenan tugged at him.

"We must leave, too," he whispered urgently. "Word will get out and we shall be blamed!"

Val almost argued with him but thought better of it. They could proclaim their innocence but to a mob looking for satisfaction, they would more than likely be ignored. He looked at the man with the bad shoulder injury, realizing that man was his only witness that he, in fact, had not killed the archbishop. He had the presence of mind to understand what needed to be done and he gestured to the man.

"Take him," he told Kenan. "He may be our only hope. Let us get him to a physic and return him with us to Winchester. Henry will need proof of what has happened."

Kenan grimly agreed, collecting the man and passing him over to two soldiers as the group of them fled the corridor and moved out into the cold night. The soldiers backed out, all of them fleeing back towards Christ's Gate where their horses await, but Val remained for a moment.

Standing over Canterbury, he just stood there and stared. Something in that man on the floor cut him to the bone. Perhaps it was because he knew how devastated Henry would be, losing an old friend in such a terrible manner. Perhaps it was because he knew he was going to be blamed for this, no matter what really happened. He was to be responsible for four knights who lacked self-control. Whatever the outcome of all of this, it was going to be devastating for all concerned.

Val knew the worst was yet to come.

He was the last one out of the corridor, racing across the courtyard of the cathedral and back to Christ's Gate where Kenan and one other soldier were the last ones waiting for him. Everyone else had already fled.

Leaping onto his steed, he spurred the horse out of Canterbury, finally catching up to his men somewhere in the dead of night. They continued to ride through the night, stopping near dawn to rest the horses for a few hours before continuing on to Selborne. On their last leg of the journey, it snowed all night, covering the ground with a blanket of snow and slowing down their travel.

Winter had finally arrived, signaling – it was whispered by many – the death of a martyr.

Canterbury was dead.

CAHPTER THIRTEEN

Eynsford Castle
One Week Later

SITTING BY THE window in Lady Eynsford's solar, Vesper could clearly see the bailey of the castle, now covered in about a foot of snow. It was the first real snow of the season, so the soldiers had taken to building an army of snowmen to fight each other. It was rather funny to watch and Vesper had been enjoying the antics all morning, even when she almost got hit with a snowball from the snowman siege. The windows of the solar were only on the second level and a far-reaching throw could easily hit the keep.

Even though the snow had come all night, the day had dawned cloudless and bright. So it was a beautiful sight to look out over the winter-white landscape even though Vesper had no real desire to go out in the snow. She was content to sit by the window in the overly-warm solar and sew on the bodice of a new gown for Lady Eynsford.

But the truth was that since her return to Eynsford, she hadn't had much drive or energy to do much of anything other than sit and sew. It was as if the memory of Val was too heavy for her to move around, the weight of it crushing her. He was the last thing she thought of at night and the first thing she thought of in the morning. And all of the space in between, she was either reliving her short memories with him or dreaming of him. Everything about Val de Nerra was closing in on her until she could hardly think.

Misery was an apt word.

She began to second guess herself, too. Perhaps, she shouldn't have suggested the separation. Perhaps, she should have let him sup with her the night before she departed Bishop's Waltham for Eynsford. Perhaps, she should have kept the necklace. All of these thoughts rolled around in her mind, causing her to doubt her decision, but she hadn't wanted to make a mistake and she hadn't wanted Val to make one, either. That would have been worse had they acted hastily. Now, they were separated to decide whether or not to pursue this courtship.

Vesper was in favor of pursuing.

Separation from Val had made her forget all of her reasoning for their separation in the first place. She had been afraid that his association with a murdering family would become common knowledge and ruin him. But now she was convinced that their feelings for one another could see them through anything. At least, she hoped so. She'd known the man such a short time that it was difficult to know just how strong their bond was, but as far as Vesper was concerned, it was like granite.

She missed the man with every breath.

"Good day to you, Vesper," Lady Eynsford suddenly entered the solar with her two old maids trailing after her. "It seems that I have slept very late this morning. The cold always makes me so sleepy that I never want to get out of bed."

She giggled and Vesper smiled. Lady Eynsford was her age, a giggly and sweet girl lacking any brains. Her name before she married the elderly Lord Eynsford had been Lady Maude FitzStephen and, much like Vesper, had been a ward of the first Lady Eynsford. But the first Lady Eynsford, Isabella, had died of a fever two years ago and barely six months after her death, Lord Eynsford married Maude. She was younger than his daughters with Isabella, creating something of a family flap, but she was a genuinely kind girl so the resistance of Lord Eynsford's children to her was waning. Not much, but a little.

Family animosity had been a difficult thing for Maude to live with.

Rumor had it that Lord Eynsford was trying to impregnate his young wife and have more sons. But in the eighteen months since their marriage, Maude had yet to conceive. However, the woman spoke of her bedroom activities with the lord, running off at the mouth constantly, and Vesper had probably learned more about marriage and sex in that time than most people learned in an entire lifetime. Maude wasn't shy about confiding in Vesper and the two other wards, Lisbet d'Vant and Eloise l'Aigle, of her husband's inability to perform and how Maude would spend hours tugging at his limp manhood in an attempt to arouse him.

It was enough information to embarrass any maiden, Vesper included.

Nay, she wasn't eager to hear more of that this morning because she knew just by Maude's tone that it had been another long night of a husband who had kept her up to feed his desires. Vesper knew that as long as the old maids were around, two women who had been brought by Lord Eynsford from Maude's home to tend her every need, that Maude wouldn't speak of the dirty details of the bedchamber. But that changed quickly when Maude sent the women out to bring her food. Once they were gone, Maude sighed with exhaustion.

"Finally, they are gone!" she said with relief. "Where are Lisbet and Eloise?"

Vesper shook her head. "I believe they are in the kitchens dyeing thread. At least, that is what they told me they were going to do after we broke our fast in the hall. Shall I send for them?"

Maude shook her head. "Nay," she said. "I will tell you, Vesper, but you must not tell them anything!"

Vesper knew that was a farce; Maude would tell them everything, anyway, because she could not keep her mouth shut. But Vesper was genuinely in no mood for sordid talk this morning.

"You know that I do not repeat what you tell me," she said evenly. "But… why don't you wait until they return? That way you will only have to tell your story once. Meanwhile, come to the window with me and see what the soldiers have done. They have created two armies of snowmen."

It was enough of a lure to distract Maude briefly, but only briefly. She went to the window to see the snowman armies but it did not hold her attention for long.

"Last night was terrible, Vesper," she moaned. "He tried something new and I have never been so ashamed in my life."

Vesper tried not to roll her eyes. "My lady, I am quite sure that Lord Eynsford would not be happy if he knew you spoke of your private life with him. What if he did the same about you? Told all of the men of his bedchamber conquests?"

Maude looked at Vesper, stricken. "Does he?"

Vesper nearly laughed at the question. It was evidently acceptable for her to speak on her husband's sexual habits but not the other way around. "I do not know," she said, shaking her head. "I am simply trying to think of the lord's feelings. And your feelings as well."

Maude appeared hurt. "Do you not want to hear? But I have no one to talk to. I must share this with someone. I cannot talk to my lord."

Vesper sighed heavily and returned her focus to her sewing. "Then speak if you must," she said reluctantly. "I know that you find yourself in a lonely position these days."

Maude remained by the window, gazing out over the bailey that was quickly turning into a sea of muddy snow. "I did not want to marry him, you know," she said quietly. "I was hoping for a young, handsome husband, like Des. I can see him from here – he is by the gatehouse."

Vesper looked up from her sewing, watching Maude's expression. She knew that Maude had always been smitten with one of Eynsford's knights, Sir Desmond de Marmande. Desmond had been fond of her, too, until the first Lady Eynsford died and Lord Eynsford swept Maude away from Desmond. Vesper was fairly certain that Desmond's heart had been broken, but he'd never been anything other than polite and seemingly happy for the wedding of his lord to the woman he'd been fond of.

But it was something they didn't speak of much these days because it hurt Maude to think of it since she had been very fond of Desmond, too. Vesper was surprised the woman had brought it up.

"You married well, my lady," she said, returning her focus to her sewing. "Lord Eynsford is very fond of you and you have wealth and position. It is a fine marriage."

Maude's features softened as she beheld her once-favored knight through the window. "Sometimes, when William touches me, I imagine that it is Des," she murmured. Her tone turned sorrowful. "Sometimes, I do not think I can take his touch one more minute, Vesper. He is old and fat, and he smells terribly. He forces me to lie on my back while he covers me with his big, hairy body and rubs himself all over me."

Vesper was sorry for her friend but hearing the wistfulness in Maude's tone when she spoke of Desmond made her think of Val. Was that how her life was going to be, also? Spending her time pining away for the man she adored? It was tearing at her heart.

"Maude, don't…," she begged softly.

But Maude wasn't listening. "All he cares about is having another son," she said, close to tears. "I spend hours pulling at his slimy, stubby manhood until it is hard enough for him to bed me. And it hurts, Vesper – he rams it into me and grunts like a pig. I do not know how much longer I can stand it."

Vesper sighed sharply and looked up at her. "No more, Maude," she said quietly. "Please. Someone will hear you and it will get back to our lord. You are his wife now and you must do as he wishes."

Maude knew that. Her fair face crumpled. "I am so miserable, Vesper," she wept softly. "Whatever shall I do?"

Vesper had no answers. She was fairly miserable herself. Before she could come up with a reply that would both ease Maude and, hopefully, convince the woman to shut her mouth, Maude suddenly spoke.

"There is someone entering the gatehouse," she sniffled, wiping at her eyes. Then, she blinked, peering at the activity at the gatehouse. "Vesper, it looks like your father!"

Vesper was on her feet, racing to the window where Maude stood and practically shoved the woman aside. In disbelief, she could see what had Maude's attention – there was no mistaking the man who had come through the gatehouse on foot, dressed in clothes she'd seen on her father since he'd come to Eynsford those weeks ago. Dirty woolens and a torn, dirty cloak. The man's head was uncovered and his bushy, dark hair was illuminated in the bright sunlight.

McCloud d'Avignon had returned.

Shocked, Vesper could hardly grasp what she was seeing. McCloud was speaking to the men at the gatehouse pleasantly. They knew him as Vesper's father from his recent visit to Eynsford.

What they didn't know is why Vesper had returned without him because she'd never said a word about her father. When people asked, all she'd said was that he'd been forced to return to Durley to tend the farm. She didn't want anyone to know what had happened but here he was, returned to Eynsford, when he had promised to leave her alone. After Vesper's initial shock faded, anger took hold. Damn the man!

He was here!

"You will excuse me," she said to Maude. "I must see why my father has come."

Maude started to follow her. "Mayhap he will join us before the fire," she said hopefully. "He was very pleasant when last I saw him. Ask him if he will come in and sit with us for a time and tell us stories of his knightly adventures."

Vesper didn't even reply; she couldn't. She was afraid that anything out of her mouth might clue Maude in on the fact that she didn't want her father here. Rushing from Maude's solar, she made her way to the stairs that led to the entry level, taking them far too quickly. Oddly enough, the keep and inner structure of Eynsford were still mostly made of wood and the stairs creaked as she rushed down them. To the entry door she went, bolting from the keep with her skirts gathered so she wouldn't trip on them.

With every step, her anger grew. He had promised to stay away from her, but here he was, already breaking that promise. Vesper was so furious that she could hardly see straight, rushing through the snowy slush to tell her father exactly what she thought of his unannounced visit. She was just nearing the main gates when Desmond, speaking to McCloud, caught sight of her.

"Ah," Desmond said pleasantly. "Here she is. Lady Vesper, your father has surprised us with another visit."

Vesper forced a smile at Desmond, a genuinely nice man, but very quickly that smile turned to a grimace as she beheld her father. "So he has," she said through clenched teeth. "What are you doing here, Papa?"

It was a rather neutral question and McCloud faced his daughter with a good deal of trepidation. The moment their eyes met, he could see her confusion and rage. Not that it surprised him; he rather expected it. In fact, it was a far calmer action than he had expected.

"I… I have missed you," he said simply. "And I come bearing some news. I thought we might speak privately."

Vesper was all in favor of that. She had a few things she wanted to say to her father, too, and none of them pleasant. She took him by the arm, leading him away from the gatehouse.

"Please excuse us, Des," she said.

Desmond waved them on and Vesper practically dragged her father away, heading for the keep when she really had no intention of taking him there. She simply wanted to take him to some place without prying ears, which was a spacious area near the keep with a yew tree in the middle of it. People might see them there but they wouldn't hear what was being said. She pulled him right underneath the tree before releasing him.

"Now," she hissed. "You will tell me why you have come. You promised that you would stay away from me!"

McCloud held up his hand to calm her. "I did," he said quickly, "and I am sorry. Please do not be angry, Vesper. You are all that I have now and I had to come."

Her eyebrows flew up in a rage. "I am nothing to you!" she said. "I was a girl-child you cast off when my mother died and you've only had contact with me twice since then. I am nothing to you!"

McCloud gazed at her, knowing what she said was true. She had every right to be angry. He tried not to feel too foolish and too remorseful, for he'd had the entire trip from Durley in which to feel every emotion he could possibly feel – regret for his life, remorse for his relationship with his daughter, and guilt that he wanted to mend it. He knew she wanted nothing to do with him but he was here to press his case, anyway. Perhaps it was because he simply didn't want to be alone.

"And I am sorry for that," he said quietly. "It is true that I left you at Eynsford when your mother died, but that was because I was heading to France to fight. I could not remain home and take care of you and I certainly could not leave you with your brother. Can you not understand that?"

Vesper was vastly impatient with him. "I will not discuss this with you," she said angrily. "You said you would stay away. What is so important that made you break your word to me?"

McCloud sighed faintly. "Everything," he muttered. "I have had time to think since your brother's death, Vesper. Burying my son did something to my soul… as if a flame had been blown out and all that remained was smoke. There was darkness there but, soon enough, I could see through it. I could see what I had done."

Vesper grunted. "A pretty speech."

McCloud shook his head. "It is not a speech. I have not always been a man of dishonor, Vesper. Once, I was a man of great honor and trust. Men looked up to me. But somehow… somehow poverty and starvation changed that man. Val remembered the man I once was, which is why he was so receptive to seeing me again. You must believe that your papa was once a great man."

Vesper was still impatient. "And you have come all the way to Eynsford to tell me that?"

McCloud was starting to wonder if she could even understand what he was trying to tell her. "I have come to tell you how sorry I am," he said. "It… it is not easy for me to speak those words, but I find that I must. I have forsaken you, which I am extremely sorry for. I… I came to ask your forgiveness, Vesper. I understand if you do not wish to know me any longer, but I find that it is important to me to have your forgiveness. I have wronged you and, for that, I am sorry. I have shown you a man that I do not wish to be."

He sounded quite sincere, enough to douse Vesper's fire somewhat. She was innately compassionate but she didn't want to be made a fool of. After everything that had happened, she wasn't sure she could ever trust him.

"Mayhap all you say is true," she said. "But had my brother not been caught, you would still be heading down the same path. You would still be conspiring to marry Lady de Nerra and eager for me to wed Val simply so you could have access to their money."

McCloud cocked his head. "Mayhap that is true," he said honestly. "But an event such as your brother's execution has a way of forcing a man to re-think his life. I have been forced to take a look at mine and I do not like what I see. I wanted you to know that."

His sincerity took her anger down another notch. She honestly wasn't certain how to reply. "So now you have told me. Now what?"

"I suppose that is up to you."

"Then I want you out."

McCloud hung his head but he didn't argue. He simply nodded his head, turning for the main gate. As Vesper watched him go, head down, she began to feel a wave of remorse. He was her father, after all. He'd made mistakes. Perhaps he was genuinely trying to atone for them. She'd always believed herself to be a forgiving person but, in this case, she hadn't shown much. Self-protection had seen to that. But, perhaps, she was being too hard on a man who was sincerely trying to seek forgiveness for his past.

Indecision clawed at Vesper as she watched her father walk away, dragging his feet through the dirty snow. He looked so beaten, so subdued. A once-proud man who had ruined his life. It was enough to force her to call out to him.

"Papa," she said. "Wait."

McCloud paused, turning to look at her. "What is it?"

Vesper wasn't sure what to say at that point. Did she forgive him? Or did she not? She grasped at the first thing that came to mind.

"You said you had news," she said. "What news?"

McCloud shook his head. "I did not have any, really," he said. "I only said that so Sir Desmond would not suspect the reasons for my visit."

"So he would not suspect that you'd come to apologize to me?"

McCloud averted his gaze. "Aye," he said. "I was not sure if you had told anyone what happened with your brother."

Vesper frowned, closing the gap between them. "Why would I do that? Why would I bring such horrible shame to myself? Nay, Papa, I have kept my lips closed and you will as well. No one here knows what happened with Mat and no one ever will. Do you understand me?"

McCloud nodded. "I am pleased you did not tell anyone."

Vesper eyed the man; he looked quite exhausted, which he should have been considering he'd been traveling on foot for days on end. He had no money; she knew that. He probably hadn't eaten much, if at all. Now she was starting to feel the least bit sorry for him. He was still her father even if he was a stranger who had been complicit to terrible crimes and had a conniving way of thinking. But men had a right to be forgiven if they were truly repentant, she supposed. With a sigh, feeling frustrated and weak, she reached out and took him by the arm.

"Come with me," she said, resignation in her tone. "Come have something to eat and then I will find you a place to sleep. When you have rested, we will speak again."

McCloud looked at her, knowing she was only doing this out of duty. He doubted there was instant forgiveness in her heart for him and he understood that. But he was sincere in his words and it was something only time would tell. He hoped she would at least give him the chance to reclaim that man he'd lost.

"I would be grateful," he said. "And I am quite hungry."

"I thought you would be."

"Not much is growing this time of year that is edible, so I have had to beg scraps for the past few days. The coinage Val gave me is long since gone."

Val. There was that name. Vesper had been doing a good job of putting thoughts of the man aside until that moment and, now, he was in her head again. Her thoughts began to turn from her father to Val, of the doubts she had in insisting upon their separation. It had been many days since she'd last heard from him and he hadn't sent her the necklace yet, the sign that he still wanted to court her. Now, that was all she could think of.

Her father knew Val, didn't he? Perhaps he would have some answers.

"A man like Val...," she said, pausing a moment before continuing. "He has a great many duties, does he not? What I mean is that he would be very busy, all of the time... would he not?"

McCloud trudged through the mud beside her, feeling the icy dampness against his frozen feet. "He is a man with great responsibility," he said. He eyed her. "I do not know what was said between you two after I left to bury your brother. Did he speak further to you about your future together?"

Vesper shrugged. She wasn't sure she wanted to tell her father everything. Although she wanted his insight, she didn't want to give the man a confession in order to get it. She glanced up at him.

"You do not blame him for Mat's death, do you?" she asked. "You know that he had no choice. He told you that."

McCloud's features seemed to tighten as memories of that day returned. He paused thoughtfully before replying. "Had the situation been reversed and it was his son I had stood in judgement over, I would have done all I could to spare his life. I thought Val was my friend. He should have... he should have spared him."

Vesper frowned. "Papa, he was surrounded by a mob and by men of the law who were looking to him to dispense justice," she said. "I do not know much about the law but I know that if Mat had been anyone else, Val would have been compelled to do the same thing. Just because he was your son did not give him any special protection for what he had done because the man was guilty. Surely you understand that."

"Mayhap I do, but I am still reconciling myself to the fact that my old friend would execute my son. *My* son."

"And I am sure Val is having a difficult time reconciling how you lied to him and tried to woo his mother. Therefore, you have no right to be angry with a man you tried to dupe."

She was correct. God help him, McCloud knew she was. But he couldn't bring himself to say it. Val had done his duty when it came to Mat and McCloud was trying not to hate the man for it.

"But I have realized my folly," he said quietly. "Will he realize his?"

Vesper shook her head at her father's sense of justice. It made her realize that, perhaps, he truly hadn't understood the depth of his betrayal or how, as he put it, he became a man he did not like. She was starting to think that her father had a twisted sense of right and wrong in general.

"You have come to me asking for my forgiveness," she said, pausing before they could enter the great hall. "If you truly want it, then forgive Val for doing his duty and ending the terror of a murderer. I do not care if he was my brother or not. Val did the right thing when you would not. If you do not see that, then I do not believe you are sincere in wanting my forgiveness. I think you are being selective in this soul purging you seem to be doing."

McCloud wouldn't look at her, wiping at his frozen nose with the back of his hand. After a moment, he lifted his gaze. There was something warm twinkling in the depths. "Is that what growing up has done for you?" he asked. "Has it truly made you wiser than your father?"

Vesper struggled not to smile. "I have been wiser than you since I was born."

"Is that so?"

"It is. Only you did not notice."

"I am noticing now."

"Swear it?"

"I do."

That seemed like a step in the right direction as far as Vesper was concerned. The mood was lighter and she felt better about the situation in general. As she led her father into the hall for a much needed meal, she failed to see a group of riders bearing the blue and white of Canterbury enter the gates of Eynsford.

Eynsford was on the road between Canterbury and London, depending on which road one took, but the castle was situated to the west of Rochester and just south of the Dartford crossing, a major ferry crossing across the River Thames that led directly into London on the other side. Because of that, Eynsford had its share of traffic, of travelers passing through, and it was a very busy place in that regard. A group of allied soldiers was nothing new in the sights of Eynsford Castle.

Which is why Vesper paid no attention. Even if she had seen them, she wouldn't have given them a second thought. She sat with her father in the great hall of Eynsford, another wooden building with a steeply pitched thatched roof, and watched him wolf down bread, cheese, and a type of stew called *engoule*, which was made with barley, milk, and beef broth. McCloud had three bowls of it before he even started to slow down, taking the time to emit a very large burp before continuing with his meal at a more leisurely pace.

All the while, Vesper sat across the table from him, letting him eat and not interrupting him with dialogue. In truth, she needed time to think on their conversation and decide if she truly wanted to give the man another chance in her life. She was coming to think that it would be better if she did because she didn't want to spend the rest of her life regretting her coldness towards her father.

He was making a great effort so perhaps she should, too.

As Vesper continued to watch him eat, the door to the hall opened and the four soldiers bearing blue and white tunics spilled forth. Desmond was right behind them.

"Sit," Desmond instructed the soldiers, pointing to seating far down the table from Vesper and her father. "I will have food and drink brought to you."

The soldiers moved to claim their seats but one of them, spying the lovely Lady Vesper, decided not to sit so far down the table. When Desmond left the hall, he managed to scoot in her direction, eyeing McCloud as he did. Not knowing if the man was her husband, father, or no one at all, he proceeded carefully.

"Greetings" he said to both of them, although his focus was on Vesper. "It is a very fine day today, even with the snow. It looks as if you have had a great deal here."

Vesper didn't want to strike up a conversation with a strange soldier, bold as he was. As she deliberately looked away, McCloud spoke with his mouth full.

"Be on your way," he grumbled. "Our conversation is private."

The soldier seemed contrite, but only slightly. He stopped his advance and backed off. "Of course it is," he said as if to beg pardon. "I did not mean to interrupt anything. I was simply being friendly. My comrades and I have traveled a long way today, bearing important messages for all of London."

Vesper still wasn't looking at him but McCloud turned to him. "If that is true, then you had better do your duty and keep your mouth shut until you are with the man you are supposed to deliver the message to," he said. "What fool would spout off about the important messages he is carrying to people he does not even know?"

The soldier, who had been very friendly and bordering on jovial, lost his humor. "Because this is a message that the entire country will want to hear," he said, a hint of threat in his tone. "The Archbishop of Canterbury was murdered by men sent by Henry. We bear this news to take to the sheriffs to the north."

McCloud was already looking at the man but Vesper turned to him, shocked by what she had heard. "Murdered?" she gasped before she could stop herself. "When?"

The soldier turned to her, the lovely woman with the high cheekbones and the pale eyes. "A week ago, my lady," he said, pleased that she was being friendly. He wanted to show her how important he was and how much he knew about this terrible deed so he began running off at the mouth. "The archbishop was ambushed by at least six knights and several soldiers, men loyal to the king."

It was an astonishing bit of news. "Sweet Jesù," she said, stunned. "They killed him?"

"*Assassinated* him, my lady."

"And it was Henry's men for certain?"

The soldier lifted an eyebrow. "The men bore the colors of de Nerra, who is Henry's justice in Hampshire," he said, leaning towards Vesper and McCloud as if he was divulging deep and dark information. "Do you know who I mean? Surely you have heard of the man here at Eynsford. It is very close to Hampshire. Lord Eynsford must have had dealings with him."

Vesper suddenly couldn't breathe. *De Nerra!* The room started to sway and she grabbed hold of the table as if it would prevent her from slipping away. Everything was spinning around her as she struggled to right herself.

"De Nerra?" she repeated, her voice sounding oddly strangled. "How… how is that possible?"

The soldier didn't seem to notice that she'd gone pale. "No one is sure. But my lord, the garrison commander at Canterbury Castle, thinks that de Nerra came to take Canterbury back to Winchester Castle to face Henry because Winchester is in the Hampshire jurisdiction. When Canterbury refused, de Nerra killed him."

Vesper was still holding on to the table, overwhelmed with what she was hearing. "It cannot be," she breathed to herself before lifting her voice in response. "I… I can hardly believe it."

The soldier nodded confidently. “Believe it, my lady, for it is true. All of Canterbury is in an uproar right now and it is swelling outward, like the ripples on a pond. Soon, all of England will know what has happened.”

Vesper had visions of Val swinging his sword at a resistant priest, following orders from a petty king. She was beginning to feel nauseous. “But… but if it is true, then he was only doing his duty, don’t you think?” she breathed. “Surely he would have only done such a thing on Henry’s order.”

The soldier shrugged, reaching out to snatch a cup of wine when a servant appeared with a pitcher. “That is what my garrison commander believes, also,” he said. “But the murder was witnessed by many and I have it on good authority that de Nerra cut Canterbury’s head off!”

He said it with relish. That was enough for Vesper. She let out a strange choking sound and leapt to her feet, staggering from the table and heading for the hall entrance. McCloud, who had been listening to the despicable tale with great amazement, took off after her. He grabbed her before she could reach the door.

“Vesper!” he demanded in a harsh whisper. “Where are you going?”

Vesper was in a panic. She was starting to weep uncontrollably. “I… I do not know,” she said. “I… I could not listen to anything more. Papa, did you hear what he said?”

McCloud nodded grimly. “I heard.”

“But it cannot be true!”

McCloud was a bit more worldly than his daughter was. He understood the depths of the politics in England and to hear that Henry gave such an order, to Val no less, did not surprise him.

“One cannot deny the facts if there were witnesses,” he said. “It was only a matter of time that such a thing could happen with the relationship between Henry and Canterbury. Henry must have ordered Val to do it and, of course, he could not refuse.”

Vesper was struggling for calm, wiping at the tears that were popping from her eyes. “It must have been horrible for him.”

"I am sure he did not relish the task."

"Then he must be in a great deal of trouble now," she said. "It does not matter if the king ordered him to do it. Everyone will be after him to punish him!"

McCloud knew that. His thoughts drifted to Val, a man who had enjoyed the king's respect and the respect of his peers for so long. He was a paragon of virtue, a man with the world at his feet.

But now… God help the man if he really did kill the archbishop. There were enough royal guards in England to protect him from the rage of the faithful when they discovered who killed the head of the church.

Val de Nerra would be a man with a target on his head.

"Then let us pray that Henry intends to protect him," he finally said. "Surely the king has realized that Val will be the target of everyone's anger in spite of the fact that Henry gave the order."

Vesper had succeeded in calming herself, but only mildly. All she could think of was Val and the trouble he must surely be in. These soldiers had been sent to spread the word of the assassination and, with it, name the man who had accomplished it.

De Nerra.

"No one will care that he was carrying out Henry's wishes," she said, her nausea coming in waves. "Soon enough, Val's name will be spread all over England, relegated to the ranks of men such as Brutus and Cassius, or of the Romans who put Jesus Christ upon the cross. Assassins who were the most hated of men. Val does not deserve to be among them, Papa, if he was only doing his duty. It is not fair."

McCloud sighed faintly. "Nay, it is not," he said. "But we cannot help him. I wish I could."

The weight of Val's troubles was sitting heavily on Vesper, her heart aching for the man so desperately. She couldn't stand that he was in such terrible trouble. Whether or not he'd been operating under Henry's orders wasn't the issue; it was the mere fact that Val, the sweet and intelligent and generous man she'd come to adore, was in terrible trouble.

She had to go to him.

"I am going to Selborne," she said, suddenly pushing past her father and heading out into the bright winter's day. "I must see Val. He must know that there is one person in this country that does not hate him."

McCloud stumbled after her. "Wait," he said, trying to grab at her as she walked. "Vesper, wait. You cannot go, child. You must remain here, safe at Eynsford."

Vesper was walking faster than he was, avoiding his snatching hands. "If I was in trouble, I am sure he would come to me," she said firmly. "I will not let him go through this alone, Papa. He must know that he has my support."

McCloud managed to get a hand on her, pulling her to a halt. "*Wait*," he said again, getting a grip on her with his other hand. "You are not thinking clearly. If you go to Selborne, you will put yourself in harm's way. Val is in the middle of a tempest and the last thing he needs is to worry about you. You must leave him to fight his battle, Vesper. Think of yourself and understand that you must remain safe."

Vesper pulled herself from his grasp, her expression something short of anger. "I have spent my entire life safe," she said. "Safe here at Eynsford, living a good and pious life. But that ended when you came to me those weeks ago and told me what was happening with you and my brother, and how you expected me to make a good marriage in order that you and Mat should not have to live like animals. It was *you* who cruelly took me out of that safe world, Papa, and when you did, I met Val. The days I spent with him were the best days of my life and I thought the joy therein was something I could never repay him. But now, I see how I can repay him – I can show him my support when all of England is turning against him. I am going to him and you will not stop me."

McCloud could see her determination. She was like stone; hard and unmovable. He knew he could plead with her until there no more breath left in his body but, still, she would go to Selborne. There was no changing her mind but, in truth, he understood her point of view and he appreciated her staunch loyalty.

Loyalty, as Val had shown him without question for their entire association until that fateful day with Mat. McCloud thought that Val had executed his son because he had no more loyalty towards him, but that wasn't the truth. It was McCloud who'd had no loyalty to Val as he'd tried to scheme against him. He'd greatly wronged the man. Realizing that, McCloud knew what he had to do.

"If you are determined, then I shall go with you," he said quietly. "I've not done much for you in your life, Vesper… now that you are all I have left, I shall not let you go alone. And if I can lift my sword for Val, then mayhap I owe it to him. He has always been a good friend to me."

Vesper watched her father's expression, wondering if he was being truthful. "Do you mean that?" she asked. "In spite of the judgement he showed my brother?"

McCloud cleared his throat softly, speaking on an uncomfortable subject. "That is something I must reconcile," he said. "I know in my mind that Val had no choice but my heart is a different matter. I miss my son and ever shall, but in the end… I know it was not Val's fault. It was mine. Now, Val is in trouble. If you are going to him, then I shall go, too."

Vesper began to realize that there might be hope between them, after all. Her father's broken moral compass might possibly be fixed. Time would tell. But knowing he was coming with her made her feel better, somehow.

"Then wait for me," she said. "I must gather a few things and then I will ask Lady Eynsford if we may borrow a pair of horses. I am sure she will give permission. Go back into the hall and wait for me to return. I shan't be long."

With that, she was off, but not before giving her father a pat on the arm. That small touch meant so much to McCloud. Perhaps his daughter would, indeed, forgive him for what he'd done. Now, they were united in their mutual support of Val and he couldn't have felt more pleased.

Perhaps that support of Val would somehow heal what was broken between them.

McCloud could only hope.

CHAPTER FOURTEEN

Winchester Castle
Several days later

HE WASN'T THROWING things this time, but it was clear that he was devastated.

Henry sported a full beard to go along with his dark red hair that tended to look like straw at times, unkempt and uneven. But the man didn't give a hang about his appearance so the hair remained dirty and on end, as did the beard at times. At the moment, that scruffy beard covered up a ruddy complexion that was red with fury and distress as he listened to reports from Canterbury soldiers who had only just arrived at Winchester.

Spouting tales of murder and mayhem, the soldiers had worked their way through four different men at the castle, from the gatehouse guards to the king's Captain of the Guard, repeating the same story until they were finally permitted to see the king.

It was a tale that no man under Henry's command wanted to repeat to him.

Therefore, the soldiers were thrust at Henry like sacrificial lambs to take the brunt of the king's distress for the news they bore. In the hall of Winchester and surrounded by some of his advisors, at least the ones who had gone hunting with him after Christmas and had only just returned, Henry had listened to a shocking tale of the murder of

Thomas Becket. According to the soldiers from Canterbury Castle, a royal garrison for Henry, witnesses spoke of men cornering the archbishop before Vespers before proceeding to kill him. The witnesses were traumatized, naturally, but more than one swore that the archbishop was murdered by four knights before being joined by two more and about ten soldiers, most of them wearing tunics of the Itinerant Justice of Hampshire.

De Nerra.

By the time the soldiers were finished delivering their message, Henry's face was so red that those nearest him thought he truly might burst. It wasn't enough that the king had suffered years of long battle with Becket; what mattered was that a man who had once been as a brother to him had been murdered by an itinerant justice loyal to the king. Henry was beside himself at the news, as if he'd never had a quarrel with Canterbury in his life.

He was shattered.

"This cannot be," he said when the soldiers finished their story. Then, louder. "This cannot be! It is not possible!"

The soldiers from Canterbury, three of them, cowered at the sound of Henry's booming voice. The king's tendency to rage was well-known.

"Our garrison commander, Sir Owen Hampton, interviewed many monks who claimed to have seen the murder, my lord," the older of the three said steadily. "We were told that four knights instigated it and had killed the archbishop by the time more de Nerra men arrived. In fact, the men that arrived later stopped what could have been an utter butchering of the archbishop, so his body remained intact for burial."

Henry was quivering with emotion, both rage and disbelief. "But he is surely dead?"

"Aye, my lord, Canterbury is dead."

Henry just stared at them after that, unmoving, seemingly paralyzed. It was difficult to know just how the man was going to react, but everyone in the room was trying to gauge him. Such terrible news would surely have consequences. There were several senior nobles around him, watching him closely for his eventual reaction, including Tevin du Reims.

The Earl of East Anglia had gone hunting with the king when they'd arrived at Winchester right after Christmas simply to appease the man, but he had intended to return home on the morrow. He had a wife and children and grandchildren who were demanding his return. But after hearing the shocking news from the Canterbury soldiers, Tevin was quickly starting to reconsider his plans to leave.

Being one of the king's most trusted men, he had privileges in speaking and action that others did not. Henry seemed to tolerate almost anything from him. Therefore, Tevin didn't give thought to stepping into the conversation about something that had the entire chamber reeling.

"It makes no sense that Val de Nerra should go to Canterbury to assassinate Becket," he said in disbelief, mostly speaking to Henry but in part to the soldiers who had accused de Nerra of precisely that. "Did anyone see de Nerra there? Can anyone place him at the scene?"

The three soldiers shrugged, shaking their heads, looking at each other in confusion. "If he was, no one has identified him, my lord," the older soldier said. "But witnesses place his men there. They described men bearing his colors."

Tevin didn't like the sound of that at all. "His colors, aye, but not him," he pointed out. "It is possible these men were acting without de Nerra's knowledge. And you said that only some of the men were wearing de Nerra colors? What about the others? It is entirely possible that there are other lords involved in this… this disgrace."

The older soldier, a man with a dirty face and a bushy beard, simply shook his head. "We were not there, my lord, and did not see the men who killed the archbishop," he said. "All I can tell you is what witnesses have told us."

"Then how did you know it was de Nerra?"

"A crimson and white tunic with a gold lion, my lord. It was identified by Owen Hampton as a de Nerra standard, as he has many dealings with the Itinerant Justice of Hampshire because of the close proximity of Hampshire's jurisdiction to Canterbury."

Tevin stared at the man a moment, realizing the identification had been true. He knew de Nerra's colors and they were as the soldier said. He was starting to get a sick feeling in the pit of his stomach as he looked at Henry.

"This makes no sense, my lord," he said. "You know that Val de Nerra would not have done such a thing unless you ordered it. He is not an unreasonable man. He would not act on his own in such matters."

Henry was still trembling, still red in the face. His dark-eyed gaze was on the soldiers who had come bearing such awful news but, after a moment, he turned away, a desolate mood that had him staggering.

"My God," Henry breathed. "It is possible? Is it truly possible that my brother has been murdered by a rogue knight?"

It was clear from his words that he was not considering Tevin's words about de Nerra. He didn't want to entertain logic at the moment, only facts. As he wandered aimlessly, men moved away from him. No one wanted to be near when the legendary Plantagenet temper let loose. No matter what the differences between Henry and his former friend, an assassination somehow made men forget about their quarrels. It only brought forth the realization that apologies and reconciliations would never come. It was the moment that men such as Henry would live with regrets of a relationship and brother lost.

Tevin knew that; he'd seen men lose brothers and suffer for it. But he didn't want a possibly innocent man to be accused of such a terrible crime, especially a man he didn't believe capable of such a thing. There had to be another truth behind all of this.

"My lord, allow me to question the witnesses myself," Tevin implored. "I must go to my home at Rochester and it is very close to Canterbury. Permit me to get to the bottom of this situation and seek justice for all."

Henry had wandered to a lancet window, his gaze moving across the bailey of Winchester as the lines of grief crept into his face. "Val has been identified, Tevin," he said with unusual calm. "Men saw his colors and identified him."

Tevin watched the king as the man leaned against the window. In truth, Henry was showing far too much calm for Tevin's taste. It made him nervous.

"But you cannot believe de Nerra is behind this," he said. "That is not the Val you know and love; it is not the Val any of us knows. There are a hundred other men I would suspect of an assassination before I would suspect Val de Nerra."

The redness to Henry's cheeks seemed to be fading as the reality of the situation settled in. More than anything, he seemed to be particularly shaken above all – not angry, not wildly grief stricken. Simply shaken.

"Then mayhap the questions you have should not be for the witnesses," he said. "Mayhap they should be for Val. In fact, I want to ask him myself. I want to find out why he killed my old friend."

Tevin was starting to think that there may not be justice for Val de Nerra at all. His colors had been identified at the scene and Henry seemed to be fixed on it, but the Val de Nerra they all knew, including Tevin, was a man of supreme character and restraint, a seasoned knight with great wisdom. That was why Henry appointed him as his itinerant justice. What the Canterbury soldiers were telling them just didn't seem to make sense.

"Let me speak with him before you bring him here, my lord," Tevin asked. "If I feel he is guilty, then I shall bring him back to Winchester myself."

Henry acted as if he didn't hear him. "Send my knights for him," he said. "Where is de Morville, in fact? He did not accompany us in our hunting and I've not seen him since my return to Winchester. Where *is* the man?"

Tevin didn't know the answer to that but he turned to one of Henry's knights who had, in fact, remained behind in command of

Winchester while the king was away. Sir Dacian d'Vant, a tall and competent man, was standing near the entrance to the solar.

"D'Vant," Tevin said sharply. "Where is de Morville?"

D'Vant shook his head. "In truth, he and FitzUrse, le Breton, and de Tracy disappeared after our stay at Saltwood Castle," he said. "We did not realize that until a few days later. At first I thought they had gone on ahead to Winchester, but they did not and no one has seen them. I have sent men to look for them."

Tevin's brow furrowed as he pondered that, turning to Henry with a rather puzzled expression. "That seems odd," he said. "De Morville is quite loyal to you, my lord, as are the others. They are most wanting for royal favor. So it seems very strange that they would simply disappear."

Henry wasn't particularly interested in four missing knights. At the moment, he was fighting off crippling grief.

"Mayhap, they have been murdered as well," he said. "Mayhap, they have fallen victim to de Nerra's sword. My God, du Reims, what if de Nerra is systematically attempting to destroy everything that is precious to me? What if I am next? Send men to bring him to me immediately. If I have a viper within my household, then I would know of it."

Tevin knew he couldn't disobey a direct order from the king. He could see that Henry was becoming paranoid in his grief and that would not be a healthy thing for anyone. But rather than argue with him about it, he simply agreed.

He had to find out what really happened before the king did.

"Aye, my lord," he said. "I shall see to it personally."

Henry didn't even respond; the grief he'd been struggling against overwhelmed him and he slumped against the window, a hand over his face. Tevin chose that moment to quit the chamber, but not before pausing to pull d'Vant along with him. He had something to say to the man. Once they were alone in the corridor outside the solar, he came to a halt.

"Listen to me," he hissed at Dacian. "Give me a day before you gather your army to bring Val de Nerra to Henry. Something is not right about this entire situation and I must speak to Val before Henry's men throw him in chains and drag him to Winchester. Will you do this?"

Dacian nodded, his fair face tight with concern. "I know Val," he muttered. "He is not capable of doing what he has been accused of. He is a decent man, more than most."

Tevin was relieved to find an ally in Henry's Captain of the Guard. "I agree," he said quietly. "A day, Dacian. Give me at least that."

Dacian simply nodded. "I will do my best, my lord."

Tevin nodded his thanks, dashing into the darkness of the corridor and taking the stairs down to the entry level of the keep. Beyond were the vast bailey and the stables where his horse was tethered. It took him little time to gather his belongings and depart Winchester for Selborne, a fortress that was less than twenty miles away, something that would take him most of the day to reach if he pushed his horse. He had to make it to Selborne to discover if Val knew anything about the assassination of Becket.

As Tevin cantered from the gates of Winchester, there were two predominant thoughts on his mind – if Val was, indeed, involved, he wanted to know the reasons behind it. And if he wasn't, then someone was going to a great deal of trouble to implicate an innocent man. Surely Val, as an itinerant justice, had his fair share of enemies. Perhaps one was finally seeking revenge against him in a most audacious way. But if that wasn't the case and Val had truly acted on his own… God help him.

God help them all.

CHAPTER FIFTEEN

Selborne Castle

HOME HAD NEVER looked so good to him.

Most of the snow from the post-Christmas storm had melted, leaving the land frozen and the roads soupy, so traveling home had been something of a muddy mess, but Val didn't much care. He's slugged through it, pushing the men and horses, sleeping very little and stopping only when absolutely necessary. A trip from Canterbury that, with better weather would have taken four days, took only slightly longer.

He just wanted to get home.

Even now as they passed beneath the gatehouse of Selborne, Val felt a sense of relief. He looked up into the sky and appreciated the colors of sunset, seeing the beauty that was his ancestral home. But he didn't intend to stay for long; he had a trip to Winchester to make so he could inform the king of what had happened at Canterbury Cathedral. He was certain that Henry would be furious with him for the actions of de Morville and the others, but he'd come to the conclusion that the king's anger couldn't be helped. The orders had been his and Val was ultimately responsible for the men in his command, even Henry's knights. Therefore, he had to face Henry like a man and own up to his responsibility.

His failure.

Entering the bailey, he and his party were immediately met by several men, including Calum. Mayne was on the wall, waving down to him, and Val managed to lift a weary hand to the man. Calum came up alongside him and began stripping his saddlebags off his war horse before the animal was taken away.

"Thank God you have returned," Calum muttered so the men around them wouldn't hear. "A visitor has come to see you."

Val looked at the man, seeing that he seemed rather rattled. "Who?"

Calum slung the saddlebags over his shoulder. "The Earl of East Anglia is in the small hall with your mother," he said. "He arrived about an hour ago but he would not tell me why he had come. All he said was that he needed to speak with you urgently and I told him I did not know when you would return, so thank God you came when you did."

Val's brow furrowed. "East Anglia is here?" he repeated, puzzled. "Du Reims?"

"Aye."

Du Reims was a man that was deep within Henry's inner circle so the fact that he was here did not surprise Val. Suspecting East Anglia's visit had something to do with Henry's command to arrest Canterbury, he wasn't relishing what he had to tell him. In fact, he resisted the urge to jump on his horse and ride off. But he held his ground, taking his saddlebags from Calum.

"Very well," he said calmly, turning for the keep. "I shall see the man. Has your brother been here, by chance?"

Calum followed him as he began to walk towards the keep. "Nay, he has not. Why?"

"Then you have not seen him since he came here to deliver Henry's missive?"

"Nay," he said. Then, anxiously: "Why do you ask? Has something happened?"

Val wasn't sure how to tell Calum the truth but he wasn't going to spare the man. He had to know what his brother had done. In his exhaustion, he sounded rather harsh as he spoke.

"I have sworn Kenan to secrecy on this and I shall swear you to it, also," he muttered. "You will not repeat this. Give me your vow."

Calum nodded seriously. "Of course, Val. What is wrong?"

They were nearing the keep now, the long shadows of sunset falling around them. "I went to the inn in Canterbury that Hugh had mentioned, but Hugh and the others were not there," he said quietly. "It was nearing Vespers so I assumed that they had gone on ahead to the cathedral to confront the archbishop. My instincts were correct; there is no easy way to tell you this, Calum, so I will come out with it – your brother murdered Thomas Becket."

Calum grabbed him by the arm and when Val paused to look at the man, he could see that he'd gone as pale as snow.

"Oh… God, no…," Calum stammered. "Tell me… tell me it is not true!"

Val could see the man's anguish. "I am afraid it is," he said. "Hugh told me that he had tried to arrest the man but when Canterbury resisted, your brother snapped and killed him. I found them just as they were bashing Canterbury's brains out all over the stone. Had I not come when I did, then I have no doubt they would have chopped the man to pieces. Now I must tell du Reims, who has undoubtedly come on behalf of the king, that Canterbury was murdered by four knights who could not control their zealous loyalty to Henry."

Calum was shaking his head, back and forth, like a madman. "He did *not* do it!"

Val sighed heavily. "Ask Kenan if you do not believe me. I told Hugh to go back to Henry and tell him what he had done so mayhap that is why du Reims is here, but something tells me that your brother has not returned to Winchester. If he did not stop at Selborne to tell you what he'd done, then I seriously doubt he's gone to Winchester to admit it to the king. Any man who would murder like that… I cannot imagine he would willingly announce what he has done."

Calum was beside himself. "But… why would my brother do such a thing? I do not understand!"

Val resumed his walk for the keep. "Nor do I," he said. "But he did. There were many witnesses to it, in fact, not just my men. I brought a wounded monk with me to verify my story for Henry but the man did not live past Guildford. He died last night of the wounds he sustained in the attack. So, now it is up to me to explain what happened when I do not even understand it myself."

Calum was following him as he took the stairs up to the entrance. "My brother," he mumbled. "I must find my brother. If he has not come here and he has not gone to Winchester, then I can only imagine he must have gone north to my father's holdings. He would have nowhere else to go."

"If I were Hugh, I would flee, too. Henry's wrath shall be severe."

Much like Val, Calum could see the long-term implications of his brother's actions. "Not only on Hugh but on you as well, Val. Henry will want to know… my God, I cannot fully grasp all of this."

The entry to the keep loomed before them and Val came to a halt, putting a hand on Calum. He could see that the man was deeply shaken with the actions of his brother, much as Val had been when he'd witnessed the bloodlust that Hugh was capable of. Hugh de Morville had been a man of honor and trust up until that point. Now, he was a murderer.

It was difficult to take in.

"Tell no one," Val reiterated softly. "Let me speak with du Reims and I will tell you the outcome. Meanwhile, go to Kenan and hear what he saw your brother do. He will tell you the same thing I did."

After that, he tried to move forward but Calum wouldn't let him. He held on to him, his features lined with grief. "I am sorry, Val," he whispered. "I did not know my brother… I never thought he would do something like this. I am so sorry for the position he has put you in."

Val patted the man on the cheek. "It is not your fault," he said. "I do not compare you to your brother, you know that. Now, let me go inside and face du Reims."

Calum let him go, watching him enter the dark keep and disappear inside. But his movements were not those of the Val he knew; they were lethargic, dragging. Calum didn't blame him. But he did blame his brother. On the heels of his deep shock came anger such as he'd never experienced before. It was consuming as well as terrifying, especially when taken in context with what the future held.

His brother was going to sink them all.

CHAPTER SIXTEEN

"AT LEAST YOU have grandchildren," Margaretha was saying to Tevin over a pitcher of very fine red wine from Spain that she only brought out for special guests. It was very sweet and she'd had too much of it. When Tevin mentioned his multiple grandchildren, Margaretha seized on it. "Valor is thirty-four years of age and has not even married yet. I will be in my grave before I ever see my first grandchild at the rate he is going."

Tevin had known Lady de Nerra through her husband, Sir Gavin, although he'd not seen her in years. She was a handsome woman with pale eyes and smooth skin, and she was also quite forthright, something that reminded him a great deal of his own wife. He'd been sitting with Lady de Nerra for the better part of an hour and found her to be quite funny at times.

"Give him time, Lady de Nerra," he said patiently. "Most knights that I know do not have marriage on their minds, merely glory. Val has a very important royal appointment and it is good that his focus is on that for now."

Margaretha frowned. "Pah!" she said. "He is more loyal to Henry than to his family."

"I doubt that."

"Then where are my grandchildren?"

Tevin couldn't help but chuckle. "Then mayhap you should help him," he suggested. "Find him a wife."

Margaretha rolled her eyes. "I could bring him the most beautiful and eligible woman in England and, because I selected her, he would turn his nose up at her," she said, watching Tevin laugh. "You have sons of your own, my lord. Tell me they would not do the same thing if you selected their bride."

Tevin thought of his own sons, five of them, in fact. "My three eldest are married," he said. "I helped arrange the contract but I allowed my sons the final word. My younger two have not yet married, but I am sure they will at some point."

Margaretha cocked an eyebrow. "Were any of them thirty-four years when the married?"

Tevin shook his head. "Nay," he said. He drained the wine in his cup. "This is very fine wine, by the way. Where did you acquire it?"

Margaretha's eyes narrowed. "Do not change the subject," she said. "I implore you, as a father of five sons, how would you handle any son that did not wish to marry at the advanced age my son is?"

Tevin was coming to feel rather bad for Val, with such a persistent mother. But before he could answer her, he heard boot falls at the chamber entrance.

"Good God, Mother," Val entered the room, his unhappy gaze on his mother. "Is *that* what you have been discussing with Lord du Reims in my absence? I cannot tell you how ashamed I am."

Tevin stood up as Val approached, grinning at the man. "Do not be," he said. "My wife does the same thing. 'Tis good to see you, Val. You are looking well."

Val smiled wearily at the old earl, a man he genuinely liked. When Tevin extended a hand to him, Val took it strongly.

"My lord," he greeted amiably. "We are deeply honored by your visit. It has been some time since I last saw you."

Tevin nodded, shaking Val's hand a moment before releasing it and moving to reclaim his seat. "It is unfortunate, I know," he said. "I usually spend my time at my home of Thunderbey Castle, but Henry has had need of me as of late. In fact, I have just come from Winchester. I realize you have only just arrived home and surely have many pressing duties, but I wonder if I might have a private conversation with you before the evening is out?"

So much for pleasantries; du Reims wanted to get right to the meat of his visit, which Val appreciated. He, too, wanted a serious conversation with the man and there was no time like the present. These were men of business and of action, and social proprieties took second to those things of importance in their lives. He motioned for Tevin to follow.

"Of course," he said. "My solar is more comfortable. Let us speak now so no one will say I kept the great Earl of East Anglia waiting."

As Tevin stood up again, Margaretha spoke. "Valor?" she said, her tone anxious. "Are you… are you well, my son?"

Val paused to look at her, hearing the concern in her voice. She knew where he had been and the serious nature of it, although she clearly had no clue as to what had actually transpired. Still, she was concerned for her son, as a mother would be.

"I am well," he said. "I am sorry I did not greet you properly when I entered. Let me speak with Lord du Reims first and then I shall attend you."

Margaretha shook her head. "No need," she said. "If you are well, then I am content."

Val's gaze lingered on her a moment, knowing how worried she had been for him. He thought he might have even caught a glimpse of a tear. But Tevin was right beside him and he would not keep the man waiting, not even to show some concern for his mother, so he took the man into his solar, which was cold and relatively dark. He quickly went about lighting the bank of tapers near his table before moving to the hearth to ignite that as well.

"Thank you for being kind enough to receive me, Val," Tevin said as he stood by Val's big table. "I know how busy you are. Administering justice for Henry must take a good deal of your time."

Val glanced at him, grinning, as he moved from the bank of tapers to the hearth. "Did my mother tell you that?" he asked, listening to Tevin chuckle. "I do apologize for her. She is singular-minded these days about the lack of grandchildren. I am surprised she did not ask you if you have any eligible daughters."

There was a seat next to the table and Tevin took it. "She did not, but I am under the strong impression that the conversation was heading in that direction," he said. "Alas, I have two daughters and they are both spoken for."

"Excellent," Val said firmly. "As much as I would like to be related to you, I will not have my mother press the both of us in that regard."

Tevin watched him as he sparked the kindling in the hearth. "I will admit, I wish I had another daughter for you," he said. "You are a fine man, Val. I have always thought so."

Val could sense that they were coming to the root of Tevin's visit; something about the look on his face bespoke of both admiration and sorrow. "And I have great admiration for you as well, my lord," he said. Then, he stood up and faced him. "Did Henry send you here to discover if I have arrested Canterbury?"

Tevin's brow furrowed slightly, confused. "*Arrest* Canterbury? What do you mean?"

Now it was Val's turn to be confused. "Did Henry not tell you that he sent me a missive commanding me to arrest Canterbury and bring him to Winchester?"

Tevin's eyebrows lifted. If he was only slightly confused before, now that confusion was growing by leaps and bounds. "A missive –?" he repeated. "*Henry* sent you a missive to arrest Canterbury?"

Val nodded, seeing the surprise in the man's features. "Evidently, he did not tell you," he said. Then, he moved to the saddlebags he had placed upon his desk and opened one, then the other, finally coming across the rolled piece of vellum he sought, the key to all of his troubles. He extended it to du Reims. "See for yourself, my lord."

Tevin took the vellum and quickly unrolled it, reading the contents once, then twice. Then, he simply stared at it. "Val," he said after a moment, hesitantly. "When did you receive this?"

"Over a week ago."

"*Who* brought this to you?"

Val didn't sense anything other than raw confusion from du Reims, which was understandable if the man knew nothing about the missive. "Hugh de Morville," he said. "He came to Selborne and delivered it. Henry truly did not mention any of this to you?"

Tevin was still looking at the missive, an overwhelming sense of foreboding filling him as he stared at it. He recognized the writing as that of one of Henry's clerks and the seal was most definitely Henry's. Even the signature looked like Henry's. But he knew for a fact that Henry didn't write it. He began to feel a rock in the pit of his stomach, weighing down on him, as he struggled to figure out what had occurred.

"Val, tell me what happened from the beginning," he said. "I want to know what de Morville said when he delivered this missive. Tell me everything."

Now, Val was starting to wonder if there wasn't something wrong in all of this. He thought du Reims looked rather pale.

"I was not at Selborne when Hugh delivered this, but his brother, Calum, was," he said. "You know Calum, do you not? He has been my second for two years now, a very fine knight. But I digress; it was Calum that took the missive and spoke to his brother. Hugh told Calum that he and FitzUrse, le Breton, and de Tracy were to go ahead of me to attempt to talk Canterbury into surrendering to me. After receiving the missive, I followed as quickly as I could but by the time I got to Canterbury… my lord, I thought that you had come on behalf of Henry to discover what happened when I went to arrest Canterbury. In fact, I was going to head to Winchester myself this very day to inform the king personally."

Tevin was looking at Val with great distress on his features. "Canterbury is dead," he said. "Henry was told of it this morning by soldiers from Canterbury Castle. That is why I am here, Val. My God… I do not even know where to begin with all of this."

Val was coming to sense that something was very, very wrong but he wasn't sure, exactly, what it was. "What do you mean?" he asked. "My lord, I know I failed in my duty to arrest Canterbury. I have no excuse other than I did not arrive in time to prevent de Morville from murdering the man. Hugh told me that Canterbury resisted arrest and, in the process, Hugh and the others killed him. I will take responsibility for that if I must, since I was ordered to arrest the man, but…."

Tevin threw up a hand to quiet him. "Val, listen to me," he said urgently. "The soldiers from Canterbury Castle that came to deliver the news of the archbishop's death said that *you* were the murderer. The men involved in the assassination were wearing de Nerra tunics. Nothing was said about de Morville and the other knights."

Val wasn't particularly shocked by that. "I brought a contingent of men with me who were, indeed, wearing my colors," he said. "But we stopped de Morville from hacking Canterbury to pieces. By the time I got there, Hugh and Reg and William and Richard had already killed the man."

Tevin's mouth hung open; he couldn't help it. Now, the pieces of the puzzle were starting to fall together and he was having a difficult time comprehending it all. Something dark and horrible had been afoot, an undercurrent of treachery that no one had sensed from knights who had closely served Henry. But now, it was starting to come clear and the realization was devastating.

"Oh… God…," he breathed. "So that was where those four went. De Morville, FitzUrse, le Breton, and de Tracy… we were only speaking of them this morning because Henry had not seen them. No one seemed to know where they had gone."

Val cocked his head curiously. "Gone? Who? De Morville and the others? They went to Canterbury on Henry's orders."

Tevin was shaking his head slowly, back and forth. "Nay, Val. *Not* on Henry's orders."

Val looked at the man a moment, dumbfounded, before his eyes widened. "Then on whose orders?"

Tevin sighed sharply. "I am not sure how to tell you this," he said, holding up the vellum in his hand, "but Henry did not sign this warrant. He never gave these orders. You have been lied to, Val. Someone has pulled you into a plot to assassinate Canterbury and now they are trying to name you as the murderer."

So there it was, out in the open. *An assassination plot*. Now, Val was coming to understand why Tevin had been so distressed and why this entire discussion had been so confusing. But on the heels of that realization came another, more devastating realization – Henry hadn't ordered the arrest of Canterbury. Henry never gave the command that Val had so diligently carried out.

An assassination plot!

Val looked at Tevin as if his entire world had just come crashing down around him.

"Sweet Christ," he muttered. "Are you certain of this?"

Tevin nodded, feeling ill. "Aye," he said. "Henry did not order Canterbury arrested or assassinated. He only learned of the man's death this morning and had you been there, you would have seen how shocked he was. It was not a performance; it was the truth."

Val was still trying to grasp at the last traces of hope that this might not be some grand plot he'd fallen in to; he was in denial. Surely this could not happen to him.

Surely there was another explanation!

"But if he wanted to keep it secret," Val said, sounding as if he was pleading. "Surely he would have known that his advisors would have taken a stand against Canterbury's arrest. Mayhap he sent the warrant and you simply did not know of it."

Tevin could see that Val was trying to find justification for that which could not be justified. He shook his head. "When we received the word of Canterbury's death this morning, no one was more shaken than Henry," he said. "I do not believe he sent that missive. But you must come with me to Winchester immediately to clarify all of this, Val. There is some kind of plot afoot and you have been pulled into it. Henry will want to hear this."

Val was had gone from denial to the horror of realization all in one breath. So, it was true… Henry really hadn't sent the missive. The more he thought of it, the more devastated he became.

"I had no reason not to trust Hugh when he delivered the missive," he said, a hint of pain in his voice. "He has delivered dozens of warrants from Henry and this was just another one, although the seriousness of it did strike me. I thought to confirm it with Henry, in fact, but Hugh and the other knights had already gone on ahead to Canterbury and I was convinced that Henry wanted this warrant carried out swiftly, so I went ahead with it. You can see for yourself in the missive that I am threatened if I did not carry out the orders."

Tevin nodded, looking back to the missive and seeing the clear threat within. "I understand completely," he said. "As you saw it, you had no choice."

"And now you are telling me that Henry did not send the missive?"

"I truly believe he did not."

Val turned away from the man, pacing across the floor and snapping his knuckles with agitation. "I cannot believe it," he muttered. "I have been tricked."

"You have, indeed."

Val swiftly turned to Tevin. "It must have been Hugh," he said, teeth clenched. "He was the one who demanded I follow through on the orders so quickly and he is the one I saw delivering the death blow to Canterbury. He must have been the one who forged this missive to me. But why? Damnation, *why?*"

It was a cry of anguish, something that seemed to go right through Tevin, piercing his heart with the power of Val's agony. He stood up, facing Val.

"I do not know," he said honestly. "But you know Hugh… he is rabidly loyal to Henry, always one to seek royal favor. Mayhap, he thought he would be given the king's favor by ridding him of a man who has caused Henry such grief."

Val was so angry that he was trembling. "Except he sought to pin any blame on me," he said. "If I have the arrest warrant, then I am responsible. Hugh could say he was simply following my orders."

"Possibly," Tevin nodded. "In any case, we must go to Henry immediately. He… he is sending men to arrest you and bring you to Winchester, Val. It would be better if you went to him before he sends his army to remove you in front of your own men. You do not want your men to see you being arrested."

Val shook his head. "Nay, I do not," he said. Then, he paused, thinking on the situation he now found himself in. It was like a nightmare. "I have lived my entire life in service for Henry. I have done everything right. I have chosen the right path. I have demonstrated my fealty to the best of my ability. And now this. I feel like everything I am and everything I have worked for is unraveling before my eyes and I cannot stop it."

Tevin went to him, putting a hand on his shoulder. "Henry will understand when he sees that missive," he assured him. "Do not lose faith, Val; that missive proves that you were unknowingly pulled into something you believed Henry wanted."

It was difficult for Val to have faith at the moment. He felt like a piece of fragile ice that had just been smashed into a thousand pieces, leaving remnants of what he once was. He wondered if he could ever pull himself back together again.

His professional life was ruined.

"Please… do not tell my mother," he finally muttered. "I would not have her know what has happened. It will only destroy her and will serve no purpose in the long run. We will simply tell her that we are going to see the king."

Tevin nodded. "We will do whatever you feel is best."

Val's mind was off in a thousand different directions, just like those smashed pieces of what he once was. He smiled thinly.

"Oddly enough, I do not want my mother to lose faith in me," he said. "I know it sounds strange, but she has always been very proud of me. I could lose that if she knew what has really happened. That I have been made a fool of."

Tevin was feeling deeply sorry for his friend. "She loves you," he said. "She would never lose faith in you, but I understand. She will not hear this from my lips."

Val simply nodded, feeling emptier inside than he'd ever felt in his life. There was a big, gaping hole where his heart and soul had once been, indicative of the depth of the betrayal he felt. But upon thoughts of treachery, and his mother's admiration, something more heady came to mind. Thoughts that had been his constant companion for weeks now, so much so that he couldn't even remember when they hadn't occupied nearly every waking hour.

Vesper....

She was waiting for him to send her the necklace he'd purchased for her, a symbol of a future between them... or not. Could he even send that to her now when his entire life was verging on destruction? Was it fair to her to pull her into this maelstrom he found himself in the middle of? With increasing sorrow, he knew what the answer was.

He could not.

"There is also another young woman whose respect means a great deal to me," he said quietly. "I had hoped... I suppose it does not matter what I had hoped. I must clear my name before I can even think of her."

Tevin looked at him with some interest. "I was not aware that you had a young lady," he said. "Your mother acted as if you did not."

Val lifted his eyebrows in resignation. "She does not approve of her, I think."

"Who is it?"

Val considered telling him but ultimately decided not to. Perhaps it was the best thing he could do, keep Vesper removed from what was happening to him. He didn't want her name associated with his right now. He waved Tevin off.

"It does not matter," he said, quickly changing the subject. "There are other men who know of the missive, who went with me to Canterbury to arrest the archbishop. I should tell them what has happened so they understand. They were part of this, too."

Tevin squeezed his shoulder, respecting his wishes when it came to not revealing a young woman he was evidently fond of. "Your men should accompany us to Winchester to give their accounts to Henry of what they saw," he said. "That can only work in your favor."

Val took a deep breath, struggling to pull himself together. "Then I shall find Calum and Kenan and inform them of our plans for going to Winchester," he said, his tone dull with sorrow. "But it is growing dark now. Would it be acceptable if we left before dawn?"

Tevin gave him a final pat on the shoulder and released him. "Not only acceptable but preferable," he said. "I am famished, so a good meal and a warm bed would be most welcome. I am an old man, Val; I need my rest."

Val glanced at Tevin; even at his advanced age, he was still powerfully built. He smiled weakly. "You are not so old that you could not fight men half your age and still win," he said. "I will not fall victim to your pleas of old age."

Tevin grinned. "You flatter me."

"I speak the truth."

Tevin gave him one last pat on the back and handed over the vellum he still held. "Speaking of truth, I would not let that out of your sight," he said, indicating the vellum that Val was still holding. "Let us go now and speak to the men who accompanied you to Canterbury. We must tell them what has happened. I would also like to hear what they have to say about it."

"Gladly."

With that, Val and Tevin quit Val's solar and headed out into the deepening night where the smells of the evening meal were heavy upon the cold air.

All the while, however, Val was entrenched in perhaps the greatest inner turmoil he'd ever experienced, knowing he'd been lied to by men he had once trusted. He also thought of McCloud, another old friend who had fooled him greatly. Was it possible that he was becoming too trusting of men in general? His mother was such a cynical, mistrustful woman, but she was also a good deal older than he was. Perhaps she'd learned what it meant to be wary of men in general. And Val, who seemed to have faith in honorable men, now found himself in a terrible position that could cost him everything.

Something in him, at that moment, changed forever.

CHAPTER SEVENTEEN

In the midst of the winter's dark night, the torches from the walls of Selborne made it seem as if there was hope in that darkness, piercing the night with tiny pricks of light.

Vesper and McCloud could see the torches of Selborne in the distance as they approached under a clear night, a half-moon in the sky lighting their way. It was a comforting sight. The road was muddy from the melting snow and travel had been slow, but they'd managed to make it to Selborne in two days, riding long into the night as they had.

Vesper, who had some money of her own that she'd earned from sewing garments for Lady Eynsford, had brought her coinage with her and they'd slept at a tavern the night before. At least, she'd had a bed but McCloud had slept in the common room. His daughter had paid for his meal but he seemed strangely against allowing her to rent him a bed, so he'd slept on the floor by the enormous hearth quite happily.

They'd pushed onward early the next morning to Selborne and were now arriving as the evening meal was being served. The smells of cooking meat were wafting upon the cold air, a pungent and delicious smell. Having not eaten since the morning, Vesper and McCloud were both famished. With rumbling stomachs, they proceeded up the road leading to Selborne, a road that seemed to go on forever until, finally, the great gatehouse arose in the darkness before them.

The castle was bottled up tightly at this time of night but it took very little for the soldiers on watch to open the gates to two lonely travelers. In fact, Mayne, who was still on the wall, noticed that it was Lady Vesper and her father so he quickly had the men usher the pair in. By the time they passed beneath the gatehouse and into the bailey, Mayne had come down from the wall to greet them.

"My lady," he said, motioning men to come forward and help the lady from her horse. "I apologize that we did not meet you out on the road. We were not advised of your arrival."

Vesper climbed off her horse, stiffly. She'd been sitting in that saddle for hours and her legs were like jelly. "We did not send word ahead," she said. "Is Sir Val here?"

Mayne nodded. "Aye, my lady," he said. "He is in the great hall. Will you permit me to escort you there?"

Hearing that Val was at Selborne filled Vesper with relief; she honestly didn't know if he would be there. She half-expected to come to a castle empty of him and trying to explain her presence to Val's mother. Not knowing if the woman knew about the events over the past few weeks, it would make for a delicate conversation.

Fortunately, she didn't have to worry about that, at least not at the moment. As Mayne politely took her elbow to escort her to the hall, a soldier handed over her satchel, which had been strapped to the saddle of her horse. With her bag in-hand, Vesper didn't waste any time. She headed for the hall, practically pulling Mayne and her father along as she marched.

With every step, thoughts of Val grew. Vesper had already planned what she was going to say to him. In fact, it was all very simple. She would tell him that it didn't matter what she'd heard because she didn't believe any of it. Thinking of tall, proud Val, she was fully willing to believe that the news from Canterbury had been a lie because the Val she knew was not capable of what that horrible Canterbury soldier said he had done and nothing in the world could convince her otherwise. That was her official position on the matter.

Still....

Val had executed her brother, so she knew he would do his duty no matter what. He was, indeed, capable of deadly force. But to kill the archbishop on Henry's command? Val wasn't an assassin. He was a man who enforced laws, a man respected and loved. He wasn't a man who could be paid to kill like a mercenary. But if Henry had asked such a thing of him, to kill the king's nemesis, then Val would have to do as he was ordered.

So… perhaps he was capable of such things.

It was the argument she'd been rolling around in her head for days, ever since she'd heard the tale of the archbishop's assassin from that despicable soldier. All she knew was that she had to reaffirm her support to Val, so much so that she'd fled Eynsford, traveling in winter to reach the man she clearly adored. She'd been so very foolish, denying her feelings for Val and floundering in confusion because of it. But those days were ended – no more separation, no more ridiculousness. It was time to confess what was in her heart and stand by it.

No matter what.

Vesper approached the entry to the great hall with Mayne on one side of her and her father on the other. The doors were slightly cracked, heat and light emitting from the interior. She could hear voices beyond, men drinking and laughing, and her heart began to race. She was so excited to see Val that she simply couldn't help it. When Mayne finally opened the door for her, she realized that she was trembling. He was here, somewhere.

She had to see him.

The stale heat from the hall slapped her in the face as she entered, her gaze going immediately to the alcove where they had sat the last time she was here. But there were two tables full of men between the door and the alcove, and it was difficult to see that side of the hall in general. Mayne pointed towards the alcove, in fact, and walked her around the edge of the room to protect her from any drunken soldiers who might try to take a swipe at her. They were halfway to the alcove when Val was suddenly appeared.

"Vesper!" he said, sounding stunned. "God's Bones… is it really you?"

His abrupt presence startled her. Vesper found herself gazing up into that handsome face, more handsome than she had remembered, and her voice caught in her throat. She opened her mouth to speak but nothing would come forth. Tears stung her eyes, hearing his beautiful voice fill her ears. All she could do was nod, eagerly.

"Aye," she finally managed to say. "I… I hope I am welcome."

Val looked at her as if that very question pained him. He put his hands on her arms, something that might have been considered an improper touch. She was a maiden, unpledged, and he was an unmarried man, and the two simply did not touch in public. But Val had a grip on her, so tightly that it was as if he never intended to let her go.

"Of course you are welcome," he said gently. "You are more welcome than you know. But what has happened? Why are you here?"

Vesper didn't want to give her reason aloud; she looked around, nervously, seeing unfamiliar men looking at her but no sign of Margaretha. She swallowed hard.

"Nothing has happened to me," she said, her voice trembling. "But… Val, I must speak with you. May we go someplace private?"

Val nodded before the question even left her mouth. "Of course," he said. Then, he eyed her. "Are… are you sure you are well?"

"I am well."

"Then it must be very important if you have traveled all this way from Eynsford."

"It is. Very important."

Val nodded again, managing to pull his gaze from her in his quest to locate someplace private where they could speak but, in doing so, he caught sight of McCloud standing a few feet behind his daughter. His expression shifted from soft and warm to suspicious and cool.

"What is your father doing here?" he asked.

Vesper turned to look at McCloud, who was looking at Val warily. "If you will feed him, I will tell you everything," she said to Val. "He means no harm, I promise."

Val's expression didn't change. "You will forgive me for being wary of that statement."

Vesper nodded, putting her hand up to touch his wrist. "I know," she said softly. "Please, Val. Feed him and allow me to speak with you."

Because she asked it of him, he agreed. Motioning to Calum, who was sitting at the table in the alcove with his wife, he indicated McCloud to the man and Calum understood to keep watch of him. As Calum took Vesper's father in-hand, Val took Vesper by the hand and quickly led her to the far end of the hall where the stairs led up to the loft above. The *clavichordium* was up there, but the instrument wasn't his focus. The loft was a private place to speak as the noise of the hall went on below them.

The darkened stairs dumped them out into the cluttered loft. It was warm up here and smoky from the fire blazing in the hearth. Val took Vesper over by the *clavichordium* simply because there was a stool there. He set her upon it, still holding her hand, and she perched on the stool gratefully. But he watched her as she shifted around on it, trying to find a comfortable position. When Vesper noticed that he was observing her with some concern, she smiled weakly.

"We have been riding since before dawn," she said. "My backside is a bit sore."

Val understood. "That has happened to me on more than one occasion," he said. Then, he crouched in front of her, still holding her hand. His gaze upon her was intense. "I still cannot believe you are here. I… I am truly speechless."

Vesper smiled weakly. "I understand your surprise," she said. "I know you did not expect to see me so soon, if ever."

He shook his head. "I knew I would see you again, but you are correct – not so soon."

Vesper wasn't quite sure how to begin the conversation after that. "I had everything planned out in my head as I would say it, but now as I look at you… I have never been very good at the coy games that men and women play. I have always spoken what is on my mind, so I am afraid that what I say will not be pretty or eloquent."

He squeezed her hand. "I would prefer honesty to pretty speeches and unnecessary words," he said. "But before you say anything, I must speak. If you are here about the necklace, I have not sent it to you not because I did not want to, but because I have not had the opportunity. I have not changed my mind about you or about anything else. I still feel the same as I did that day we parted in Bishop's Waltham."

Vesper sighed heavily, so heavily that she closed her eyes, hanging her head with relief. Sweet Jesù, she had hoped to hear those words.

"I am so very glad to hear that," she said softly. "Because that is why I have come. I know the day of my brother's execution was a chaotic day at best. We were thrown into a great deal of turmoil, both of us, and I suggested we part company to think on our true feelings for each other because I thought it was the right thing to do. But I must admit that I was wrong. No amount of separation could change my feelings for you. I did not mean to chase you away on that day."

A smile filled his expression. For all of the relief she was feeling, he seemed to be feeling the same. "You did not," he said, bringing her hand to his lips for a gentle kiss. "And no amount of separation could change my feelings for you, either. But you did not have to come all the way to Selborne to tell me this; you could have sent a missive and I would have moved heaven and earth to come to Eynsford to see you."

His tender kisses were sending bolts of lightning up her arm and her heart, already racing at the sight of him, was in danger of bursting. "I would have," she said. "But I came because I heard some very troubling news at Eynsford. I felt compelled to come to you, to tell you that no matter what happens, I will stand by you. You must know that there is at least one person in England who still believes you are noble and wise."

The smile faded from his lips. "What did you hear?"

"That you assassinated the Archbishop of Canterbury," she said. Then, quickly: "I do not care if it is true. I did not come to ask you that.

But soldiers from Canterbury Castle stopped at Eynsford on their way to London bearing the message that you had assassinated the archbishop. I thought they were lying and told them so, but if they are spreading such lies, then surely others are, too, and many people will hear. I thought… I thought that it would bring hateful people to you, trying to harass you, and I wanted you to know that I do not believe their lies. I thought you would want to know that someone in this world still has faith in you."

Her words melted his heart. He settled back on his buttocks, sitting on the wooden-planked floor of the loft while still holding her hand. He averted his gaze a moment, trying to think on what he should tell her, exactly, but because she had been forthright with him, he decided the best course of action would be to be equally forthright with her.

It was time for total honesty.

"That you would risk yourself to come here tonight tells me all I need to know about you," he murmured. "You are a woman of great bravery and great loyalty, and that makes me the richest man in all of England. It is true that I was there when the archbishop was murdered but I did not kill him. It is a great mistake that I am being blamed for, however. I am sorry you had to hear about it from others."

Vesper had to admit that she was hugely relieved to hear that he was innocent. "May… may I ask what happened?" she asked. "I know I said I did not come to ask you if it was true, but I cannot understand how you could be mistaken for an assassin."

Val shifted position, turning so he was sitting alongside her as she sat on the little stool. Very carefully, he lowered his head onto her lap in a moment he would remember for the rest of his life. It was sheer bliss, the softness and warmth of her surrounding him, easing his troubled mind. He'd spent the past several days in such turmoil that he was certain he'd never feel any comfort in his life again, not ever.

Up until the moment he saw Vesper coming through the doors of the great hall, he continued to wallow in that turmoil, his thoughts on riding to Winchester on the morrow to face Henry. His life, his reputation, was in so many pieces that it would be difficult to put them back together again. But the moment he saw Vesper, everything changed.

There was light and beauty and warmth left in the world.

He couldn't believe he'd been foolish enough to think that he would distance himself from her simply to keep her away from the troubles that were descending on him. Perhaps he was weak in not sending her away this very moment, letting his emotions rule him and not his head. But her support meant so very much to him that he couldn't send her away, not now. Not when he needed what she was offering.

With his head in her lap, it was comfort such as he'd never known and when her hand timidly touched his head, stroking his dark hair, all was right in the world. He never wanted to be separated from her, not ever. Therefore, he dreaded saying what he needed to.

"What I tell you must never leave yours lips," he murmured.

Vesper cradled his big head on her lap, her fingers in his wavy, dark hair. "I would never repeat what you tell me, I swear it."

He believed her and continued on with his sordid tale. "There was evidently a plot to murder Canterbury and I was unknowingly caught up in it," he said. "Now, whoever has created this plot is attempting to make me guilty for it. Tomorrow, I must ride to Henry at Winchester Castle and tell him what has happened. I saw four knights, men who I thought were honorable men, murder Thomas Becket. I did not participate. In fact, I stopped them from doing worse damage. But because I was placed at the scene by witnesses, I am being blamed."

Vesper closed her eyes briefly, indicative of the anguish of his confession. "I am so sorry," she whispered. "You are a true and noble man, Val. For these evil men to try and blame you for such a thing… it will not work. I am confident that God knows of your innocence and He will not let you fall."

Val sighed faintly. "I am not concerned with God at the moment, only Henry," he said. "He and Canterbury were friends from long ago. Although they have been in contention for the past several years, it was not always like that. I fear that Henry will take Canterbury's death very hard and will seek to punish those involved."

"Like you?"

"Possibly."

Vesper didn't like the sound of that at all. Fear began to clutch at her. "But Henry knows you too well, does he not?" she said. "He appointed you his itinerant justice, which means he must trust you greatly. Do you truly think something like this would change his mind regarding you?"

Val was feeling so much comfort as she stroked his hair that he was becoming drowsy with it. He'd hardly slept the past several days and, now, all of his exhaustion was catching up to him. Something about her touch, her mere presence, built a cocoon around him that made him feel as if everything in the world was right, just for that brief moment.

"I cannot know," he said. "I wish I could predict how he will react, but I truthfully cannot know. But one thing is for certain, Vesper – if he punishes me, then I do not want you to be punished also. It would break my heart if something happened to you because of me."

Vesper could feel the sorrow radiating from the man. The fingers in his hair moved to his cheek and she put a soft, warm palm on his face.

"I am not afraid," she said quietly, firmly.

Her touch was like heaven and he closed his eyes to it, savoring it. "I know you are not. But I am. As much as it pains me to say this, for now, you should distance yourself from me. I am not the itinerant justice you knew when we first met. Now, I am a suspect in a murder that will shake England to its very foundation. You should not be associated with me."

"And, yet, here I am."

"But…."

She cut him off gently. "Let me tell you what I have learned during our separation, Val," she said. "When I left you at Bishop's Waltham, I told you that I was afraid for your reputation should you be associated with a family of murderers. I was afraid of how it would reflect upon all you have built for yourself. I told you that something dark and terrible had happened to damage our relationship and you said that you felt it could be mended. You never wavered on that opinion. Now, I tell you – whatever plot you have been pulled in to and whatever the rest of England may think of you, I know differently. I am not afraid or ashamed to be associated with you. You once told me that you were unconcerned being related to the House of d'Avignon. I tell you now that I am unconcerned being related to the House of de Nerra. Whatever happens, I will stay by your side."

It was a speech that saw Val's own words turned against him. Once, he'd told her all of that. He would not have been ashamed to have been associated with the House of d'Avignon and he meant it. But now, Vesper was in a similar position and telling him exactly what he had told her. He had no recourse to deny her, but that didn't mean he wasn't terribly worried for her still. Sitting up, he looked at her.

"You have lived a protected and genteel life, Vesper," he said, trying to force her to understand what she was committing herself to. "What I am about to face… people have been executed for less. I cannot even promise that will not happen to me if Henry is enraged enough."

Vesper studied his handsome face, so wrought with distress, and she smiled. "Then if you go, you do not go alone," she whispered. "Let me stand with you. It will be the proudest thing I have ever done."

Val stared at her a moment, her words pounding into him like a battering ram. *It will be the proudest thing I have ever done.* Was it really true that she understood the depths of the situation and what it might entail? He didn't think she did. But he could not refute such sweet devotion. He lifted a hand, cupping her face.

"I do not know what I have done in life to warrant a reward such as you," he said softly. "Although I know I should deny you, in my heart I cannot. You will be the very source I draw my strength from in the dark days to come."

Vesper's smile broadened. "I hope so," she said. "I will not leave you, not ever."

Val forced a smile. He felt so guilty for permitting her to be with him during this time but he couldn't help it. He needed her. He felt better simply knowing she was here, with him, supporting him. Leaning forward, he kissed her sweetly on the cheek before his lips moved to her mouth, slanting over them gently.

The moment he tasted her, however, his kisses grew hungry and he pulled her off of the stool and into his arms, feasting on her with a fervor that was borne from his very soul. Something about the woman fed him as nothing else ever had. Although he'd never been in love before, he suspected that was exactly what he was feeling. This strong, beautiful, and brave woman belonged to him.

He loved her.

"Marry me," he whispered between heated kisses. "If Henry sends me to the executioner, at least I will know you will be well taken care of as my widow. You will inherit everything, including Selborne."

Vesper, who had been consumed by his kisses, suddenly pulled away and looked at him, startled. "Nay," she said. "That is not why I would marry you. I do not care about your money, Val. All I care about his you."

Val could see that he'd insulted her. "I did not mean to offend you," he said. "I simply meant that it would give me comfort to have you by my side, as my wife, and to know that if anything happened, you could live out your days in comfort. It would mean a great deal to me."

Vesper understood his position, sort of, but she was still incensed. "I was never interested in you for your wealth," she said, brow furrowed. "In fact, if I marry you, I do not want your money. Donate it to the church for all I care. I do not marry you for the security you can give me. I marry you because I love you."

He eyes widened. "You… you *love* me?"

Vesper hadn't really thought about what she was saying before she'd said it because she was trying to prove a point. Realizing she told the man that she loved him, she looked at him rather hesitantly because of his reaction. Was he shocked? Was he pleased? Seeing his astonished expression, something told her he felt the same way she did.

"Of course I do," she said after a brief pause. "Why else would I have ridden all the way from Eynsford on a borrowed horse to see you? Either I am foolish or I am in love. And I do not believe I am foolish."

Val stared at her a moment longer before pulling her against him, his big arms around her slender body as he hugged her fiercely. "As I love you," he whispered. "I know it seems foolish that we should find love after hardly knowing one another, but I cannot help how I feel. Something brought us together, Vesper. I do not believe in coincidences. I believe that I was in Whitehill chasing that fugitive on the very day you were there because we were meant to meet. We were meant to be together, you and I."

Vesper had her arms wrapped around his neck, her face buried in his hair. "It was a violent day," she giggled softly. "Do you recall? There was an enormous fight going on with you in the middle of it. I will admit that you impressed me that day. I'd never really seen a fight before and you took to it so easily."

He grinned, pulling back to look at her but not releasing her from his arms. "I have been doing it for many years," he said. "A battle draws me like water draws a duck. But trouble does not usually follow me as it has as of late. It seems that you and I have had our share of misfortune in the short time we've known one another."

"That would be a fair statement."

"In speaking of misfortune, why *is* your father here?"

The conversation shifted focus and Vesper thought on her father, of the conversation over the past couple of days that she had shared with him. "He came to Eynsford a few days ago and begged for my forgiveness," she said. "He says that he realizes the error of his ways and that, with my brother gone, I am all that he has left."

Val wasn't so willing to believe McCloud after what he'd been through with the man. "How do you feel about his change of heart?" he asked.

She shrugged. "I cannot say that I am willing to trust him just yet, but it seems as if he is sincere. He was with me when the soldiers from Canterbury came bearing news of the archbishop's murder and he came with me to Selborne because he would not let me travel alone." She sat up so she could look him in the face. "You have known my father for many years and he was a good friend to you. There is no doubt that you know him far better than I do. Do you believe me means what he says? That he is truly sorry for his behavior?"

Val didn't want to completely discount McCloud but he wasn't going to let the man fool him twice. "I do not know," he said honestly. "The man I knew in France was a different man than the one you see today. The man I knew then was truthful to a fault and would risk his life for his comrades. He was not subversive in any way. But your father has changed a great deal since then, as I have come to see. My mother saw it first but I refused to believe her and now I feel foolish because of it. Is your father sincere? I suppose only time will tell. But I will say this – I will be very careful before trusting him again completely."

Vesper considered his advice carefully. "As will I," she said. "I do not want to be associated with the man he has become but I cannot completely walk away from him. Isn't everyone worthy of forgiveness once?"

Val nodded faintly. "Once, aye," he said. "But I am under the opinion that men who have tasted darkness never really do change, so if you decide to forgive him, I will support you. But my relationship with him will be different."

Vesper nodded. "I know. I realize what he has done to make you leery of him and I do not blame you."

Val put a hand on her head, an affectionate gesture, and ended up toying with her silken dark hair. "Then let us speak of him no more. I would rather speak of us. A man asked you to marry him only a few moments ago and he has not received an answer yet."

Vesper's grin was back and she averted her gazes, shyly. "I thought it was assumed that I had agreed. I did not tell you I loved you as a jest, you know."

He snorted, leaning forward to kiss her on the temple. “I do not wish to assume. Give me your answer so that I may hold it against my heart.”

Vesper gazed at him, into that handsome face that she was coming to love so well. “I will marry you, Valor de Nerra,” she whispered. “The question is whether or not your mother will let me.”

Val laughed softly. His heart was light with her acceptance, delight filling his soul that he’d never experienced before. Now, officially, she belonged to him and nothing would ever separate them save death. He felt as if he could walk on air.

“She will be thrilled that I have finally chosen a bride. But you should know that she will demand grandchildren right away,” he said. “Only this evening did I hear her lamenting her lack of grandchildren to an old friend of mine. She will spout off at anyone who listens that she has no grandchildren and that I am to blame.”

Vesper eyed him with feigned suspicion. “Is that why you have asked me to marry you? To appease your mother?”

He grinned, shaking his head. “I have asked you to marry me because it would be the greatest honor of my life to call you my wife and for no other reason than that.”

It was such a sweet thing to say and Vesper’s heart was leaping for joy within her chest. “I shall endeavor to be worthy of you, my lord.”

He grasped her by both arms, pulling her against him. “Not ‘my lord’. Say my name. Say it and mean it.”

His mouth was hovering above hers, his heated breath on her face. It was enough to melt Vesper completely. “Val,” she whispered. “My darling Val.”

His mouth slanted over hers again, sucking the breath right out of her. Vesper collapsed against him, feeling so small and insignificant against the power of his arms. The more he held her, the more she liked it, and soon her arms went around his neck again, holding him tightly against her as their lips melded. It was a kiss that turned her body to liquid fire, coursing through her, building into something that made her heart race like mad. All she knew was that Val's lips were stoking a fire in her that she'd never known before, something that begged to be quenched in a way she'd not yet experienced.

But Val knew how to sate it. He was experiencing the same fire.

As the noise of the hall went on down below, Val and Vesper engaged in a heated kiss, hidden by the clutter that had built up in the loft. No one could see them where they were; Val knew that. He also knew that his feelings for Vesper were stronger than he could control.

Facing an unknown future, he was not in command of his emotions as he usually was. He began to think about tomorrow and facing Henry. What if Henry did, indeed, throw him in the vault, or worse? What if he ordered him executed for having a part in Canterbury's death? There would be nothing left of him, no wife or children or family left behind other than his mother, who would surely curse him for not giving her grandchildren to carry on the de Nerra name. He could easily see his mother going mad because of it, living with terrible regrets.

He didn't want to live with any regrets, either.

And Vesper… this sweet, beautiful woman he found himself so enamored with. What about her? She could marry him tomorrow before he left for Winchester. Or, she could go with him to Winchester and they could be married at the cathedral. But would he have time to consummate the marriage, to spend a few precious minutes with her to demonstrate how much he adored her? He couldn't be sure that there would be time at all, at least not like they had at this moment. Right now, the timing was perfect to do precisely that – make her his own, forever.

God, he had such need of her. In her, he saw his salvation.

Laying Vesper back on the dusty floor, he loomed over her, gazing down at her and drinking in her beauty. With her sculpted cheekbones and bright eyes, she was as perfect a woman as God could have ever made. When he saw that she was inspecting him just as he was inspecting her, he smiled faintly.

"I was wondering if our children will look like you," he murmured, kissing her cheek gently. "Or mayhap they will look like me."

Vesper reached up, touching his face. "You mean the grandchildren your mother wants so badly?"

"The same."

She grinned. "They will have to look like you or I doubt she will accept them."

Val laughed deeply, kissing her on the cheek again. "I would not be surprised if you were correct."

His kisses grew stronger and, soon, his mouth was capturing hers again, one big arm around her while the other roamed. As he kissed her lips and suckled on her chin, his right hand drifted down her arm and onto her torso, lingering on her belly. But the kisses grew more heated and that same hand moved up her body, gently closing around a breast. Vesper's eyes opened wide and she looked at him in surprise. Val simply kissed her chin again and squeezed her breast softly.

"Does this disturb you?" he asked softly.

Vesper wasn't sure how to answer, but it was clear that she was trying to pretend as if she wasn't bothered by it at all.

"Nay," she said quickly; perhaps *too* quickly. "You are to be my husband and it is your right. But…"

He leaned down, nuzzling her neck. "But what?"

"We are not married yet."

It was the maidenly virtue speaking, the virtue that had been drilled into the head of every young woman. One was not to participate in the pleasures of the flesh until after marriage, but that was a myth in many cases. There were plenty of young women who indulged because Val had been with a few of them. There had been one of the ladies of the Countess of Gloucester, and then a distant de Bohun relation he'd met at a masque in London, and….

"I will summon a priest tonight," he said, already feeling his manhood growing rigid for want of her. "If it makes you uncomfortable, then I will stop. But know this… I depart for Winchester tomorrow and there is no knowing if I will return. You know this. If I am to spend a last night of freedom, then I would very much like to spend it with you. There is no telling what tomorrow will bring for us both."

Vesper met his gaze, her hazel against his brilliant green. She bit her lip. "That sounds very much like a manipulative statement I heard once when a certain knight I was trying to fend off sought to play on my sympathies."

Val's eyebrows rose in surprise. "And?"

"And *what*?"

"Did it work?"

She scowled. "Of course it did not work!"

He started laughing again, low in his throat, and Vesper couldn't very well be angry with him because she could see that he was jesting with her. Even so, there was truth in his words. He was going to face something unspeakably frightening tomorrow and it was very possible she would not see him for a very long time, if ever. That thought scared her to death.

She loved Val, wildly so. With time, it was a love that would deepen and grow roots, becoming something rich and binding. But now, her love for him was new and exciting and full of the dreams that all young women had – a handsome husband, a home, and children. Perhaps those were Val's dreams, too. If they were, she didn't want to leave them unfulfilled.

Taking his hand, she put it back on her breast.

"For whatever comes tomorrow, let us live tonight as if there is nothing ahead of us but our future together," she whispered. "For tonight, pretend that I am your wife and I will pretend you are my husband. And when tomorrow comes, we will be grateful for this time together – either as our last time together or as our very first of many to come. Either way, I am yours."

The smile faded from Val's face as he looked at her. She was so rational and wise, and he appreciated that about her. Everything about Vesper d'Avignon was perfect in his eyes.

He couldn't wait to make her his own, forever.

"Until I die, I will love you and only you."

"And I, you."

The hand on her breast fondled her gently as his mouth found hers yet again. Vesper was becoming accustomed to his kisses now and she had quickly learned to crave his warm lips. He had stubble on his face, scratching her tender skin, but she didn't care. There was nothing about him that she didn't love.

His kisses became more forceful and the hand on her breast began to unlace the stays of her shift beneath the lower neckline of her surcoat. His mouth moved from her lips to her neck and finally to her chin, along her collarbone and to the swell of her breasts. Vesper had just become accustomed to his hand on her breast when he suddenly peeled the fabric back, exposing her left breast. Her nipple hardened when the warm air hit it and as Vesper tried not to become embarrassed by the fact he'd just pulled her clothing down from one breast, Val's mouth descended on a taut nipple.

It was a sensation like none other. Vesper was overwhelmed by his hot mouth on her breast and her back arched in surprise, in pleasure, giving herself over to the newness of the experience. Val's body was half-covering her, the weight of him pressing upon her, but it was a touch that stoked the fire his kisses had started.

The noise from the hall below was a quiet rumble, reminding them that they were not alone in this tryst. Although men could not see them, any sounds from the loft might surely be heard, so Vesper put a hand over her mouth as Val pinched her nipple between his teeth. It was enough to cause her to cry out but the hand over her mouth prevented any noise from escaping. Still, his hands were moving over her, his mouth on the flesh of her breasts when she could feel one of those roaming hands snaking up her skirt.

As a woman who had never known the touch of a man until this moment, Vesper should have been fearful of the hand on her thigh, moving upwards, but the truth was that she wasn't afraid. She was curious and eager to learn, and everything Val had done to her until this point had been thrilling and pleasurable. Therefore, she wasn't afraid. She liked his mouth on her breasts so much that she was quite willing to see what he would do next, something more to give her such pleasure.

What she wasn't prepared for, however, was the shock of his fingers probing her woman's center. She barely touched herself down there, only to wash and to tend to necessary woman's needs, so to have a man touch her there – even a man who would be her husband. She was growing embarrassed and Val must have sensed that. His hand came to a halt and he stopped nursing at her breasts, lifting his head to look at her.

"Did I hurt you?" he whispered raggedly.

Vesper shook her head. "Nay," she said. "'Tis just… I have not…"

He could see how embarrassed she was and he leaned forward, kissing her on the chin. "You needn't be ashamed," he murmured. "This is a wonderful and natural thing. You will enjoy it, I promise. Will you trust me just a little?"

She had liked what he'd done to her so far so she nodded. "Aye," she murmured. "But… but there are men in the room below us…."

He kissed her again. "They will not hear us if we are quiet," he said. "And they cannot see us, even if the come up the staircase. But if you are still uncomfortable, then I shall stop."

She quickly shook her head. "Nay," she said softly. "You promised that I would enjoy this. I am waiting."

He gave her a half-grin, kissing her once more as he resumed his heated kisses on her shoulder. The hand on her thigh remained still for a few moments longer before beginning its exploration once more, moving to the dark curls between her legs. He probed her gently, causing her to twitch and buck, because his fingers made some kind of magic happen down there. There was a certain spot he would touch that nearly brought her off the floor. It made sparks fly, causing her legs to tremble, but it was oh-so-pleasurable.

Val had been right; she liked it a great deal. It was the most amazing sensation she'd ever known. As she lay there, thoroughly enjoying his attention, Val pulled her skirts up to her waist and settled himself between her legs. Then, she could feel him fumbling with his breeches as something very warm and very hard suddenly pressed against her womanly center.

Vesper didn't have time to think on what he was doing; she barely had time to breathe before he was slanting his mouth over hers again while at the same time, thrusting his hips forward so that his manhood slid into her waiting body. Vesper gasped at his sensual intrusion, groaning softly as he tried to muffle the sounds with his kisses. Three gentle but firm thrusts and he was seated to the hilt, having broken through the barrier of her virginity. The flash of sharp pain told Vesper she was no longer a maiden, but true to Val's word, she was enjoying it. Oddly enough, the pain hadn't been enough to frighten or distress her. It had quickly come and was quickly gone. As Val gathered her up against him, his hips began to move.

Vesper's arms were around his neck as he thrust into her repeatedly, a gentle rhythm at first to allow her to become accustomed to him, but Vesper very quickly discovered that his pelvis against hers caused those sparks to fly again. It was that pleasure he spoke of, overwhelming her, and she closed her eyes as the sparks grew hotter and more intense. All she could do was hang on to Val as he had his way with her but she didn't care a lick; not a bloody lick. Had Henry's army stormed the loft at that moment, she wouldn't have let go of Val and she wouldn't have let him stop, not for anything. This was what she was born to feel with the man she was born to feel it with.

Every stroke, every kiss, was pure magic.

Somehow, the sparks he was creating in her exploded into a shower of stars and ripples of pleasure coursed through her body as she experienced her first release. As Vesper went limp in his arms, gasping for air, Val took his own pleasure, releasing himself deep. In truth, his mind had been a miasma of lustful thoughts from the moment he entered her until this very second when he climaxed so hard that he bit his lip. Now, reality was settling along with the taste of his own blood and the smell of her, the feel of her, was filling the very air around him. Even after he released, he continued to move his hips gently, his body joined to hers, the feel of his seed making her hot and slick against his flesh.

His seed… God, he'd never imagined he would wish for a woman to conceive his child but, at this moment, he prayed for that. He prayed that his seed would find its mark and take root, and a son in his image would be born. He couldn't imagine a better mother for his child, the wise and beautiful Vesper, a woman he adored deeply. If he went to Winchester tomorrow and Henry decided upon a punishment that would see him leave this earth, then at least there was a chance that something of him would live on.

That's what this night meant to him. Hope for his destiny.

"Vesper?" he whispered, his face in the side of her head. "Sweetheart? Are you well? I did not hurt you, did I?"

Vesper shook her head, tickling his nose with her hair. "You did not," she murmured. "I am well. More than well."

He smiled. "Then I kept my promise? You enjoyed it?"

She nodded. Then, she pulled back to look at him, putting a hand on his cheek and watching him as he kissed it tenderly. There was reverence in his movements.

"I did," she said, trying to think of a way to voice her thoughts and not sound foolish. "I have never felt so close to anyone, as if we were made for each other. As if you are a part of me and I am a part of you. Val… let me go with you tomorrow when you go to Winchester. Please."

His smile faded. "Nay," he said with regret. "I would have you remain here with my mother. If Henry should punish me, then I should not want you there."

Vesper didn't like that answer. "But you are going into a den of men who only seek to harm you," she said. "Let me go as the one person who would support you."

He touched her face, kissing her on the cheek. “It is out of the question, so please do not ask me again,” he said. “I feel strongly that you must remain here. Whatever I must face with Henry, it will bring me comfort knowing you are here and you are safe. Will you please do this for me?”

Vesper was unhappy about it but she didn’t want to spoil the mood. He seemed sorrowful enough without her pleading, so she simply nodded her head. “If you wish it.”

“I do.”

“Then I shall do as you ask.”

There wasn’t much more to be said after that. Val continued to hold Vesper in his arms for a few minutes longer, knowing that they should return to the feast below before someone did, indeed, come looking for them. They’d already been gone overlong. Therefore, he kissed her gently once, twice, and sat up, pulling up his breeches and helping her smooth her skirts. There was some evidence of their activities on the back of her gown, but the fabric was dark and masked it quite well. No one would ever know of their encounter.

But they certainly knew.

The taste of Vesper lingered on Val’s lips. All he had to do was lift his hands and smell her on them. It was a glorious smell. As he returned her to the feasting table in the alcove where he introduced her to Tevin du Reims, all Val could think about was their tryst in the loft. It made it most difficult to focus on conversation, which he struggled to do after that. Vesper was so heavily on his mind that he couldn’t shake her.

Marriage…

He made up his mind as he watched Tevin make conversation with Vesper that he would marry Vesper on the morrow before they departed to Winchester. He hadn’t wanted to delay that trip but he wasn’t sure if he’d have the opportunity to marry her once he reached Winchester, if ever, so his marriage to Vesper became the priority. It was all he could think of as he watched Vesper deep into the evening, nearly ignoring everyone else at the table because of her. If Tevin and Calum and the other men didn't realize he was in love with McCloud's daughter, they certainly did by the end of the night.

It was obvious.

In fact, once Vesper had retreated to bed for the evening and McCloud wandered off to play gambling games with some of the soldiers, Val sat up with Tevin, Calum, Kenan, and Mayne to discuss what would happen on the morrow. Val made it clear that he wanted to marry the lady before he left, sending Mayne to summon a priest from the small church in the village that skirted Selborne.

Mayne charged out in the middle of the night, knowing that time was precious, as Calum and Tevin tried to talk Val out of such an impulsive move. They were thinking of Vesper mostly, concerned that Val was acting so rashly, but the man's mind was set. He would marry her and then he would face Henry. There was no convincing him otherwise.

But the truth was that they understood his determination and, in particular, Tevin understood. He was an old man and he'd been married to his wife for many years, a woman he'd fallen madly in love with so long ago. He understood what it was like to want to marry a woman and not be able to – aye, he very much understood that need.

So, Tevin retired to sleep a few hours before dawn, leaving Val to seek his mother and wake her up with the news that he was actually doing something she wanted for once – he was getting married. He roused Margaretha from a sound sleep to tell her many things – of his decision to marry, of the details of the plot he'd evidently been pulled into, and of his intention to face Henry on the morrow to clear his name. It had been a difficult conversation with the woman because he'd tried to spare her all he could, but the truth was that he could spare her no longer.

She had to know.

But Margaretha was a strong woman, something she exhibited as Val told her what had happened when he'd reached Canterbury and why Tevin du Reims had really come to Selborne. Now, much of what was going on made sense and she understood the situation. She also understood her son's desire to marry a woman he hardly knew, although he did profess to love her.

Margaretha wasn't in complete approval of the marriage but Val was determined so she didn't argue with him. Perhaps she should have; perhaps she should have even tried to stop him because she didn't believe that he was thinking clearly, but she couldn't bring herself to do it. Her beautiful boy was about to face, perhaps, the worst crisis of his life and she would not make it worse by arguing the details of the life he wanted for himself. Whatever he wanted, she simply agreed with him, and Val left her chamber feeling relatively good about their conversation. At least his mother hadn't fought him on his desire to wed Vesper. She had been remarkably stoic about the entire situation, giving him the strength to face the morrow.

And Margaretha knew that. She may have been a shrew and a nasty old woman at times, but she knew how to choose her battles wisely. This wasn't one she could win and she didn't want to burden her only child with animosity between them when he was, quite possibly, facing a death sentence on the morrow. Certainly, the day would come and then they would have their answers, but until then, they were all living in apprehension.

No one knew what the morrow would bring, least of all Val.

Realizing that everything her son had worked for might be coming to an end, Margaretha tried to remain strong long after he had left her. She tried to tell herself that all would be well. It wasn't even the marriage she was concerned about but Val's future as a whole. But her attempts to be brave didn't work; her heart was breaking for her only son. Was this to be the last of her great son, the vestiges of Valor de Nerra never to be reclaimed? She could only pray it wasn't so.

In the wee dark hours of the morning, Margaretha wept.

CHAPTER EIGHTEEN

IT WAS ABOUT an hour before dawn. The grounds of Selborne Castle were quiet for the most part as soldiers went about their rounds and the servants starting cooking fires to prepare for the morning meal. It was cold this morning, with a thin layer of ice on the ground, and smoke hung heavy in the air because of the cloud layer, causing the men on the wall walk to cough intermittently, their eyes stinging in the mist.

In the stables against the western wall, McCloud was saddling the horse he'd borrowed from Eynsford. He also had a sack of food to take with him, provisions he'd requested from the servant who had shown him to his bed the night before. It sat on the ground by the end of the stall as McCloud prepared the horse, cleaning out the hooves by the light of an oil lamp and making sure the leather straps on the saddle were secure.

But his movements were slow and lethargic. He moved with a heavy heart, for many different reasons. In spite of traveling with his daughter for the past two days, he wasn't entirely sure Vesper was forgiving of his actions and he wasn't sure she was willing to put everything behind them. Worse still, Val, who had been a close and trusted friend, wouldn't even speak to him last night. He'd simply glared at him when he arrived and then ignored him the rest of the time, so Val's behavior had been wearing heavily upon him.

It hurt more than he thought it would.

Not that he deserved the man's friendship. He knew he didn't. But he'd come to support Val when it seemed as if the whole of England would very soon be against the man. He was both hurt and angered that Val wasn't willing to forgive him, a man he'd known for years, especially when Val was finding himself in a rather precarious position. He would need all the friends he could get. At least, that's how McCloud saw it.

Therefore, he brooded as he saddled the horse, thinking that he would simply return to Durley and try to eke out an existence there. He had nowhere else to go so returning to Durley seemed to be the best option. He would leave his daughter to Val, since the man was clearly enamored with her, and that would be the end of all things as he knew it. He would have to try and rebuild his life without his only living child or friends from long ago.

"McCloud."

A deep voice pierced the darkness and McCloud turned to see Val entering the stable. His heart leapt a bit at the sight of the man, wary of his presence, hoping that Val hadn't come here to tell him how disappointed he was in him. Nothing Val could say could be any worse than McCloud had already said to himself, so he braced himself as Val came towards him.

"Val," he said evenly. "You have risen early."

Val came into the weak light of the lamp. "I did not sleep," he said. "I saw you come into the stable. We must speak and there was no opportunity last night."

McCloud sighed faintly, returning his attention to the horse. "If you've come to scold me, then get on with it," he said. "Whatever you must say to me, I have earned it."

"I have come to speak with you about Vesper."

McCloud paused, looking up at him. "Oh?" he said. "What about her?"

Val hesitated a moment before continuing. "I am going to marry her this morning, as soon as the priest arrives," he said quietly. "I wanted you to know that."

"I assumed as much."

"You said once that you were agreeable if I courted her."

"I am."

"Then I assume you are agreeable with marriage."

McCloud's gaze lingered on Val a moment, perhaps sensing more behind that statement. Perhaps Val was thinking on his current situation and his uncertain future but he didn't want to voice such things. McCloud turned back to the horse again.

"Val, I know of the rumors regarding you and Canterbury," he said. "I was there when the soldiers from Canterbury Castle arrived and told Vesper of the assassination. I can only imagine that you are now in a rather precarious position because of it."

Val watched the man pick out the hooves of the horse. "I am going to Westminster to discuss just that very situation with Henry right after I marry your daughter," he said. Then, he paused a moment. "You have not asked me if those rumors are true."

McCloud shrugged. "It is not my business."

"Do you believe them?"

McCloud faltered. "I know you are a man of duty," he said simply. "If Henry ordered you to kill Becket, then you would obey him. Do I believe you are capable of such things? I know you are. I saw what you did to my son. But if there is one thing you are not, Val, it is foolish. You are no fool. I am sure you had a very good reason for what you did."

"I did not do it."

McCloud looked at him. "Then why do men say that you have?"

Val sighed, leaning against the wall of the stable. "Because I was sent a forged missive ordering me to arrest Canterbury. The same knights who delivered it are the ones who killed Canterbury. Now they are trying to blame me for it."

McCloud was looking at him seriously. "Does Henry know this?"

"He will when I see him this morning. You saw the Earl of East Anglia in my hall last night? He will help defend me against Henry's anger. McCloud, I know that you and I have had our problems over the past few weeks and I cannot say that I will ever trust you again, but you are Vesper's father. She is to be my wife. I should like it if we could at least live peacefully."

McCloud wasn't sure if he felt much hope in Val's words but at least the man didn't outright hate him. "I should like that as well," he said. "Mayhap someday… someday I will earn your trust again. I am sorry to have destroyed it in the first place."

Val didn't reply right away. Still leaning against the wall, he averted his gaze, staring pensively off into the dark stable. After a moment, he spoke.

"Was it pride that kept you from coming to me when your farm dried up and you could no longer feed yourself?" he asked. "I have been trying to figure that out – what would make a man turn as badly as you did. Selborne is a day's ride from Durley. Mayhap we are not as good of friends as I thought we were since you did not turn to me for help. I can think of no other reason."

McCloud was looking at the horse but not really seeing it. He was feeling a great deal of sorrow over Val's question. He could only think of one answer.

"I am not your responsibility," he muttered. "It is not your duty to feed and clothe me. How weak would I have looked to you had I come crawling for help?"

"So it was easier to permit your son to run amok, murdering at will?"

McCloud didn't really have an answer for him. "A man's pride is a complex thing," he said. "With Mat… I knew what he was doing was wrong. But he was my son. I had not the heart to punish him. It was easier to pretend he was not murdering rather than face the truth. Val, I have no real excuse to give you. All I can say is that I am sorry you have lost faith in me."

Val watched the man as he turned back to the saddle to make sure it was secure before moving to put the bridle on the horse.

"So am I," he said quietly. "But I do appreciate that you escorted Vesper to Selborne. I am grateful."

McCloud snorted. "She would not stay away. She was coming and there was no discouraging her."

"She is a determined young woman."

"Very much so."

The horse's bridle was on and secured, and McCloud led the horse out of its stall. He picked up the food sack on the ground and secured that to the rear of the saddle. When he was finished and the horse was ready to depart, he paused to look at Val one last time.

"Take good care of her," he said huskily. "She is a good girl. She did not deserve what I brought her. I pray you can give her something much better than I ever could."

Val could sense that the mood was turning serious, something that pained him more than he thought it would. "I wish I could believe you were sincere," he said. "This is like a nightmare, McCloud. Everything I thought was the truth has, mayhap, been a lie all this time. Marrying your daughter should make me very joyful because you would become part of my family, but now… all I can tell you is that I do not hate you. But I am disappointed. Mayhap it is something that can be mended in time, as you said."

McCloud nodded, but he was staring at his feet. "I will admit that I am not quite over the fact that you executed my son," he said. "I understand why you did it. I understand you were following the law and that you had every right. But I had hoped for special consideration, I suppose. I had hoped you would protect him."

Val has a suspicion that McCloud was harboring some resentment towards him but he was unrepentant about it. "Had you come to me in the very beginning, when he'd made his first kill, mayhap I would have," he said honestly. "But you let it go on to the point where there was nothing I could do once he was caught. Had I not punished him, the entire town would have turned against me and St. Lo's men more than likely would have, too. I was in no position to show mercy that day. Even if I had been, I would not have. Your son deserved the most serious punishment I could deal out and, for the fact that you were his accomplice, I should have punished you, too. But I did not. Consider that my protection, McCloud. You received my mercy when you should not have."

McCloud was feeling scolded, ashamed. "Have you never made a mistake, Val?" he asked, growing defensive. "Are you always so perfect? I see now that you are in trouble with Henry so it seems to me that you are not as perfect as you pretend to be. Mayhap you should have more understanding for imperfect men."

Val shook his head. "I find myself in this position through no real fault of my own," he said. "But you were clearly at fault. You made the choice, McCloud. No one forced your hand."

McCloud gathered the reins of his horse. "Then there is nothing more I can say," he said. "I have asked for your forgiveness. It is your choice whether or not you choose to give it. Meanwhile, you have my blessing to marry my daughter but you already knew that. I pray the marriage is good to you both."

With that, he began to lead his horse out of the stable and away from Val. Val continued to lean against the wall, watching the man depart and knowing very well that their relationship might not ever be repaired. It was a sad thought but one that couldn't be helped. Too much had happened for them to return to the great friends they once were. As he pushed himself up off the wall, preparing to follow McCloud from the stable, a soldier entered the structure.

"My lord," he said, addressing Val. "We have sighted an incoming army on the horizon, coming from the west."

Val's brow furrowed curiously. "An army?"

The soldier, a young man and rather excitable, nodded. "Aye, my lord," he said. "At least one hundred men, mayhap more. Sir Kenan told me to tell you."

"Is Kenan on the night watch?"

"Aye, my lord."

It sounded like something Val needed to see for himself. As McCloud headed towards the gatehouse to depart south, Val followed the soldier at a jog across the bailey and to the ladder that led up to the wall walk. He mounted the wooden ladder, emerging onto the wall and moving towards the west side just as Kenan appeared out of the early dawn, heading towards him. They came together quickly.

"It is Henry," Kenan said, his voice low. "It has to be. The contingent is bearing torches and banners."

Val wasn't so quick to panic like Kenan was. "Can you make out the colors?"

Kenan shook his head. "Not yet," he said. "It is still too dark but we can see them coming because of the torches. Val, Henry is coming for you… you must run."

Val grinned; he couldn't help it. "Are you serious?" he asked in disbelief. "You cry like an old woman, Kenan. Get hold of yourself."

Still grinning, he pushed past Kenan, who followed. "I am completely serious," he said, trying to keep his voice down so the soldiers wouldn't hear. "It is madness if you remain. If you will not flee, then at least hide. I will tell them that you left and I do not know where you have gone."

Val kept trying to push him away. "Du Reims is here," he pointed out. "He has seen me and he knows that I have not fled, as does everyone else at Selborne. Nay, Kenan, I will not flee. If it is Henry, then let him come. I have nothing to fear."

Kenan wasn't so sure. After being told yesterday that the warrant they'd based their trip to Canterbury on was a forgery, he was convinced that they were all going to be punished by Henry, but Val didn't seem to think so. Kenan had spent all yesterday in a rage towards the knights who had brought the missive, so much so that he'd nearly come to blows with Calum over it. It was Calum's brother, after all, who had brought the suspect missive and who had murdered Canterbury. Now that brother was trying to frame Val for it. It was a volatile situation that had seen the soldiers separating the two knights during the night.

Therefore, Kenan was on edge even as Val brushed him off. He followed Val down the wall walk as Val went to see the incoming army for himself. It was drawing closer to sunrise so the sky was starting to lighten, the clouds above turning shades of lavender and gray. It was easier to see the landscape beyond the wall now, the sloping of the hill leading away from Selborne and the road beyond. This particular road traveled east-west, almost continuously from Selborne to Winchester and beyond.

"Val, please," Kenan said softly. "They are coming for you. Will you not save your own life?"

Val was watching the pinpricks of light in the distance, light that represented many torches of an army that had moved out in the dark. "I would agree that it is probably Henry," he said evenly. "There are no other castles in the area that could put so many men on the road at this time of the morning. In fact, they must have left Winchester in total darkness to arrive at Selborne by dawn."

He was acting like he didn't hear Kenan, who stopped trying to talk to the man. He knew there was only one person who might be able to get through to Val so he abruptly left the wall without a word, making his way quickly down the ladder and then heading across the bailey. Val hadn't paid much attention to him until he happened to casually turn and see that the man was making his way to the keep. That sight spurred him into action.

Realizing that Kenan was more than likely going to tell Margaretha what was happening, Val bolted off the wall, taking the ladder far too quickly in his attempt to catch Kenan before the man made it into the keep. But Kenan was too far ahead of him, rushing into the keep just as du Reims was exiting. Kenan came to a halt when he saw that it was the earl and, in desperation, he spilled his message.

"My lord," he addressed him, breathlessly. "Henry is approaching with a small army, undoubtedly to arrest Val. I have told Val that he must flee but he does not seem to think he should. Mayhap you can convince him otherwise."

Tevin, looking a bit sleepy at this early hour, turned to Val in shock as the man came racing up the stairs to the keep. "Is this true?" he asked Val. "Henry is here?"

Val glared at Kenan before answering. "That is the assumption, aye," he said. "In spite of what this idiot thinks, I am not running to save myself. That would be the cowardly thing to do, an admission of guilt, and I will not do it. I am not guilty and I will prove it."

Kenan was miserable; Tevin could see that. He could also see that the bailey of Selborne was coming alive as the army approached, with soldiers rushing about and men on the walls yelling at one another. Servants, alerted by the soldiers, had come out to see what the fuss was about. Everyone seemed to be concerned that a small army was approaching Selborne.

Everyone except Val, that is.

But Tevin saw the seriousness of it much as Kenan did. He growled unhappily. "Damnation," he hissed. "D'Vant said he would give me at least a day. It seems that I have not been given even that."

Val looked at him curiously. "What do you mean?"

Tevin began to take the steps down to the bailey, pulling Tevin with him. "I did not want him coming to arrest you for all to see," he muttered. "I told him that I would bring you to Winchester but it seems that was not good enough. Henry must be angrier than I thought he was, so unless you wish for your men to see you placed in irons, I would suggest you ride out to meet d'Vant on the road. Will you do this?"

Val nodded without hesitation. "Of course," he said, coming to a stop. "I must gather my things, including the missive that started this entire mess, but I am more than willing to meet them on the road."

"Good," Tevin said quickly. "For now, I shall ride out to stop them from coming any closer. You will bring my things along with yours, please. We shall not be returning to Selborne."

Val nodded, feeling a sense of urgency from the earl and struggling against the apprehension it provoked. "I… I had hoped to marry Vesper this morning before I went," he said, regret in his tone. "I suppose that is not possible now."

Tevin looked at him. "Has your knight returned with the priest?"

"Not yet."

"Then we cannot wait. Tell your lady that the marriage will have to wait until you are able to return home."

There was a great seriousness in Val's expression. "Be honest, my lord. Will I ever be able to return home?"

Tevin met his gaze. "I believe so. You have the missive you were given and you have witnesses. You said that your knight, Kenan, was there as well? Then bring him. And bring the men who accompanied you. We will hear all of their testimony to prove you were tricked into this. Go, now; hurry. Henry will not wait."

Val didn't waste any time. He rushed back into the keep, nearly plowing into Kenan who was still standing in the doorway. It reminded him how angry he was with the man for making the attempt to run to his mother with the news of Henry's army.

"I will beat you within an inch of your life at a later time, but for now, you will ride with me to Winchester this morning," he said. "Gather the men who also witnessed Canterbury's murder and do it quickly. We are going to meet Henry's army on the road and there is no time to waste, so fly as if you have wings, Kenan. I will meet you in the bailey in a few minutes."

Kenan nodded, relieved that there would at least be some action in this situation. As he went to find the soldiers who had witnessed the assassination of the archbishop, Val raced up the stairs that led up to his chamber.

The keep was just awakening at this hour, perhaps spurred on by the shouts in the bailey of the approaching army. Servants were already in the small hall, filling it with fresh bread for his mother, but Val wasn't paying any attention. He was concerned with retrieving his possessions, Tevin's possession, and bidding farewell to Vesper. His heart ached that he could not marry her before departing to Winchester, but it could not be helped. He hoped she understood.

His chamber was right above his solar, on the same level as his mother's chamber but his could only be reached by a small stairwell. He made it into his chamber, tossing aside the clutter to find his saddlebags and the missive contained therein. He already had on his mail and then a tunic over that, but he found his heavy fur-lined robe and tossed that on over the top to protect against the icy morning.

Grabbing his helm, he headed back down the stairs and rushed over to a larger stairwell that gave him access to most of the keep above, including his mother's chamber and Vesper's chamber. Tevin had been put on the very top floor so he pounded up the stairs to collect Tevin's saddlebags.

Val was fairly certain that Tevin was putting rocks in his saddlebags with all of the weight in them. He slung them over his broad shoulder while collecting the man's weaponry, which was against the wall. With all of these things in his arms, Val headed back down to the level below Tevin's, the level with the women's chambers. He was just coming off the stairs when one of the panels opened and Vesper was suddenly standing in the doorway.

Wrapped in a heavy woolen robe against the cold temperature, her long hair was splayed over her shoulders, giving her a rather ethereal and angelic appearance. Before Val could say a word, she spoke.

"What has happened?" she asked. "Why are you running up the stairs like a madman? Why are the men shouting outside?"

She seemed worried and he sought to ease her. "Good morn to you, my lady," he said softly, avoiding her questions. "Did you sleep well?"

He was smiling at her so sweetly that the worry faded from Vesper's face and she smiled, her cheeks flushing. "Very well, thank you. And you?"

"Hardly at all for dreams of you."

The pink in her cheeks deepened. "I suppose I should be sorry to hear that but I am not," she said. "I am glad you were dreaming of me."

Val just stared at her, grinning like a fool. Simply looking at her made all of his troubles fade, for she had that effect on him. His heart seemed more at ease. But more shouting caught his attention; he could hear it coming in from her windows, which faced the bailey. It reminded him that time was of the essence. His expression sobered.

"I am afraid that I must go to Winchester sooner than we had planned," he said quietly, not wanting to frighten her. "Henry's army has been sighted approaching Selborne and I can only surmise that they are coming for me, so I must go with them to Winchester to explain to Henry what happened in Canterbury. Your father has already left Selborne and I would have you remain here with my mother while I am gone. I will send word to you when I can."

"Why is the army coming for you, Valor?"

The question didn't come from Vesper. It came from Margaretha as she emerged from her chamber down at the end of the short corridor. She, too, had just arisen and her hair, usually so tightly wimpled, was in a thick, gray braid that trailed down her back. She was wrapped heavily in a shawl, her gaze upon her son most piercing.

Val looked at the woman; she looked terrible. Her eyes were red-rimmed, something he'd never before seen on her, and his heart sank. He could see that she'd been crying. No matter that his relationship with his mother could be contentious at times and no matter that there were times he wanted to gag her, she was still his mother and he loved her. He was so very sorry to see how upset she was.

"As I was just telling Lady Vesper, I believe Henry is demanding my appearance and he does not want to take a chance that I will not come to Winchester sooner rather than later, so he is sending his army to escort me," he said steadily. "Please do not worry, Mother. Lord du Reims is positive that once evidence is presented in my defense that I shall be absolved of any crimes against Thomas Becket."

Margaretha came towards him, seemingly pensive, but her gaze moved to Vesper as she drew near. Now Vesper had her focus.

"I did not realize you were here, my lady," she said. "I retired early last evening. When did you arrive?"

Vesper, too, could see how overwrought Margaretha appeared. This was not the stern, firm woman she'd first met when she had come to Selborne. "At the evening meal, my lady," she said politely. "My father escorted me from Eynsford Castle. We had heard of the archbishop's assassination and... and I had to come. I had to tell Val that he had my support in this matter. I felt that it was important."

Margaretha's gaze moved over the young woman's features as she took a second look at her. Vesper was certainly lovely and well-spoken enough. She'd seen that from the beginning. Margaretha also remembered her level-headed decision making in the wake of her brother's execution, something Margaretha had admired. In spite of everything, she had some respect for the young woman who seemed to be caught up in a terrible circumstance with her father and brother. But for the fact that the woman had come to support Val... that action couldn't help but touch Margaretha's heart.

"I am sure Valor appreciates your devotion," she said. "I am sorry I did not know you were here until now. I would have made more of an effort to show you the hospitality of Selborne."

Vesper forced a smile. "My appearance was rather sudden," she said, looking at Val. "Your son was kind enough to be quite hospitable."

There was some expression that passed between the two that Margaretha caught, something warm and liquid. She couldn't help but think how much like his father Val looked at that moment as his pale eyes glittered at Vesper. She'd seen that expression on Gavin de Nerra's face, many times, and the meaning was very special to her. To see it in Val's features touched her more than she realized.

Mayhap he truly is in love with this young woman....

But thoughts of warmth and love were going to have to wait. There was an army approaching for her beloved boy and she couldn't shake the sense of foreboding she felt. It was becoming more weighty by the moment.

"Then I am glad he showed you such hospitality, for you are always welcome at Selborne," she said. Then, she turned her attention to her son. "As for Henry, I fear that he wants more from you if he is sending his army to escort you. Had he simply demanded your appearance, he would have sent a missive. Nay, this is more than that."

"What more?" Vesper asked, worried again as her gaze moving between Val and his mother. "What do they want?"

"To arrest him," Margaretha answered for her son. "That would be the only purpose of sending an army here. If Val refuses to surrender himself, then they will lay siege. Val thinks that I do not know this, but I do. They want my son and they want him badly."

Vesper looked at Val with increasing horror. "Is that true?" she asked. "Are they here to arrest you?"

Val cast his mother a long look, exasperated that she should be so blunt about the situation. "I am not certain," he stressed to them both. "But I must go to them. Mother, will you please entertain Lady Vesper until I return? She will be your daughter soon so I would like for you to get to know her."

Margaretha looked at Vesper again, who was looking up at Val with an expression that suggested she was verging on tears. Perhaps Margaretha wasn't thrilled with the swiftness of the marriage but, ultimately, she had to trust her son. If he thought the lady was worth his affections, then Margaretha would give him that benefit. Already, she liked the woman. Moreover, if she was to lose her son, then Vesper would be her last connection to him.

God, please do not let this be the last time I see my son….

"She will be my guest," Margaretha finally said. "I look forward to her company."

Val knew it was hard for his mother to say that. She wasn't happy with any part of the situation so he appreciated the fact that she didn't try to argue with him about it. When the situation was serious, as it was now, Margaretha knew how to behave. She didn't push. She simply accepted.

"Thank you," he said to his mother. "Now, I must go down to the bailey. Lord du Reims is waiting for me so we may ride out to meet the incoming army. Know that I will send word when I can, but I imagine I will be at Henry's mercy for the foreseeable future. You must not worry about that."

It was a futile statement considering both women were already worried. "You are Henry's cousin," Margaretha reminded him. "Do not let him forget that. He must treat you more fairly than most."

"I will not let him forget, Mother."

Margaretha had nothing more to say to him. Everything was in the hands of Fate now and there was nothing left to do but for Val to face what was coming. Lifting her hand, she put her warm palm on his cheek.

"Then God be with you, Valor," she said. "I shall pray for you."

Val smiled at his mother, bending down to kiss her cheek. He looked at Vesper and hesitated a moment before bending down to kiss her cheek, too. Perhaps, he shouldn't have done it in front of his mother, but that couldn't be helped. He wanted to make this a parting well-made, and that included a proper farewell to the woman he was in love with. He made his way to the stairs, leaving the stricken women behind him. He took the first step and then paused.

"Mother," he said, not looking at her. "I love Vesper. You will treat her as you would treat me. That would make me happy."

Vesper's eyes widened and she dared to look at Margaretha, who was looking at her son. "If you love her, then I shall, too," she said. "Go, now. Do not keep Henry waiting."

Val continued down the stairs without another word, leaving Vesper and Margaretha standing in tense silence. Margaretha finally turned to Vesper, who was looking at the dark stairwell where Val had disappeared. She could see the utter devastation in the young woman's features, the fear for the man she loved heading off into an uncertain future. Margaretha understood her fears very well, for she had them many a time when Gavin would head off to battle.

"Would you join me for the morning meal, my lady?" she asked. "If we are to know one another, we may as well start now."

Vesper knew she should accept. She should be gracious and polite and impress Val's mother. But she couldn't seem to manage it.

"Nay," she said after a moment, looking at Margaretha. "Forgive me, my lady, but I… I am going to Winchester with Val. I cannot let him go alone."

With that, she abruptly turned into her chamber and rushed to her satchel, hauling it up onto the bed as she began yanking clothing out of it. Margaretha, surprised by her declaration, followed her into her chamber but stopped just inside the doorway.

"My lady, that may not be wise," she said, struggling not to show her anxiety. "Valor would have asked if he had wanted your company."

Vesper didn't look at the woman as she yanked off the robe she was wearing to reveal a soft shift beneath. "He is trying to protect us," she said. "Of course he would not ask for our company. But I do not need to be protected. I have been alone my entire life, Lady de Nerra. I have spent eight years at Eynsford, living what Val called a polite existence. That is true. But that does not mean I am complacent. If the situation were reversed, Val would not let me go alone. He would not let you go alone. He would go with us and fight for us, and that is precisely what I mean to do. I have never in my life known anyone worth fighting for, but I do now. Val will not go this alone, I swear it. If anyone tries to separate us, I will kill them."

Margaretha watched as Vesper pulled a dark blue woolen gown over her head, struggling to fasten the stays as she pulled a pair of shoes out from beneath the bed. The woman was working furiously, trying to prepare herself to go after Val. Margaretha couldn't decide if it was a foolish venture or a brave one.

"But what can you do?" Margaretha asked, trying to be logical even though there was a large part of her that wanted to go with Val, too. "As much as I would also like to attend him, I fear that I would only get in the way. Valor does not need the added complication of an emotional female. And I fear that insisting on going with him might make him feel emasculated, as if he cannot defend himself and need's a woman's help."

Vesper was trying to fasten her dress and pull a shoe on at the same time. "If that is true, then I must take that chance," she said. "I cannot simply sit back and pray for the best. I must do all I can to ensure Val has someone to fight for him, to support him in his darkest hour. I cannot explain my feelings on the matter any better than this… I had no one until I met Val. I shall not let him go so easily. As he loves me, I love him, and I will fight for that love."

In spite of herself, a smile spread across Margaretha's lips. She was coming to like this girl a great deal, a lass who would fight for her son so fervently. A lass who loved him, perhaps not as deeply as Margaretha did, but that would come in time. But they needed to *have* that time. She walked up behind Vesper and pushed her hands away so she could finish fastening the dress.

"I have a dagger you can bring with you," she told Vesper. "Keep it on you but do not let anyone know you have it. That will be your secret in case it is needed. Do you have gloves and a cloak?"

Vesper pulled on her other boot as Margaretha finished her stays, pleased that the woman was helping her and not trying to stop her. Not that she had any doubts, to be truthful. Margaretha struck her as fierce that way. "I have a cloak but no gloves," she said.

"I have some you may borrow. It is cold outside. Wait and I shall return."

Margaretha darted from the chamber as Vesper quickly found her comb. Running it through her dark tresses, she braided her hair, tying off the end with a ribbon she had in her satchel. She was just swinging her cloak over her shoulders when Margaretha rushed back into the chamber and handed her an exquisite dagger with a bejeweled hilt, tucked into a small leather sheath. When Vesper took it from her, she looked at the woman, seeing an ally in this battle she was about to face.

"Thank you," she murmured sincerely. "I will not let Val out of my sight, I promise. I will fight for him until the death if I need to."

Margaretha hadn't really allowed herself to feel the fear of her son's situation until she realized how far Vesper was willing to go in order to protect him. She fought the tears that were trying to resurface.

"He is very fortunate to have someone like you, Vesper," she whispered tightly. Reaching out, she put her hands on the woman's shoulders and kissed her on the forehead. "If I were any younger, I would go with you, but I fear I will only be a burden. Go with my blessing and fight for my boy. You have my undying admiration for doing so."

Vesper looked into the face of the woman she had only known to be a grim shrew. But now, in this moment, she simply saw a mother who was terrified for her son. On some level, she felt bonded with the woman over their mutual love of Val. She forced a smile.

"I will do my best, I promise," she said.

Margaretha simply nodded her head, standing aside as Vesper rushed from the chamber. She could hear the woman moving swiftly down the stairs but, after that, the sounds faded and there was nothing but that terrible silence. It would kill her, she knew it. She couldn't simply stand idly by while Val was in such danger. Even if she was old, as she'd told Vesper, it didn't mean she shouldn't do the same thing the young woman was doing.

To fight.

Henry was about to have a battle on his hands.

CHAPTER NINETEEN

"I THOUGHT I asked for at least a day, Dacian," Tevin said sternly. "Why are you here? And why have you brought so many men with you?"

Less than a quarter of a mile from the front gates of Selborne, Tevin had met up with the incoming army from Winchester with d'Vant leading the contingent. But they'd come to a halt, with du Reims blocking their path, and Dacian pulled off his helm, propping the thing on his saddle as he faced the immovable force of the Earl of East Anglia. He ran his fingers through his blonde hair in a weary gesture.

"I had no choice," he said, reining his horse closer to Tevin and lowering his voice so the soldiers behind him wouldn't hear. "Over the past day, the news of Canterbury's death and of Val's involvement has spread like wild fire. Henry wants answers and he would not be put off, even when he knew you'd come to Selborne. He wants Val at Winchester to answer for what has happened."

Tevin sighed heavily. "Val did not do it," he said. "Do you recall how we were wondering what had happened to de Morville and FitzUrse and le Breton and de Tracy? I discovered that when Henry went hunting after Christmas, they delivered a forged message from Henry to Val demanding the arrest of Canterbury. Since Val had no reason not to trust them, he followed them to Canterbury where those four knights proceeded to murder the archbishop before Val could stop them. Now they are trying to push the blame on to Val when he is the one who has been wronged."

D'Vant looked at him in shock. "Are you certain of this?"

"Val has the forged missive with him. Those four have deflected the blame on to the man in a most atrocious way. Have they returned to Winchester?"

D'Vant shook his head. "Nay, they have not."

"Then they are on the run. They know that Val will prove his innocence to Henry and name the real assassins."

D'Vant's mouth popped open in astonishment as he digested the information. "My God," he finally hissed. "Those four have always been zealots for Henry, always trying to gain his favor, but I never imagined they would do anything like this."

"Nor did I."

"But why pull Val into it?"

"When you read the missive, you shall see. As Henry's law in Hampshire, he was ordered to arrest Canterbury and bring him to face Henry at Winchester Castle. There is nothing unusual about that request other than it was fabricated. Val went to arrest Canterbury but those four killed the man before he could."

D'Vant was beside himself. "Henry must know of this," he muttered. "Other than the missive, has Val any additional proof? Witnesses, mayhap?"

Tevin lifted his eyebrows. "Eleven men who witnessed the murder plus Hugh's brother, Calum, who spoke to Hugh when Hugh delivered the missive. I have never seen a less ambiguous case, Dacian. Val is innocent."

D'Vant believed him implicitly. "I must still take him to Winchester, now, to tell Henry the truth," he said. "It is imperative that Henry know."

Tevin nodded. "I know," he said. "Val will be here shortly with his witnesses. He is completely willing to go to Henry and tell him everything."

"What a quagmire this is."

"That is an understatement."

D'Vant abruptly caught sight of something over by the gatehouse of Selborne and Tevin turned to see men spilling forth on horseback, including Val, Kenan, and Calum. There were several soldiers with them but Val was in the lead, charging towards Tevin and Dacian. The sound of thundering hooves made some of the other horses nervous, made worse when Val finally pulled his horse to a halt and sprayed mud and rocks all over the legs of the other horses. Unhappy animals and frustrated men shuffled about, vying for control.

"Dacian," Val greeted the man evenly. "This must be serious if Henry has sent his Captain of the Guard. I would presume you have come for me?"

Dacian was trying to soothe his excited horse. "You presumed correctly," he said, trying to ascertain Val's state of mind – was he angry? Relieved? Fearful? "Lord du Reims just told me what happened with de Morville and the others. Do you have the forged missive with you? Henry will want to see it."

Val nodded, reaching over to hand Tevin his possessions. "I have it," he said. "Did he tell you everything?"

"I did," Tevin said as he settled his bags on the back of his horse. "He knows that de Morville delivered it to you. He knows that it was de Morville who killed Canterbury."

Val nodded, looking to d'Vant and seeing the man's bewilderment. "The missive was delivered by men who had delivered such missives to me before, Dacian," he said simply. "There was no reason not to trust them."

Dacian could see what a terrible misunderstanding this had been, a betrayal of Val and of his reputation. "There was no reason you should have," he said, disgusted. "That they used your trust to betray you… I am having a difficult time accepting that. These were men in my command for many years."

"And they were my friends for many years," Val said with a hint of regret. "But what they did… even if I am declared innocent by Henry, still, rumors are flying that I murdered Canterbury. It will take years to clear my reputation."

That was a very true statement and d'Vant felt deeply for him. He shook his head sadly. "I am sorry, Val," he said, his gaze moving to Calum, who was slightly behind Val. His ire rose. "Your brother did this. What do you have to say for him?"

Calum knew the anger wasn't directed at him, personally, but he still took it that way. His brother had made him look like a fool. "Nothing," he said flatly. "He sat with me in Val's solar and looked me in the eye when he told me his lies and handed me the missive that ultimately sent Val to Canterbury. Never, at any time, did I see any hint of mistruth as he spoke. I am as disgusted and astonished by his behavior as anyone else."

D'Vant didn't say anything more; this was not the place and now was not the time. They were not going to air all of this now because Henry was waiting for Val and the truth of the matter. D'Vant turned to Val.

"I have come to arrest you," he said. "You know this."

Val nodded. "I do."

"But after what I have been told, I do not feel right doing so. You are an innocent man, Val. I will not treat you like a criminal."

Val looked at the army behind d'Vant, at least a hundred men, who were all looking at him as if he was someone of suspect. He nodded his head in the direction of the army.

"Your men may feel otherwise," he said quietly. "Until Henry has declared me innocent, in their eyes, I am still a suspect. You had better restrain me until we reach Winchester or it may go badly for you."

"But…."

"Carry out Henry's orders, Dacian. You are to arrest me. Do it."

Dacian sighed heavily and looked to Tevin, who nodded reluctantly. He understood what Val had said, that it was better to fulfill Henry's orders for the moment. With great sorrow, Dacian then turned to the men beside him, who had heard everything. They, too, believed in Val's innocence, but Val had a point – the rest of the army didn't. They could certainly spread the word but until Henry absolved Val, there would still be those who would consider him a murderer. It was safer for Val if he was, indeed, treated like a criminal, at least until they reached Winchester. Therefore, the man next to Dacian reluctantly handed over a pair of shackles for Val's wrists.

Val saw the restraints and held his big arms out, extending them for Dacian. Begrudgingly, Dacian put the shackles on – they were two horseshoe-shaped iron bars for each wrist with a bigger bar that went through the loop ends of them, secured on one end with a big iron lock so the bar couldn't be pulled through. Everything was proceeding peacefully until another horse emerged from the gatehouse of Selborne, thundering down the road towards them.

Val and the others turned to see Vesper charging into their midst, kicking aside the men and horses that didn't move out of her way fast enough. She was smacking rumps of the horses that didn't move and slapping aside at least two men who tried to grab her. One man got too close to her and she clawed a hand, scratching his face.

Shocked, Val could hardly believe his eyes. He had no idea why Vesper was here, scratching and kicking men, but he soon found out. She planted herself between him and Dacian, pulling a dagger on Henry's knight. As Dacian's eyes widened with surprise, Vesper leveled the weapon most menacingly.

"Get away from him," she hissed. "If you touch him, I will kill you!"

Val was astonished. "Vesper," he said, reaching out and trying to pull her back. "Sweetheart, what are you doing? Where did you get the dagger?"

Dacian lifted his hands, slowly, to prove to the lady that he had no weapons. "My lady, I assure you that I have no intention of harming Val," he said. "Quite the contrary."

Vesper heard the question from Val but she was singularly focused on the knight who had evidently arrested him. She completely ignored

Val and his attempts to pull her away. "Then why do you shackle him?" she demanded. "He is not guilty of that which he has been accused. Honorless men assassinated the Archbishop of Canterbury and are trying to turn the guilt on to Val. He did not do anything except follow what he believed were Henry's orders!"

Dacian nodded patiently. "I know, my lady," he said. "Lord du Reims told me. Uh… may I have your name, please?"

"Lady Vesper d'Avignon," she said without hesitation.

"She is to be my wife, Dacian," Val said, trying to decide how he felt about Vesper's sudden and violent appearance. Truthfully, he was still shocked because he never would have imagined such a thing from her. "We were hoping to marry this morning but your arrival thwarted those plans."

Dacian understood a little more now. "Ah," he said. "So she is upset that her wedding was moved aside. That is understandable."

Vesper scowled. "That is *not* why I am upset," she said. "I am upset because an innocent man is being treated like a criminal. Remove those shackles from him immediately."

Dacian looked to Val, who shook his head faintly at the man. His shock was starting to wear off and he realized that he was very touched by her desire to protect him. The woman had a vast wealth of courage he couldn't even begin to comprehend, bravery she'd proven at every turn since their introduction. But this… this was beyond even what he believed she was capable of and his admiration for her grew.

So did his love.

"Vesper, sweet," he said. "Look at me."

Vesper shook her head. "I will not take my eyes from him," she said, referring to Dacian. "He means to harm you. They *all* mean to harm you."

Val was trying to calmly defuse the situation when one of Dacian's men, who was relatively close to Vesper, reached out to disarm her. She caught the movement and slashed at the man, who came away with a nasty gash to his wrist. Then she used her horse to push Val away from

Henry's men, all the while keeping herself between them.

"I will do the same to any man who tries to harm Val," she said loudly to the group. "If you would all like your flesh carved into, then by all means, try that again."

Val's astonishment returned as he watched her threaten an entire army with a dagger, but he felt enormous pride as well. This reasonable and wise woman had what men had – *valor*, he thought. *She has great valor*. But in this case, it was misplaced. It was also dangerous. She fully intended to use that weapon on his behalf and he simply couldn't allow it. Reaching out, he managed to get hold of her sleeve.

"Come here," he said quietly, tugging on her arm. "Give me that dagger before you kill someone."

Surprisingly, Vesper pulled away. "I will not," she said. "I am sorry if it displeases you, but I cannot let these men harm you. The only way I know to prevent that is to go with you to Winchester. Do not tell me to remain here at Selborne because I will not. I am going. I discussed it with your mother and she is in support."

Val's heart broke, just a little. He could see how frightened she was, which had spurred her bravery. "It is not necessary, I promise," he said calmly. "The man you pulled your dagger on is Dacian d'Vant. He is Henry's Captain of the Guard. He will ensure I have very fair treatment so you needn't worry, I swear it. And look – Lord du Reims will also ensure my protection. You trust him, do you not? Now, please, give me that dagger."

Vesper's gaze moved to Tevin, who was several feet away from Val and watching the entire scene with a good deal of sorrow. She could see it in his face. But her focus returned to Val and she shook her head, her eyes welling with tears, tears she tried very hard to chase away.

"Nay," she said tightly. "I will not. I will protect you until we reach Winchester. If you tell me to stay behind, know that I will simply follow you so you may as well accept my presence. I will be your guard."

Val thought it was about the sweetest thing he'd ever heard. He'd never had anyone in his life willing to protect him so, but he also knew that she had no idea what she was really getting herself in to.

"Sweetheart, listen to me," he said quietly. "I promise you that Dacian and Lord du Reims will protect me. I will not be mistreated. But every one of those men has a sword much bigger than that dagger you hold and if they really wanted to get at me, they would carve right through you. I do not wish to see you in such danger, not when I am fighting for my very life. I would sacrifice all to protect you and, in the end, mayhap one of those swords would carve through me instead. Do you understand what I am telling you? I love and admire you for your fierce support, but it would be much better if you gave me the dagger and returned to my mother. She will be in need of your comfort right now."

"I have never heard anything so ridiculous."

The voice came from behind and Val turned to see his mother riding up on one of her small gray palfreys. Swathed in gray wool from head to toe, she blended with the cloudy morning and gray sunrise. At the sight of her, Val's men instantly parted and permitted her to pass between them, for no one wanted to get in Lady de Nerra's way.

Val didn't think he could be any more astonished but he was wrong. As he watched, his mother pulled out his father's broadsword, something she'd slept with since his death. It was fairly heavy but she laid it across her lap as she rode up between Val and Vesper.

"God's Bones, Mother," Val said, shaking his head. "You must have the hearing of a dog to hear what I just said to Vesper. What on earth are you doing here?"

Margaretha eyed her son. "Your voice carries and, believe it or not, I am very familiar with it," she said. "I have heard many things you thought I could not."

"I would believe that."

Margaretha's gaze lingered on her son for a moment before turning to Tevin. "And you allowed them to put shackles on my son?" she asked the earl. "I thought you were going to protect him."

Tevin sighed heavily, not wanting to agitate the women who had rushed forth to save Val. He understood that they were frightened and, in truth, he could see his own wife doing the very same thing, which was why he was so patient with the interruption. "It is necessary for now, Lady de Nerra," he said. "No one means to harm him, I swear it. And I will protect him with my life if that is the case. You have my word."

Margaretha was mildly comforted by his declaration but not entirely. Her focus moved to d'Vant. "Dacian, I am displeased," she said in a tone that all men feared. "You have shared my table many times. I know your mother. Why have you come to arrest my son? He is innocent of the murder of Canterbury. If no one has told you that, then I will."

Dacian would rather face all the armies in France than the formidable Lady de Nerra. "I have been told, my lady," he said. "And I am under orders from Henry. I must return Val to him so that Henry, too, may know of his innocence."

Margaretha glanced up at the sky, now considerably brighter with the sun just peeking over the horizon. "Then let us waste no more time," she said. "Lead on, Dacian. We will follow."

"Wait," Val said, his tone bordering on frustrated. He looked at Dacian. "Please, move the army out. I will join you shortly. It seems that my womenfolk are bordering on rebellion and if I do not stop it, they will threaten everyone."

Dacian was glad it wasn't him having to do the duty, especially not against Lady de Nerra. Quickly, he reined his horse around and motioned to the men. "Gladly," he told Val. "You will hurry, please."

Val didn't respond; his gaze was on Vesper and his mother. Margaretha was looking at him quite stubbornly while Vesper was looking at Margaretha, seemingly surprised by her appearance. Val was coming to think that Vesper didn't know of Margaretha's plans simply by the expression on her face.

But no matter; he had to end this before it got out of hand. As Tevin, Calum, and finally Kenan were the last men to follow Dacian and the soldiers several feet down the road to wait, Val endeavored to convince his mother and Vesper to return to Selborne.

It wasn't going to be easy.

"Ladies," Val said, trying to be very understanding and patient with them because he knew that anything else wouldn't work. "I admire your bravery more than I can say. I am deeply touched that you are trying to protect me. But I do not require your assistance at this time. I would appreciate it if you would please return to Selborne. That is my wish."

Margaretha, who was unimpressed by his words, turned to Vesper. "Coming from a man with shackles on his wrists, I take no stock in his assurance," she said. "Shall we go, my lady? If you will ride on his other side, we shall make an excellent escort, you and I. No one will dare cross us to get to him."

Vesper nodded eagerly, reining her horse to Val's other side. When he looked at her, baffled, she slapped the butt of his war horse and the animal bolted forward. "Your mother and I intend to escort you and there is nothing you can do about it so you may as well accept it," she said as she trotted alongside him. "I am not trying to be disrespectful, Val, but surely you cannot expect us to simply wait for you and pray that Henry forgives you. It would drive me mad to wait and I am sure it would not do your mother any good, either. Do you not understand that we do not want anything to happen to you?"

Val was reining his horse back, slowing it down as Vesper's slap on the rump had jolted it. "And do you not understand what a fool I will look like with two women as my escort?" he shot back softly. Seeing her face fall, he hastened to apologize. "I am sorry, sweet, I do not mean to be cruel, but you are not helping me. You are making me the laughing stock."

His words cut her but she would not surrender. "Better a laughing stock than the admired dead," she said, wounded. "As long as your mother and I ride with you, those men will not dare harm you."

Val couldn't believe he was debating this with her. "Why? Because of that dagger?" he asked, pointing out the obvious. "I have already told you that they have swords much bigger than that dagger, Vesper. They will slice through you quite easily. Is that what you want me to see? My future wife slain before my eyes?"

"They will not touch her," Margaretha said. "I will take out the first man who tries. If you do not believe me, then watch and see. I am not so feeble and old that I cannot swing this sword. Since no man wishes to die by a woman's hand, it will keep your haters at bay, at least until we reach Winchester."

Val was on the end of a losing battle. Shaking his head, he grunted unhappily, lifting a hand to wipe at his face because this situation was so unbelievable. "So you are telling me that simply because a man does not want to have the shame of being slain by a woman, that alone will keep me safe?"

"Exactly."

Val hated to admit it, but there might actually be some truth to that. A man's pride was funny that way. But he had to try one last time.

"Mother, please," he begged softly. "Think of your bad heart. Of your health. This trip will be most taxing. Will you not go home? *Please*?"

Margaretha was facing forward, looking at the waiting army up ahead with the sword still laid across her lap. "I cannot," she said after a moment. "I have my future grandchildren to protect, and my legacy, so I must see this through regardless of my health. Henry will listen to the evidence presented. If he does not, he will be very sorry."

Val cocked a disbelieving eyebrow. "Are you actually going to threaten the king if he does not release me?"

Margaretha didn't look at him. For a moment, she didn't reply, seemingly lost in thought. "It is said that Rosamunde travels with Henry these days as part of his court," she said, almost casually. "I know the girl. I met her at Winchester two Christmases past. Do you recall?"

She spoke of Rosamunde Clifford, Henry's beloved mistress. That talk made Val nervous because Margaretha was a friend of Eleanor of Aquitaine, Henry's wife. Val's mother and father had shared a monogamous marriage and, as far as Val knew, his father had never taken a mistress, but any talk of mistresses upset his mother greatly. She felt very strongly that a mistress or concubine was immoral.

"What about Rosamunde, Mother?" he asked suspiciously.

Margaretha looked at him, then, and Val didn't like what he saw in her expression. In fact, it frightened him. Such black determination there, something unmovable and… wicked. Aye, it was wicked.

"If Henry does not release you of all charges, it would be a shame if the dagger that Vesper holds finds its way between Rosamunde's ribs," she said. "It would make one less whore in court."

It was a cold thing to say, shocking and cruel, but not something out of the realm of possibility when it came to his mother. Now Val understood the blackness to her expression… and he believed every word.

"I have never heard you speak that way," he said.

"That is because my son has never been threatened before. If Henry is going to condemn you, then I will make sure he pays the price."

"So you are coming with me to kill Rosamunde?" he asked, incredulous.

Margaretha sighed and looked away again. Her gaze moved over the winter-dead landscape. "Do you see this land, Val?" she asked. "This is what my soul would be should you leave me. I would be as dead as the ground in winter. Therefore, I have nothing to lose if something happens to you. And an old woman with a weapon can be a deadly thing, indeed. Remember that."

Val pulled his horse to a halt. They were nearing the army and he didn't want their conversation overheard. "Am I really hearing this correctly?" he asked. "Are you truly telling me that if Henry does not absolve me of Canterbury's death, then you will go on a killing rampage to punish him?"

"No one will suspect an old woman."

Val was stunned. Margaretha hadn't reined her horse to a halt when Val had and was continuing to plod forward, so he spurred his horse and caught up to her quickly, blocking her.

"Is that how you would have others remember the House of de Nerra?" he hissed. "A son who was blamed for killing Canterbury and a mother who went mad because of it? Because that is not how I wish to be remembered. If you are serious about this, I will have Dacian put you in irons right now. I will not let you spout threats against Henry and possibly get us all killed when I am quite sure this situation will be amicably resolved. I know you are frightened, Mother, but you must be reasonable. I need your level head. I want to return home when this is all over and marry Vesper and have those grandchildren you so badly want, but I must have your promise that if anything happens, you will not follow through with this insane threats. Promise me!"

He boomed the last two words and Margaretha jumped in spite of herself. That cool exterior she was projecting suddenly fractured as Val's anger was unleashed. She looked at her son, trying not to appear startled by his shout. After a moment, she merely nodded and looked away again but that wasn't good enough for Val. He bent over, grabbing her by the arm.

"Say it," he hissed. "Promise me you will do nothing."

"You are hurting me."

"I do not care. Promise me."

Margaretha was stubborn but she wasn't foolish. Moreover, she had always been willing to give in to Val's wishes, no matter what they were. As difficult as it was for her, she surrendered.

"I promise."

Val released her immediately, looking over at Vesper, who had listened to the entire conversation. She didn't look surprised by it; in fact, she looked as if she understood. Something about those beautiful hazel eyes conveyed understanding in Margaretha's position. *I have nothing to lose if something happens to you.* Val cocked his head at her.

"I do not have to worry about you, do I?" he asked quietly. "You will behave yourself, will you not?"

Vesper nodded, but it was reluctantly. "I will do what you wish me to do."

"Then go back to Selborne."

"Anything but that."

He started to get mad but the ridiculousness, the seriousness, of the situation overwhelmed him and he just ended up laughing about it. It wasn't a humorous laugh, either – it was one of disbelief and frustration. But the truth was that, all things considered, he knew he was a very fortunate man to have two women so devoted to him. Brave, bold women who would do anything for him, including kill for him. As foolish as it was, he was touched by it deeply. Men should be so lucky to have such rabid devotion in their lives. When he thought he'd lost everything – his reputation, his freedom – perhaps he hadn't really lost anything at all. Perhaps those things he'd taken for granted had been the better part of him all along.

The love of not one good woman but two. It gave him the strength to face what he must.

"Very well," he said, knowing there was nothing short of having them taken back to Selborne in ropes that would force them to return there. "Then stay close to me. We have already wasted too much time. The king is waiting."

Vesper and Margaretha didn't leave his side the entire ride to Winchester.

CHAPTER TWENTY

Near Winchester Castle

"I WONDER IF Henry knows."

It wasn't a question as much as it was a statement. De Morville, riding in the lead of the group as Winchester Castle came into view against the dark morning sky, hissed irritably.

"Of course he knows," he said. "Everybody knows. We have spent all of this time hiding in tiny villages and sleeping in beds that had families of bugs crawling all over them so we could stay out of sight but, still, people in these towns were speaking of Canterbury. Of course Henry knows. Everybody knows!"

Stubbled, exhausted, and feeling a great deal of remorse for his actions of that terrible night in December, le Breton's dark-rimmed eyes peered out from beneath the heavy cloak he wore.

"Val has already been to Winchester," he muttered. "He has already told Henry what has happened. He said he would. I should have never listened to you when you said we had to hide. We should have come to Winchester immediately."

Hugh yanked back on his horse's reins and reached for his broadsword with the intention of going after Richard, but Reginald FitzUrse stopped him. "Nay," he said, putting himself between the two men. "Richard is right. We should have come to Winchester right away. We should not have delayed as we did."

Hugh sucked in a deep breath, struggling to calm his frayed nerves. "We needed to think on what to do," he reiterated again. "All of you believed it to be the right course of action at the time. It was far better for us to take the time to stay out of sight and decide a course of action."

"Look at us," William de Tracy spoke. He lifted his arms beneath his worn cloak as if to make an example of himself. "We stole these clothes, sold our fine horses, and now we find ourselves on beasts that we should be eating rather than riding. No one would suspect that we are four of Henry's knights and that is how we planned it but, still, we find ourselves riding to Henry. Richard is correct; we should not have panicked and gone into hiding. We simply should have gone to Henry to tell him what had happened. We did this for him, did we not? He should be glad for what we did. If we believed he ordered us to kill Canterbury, then we should have run back to him to announce it."

Hugh was feeling as if they were blaming him for his insistence that they conceal their identities and stay away from Winchester in the days following Canterbury's assassination. He sighed heavily. "So we are returning now to tell him everything and pray for his blessing," he said. "If he does not give it, then we must make it clear that we were following Val's lead. It will be the four of us against him. That is why we gave him the forged missive, is it not? So Val would take the blame if Henry is displeased. We must insist on this."

William shook his head in disgust. "If Val has already gone to Henry, then Henry knows that we instigated it," he reminded Hugh. "Moreover, Val had several men with him who will vouch for the fact that Val did not kill Canterbury; we did. And what *of* that missive? Henry will know that it was forged and Calum will testify that we gave it to him. Henry will know that we were at the root of everything!"

Hugh was feeling his position weaken by the moment. Coming into Winchester from the south, they could see it ahead about a half a mile. The morning was gloomy and a hint of rain was in the air as Hugh finally pulled his horse to a halt. The other three followed suit, all of them looking at the city ahead.

"And so, it comes," he said quietly. "Do we enter Winchester and tell Henry that we have rid him of his nemesis? Or do we go to him and blame Val de Nerra for it?"

FitzUrse, his gaze locked on the castle in the distance, spoke. "If we believed this was Henry's order, then we should have no shame in telling the king what we have done."

Hugh looked at him. "We were convinced enough when we planned the event."

"Now I am not so sure."

Truth be told, Hugh wasn't, either. None of them were. The aftermath of the event caused them all to wonder if they'd done the right thing. Doubt was what had caused them to go into hiding. The doubt was still there, gaining in strength.

"If we tell him what we have done and he is displeased, it could mean our end," Richard said. "I am not entirely certain that Henry will be happy with what we have done."

"Nor am I," William said quietly. "Val told us to return to tell Henry, but I am not willing to meet my end today. Let us flee England and send Henry a missive from afar, seeking his counsel on our actions. Let Val explain his role in all of this; I, for one, am not ready to face Henry. Come with me if you wish, for I am leaving the sight of Winchester behind me."

He turned his horse south, for there was a road leading east a mile or so back, a road that would lead them across southern Hampshire to another road heading north into London. There, they could make an escape if they chose to because today wasn't a day for confessions. Men who had been so convinced of a royal order weren't so convinced any longer.

It was easier to let another take the blame.

One by one, the other knights followed him, all of them fleeing Winchester and the justice that awaited them. It was easier to escape what they'd done rather than face it.

Face a king who had lost an old friend by their hand.

CHAPTER TWENTY-ONE

VESPER HAD NEVER been to Winchester Castle but she'd certainly heard tale of it. Coming in from the northeast on that gloomy morning, she could see the vastly large complex to the southwest, looming above the town that surrounded it like the jewel in a crown.

The village of Winchester itself was a fairly large establishment, having been one of the places that the Duke of Normandy began laying down his foundation of conquest so many years ago. Winchester Castle had been part of that and as the party from Selborne drew near, the size and structure of the castle began to come into view. It was positively enormous, a huge fortress surrounded by a moat big enough to be a lake.

It was past the nooning meal by the time they arrived in town and most people had gone about their morning business, but there were still a great many villeins who paused before their homes or places of business to watch the gang of knights and two small women ride by.

The homes near the edge of the town were newer, of waddle and daub construction and pitched roofs, while the homes nearer the center of the town and towards the castle were older. Some weren't particularly well-kept and more than one home could be seen in the midst of repairs.

Vesper thought it was all quite fascinating, even fascinating enough for her to forget why they'd come. She's spent the last several hours in silence, riding alongside Val, keeping her dagger in her hand in case some fool tried to harm him. In truth, it had been rather exhausting to be so edgy all of the time and unable to relax, so by the time they'd reached Winchester, she was feeling a good deal of fatigue. But she pushed it aside, ignoring the aches and the hunger because she knew that, now, they were quickly approaching what would soon become Val's fight for life. Henry was waiting for him in the walls of that enormous castle and she wouldn't let her guard down until it was all over.

Until Val was free.

On the other side of Val, Margaretha hadn't uttered a word, either. She kept that enormous broadsword across her lap as she rode and Vesper was growing increasingly concerned for the older woman. Vesper knew that if she was exhausted, then Margaretha must be feeling it, too. But to her credit, Margaretha remained stoic and calm. That seemed to be her usual manner, which Vesper was coming to appreciate. But she wondered just how that calm demeanor would hold once Henry confronted Val. The very fact that Margaretha had come at all showed that she was a lioness who wasn't about to let her cub fall victim to Henry's anger.

The great gatehouse of Winchester faced east so they skirted the moat, heading for the big structure at the head of the bridge that spanned the moat. Vesper's attention was torn between the castle and its ominously big walls and the village off to the west that they had recently passed through. People were still watching them, like a passing parade, but Vesper's attention ended up on the gatehouse when they finally reached it.

That was when the situation became interesting.

Passing through the gatehouse hadn't been anything out of the ordinary, the horses' hooves creating hollow sounds as the clopped across the bridge that led into the vast bailey of Winchester. But once they reached the bailey, littered with outbuildings and another smaller set of walls that isolated the keep off to the north, it was as if a massive army was waiting inside for them.

Soldiers were strewn all over the ward and makeshift camps were dotted all through it, accompanied by the appropriate rubbish and scents. It smelled like a zoo of men. As the incoming escort came to a halt, armed men approached from the direction of the keep, making their way through the hundreds of soldiers in the bailey.

"My lord," a heavily-armed soldier bearing a crimson tunic with the royal lion on it addressed d'Vant. "Henry has sent me to bring the prisoner to him. He has seen your party coming from the east for quite some time and demands his presence."

D'Vant dismounted his war horse, turning it over to one of the grooms who had rushed out from the stables.

"No need," he told the soldier calmly. "I will escort de Nerra."

"But Henry said…."

Before d'Vant could respond, Tevin suddenly appeared from around the rear of Dacian's horse. He had just dismounted his steed and, in hearing the soldier's request, decided to intervene. He wasn't going to trust Val's safety to soldiers he didn't know. It would be a feather in the cap of any soldier to claim he was the one who killed Canterbury's assassin.

"The prisoner is not your responsibility," he snapped. "De Nerra will be taken to Henry but not by you."

The mighty Earl of East Anglia was not to be tangled with; every fighting man in Henry's service knew that. The soldier backed away somewhat.

"Aye, my lord," he said, now seemingly nervous that he had roused Tevin's anger. "Henry asked that he be brought to the hall."

"Then he shall. Now, get out of my sight."

The soldier backed away to stand with the other men he'd brought with him as du Reims charged past them, heading in the direction of the hall in search of the king and leaving d'Vant to escort Val. But the armed soldiers sent by Henry were eyeing Val quite critically as the man slid off his horse and removed his saddlebags. In spite of his shackled wrists, he went to help his mother from her mount.

Vesper, meanwhile, had dismounted, still holding that dagger as if it meant life or death for Val. There was no way she was going to relinquish it. As she went to stand next to Val and Margaretha, one of the armed soldiers that had come to take Val to Henry shouted.

"Murderer!"

Val didn't even react; he didn't so much as look up. He was in the process of trying to convince Margaretha to turn the sword over to d'Vant but Vesper heard the shout and it infuriated her. Dagger in her hand, she moved in the direction of the heavily-armed soldiers.

"Who said that?" she demanded. "Who was it? Are you so cowardly that you shout from a group of men so you can hide behind them? You should be ashamed!"

Val's head snapped in her direction when he heard her angry voice. Quickly leaving his mother, he rushed to Vesper just about the time d'Vant got to her. Dacian, too, had heard her angry challenge. Val had her by the arms as d'Vant put himself between Vesper and the armed soldiers.

"My lady, your bravery is astonishing," d'Vant said, a twinkle in his eye. "I should be so fortunate as to have such a courageous lady to protect me. But it would not do to challenge those men. They are ignorant and you would only be wasting your breath."

Vesper was so angry that she was trembling. "Why do you let men treat Val like this?" she asked. "You know he is innocent yet he bears chains as if he is guilty. Why do you let him shame himself so in public?"

Dacian looked at Val, regret in his expression. "It was not my idea, my lady, I assure you."

Vesper's brow furrowed and, puzzled, she turned to Val also. "Then why do you wear these shackles?"

Val had his hands on her arm; his wrists were chained too closely together for him to grasp her any other way. "It is better this way," he said quietly. "Dacian will not get in to trouble with Henry and men will believe I have had no special treatment because Henry has ordered my arrest. We are simply following the wishes of the king, so do not trouble yourself over fools that believe only rumor."

He was pulling her back, away from the armed men, but Dacian turned around and ordered the group away. Grumbling, they went. Once they were far enough out of range, Dacian motioned to Val.

"Come along, then," he said. "The sooner we get this over with, the better."

Val still had hold of Vesper, fearful of what would happen if he let her go. She was fully willing to attack a group of grown men with her little dagger because she believed they had slandered him.

"Agreed," he said. "Would you mind escorting my mother? I fear my hands are full."

That was metaphorical as well as literal as far as Dacian was concerned; Lady Vesper was quite a handful, to be sure. Taking a few steps in Margaretha's direction, Dacian held out a hand to her.

"Lady de Nerra," he said politely. "I would be honored to escort you into Henry's hall."

Margaretha was pale with exhaustion but her posture and the tone of her voice suggested otherwise. "Take me to Henry," she said, putting her hand on his arm. "I have a need to speak with him."

"Indeed I will, my lady."

"*Immediately*, Dacian."

Dacian was again glad that he wasn't a target of Lady de Nerra's rage and he didn't envy Henry one bit. The man was going to have trouble on his hands, very soon. Without hesitation, he began to lead the woman towards the hall that had been built in the time of the Duke of Normandy as the rest of the group, including Val and Vesper and Calum, followed. Since the duke built Winchester and the castle had served, for many years, as the seat of England, it had a long hall built of stone with a steeply pitched roof that was designed for large gatherings. Rather than a hearth to warm the space, it had a fire pit in the center of it. As the group approached, they could see smoke escaping from holes near the roofline.

It was a hall where Henry conducted business as his forefather once had. The great oak doors yawned wide to admit the entire party into the hall. The floor was covered with stale straw, ankle-high, to keep in the warmth in the cold winter temperatures, but the smell of it was quite overwhelming. Food had fallen from the tables into the straw and, if not eaten by the dogs, had subsequently rotted, so the entire hall had a rotting-food smell coupled with the scent of the dogs who were roaming the hall in packs.

The aroma was quite pungent and when Margaretha entered, she was hit by the smell and, for a moment, came to a pause and briefly closed her eyes, sickened. D'Vant thought there was something genuinely wrong with her and looked at her with concern, but she waved the man on. He took her deeper into the hall but when Vesper entered behind them, she wasn't quite as tactful in her reaction as Margaretha was. Her hand flew to her nose.

"Sweet Jesù," she gasped. "What a stench!"

Val looked around the hall for Henry, mostly, but he had a faint smirk on his face as he did so. "It is your punishment for demanding to come along," he muttered. "Now you must sit in this filthy smell. It is probably rotting the inside of your nose as we speak."

Vesper looked at him in horror, her hand still over her nostrils. "You could not have warned me?"

"Would *that* have made you remain at Selborne?"

"Possibly."

"Then I was a fool not to mention it."

He was grinning at her and, in spite of herself, Vesper started to laugh. The smell really was atrocious. But more than that, it was the first relaxed word she'd had with Val since leaving Selborne. She used her free hand to squeeze his arm.

"It would not have made me stay at Selborne," she said softly. "Please do not be angry with me for coming with you. Had the situation been reversed, you would not have stayed away from me. I cannot stay away from you."

The smile faded from Val's face. "I suppose I understand," he said. "And I do appreciate that you are so fiercely loyal."

"I would do anything for you."

His pale eyes glimmered at her, very much wanting to kiss her but he didn't dare. This wasn't the place. "Anything but return to Selborne."

She fought off a grin. "Anything but that."

He snorted softly before giving her hand a gentle squeeze. "When Henry enters, say nothing," he said softly. "Do nothing. I believe all of this can be resolved quickly with the evidence I will present, so do not make it more difficult for me with emotional outbursts. Will you promise me?"

Vesper nodded, but it was with reluctance. "Even if he is terribly wrong and cruel?"

Val lifted his eyebrows. "This is the king we speak of," he reminded her. "He can be as wrong and cruel as he wants to be. But he is not unfair or unreasonable. All will be well in the end, I swear. But mind your tongue."

"I promise."

The twinkle in his eye was back. "Good lass," he said. "Now, let us find a place to sit in this mess. I see that Dacian has seated my mother; let us go and join them."

Truthfully, Vesper was grateful for it. Although her rump was sore from riding, she very much wanted to sit on something that wasn't moving. There were three fairly large feasting tables in the hall, placed in the shape of a horseshoe, and Margaretha was sitting at the end of one of them. Vesper took a seat next to her on a bench that had splinters sticking out of it, so she sat close to Margaretha to avoid the splinters. But sitting next to the woman meant that Val moved away from her and she suddenly stood up, planning to follow him until he put a hand out to silently direct her to sit again. She did, unhappily, as Val went to Dacian and lost himself in quiet conversation with the man.

Vesper never took her eyes from him. She was feeling some apprehension now that they were in Henry's smelly hall, knowing that the king would soon make an appearance and all of the horror and rumors of the past several weeks would soon be made clear for all to hear. All that Val had suffered through would finally be resolved and she found herself praying fervently for the king's mercy so that they could be married and begin their life as husband and wife. Perhaps that was a selfish hope but she couldn't help herself.

She just wanted this to be over.

They'd been through so much since their acquaintance, things that should have ended any budding romance. Her father's manipulation, his lies, her brother's execution… any one of those things should have stopped a relationship between her and Val before it even got started, but they hadn't. Whatever bond they had between them was stronger than her father's scheming and the demands of Val's duties. It was something that was worth fighting for.

And she would fight until the very end.

Off to her right, Vesper could see Kenan and the soldiers from Selborne, men who had been present when Canterbury had been killed. They were here as Val's witnesses to the fact and her apprehension was eased somewhat at the sight of them. Surely Henry could not deny what so many men had witnessed. She could also see Calum, carrying Val's saddlebags and the forged missive contained therein that was the key to this entire terrible situation. Poor Calum. He was a pawn in this ploy as much as Val was. He had been the one at Selborne to receive that fateful message.

Thoughts of Selborne brought thoughts of her father. She hadn't seen him since last night. Val had said he'd left Selborne before dawn and Vesper wasn't sure if she would ever see him again. It was odd, however, considering how much McCloud had seemed to want her forgiveness for what he'd done. She didn't think he would have left before they at least had some understanding between them, but she couldn't think of that now. At the moment, Val's situation had all of her attention. Her father would have to wait.

"De *Nerra!*"

The hair-raising cry distracted Vesper from her thoughts. It came from the far end of the hall as a door swung open and men began to appear. Everyone in the hall turned to the source of the shout as a well-built man with dark red hair, badly cut, came into view. He wore a full beard, dark with shades of gray in it, and was wrapped in heavy woolen tunics that looked as if they hadn't been washed or mended in some time. *Slovenly* was the first thing that came to Vesper's mind when she saw him. But before she could turn to Margaretha and ask who the man was, the older woman was on her feet and heading straight for the agitated figure.

"My lord Henry," Margaretha said loudly. "I have come with my son to face your good justice. Would you disrespect me so by not greeting me first?"

Henry wasn't in any mood for pleasantries. He'd come racing to the hall from the keep when Tevin had appeared with tales of Val de Nerra's innocence but the truth was that Henry wanted to hear it from the mouth of his itinerant justice. He'd spent the past few days building up such an outrageous scenario about Canterbury's death that it was now more nightmare than truth.

Because of that, he was desperate to speak with Val but Lady de Nerra, Val's mother, would not be overlooked. To do so would be a grave mistake on Henry's part and he knew it. Therefore, he forced himself to focus on Margaretha. He smiled at her, his teeth gapped-toothed but not unhandsome. In fact, he laughed when he saw her.

"I should have known you would come, my lady," he said. "In fact, I am glad you have come. Mayhap you can explain to me what your son has done just as du Reims has tried to explain to me. What is this madness that I am hearing about him?"

At that moment, Tevin emerged into the hall right behind Henry. Having run off to find the king before the man faced Val, he'd spent the past few minutes explaining to the king what had really happened at

Canterbury. But Henry wanted to hear it from Val and had charged out of the keep before Tevin could finish his tale. Henry moved fast when he wanted to and he'd escaped the Earl of East Anglia in search of the only man who could give him the answers he sought –

Val de Nerra.

But there was the small matter of getting through Margaretha first. Before Margaretha could reply to Henry's greeting, Tevin came up behind Henry and pointed to Val. "De Nerra has been arrested just as you asked, my lord," he said to Henry. "But he should not have been. As I have told you, he is an innocent man and he can prove it. Val, tell Henry what happened and spare no detail. Do it now."

Margaretha was forgotten as all focus shifted to Val. In fact, Val found himself gazing steadily at the king. He and Henry had always shared an excellent relationship and as he studied the edgy expression on the man's face, a bevy of thoughts raced through his head, not the least of which was regretting the fact that he'd not confirmed de Morville's missive with Henry from the start. That would have prevented all of this.

… or would it?

Taking a deep breath, Val summoned his courage.

"I was away from Selborne when Hugh de Morville, Reginald FitzUrse, Richard le Breton and William de Tracy arrived bearing a missive that I believed was from you, my lord," he said evenly. "I have brought the missive with me so that you may see it. The missive instructed that I was to arrest the Archbishop of Canterbury and bring him to Winchester to face your justice. The missive threatened to strip me of my appointment should I refuse, so naturally, I obeyed."

Henry was listening to Val intently, soaking up every word from his mouth. Upon the mention of the missive, he interrupted Val from continuing.

"This missive," he demanded. "Where is it?"

Val turned to Calum, who had his saddlebags. Swiftly, Calum came forward and laid the bags on the table nearest Val, untying the flap before digging in to the pouch. But Henry recognized the knight and his eyes narrowed.

"De Morville Secundi," he said, referring to the fact that Calum was Hugh's younger brother. "What do *you* know of your brother's actions?"

Calum knew this moment would come. He swallowed hard as he pulled forth the fateful vellum that his brother had given him, more fearful than Val was in a sense. It was his brother who started this and Calum who gave the missive to Val. Aye, he was guilty as much as Val was. He prayed that Henry didn't see it that way.

"My lord, I can only tell you the same thing that Val can," he said. "I was the one my brother gave the missive to. He had me read it before Val did. When I asked him why Val should be given this duty, he told me that it was because he was the law for all of Hampshire and since Winchester is in Hampshire, it is his jurisdiction. My lord, never at any time did I have the slightest hint that he was lying to me. He and the other knights all told the same story and all confirmed that the missive came from you. There was no reason for me to doubt my brother and no reason for Val to doubt him."

Henry's expression was starting to tighten, a distinct sign that he was becoming angry. "And he told you that de Nerra was to arrest Becket and bring him to me?"

Calum nodded and extended the missive to Henry. "See for yourself, my lord."

Henry snatched the vellum and unrolled it, his eyes greedily devouring the carefully written words. Tevin was looking over his shoulder as were a few other advisors, all jockeying around behind the king to get a look at what he was reading.

Time seemed to go unreasonably slow as the king read the fateful missive. It was agonizing. But the more Henry read, the darker his face became. By the time he was finished, all of that darkness came to a head and he exploded in a bellow of sheer fury that echoed off the roof, reverberating violently against the walls. Even the men in the hall, standing around and watching the scene, were uncomfortable with the cry. It was an ugly sound.

It was a sound of utter pain.

"This!" Henry held up the vellum. "This did not come from me! I did not send this!"

Calum was starting to fear for his safety. He looked at Val, who appeared equally concerned. "We know that now, my lord," Val said, hoping Henry didn't demonstrate that anger on him and Calum. "But at the time, we had no reason to believe you did not send it. It was delivered by men I trusted, men who have delivered dozens of such missives from you. There was no reason to believe this one was any different."

Henry was so angry that he was trembling. "But this was *not* from me," he said, shaking the vellum at Val in a threatening manner. "Did you not think to confirm an order of this magnitude?"

Val had, but he wasn't going to say so. Only his complete belief in the truth of that missive would save him and he knew it. "I have never questioned an order from you, my lord," he said simply. "It was not my place to confirm an order signed by the king."

That was very true and Henry, above his rage, realized that. He was coming to see that the terrible plot he'd suspected was not something Val de Nerra was behind. He wasn't systematically trying to destroy the hierarchy of England, starting with Canterbury. Henry knew that had been a foolish consideration to begin with but a fearful man will think many things, not all of them reasonable. Clearly, Val was caught up in something beyond his control which should have eased Henry, but it didn't. He was becoming distraught.

"Tell me what happened at Canterbury," he finally demanded. "Tell me everything."

Val knew this would be the hard part. "When I returned to Selborne and read the missive, de Morville and the others were already a day ahead of me, heading to Canterbury. They said they were going ahead of me to try and convince the archbishop to surrender to me peacefully. I left immediately to follow them, taking twenty men with me as well as my knight, Kenan de Poyer. Kenan witnessed everything I did at Canterbury's cathedral, as did the soldiers I brought with me. I have eleven witnesses to what happened there, my lord. It was… not pleasant."

Henry's eyes widened with impending horror. "What? Speak, man!"

Val briefly thought on being tactful about it but decided that wasn't the course of action to take. He wanted to paint the horror of what de Morville and the others were capable of so Henry would know the depths of the betrayal and horror they were all facing.

"We arrived in Canterbury at the West Gate Inn, the location that Hugh indicated where we should meet him when we arrived," he said. "We entered the city close to Vespers and de Morville and the others were not at the inn, so I suspected they might have gone to the cathedral, knowing that Becket would be there for the evening prayer. We went to the cathedral and were heading around the side of the structure where the cloister is when we began hearing the signs of a struggle. We rushed into the cathedral, near the quire, only to see de Morville and le Breton delivering a death blow to Becket. The man's head was in pieces and his brains were all over the ground. From my perspective, it seemed to me as if they intended to cut Canterbury to pieces so I stopped them. When I asked de Morville why he had killed him, he told me that Becket attacked him with a staff and he killed in self-defense. My lord, I saw no staff on the ground so I chose not to believe him. I told him to return to Winchester to confess to you what he had done. I further told him that I would be telling you what I saw, as I am now. So help me God, this is the complete and unreserved truth. I never lifted a finger against Becket, at any time, but I was too late to protect him from those who sought to kill him."

By the time he was finished, Henry's cheeks had gone from an angry red to a sallow pale. Visibly shaken, he stared at Val for several long seconds. Even Tevin, who had not heard the detailed testimony of the event, looked taken aback, as did Henry's advisors and nearly everyone else in the hall. It was an utterly horrific description.

"And so, they killed him," Henry finally muttered, oddly calm in contrast to the shouting man from moments earlier. Now that he knew the truth, he was deeply grieved. "Thomas' blood was spilled at the very ground upon which he served. But I do not understand why these knights should do this. I did not command it. I did not ask it of them. Why should they do this in my name?"

"To please you, my lord," Tevin said, subdued. "These knights have always sought your favor. They knew of your extended trouble with Canterbury. Mayhap, they sought to seek your favor, once and for all, by ridding you of a most troublesome priest."

The words hung in the air between them, sharp and cutting, but it was enough to jolt Henry. *A most troublesome priest....*

He suddenly turned on du Reims, his eyes wide as a sense of foreboding swept him.

"Those words," he hissed. "I spoke those words, once. I did!"

Tevin nodded, realizing that a great deal was coming clear to him at that moment. It was tumbling over him like an avalanche. "At Bures Castle," he said. "I heard you say them. Everyone in the room heard you say them. In your anger, you shouted them."

Henry's mouth flew open, a gesture of astonishment as he, too, began to grasp what Tevin already understood. "They thought...."

"That you meant them. Aye, my lord, I believe they did."

"So they concocted a scheme to rid me of him!"

"For your favor, I am sure. Mayhap, they even believed you gave a command. In any case, they lied to Val and now he stands here before you, not them. He has taken their blame. Val is innocent, my lord. You must release him."

Henry was astonished by the pieces of a terrible puzzle as they came together to present of picture of appalling proportions, but one thing was for certain – it all made perfect sense. Now, he was starting to understand what had motivated these knights to kill on behalf of the king.

Words from the king himself.

Who will rid me of this troublesome priest?

After a moment, Henry turned to Val. "And you," he said. "Did they seek to deflect the blame on to you? Because they have succeeded marvelously. Everyone in England believes you have killed Canterbury."

Val watched as Tevin, standing next to Henry, snapped his fingers at d'Vant, pointing to the shackles on Val's wrists. D'Vant immediately moved forward to remove them as Val addressed Henry's statement.

"Unfortunately, they do, my lord," Val agreed, feeling some relief as he came to realize that Henry understood his role in the situation. "When I arrived to prevent de Morville from chopping Becket to pieces, I had several soldiers with me, men bearing my crimson and white standard. That is why the rumors say I killed him. Clearly, I was there."

"But you tried to stop it."

"Aye, my lord. I did."

Henry was beside himself with what had happened, the depth of the deception perpetrated in his name. Wearily, he planted himself on the end of the nearest bench, his mind overwrought with everything he'd been told.

"Then you have been treated most unfairly," he said. "You are being falsely blamed for something that is most serious while the real murderers have fled like cowards."

D'Vant finished removing the last shackle and Val rubbed at his wrists where the iron had chaffed his skin. "It would stand to reason that I should have thoughts of revenge against de Morville and the others, but I am more concerned with myself at the moment," he said. "I am afraid it will take some time to restore my reputation in this regard and it greatly concerns me, to be truthful. It will make the execution of my duties as itinerant justice far more difficult if men believe I have murdered a priest."

Henry sighed heavily. "It will make it impossible," he said. "Even if you are innocent, there will be those who cannot be convinced of it. I will do all I can, of course, to let the nobility know that you had nothing to do with Canterbury's death, but the common man… the fools who live and die by God's word… may never believe it. They may never trust you again."

Val knew that but it was still difficult to hear. He made his way to where Henry was sitting, leaning against the tabletop in a weary gesture. After a moment, he shook his head. "It is unfortunate," he finally said. "I have greatly enjoyed my royal appointment. I have executed my duties to the best of my ability and have built a great reputation. And now… now it is all gone. Everything I have worked for is gone because of men who were trying to gain your favor."

A sense of desolation filled the hall as the men began to realize that Val's life as the Itinerant Justice of Hampshire was over. It was a position of law he could never hold again, through no fault of his own, because there would always be those who doubted his credibility. He'd been betrayed and ruined by men he trusted.

It was a grossly unfair situation in the purest sense of the word.

No one understood that better than Vesper. She had been listening to everything, horrified anew by the details of what Val had been involved in, realizing as everyone else did that Val's reputation was in ruins. Although she'd promised Val she would not speak, something in her simply couldn't remain silent. The man she loved, the great and noble knight she deeply respected and admired, was seemingly at an end but she couldn't accept that. She refused to. Something had to be done but they were all standing around, looking as if they were preparing for a funeral. Well, there would be no funeral if she had anything to say about it.

"Then you must help him, my lord," she said, her voice trembling with nerves because she knew she should not be speaking. "Val is a great and noble man who has shown that greatness in just the short time I have known him. He has an infallible sense of justice and duty and it is completely unfair for such a man to be ruined. You cannot allow that to happen."

Henry looked up to see an exquisitely beautiful woman standing in his hall. He hadn't noticed her when he entered but he was noticing her now. As he watched, Val went over to her, giving her a rather disapproving look. Henry pointed.

"Who is this woman?" he asked.

Val put his arm around Vesper's shoulders as he faced the king. "This is Lady Vesper d'Avignon," he said. "We are to be married."

That seemed to bring back at least some of Henry's humor. The dark eyes twinkled. "What a right and glorious announcement," he said, looking to Margaretha, who was still standing a few feet away from him. "And you, Lady de Nerra? Does this please you?"

Margaretha was still in the throes of relief over the fact that Henry wasn't going to punish Val for his role in Canterbury's assassination. She was feeling rather lightheaded, in fact. When she realized that Henry was addressing her, she eased herself down onto the bench behind her.

"Pleased?" she repeated. "I am positively ecstatic. I shall finally have some grandchildren."

It was a light moment in a circumstance otherwise wrought with anxiety and sorrow, but Vesper wasn't willing to give in to whatever weak humor was about. She was still deeply concerned for Val and his future. She didn't want the subject turned away from Val and his situation so she sought to bring it back to that focus.

"May I tell you how dedicated Val is to his duty, my lord?" she asked, pulling away from Val and moving in Henry's direction. "My father is McCloud d'Avignon. He fought for you in France. He and Val became very good friends."

Henry cocked his head thoughtfully. "D'Avignon?" he repeated. "I know this man."

Val nodded as he came up behind Vesper. "McCloud was with me six years ago when we moved into Normandy and Brittany to reclaim your lands there," he said. "He was also with me two years later when we punished your unfaithful barons in Normandy. He was a good knight."

"Was?" Henry said. "He has passed?"

It was Vesper who answered. "He is alive, my lord, but he is not the same man," she said. "Although I do not wish to sully my father's reputation of the past, the truth is that he has changed. Recently, he met Val again after a few years of separation and plotted to take advantage of him. You see, my father has fallen into poverty over the years and my brother, who was a grown man with the mind of a child, took to murdering people and stealing their food so he and my father could eat. My father should have stopped him but he did not. When my brother was captured in the midst of a crime, it was up to Val to dispense justice since the crimes were committed in his jurisdiction. Although Val and I were becoming fond of each other at the time, Val could not let that sway his good judgment. He did what was required of him and executed my brother for murder. The point, my lord, is that Val is a man with an unbreakable sense of right and wrong. He is too good a man for you to allow a mistake to ruin him. You must help him regain what has been wrongly taken from him – his reputation."

Henry was listening to Vesper with some sympathy. She was a lovely, well-spoken woman and he saw what Val saw in her. As a man who appreciated a beautiful and accomplished woman, Henry had a rather high opinion of Vesper after hearing her speak.

"He truly executed your brother?" he asked. "A son of an old friend?"

"He did, my lord, but only because it was required of him. I am sure he took no pleasure in it."

Henry's gaze moved to Val only to see a rather ambivalent expression on his face. Certainly there was no pleasure there but there may have been a hint of regret. It was then that Henry began to understand the bond between Val and his lady, something that wicked fathers, executions, and rumors could not destroy. That kind of connection was a rare thing.

"Mayhap he did not," he said. "But any man who would execute his lady's brother is a man of duty, indeed. And you do not hate him for it?"

"I do not, my lord."

Henry nodded, his gaze still upon her. "I would believe that, because you are here with him when my order was only for Val to face me. Yet, you and his mother have come as well. This kind of thing is not for women to observe."

As Val cleared his throat softly, with some embarrassment, Vesper held up the small bejeweled dagger. "I was afraid men, in their anger over Canterbury's murder, would try to harm him," she said honestly. "I did not come without a purpose in mind. I came to protect him."

Henry's eyebrows lifted. Then, he started to laugh, a great laugh that had half of the hall grinning because of it.

"Even from me?" he asked.

She shrugged hesitantly. "Mayhap, my lord. Are you going to release him?"

Henry threw up his hands. "I am afraid of what you will do if I do not. Of course he is released, my lady. But as you know, that does not solve his problem. No matter what I say, there will be those who believe he murdered Canterbury."

"Then how will you help him, my lord?" Vesper asked anxiously.

Henry sighed heavily, his smile fading. He stood up from the bench he was seated on and pensively wandered over to the advisors who had followed him into the hall, Tevin included. He looked at Tevin, in fact, as he stroked his chin.

"What say you, du Reims?" he asked. "How can we salvage de Nerra's reputation?"

Tevin's gaze moved to Val, who was standing with Vesper, his big hand enclosing hers. He could see the apprehension in their manner although Val was trying very much not to show it. Still, he knew the man was concerned, as he should be. He felt a good deal of pity for them both.

"Val is a great knight, my lord," he said. "The man shines on the field of battle. I have seen it."

"Excuse me, my lord, may I speak?" A powerfully built man with a massive beard moved out from the rear of Henry's advisors, moving to the forefront where Tevin was standing. His gaze was on Val as he came to a halt near Tevin. "Do you remember me, de Nerra?"

Val peered at the man a moment before realization dawned. "Percy," he said, a faint smile coming to his lips. "Of course I remember you, my lord, although I have not seen you in many years. You did not have the forest growing on your face when last I saw you."

William de Percy, a cousin to the mighty de Percy family of the north and the military commander for Agnes de Percy, the family's only heiress, grinned in return. "It has, indeed, been a long time since we last met, but I never forget a man or his reputation. When I heard that you were in league with a scandal, I could hardly believe it. Now I see that my instincts about you were correct."

Val nodded sincerely. "Thank you, my lord."

William's attention lingered on Val for a moment before turning to Henry. "Mayhap, I can help de Nerra," he said. "It seems to me that the man cannot return to his duties as itinerant justice, as you have discussed, but it is through no fault of his own. That is clear. That being said, England is a vast place, my lord, with many needs. I am here because of your needs in Ireland, my lord. You have a thousand de Percy men in your bailey even now, waiting to join with other men to move out to your properties in Ireland to defend against the Irish king. I have excellent knights in my ranks but a knight of de Nerra's caliber would be not only desirable but necessary for a successful campaign. Mayhap you should consider that."

Henry's expression lit up as if a great idea had suddenly occurred to him. "Of course!" he exclaimed. "Send de Nerra to Ireland! He was invaluable to me in France for so many years and now Ireland needs the same wisdom and strong sword. A brilliant solution!"

Val was listening to the conversation with great interest and perhaps even great reluctance. He'd gone to France before when he had no wife and a multi-year military campaign hadn't been a concern to him. But now, he had Vesper to think of. He wasn't sure he wanted to leave her for years on end.

"If you wish for me to go to Ireland, then I will, of course, obey," he said hesitantly. "But… but I would still have to return to England. Men do not forgive so easily, my lord. I fear I would return to the same suspicion and anger. Moreover, my mother is here… my wife would be here also. I could not leave them, knowing how men now view the de Nerra name."

Henry and William looked at him, noting Vesper standing next to him, looking the least bit concerned. Certainly, sending Val away would be the best thing for him, but he had a point – what of the women he left behind? They would be left in the aftermath of Val's scandal. Henry scratched his chin again, thinking on a resolution to that particular issue.

"You could not take the women with you on campaign," he said. "It would not be safe for them. You know that."

Val did. "That is true, but it would not be safe to leave them at Selborne without my protection," he said. "Men know that my seat is Selborne. Zealots intent on avenging Canterbury will be looking for me there and I cannot leave them alone in a fortress that attracts dangers such as that."

William looked at Vesper in Val's grasp and then to Margaretha, who was still seated and looking rather exhausted, before turning to Henry.

"I believe I have a solution," he said. When Henry nodded encouragingly, William looked at Val. "As you know, the north of England has need of good men. Threats from the Scots abound and the de Percy family has many holdings that are in need of protection. There is a large castle that guards a strategic pass from Scotland that is in need of a strong hand. Currently, a de Percy cousin mans the castle and, although he is an excellent commander, he is growing older. The time will soon come for him to be replaced. Upon your return from Ireland, you can assume the post as the de Percy family's most respected military commander and your wife and mother will join you at that time. Meanwhile, if you do not wish to leave the ladies at Selborne Castle, your mother and wife can go to Holystone Castle and live with my two spinster sisters, a myriad of animals, and a full contingent of soldiers until you return. Northumberland is a beautiful place; I am sure they would enjoy it."

Val knew it was a good offer. It was better than anything he could have ever hoped for. Men were willing to protect him and Vesper and his mother from the vengeance of Canterbury's faithful and he was deeply grateful. But it still meant going to Ireland, something he didn't want to do. All things considered, however, it was necessary. He knew that the best thing for him would be to go away and let the fervor of the assassination die down.

In truth, he had no other choice.

"What is this castle you speak of?" he asked William.

"Black Fell Castle," William replied. "It is a big place and very strategic."

Henry, seeing Val's hesitation, knew why. But much as Val knew, he, too, knew that this was an excellent offer.

"Val," he said frankly. "Ride at the head of the de Percy army into Ireland. I will send more of my men with you and you shall be in command of all royal troops in Ireland. Black Fell Castle is in the Gilderdale Vale, which is very strategic and rich. I shall bestow the title of Baron Gilderdale upon you as well as the property of Black Fell Castle, but you shall serve the House of de Percy as their most trusted advisor. All of this shall be far from Canterbury and the terrible memories, and you may reclaim your reputation and start your life anew. This is an excellent opportunity for you to restore that which you have lost."

Val was astonished. "It is, indeed, my lord," he said. "I am more deeply honored than you can ever know. But if I go north, what becomes of Selborne? It is my mother's ancestral home. It has been in her family since before the time of the Duke of Normandy. Do we simply walk away from it?"

Henry shook his head. "Nay," he replied. "I will garrison it for the crown. Calum and your other knights can remain there, in command, but I will also put my men there. Should you ever want it back, it is yours."

That was more than fair. Frankly, this wasn't what Val had expected when he'd come here today. He'd expected anger and punishment but what he'd received was understanding and rewards. God's Bones, it was too good to believe. The chance to reclaim his honor and start anew… aye, he'd lost a great deal, but he'd not lost everything. There was still something in the destruction that had been his life and reputation that was worth saving, a hope that was greater than the darkness around it.

Val looked at Vesper. The hope that had been salvaged was something he saw in her eyes, something that couldn't be killed by rumors or destroyed by men. It was *her* hope he felt. He felt it to his very bones.

"A moment, my lord," he said to Henry.

Taking Vesper by the arm, he led her over to where Margaretha was seated. Crouching down so he was at his mother's eye level, his gaze moved between the two women.

"I do not believe I have any choice in this matter," he said quietly, "but the offer could not be more welcome. Henry is giving me a great opportunity to restore my honor. Mother, surely you can see that. I realize it means leaving Selborne, but we shall not lose it. It shall still remain your holding. And you heard Henry – he will grant me a title and my own property. As much as I am proud to inherit what you and my father have left me, to earn my own way… it has been a dream of mine."

Margaretha was gazing into her son's face, seeing how very much he wanted what Henry had offered. She had not the heart to refute anything about it.

"Then if this suits you, accept it," she said softly. "Selborne is simply a pile of stones, Valor. Do not worry about leaving it behind. The legacy

I have always spoken of is inside of you. You carry it with you by your bloodlines and your deeds. You honored the House of de Nerra and the House of Byington the day you first held a sword and wielded it with honor. Now, Henry is giving you an opportunity at rebirth – leaving the old Valor de Nerra behind and creating a new one. I do not mind you leaving to go to Ireland or even to Northumberland, but I am an old woman. I will remain at Selborne."

"Nay," Vesper said, grasping the woman's hand and holding it tightly. "You must come with me, wherever Val wishes me to go. I will not leave you behind."

Margaretha smiled at her. "Valor does not need me any longer," she said. "Don't you understand? I have done my duty with him. Now it is your turn to help him reclaim his greatness."

Vesper frowned. "He is already a great man," she said. "It is your love and support that have made him so. He cannot lose that now. Besides… if I move far away, you will never see your grandchildren."

That thought gave Margaretha pause. "You have a point," she finally said. "But you two must be married before he departs for Ireland or there will be no chance of grandchildren."

Vesper didn't dare look at Val, knowing that her statement wasn't exactly true. There was already a chance for grandchildren but that was their little secret. She wasn't quite sure what to say in response but Val didn't give her the chance. He leaned forward and kissed his mother on the cheek.

"We are a family," he said. "I could not stand leaving you behind at Selborne while sending Vesper to the north. She is right; you must go with her. You must help her and she must help you. And when your grandchildren are born… you must be one of the first faces they see. Please, Mother… come with us to embark on this new life. It would not be the same without you."

Margaretha smiled faintly. "So much like your father," she whispered, putting a hand on his dark hair. "You are so much like him at times that it is frightening. And I never could deny him his wants, either."

"Then you will go north?"

"I will go north."

Val sighed heavily, feeling more relief at her agreement than he cared to admit. He turned to Vesper, seeing that she was looking at him with an expression between apprehension and pride. It was an expression that filled him with strength he never even knew he had. Kissing her hand, he looked deeply into her eyes.

"I will be gone for a long time," he said softly. "Mayhap even years. I know this is not something you expected, but your support in the matter means everything to me."

Vesper smiled faintly. His hand was holding hers, still up by his lips, and she leaned forward to kiss his hand as he had kissed hers.

"You are a great man," she said hoarsely, fighting off tears at the thought of a long separation. "You must be allowed to restore that greatness. Wherever you go, and for however long you are gone, know that I will love you just as I do now until I die. No separation or war can destroy that. When you return to me, it will be as if you have never left."

Her words gripped his heart, squeezing it, making him feel such longing for her already that it was tearing him apart. But he couldn't think on that now; he couldn't destroy their last few hours together with his melancholy. Cupping her face with his free hand, he kissed her on her soft, warm lips.

"And I shall love you and no other, for always," he murmured. "Have no doubt that I shall return to you, Vesper. I belong to you."

Vesper was trying very hard not to weep. The tenderness of this moment was shattering her into a million pieces of longing but she fought it. "As I belong to you."

Val kissed her once more before standing tall. Still holding Vesper's hand, he faced Henry and William.

"We are agreeable, my lord," he said, trying to swallow away the lump in his throat. "I will go to Ireland and my mother and my wife will go to Northumberland. I cannot thank you enough for your generosity, my lords, all of you."

Henry grinned, that gap-toothed smile. "My wars in Ireland are already won," he announced. Then, he held out both arms as if to embrace the entire hall. "Good lords and good ladies, may I introduce you to Baron Gilderdale, commander of my armies in Ireland. Long may he live and prosper."

Val simply shook his head at the pomp and circumstance of a sometimes-dramatic king, fighting off a grin when he saw Tevin and William smiling openly at him. Somewhat embarrassed, he scratched his cheek, turning to glance at Calum and Kenan standing several feet away only to see that they were laughing at him in a joyful sort of way. That brought about his own laughter, a release of tension and an expression of delight in the course his future had taken.

Where Val thought there had been no hope, hope anew rose from the ashes. He was stronger than before, a knight bound for the glory that was Ireland, with his mother and wife safe in England, protected by friends and allies who weren't willing to see him fall from grace. Instead, they had been there to help dust him off and set him on his feet again.

Even in the darkness, there was light.

But there was also a slight problem.

"Wait," Val said, turning to Henry as the man seemed apt to hunt down food and drink now that business was concluded. "If I am to leave for Ireland, then I would like to marry Vesper before I go."

Henry flashed that famous grin. "I happen to know of a cathedral nearby," he said. "I will send word to the Archbishop of Winchester to perform the mass."

"How soon will I leave for Ireland?"

Henry sobered, just the slightest. "We are waiting for more men from Dorset and they should arrive by the morrow. As soon as they come, the army shall depart."

"Then there is no time to waste for my wedding."

And waste time, they did not. In her traveling clothes and with the King of England in attendance, Lady Vesper d'Avignon married Sir Valor de Nerra at the entrance to Winchester Cathedral that very night as a faint dusting of snow fell from the dark and swollen sky. Once the vows were taken, everyone moved inside for the great mass and the wedding blessing.

It was a night of great rejoicing and happiness, but no one was rejoicing more than Margaretha. Finally, her bachelor son had taken a bride and she couldn't have been more pleased about it. The entire wedding feast consisted of more talk of grandchildren, at least as far as she was concerned, and when the newly married couple retreated to their borrowed chamber in the keep of Winchester for the night, a slightly-drunk Margaretha made sure they understood that their purpose that night was to conceive a child.

Henry egged her on and poured more wine into her cup as Val rolled his eyes and carried his bride away. Only when he was out of sight did he grin at the sight of his drunken mother demanding grandchildren.

With his wedding night before him, he intended to do his best to obey her.

EPILOGUE

Holystone Castle
May, 1173 A.D.

IT WAS A glorious spring day, abnormally warm this far north, but Vesper wasn't complaining. The sun felt wonderful on her face as she stood at the edge of the kitchen yard, watching Margaretha stand in the middle of the fowlery where chicken and ducks and their young gathered.

But Margaretha wasn't standing there simply for something to do. She was watching her grandsons run about, chasing the newly hatched ducks and admonishing the boys to be gentle with the little creatures. Gabriel and Gavin de Nerra, identical twins born nearly nine months after their father had departed for Ireland, were just over a year and a half years of age and, as Margaretha put it, they were wicked personified. They ran around like madmen, ate heartily, hated to be bathed, and generally caused a ruckus around Holystone, which had been a quiet castle until the birth of the two ruffians.

But they were precious ruffians. William de Percy's two spinster sisters, Lady Arietta and Lady Blossom, had been disturbed by the babies at first but very soon came to tolerate and even love them. Now, they vied for time to tend them with Margaretha, greatly displeasing the woman who had waited so long for them. But the wait had been worth it; she adored the boys who looked much as their father did at that age.

Bright, sweet, and spirited, she thanked God daily for their exhausting presence.

But they needed a strong hand, one she was more than willing to lend. Even now, she stood over them as they chased chicks and ducklings, her attentive eye watching their every move.

"Gabriel," she said imperiously. "Be kind to the ducklings. That's right; be very gentle. Gentle… *nay!* Do *not* kick them!"

Gabriel hadn't made contact with the duckling but his move had been naughty, naughty enough that Margaretha grasped him by the arm and pulled him away from the ducklings. Terribly unhappy, Gabriel began to wail as his mother came to his rescue and took him from his grandmother.

"It is nearly the nooning meal," Vesper said, wiping the tears from her son's face and trying to soothe his crying. "Please bring Gavin. I believe they both need to eat and then rest for a time. Gabriel is only naughty when he is tired."

Margaretha cocked an eyebrow at the whimpering child. "Gabriel is naughty when he believes he can get away with it," she said, patting the little boy on the cheek. "Val was much that way. He will outgrow it."

Vesper simply grinned, carrying her child out of the fowlery as Margaretha followed with the equally unhappy Gavin. Both boys wanted to stay and play with the spring babies but their mother and grandmother had other ideas.

A gentle wind blew through the grounds of Holystone and Vesper tried to distract her crying son, pointing to the birds, the sky, and even the soldiers who were repairing a provisions wagon near the front gates. The castle was too small for a gatehouse but it did have an abnormally tall wall around it, great protection against the marauding Scots who occasionally made their way this far south.

But those instances were rare. In all, Holystone had been a beautiful place to live and Vesper was very happy here with her children and with Margaretha. But one thing was obviously missing.

Her husband.

Val had been in Ireland for almost two and a half years, the longest years in Vesper's life. She'd known him so short a time before he departed that, in some ways, he was like a dream to her, something from her memory during one of the most turbulent but happiest times in her life. Nightly, she closed her eyes and tried to picture his face or hear his voice, but with time, those memories had faded. It was difficult to remember what he looked like or the sound of his voice, but that didn't matter – her love for him was just as strong as it had ever been. Time hadn't been able to erase the powerful bond between them.

Every time she looked at her boys, she could imagine what Val looked like. Sometimes, they would smile in a way that would jog her memory and she would think how much they looked like him. Margaretha commented on it constantly. Ever since Val had left for Ireland, they had been companions. And they had become very close with each other. Vesper couldn't remember much of her own mother and Margaretha filled a big void for her, something she appreciated deeply. Yet, as far as a fatherly void, she'd never really had one.

McCloud had been with her all along.

"Why is my grandson weeping?"

Coming from behind the wagon that the soldiers were repairing, McCloud appeared with a tool in his hand. He'd been helping the men level off the broken wagon but Gabriel's cries had lured him away. He tossed the tool aside and headed for Vesper as she tried to soothe her grumpy, weepy son.

"It is time for his nooning meal and a nap," Vesper told her father. "There is nothing wrong with him that food and sleep will not cure."

McCloud wasn't convinced. He pulled Gabriel out of Vesper's arms and began to rock the boy, singing to him and gently swinging him around to distract him. Gabriel's cries turned to giggles as McCloud turned circles with him in the bailey. Vesper couldn't help but smile; her father was really quite good with the boys, attentive and kind. This was the man she'd remembered from her childhood before poverty and hopelessness had turned him into someone else.

She knew that now.

But she almost hadn't. She had no contact with her father until after the twins were born and, even then, it had been at Margaretha's insistence. Vesper had spent months after the birth of her boys in a depressed state and she'd lamented more than once the loss of her father and how she missed the chance to forgive him when he'd begged it of her.

At first, Margaretha hadn't been sympathetic. But over time, she encouraged Vesper to ease things with McCloud, especially now that he had grandsons. So, Vesper had sent a missive to him all the way in Durley. She had told him of the births, and of her life, and McCloud's reply had been to come to Holystone to see his grandsons. Not even a bad winter that year could have kept him away and he appeared one evening, nearly frozen to death, demanding to see his grandchildren.

He never went home after that.

Now, McCloud was a fixture at Holystone. The relationship with Vesper that had been so terribly damaged by his lies had slowly been repaired. It had taken time for him to earn her trust again, and Margaretha's trust even, but he'd work hard at it. He was fully aware of what he'd nearly lost. Nowadays, the father/daughter relationship was better than it had ever been and Vesper was grateful for his presence. He was a very wise man and, many a time, he'd give her comfort and advice on Val's long absence. Slowly but surely, more trust – and a stronger relationship – was built.

Therefore, she appreciated moments like this because her life could have so easily been different. As McCloud entertained Gabriel, Margaretha walked up leading Gavin by the hand, Gavin was rubbing his eyes and whining. Margaretha picked the boy up, soothing his irritation.

"The cook says that it will rain later today," she said. "More's the pity. It has been a beautiful two days since the last storm. Any more rain and I shall become waterlogged myself."

Vesper glanced up to the sky with not a cloud in it. "I do not know how she knows, but she is always correct," she said. "This has been a very wet spring."

The five of them began to move towards the keep, a squat, square-shaped structure that was powerfully built. Holystone didn't have a great hall but the entry level of the keep was one big chamber that served as their hall. The spinster sisters kept it very clean, with no dogs and a thrice-daily sweep. This hall was their destination since that was where they ate their meals.

"I am weary of so much rain," Margaretha commented as Gavin struggled to get out of her arms. "It is unfortunate because when the weather is good as it is now, the children can run and run until they collapse. When they are kept inside the keep because of the weather, I am not sure who goes more insane – me or them."

Vesper grinned. "Summer will be here very soon and then they can run outside to their heart's content," she said as the steps to the keep came near. "But I do hope Val returns home before they are too much older. I had so hoped he would get to see his sons when they were small."

They'd wandered to the subject of Val's absence, which was a frequent subject these days. Vesper's longing for her husband had been intense and they were all aware of the fact.

"His last message to you said that he had hoped to come home soon," Margaretha reminded her. "That was back in March. It is quite possible that he is already on his way here."

"And it is equally possible that Henry will keep him in Ireland," McCloud said, putting Gabriel on his feet because the boy was squirming so. "I have heard the soldiers speaking of what is happening in Ireland and they say that Henry has taken on a large-scale building project of many castles to keep the Irish lords at bay. Val and I were in France for four years before we returned to England, so it is possible that Val will spend more time in Ireland."

Vesper didn't like that thought. But she knew her father was only being pragmatic about the situation. Still, there were days when she didn't want to be pragmatic. She wanted to take the boys and travel to Ireland to find her husband. It was tragic that her children hadn't even met their father yet, something that very much hurt her heart. He was missing out on so much of their lives.

Without anything to say to her father, she began to take the steps to the keep only to come to a halt when Gabriel escaped McCloud's clutches and ran off screaming. Vesper and Margaretha watched McCloud as the man tried to corral the squirrely little boy, but Gabriel had no intention of being captured by his grandfather. He began to run around the wagon that was being repaired in the bailey, much to the amusement of the soldiers.

Because he was being so fussy, Margaretha set Gavin to his feet as well, holding tight to his little hand so she wouldn't be in the same position that McCloud was, but Gavin had learned a trick with his grandmother – if he bit her fingers, she would release him, so he clamped down with his baby teeth, forcing a yelp from his grandmother but she most definitely released him. He was off like a shot, running into the bailey and screaming with glee.

"That little beast!" Margaretha said, rubbing the spot where he'd nipped her. "He bit me! Again!"

Vesper couldn't help but grin at her naughty boys. "They are very clever, both of them," she said. "Would you not say so?"

Margaretha shook her head. "Naughty little beasts."

Vesper began to laugh. "I am sure Val will be very proud of their resourcefulness."

"If I do not beat it out of them before he knows what devil spawns he has fathered."

Vesper continued to laugh, turning to put her hand on Margaretha in a gesture of pity only to see that Margaretha was smiling, too.

"You are the one who wanted grandchildren," she reminded her.

"I must have been mad."

Still chuckling, Vesper headed off after Gavin, who tended to be the faster of the two. Margaretha didn't run these days as McCloud did, so chasing down the twins fell to Vesper and her father. As they tried to run down the two little boys, over by the main entrance, the men threw the big iron bolt across the gate and began pulling the gates open.

The old gates creaked and groaned on their hinges as they were opened. Seeing daylight beyond the gate, Gavin switched course and began to run for the opening. Vesper picked up her pace after him, reaching him just about the time the gates opened enough to admit men on horseback.

Vesper wasn't paying any attention to the men who had entered Holystone; she was more concerned about her sons who very much needed to eat and sleep. Gavin was screaming in her ear as she walked away from the gates, so much so that she barely heard someone shout her name. In fact, the shout came twice before she turned around to see who was calling her.

A very big knight had entered at the head of a large contingent of men, all of them looking seasoned and, quite frankly, weary and beaten. Mail was damaged, tunics were dirty, and horses were shaggy from a brutal winter. As Vesper peered at the men curiously, because some of them were still coming in through the gate, the big knight ripped his helm off.

"Vesper!"

It was Val.

Realization hit Vesper so hard that her knees nearly buckled. In fact, she almost stumbled with the baby in her arms but she caught herself, astonished to the bone as Val vaulted from his horse and began running in her direction. Vesper could hardly believe it; all she could do was stand there and gasp. *He was here!* God, how many times had she dreamed of this moment? It seemed like a million, at the very least. But when the moment finally came, it came so subtly that she found she was hardly prepared.

Was it a dream?

Was he truly here?

He called her name again, snapping her out of her shock. With a cry, Vesper forced her legs to work, running towards Val only to be intercepted by Gabriel, who had escaped McCloud and was running for parts unknown. She managed to reach out and grab her other son, who threw himself onto the ground and began to scream.

Now, she had two screaming boys in her arms as she tried to run to Val but she simply couldn't do it. Too much struggle, perhaps too much shock, had her stumbling to her knees. It didn't matter, however. Val was on her so quickly that she could hardly draw a breath before he was kissing her furiously, his arms going around both her and their screaming sons. After the first few eager kisses, Val began to roar with laughter at the first sights and sounds of his children.

His sons.

"God's Bones," he said, his white teeth gleaming beneath his dark and heavy beard. "I have dreamt of this moment. My God, I cannot tell you how much I have dreamt of this moment and when it finally comes, it is pure chaos."

Vesper was weeping with joy, laughing with Val in spite of herself. "My sweet darling," she murmured, kissing him as he kissed her in return. "This is not how I dreamt it, either. I cannot even put my arms around you because if I let go of them, they will run off and we will lose them both."

Val had tears in his eyes as he pulled Gabriel from his mother, holding the boy in front of him and looking into a handsome little face that looked very much like his own. Gabriel, however, had no idea who the strange man was and didn't take kindly to him, so he tried to kick and push him away.

But it made no difference to Val. He was instantly, and completely, in love with his child. Seeing that little face satisfied something deep within his soul.

"Which one is he?" he asked Vesper. "Gabriel or Gavin?"

"Gabriel," Vesper said, wiping the tears from her face as she watched Val gaze upon his son for the first time. "He is your second born. Gavin was first. You can tell Gabriel from Gavin because he has a big dimple in his left cheek. See it when he opens his mouth?"

Val could, indeed, see it. "Gabriel," he repeated reverently. "See how strong he is! And big! I did not imagine them to be so big!"

He said it with awe as the child tried to pull away. But Vesper forced Gavin to his feet and she took hold of Gabriel's arm, forcing the boy to stand as well even though Val still had his hands on him. She spoke firmly but softly to her sons.

"Gabriel?" she said. "Gavin? Listen to me. This is Dada. Do you remember how I read you Dada's missives? Do you remember how I told you he was fighting a great war? He has come home to see you. You must embrace him and show him that you love him."

Gabriel wasn't quite calm enough to grasp what his mother was telling him but Gavin was. He was the more introspective child, one of deep thought and feeling. He peered at Val, going to stand beside his fussing brother and looking Val in the eye. Val's gaze moved back and forth between the two boys, mirror images of each other, and his heart couldn't have been more full at the moment. It was joy beyond measure.

"Greetings, Gavin," he said to the boy who was staring at him. "You are a very big lad. Do you know how to ride a horse yet? Has your mother taught you?"

Vesper moved in close to Val, putting her arms around him and laying her head on his shoulder as he spoke to their sons. The feel of him in her arms threatened to bring tears again but she struggled against them. "I have not," she said hoarsely. "But my father has put them on ponies and led them about the stable yard."

The mention of McCloud caught Val off-guard but he didn't say anything; not now. He was too upswept in the first look at his boys to let anything spoil that.

"I see," he said. Then, he simply shook his head. "I cannot believe I am actually looking at them. I have prayed for this day since I received your missive telling me that you were with child. I have imagined the faces of my sons a thousand times over in my mind but it does not compare to the beauty I see before me. They look so much like my father that it is truly astonishing."

"They look like you," Vesper whispered, still holding him as she turned to look at him. "Why did you not send word that your arrival was imminent? I have been waiting almost two and a half years for this day and now I can hardly believe it. I always imagined what I would say to you at this moment but now I cannot recall any of it."

Val took his eyes off of the boys long enough to look at her. "Tell me that you love me as if we have never been apart."

She snaked her fingers up into his long, shaggy hair, gently caressing his head. "I love you as if we have never been apart."

"Truly?"

"Truly."

"And I love you more than I ever have. You are what has kept me alive these many months, Vesper. The thought of returning home to you and our children."

Vesper pulled him towards her, her forehead coming to rest against his mouth as he tenderly kissed her. It was a gentle and surreal moment, wrought with raw emotion between two people who had missed each other dreadfully.

"Please tell me you are home to stay," she murmured. "For if you are not, the children and I are returning with you to Ireland. I cannot stand to be away from you for another two and a half years, Val. It would kill me."

"I am not returning to Ireland," he said, his cheek on the top of her head as he felt the softness of her hair. "Henry has need of me here in England. It seems that there are rebellions afoot."

"We have heard that also."

"I am home to stay, sweetheart. I promise. Be at ease."

Gabriel took that moment to yank himself away from his father, attempting to run off but being grabbed by his grandmother, who was standing nearby. Val looked up to see Margaretha standing a few feet away, tears pooling in her eyes as she gazed upon her son. He stood up, smiling wearily at her.

"So, you finally have your grandchildren," he said as if quite pleased with himself. "Happy?"

Margaretha wasn't one to show emotion and was embarrassed when she did but, in this case, she made an exception. She accepted Val's embrace, relishing the feel of her only child. He was safe and whole, and that was all she cared about. God had answered her prayers.

"Your children scream, bite, and run about like wild animals," she said, sounding as if she was scolding him. But she quickly softened. "They are also brilliant, loving, and quite devilish. They were well worth the wait, Valor. I adore them. And you. Welcome home, my son."

Val chuckled, kissing his mother on the cheek. As he did so, he noticed that Gavin had followed him and was still looking up at him quite curiously. Gabriel didn't seem to be interested at all, but Gavin was clearly interested in him. Val smiled down at the lad.

"It has been a long time since I have been here, Gavin," he said. "Will you show me to the keep?"

Vesper was standing next to Gavin, her gaze moving between Val and Gavin. "Dada must be shown to the hall, Gavin," she said to the child. "Will you take him? There is food there. Are you hungry?"

Gavin looked as if he was considering both questions. While Margaretha began to head towards the keep with Gabriel howling in her arms, Gavin was seriously mulling over his mother's request. After a moment, he reached up and took one of Val's enormous hands.

"Come," he said simply.

With that, Gavin began to walk towards the keep, leading his father alongside him. Vesper watched them walk away, her heart melting by the sweetness of it as Val turned to look at her, winking with the sheer delight of it. He was thrilled to pieces that he was finally in the company of his sons, or at least one of them, and it showed in every curve and contour of his face.

He was finally home.

Vesper simply wanted to observe for the moment, a sight she had been praying for since the children were born. Val was here and all was right in the world again. There were no words to describe the contentment and pride that was in her heart.

"Val looks as if he has not suffered in Ireland," McCloud said softly, coming up to stand behind her. He, too, had been watching the reunion, but from a distance as he had not wanted to interfere. "I am glad he has come home, Vesper. Glad for you and the boys."

He turned to walk away but Vesper stopped him. "Where are you going?" she asked. "Come inside and eat. I am sure Val has many stories to tell."

McCloud shook his head. "You and I have made our peace, but Val and I have not. Let him have this time with his family. I will be here when he is ready."

Vesper wouldn't let him go. "Papa, you *are* family. It is true that you and Val did not part under the best of circumstances before he went to Ireland, but time changes men. I am sure he will be forgiving of your past sins. As he has been given a new start in life, a new chance to redeem himself, you must be given the same. You must at least give him the opportunity to do so."

McCloud could see the wisdom in her words. Although he was reluctant, he very much wanted to reconcile with his old friend. He was, after all, family and McCloud had come to realize that family was the most important thing of all.

"Very well," he said, forcing a smile as Vesper began to pull him along towards the keep. "Val is my son now, through you. I should like it if we can become friends once again. Do you remember, long ago, on the first night you met Val at Selborne Castle? I told you that food and wealth were the only things of importance when considering marriage. I believe I was rather cruel about it."

Vesper thought back to that night, so long ago. It was the first night she realized that she felt something for Val. "I remember," she said. "You told me that Val was trying to woo me and I did not believe you."

He looked at her. "Do you believe me now?"

Vesper laughed softly. "I do."

McCloud could see how very happy she was, happier than he'd ever seen her. Before them, the keep of Holystone loomed like a great big box against the sky. So much had brought them to this point in their lives and not all of it terrible. There had been some good mixed in with the bad. But the bad was a faded memory, like a terrible dream from long ago. McCloud patted her hands, looped through his elbow.

"I am glad you let him woo you," he said. "But not for wealth and food. I am glad because there is no finer man on this earth than Val de Nerra and he is the only man, in my opinion, worthy of you. I thought you should know that."

Vesper paused at the base of the stairs that led into the keep as she faced her father. A man she had once distanced herself from but a man now who had redeemed himself much as her husband had. Men who had once been in pieces, now made whole again by the power of love.

At least, that was how Vesper looked at it.

"Why don't you tell him that?" she asked.

McCloud did.

No finer man on this earth....

Post Script

In May 1171, Hugh de Morville, Reginald FitzUrse, William de Tracy, and Richard le Breton were excommunicated from the church by Pope Alexander III and ordered to go to the Holy Land for a 14-year pilgrimage. Their honor was never fully restored and Henry, although he didn't punish the knights, didn't really defend them, either. They never found the favor they sought from the king they had killed for.

Even though Valor de Nerra is a fictional character, let's assume that he was the only one out of that group who managed to regain his honor. We will assume he went on to fight many more years for Henry as one of the king's greatest commanders and that he became a mentor to many of the up-and-coming knights such as Juston de Royans, Christopher de Lohr, David de Lohr, Rhys du Bois, and Gart Forbes among them.

In the World of Le Veque, Valor de Nerra is the godfather of some of England's greatest knights.

Ante mortem animo

Courage before Death

About Kathryn Le Veque

Medieval Just Got Real.

KATHRYN LE VEQUE is a USA TODAY Bestselling author, an Amazon All-Star author, and a #1 bestselling, award-winning, multi-published author in Medieval Historical Romance and Historical Fiction. She has been featured in the NEW YORK TIMES and on USA TODAY's HEA blog. In March 2015, Kathryn was the featured cover story for the March issue of InD'Tale Magazine, the premier Indie author magazine. She was also a quadruple nominee (a record!) for the prestigious RONE awards for 2015.

Kathryn's Medieval Romance novels have been called 'detailed', 'highly romantic', and 'character-rich'. She crafts great adventures of love, battles, passion, and romance in the High Middle Ages. More than that, she writes for both women AND men – an unusual crossover for a romance author – and Kathryn has many male readers who enjoy her stories because of the male perspective, the action, and the adventure.

On October 29, 2015, Amazon launched Kathryn's Kindle Worlds Fan Fiction site WORLD OF DE WOLFE PACK. Please visit Kindle Worlds for Kathryn Le Veque's World of de Wolfe Pack and find many action-packed adventures written by some of the top authors in their genre using Kathryn's characters from the de Wolfe Pack series. As Kindle World's FIRST Historical Romance fan fiction world, Kathryn Le Veque's World of de Wolfe Pack will contain all of the great story-telling you have come to expect.

Kathryn loves to hear from her readers. Please find Kathryn on Facebook at Kathryn Le Veque, Author, or join her on Twitter @kathrynleveque, and don't forget to visit her website at www.kathrynleveque.com.

Made in the USA
San Bernardino, CA
15 April 2017